Dark Terror

Dark Terror

Spirit Wild Series

KATE
DOUGLAS

Beyond the Page Books
are published by
Beyond the Page Publishing
www.beyondthepagepub.com

Copyright © 2017 by Kate Douglas
Cover design by Dar Albert, Wicked Smart Designs

ISBN: 978-1-946069-22-1

Acknowledgments

Writing a book is a solitary venture, at least until the author thinks it's done. That's when beta readers and editors come into play and the party really starts! My betas on *Dark Terror,* Jan Takane, Jennifer Brame, Lynne Thomas, Rose Toubbeh, Kerry Parker, and Sue Thomas, definitely had their work cut out for them, and I thank you ladies most sincerely for your eagle eyes and nit-picky ways. What amazes me more with every book is how all of my betas will find different things—there are always a few duplicates, but each of them reads in their own unique manner, and their "catches" greatly improve my stories.

This book is dedicated to my editor, Bill Harris, who makes me a better writer without any tears, bloodshed, or ugly, messy incidents (mine, not his . . .). Bill actually makes the final edits the best part of writing a book, because the parts he cuts and the things he asks me to fix are always exactly what the story needs.

If you truly enjoy reading a book, you really need to thank the editor. The same goes for writing, and for that, Bill gets my most grateful thanks. He's helped me find the joy in telling stories again, something I was afraid I might have lost.

And to my agent, Jessica Faust. Just because . . .

1

Chanku pack headquarters, South of Glacier National Park
Wednesday, June 6, 2040, 11:45 p.m.

Goddess but she ached. The pain was difficult to describe, though one of her friends had come close. Janine said it felt just like what it was—being caught in an endless cycle of unfulfilled lust, a pain so intimate, so visceral, that it burned like an orgasm forever denied. Pain that went on, and on, and . . .

"Whatcha thinking, Mary?"

Jack Temple's teasing voice slashed through her misery. Mary floundered for an answer, took a deep breath and shot him a saucy grin instead. He'd caught her, fair and square. She *had* come out here to the pond to think.

Unfortunately, Jack was the one she was thinking about . . . in a roundabout way. All that unrequited lust was killing her. She almost laughed at that. Poor guy didn't have a clue.

Shaking her head, she shrugged self-consciously while checking to make certain her shields were up, her personal thoughts blocked. "Oh, nothing important." She patted the rock she liked best for sitting on out here, one big and flat and wide enough for two. The alpha's mate had designed this beautiful pond with secluded gardens and private walkways all around, a perfect place to find solitude on a lonely night. "You're welcome to join me in my vast mental wasteland. At least we have a gorgeous view."

As late as it was, the solar fairy lights twinkling along the edges of the pond lent a mystical, almost supernatural feel to the dark shadows beyond. The faint slice of the waning crescent moon was barely visible in the night sky, almost lost in the countless numbers of stars that swept from one mountain-studded horizon to the next.

Jack folded his big, powerful body down beside her. Odd, how she could be so afraid of men and yet never fear this one. "That actually sounds pretty appealing," he said, tweaking her long hair with his fingertips. "Today was nuts with the final testing—math is not their favorite subject. Tomorrow's the last day of school and the pups are growing restless. I can't wait to turn them over to their parents for the summer." He laughed. "I really love my job, but there are days . . ."

"I'm well aware. They're cute, but hellions, every one."

He laughed. "That's right." He bumped shoulders with her. "You were one of the chaperones on that field trip to the sheriff's department Monday. I heard it got pretty crazy."

Shaking her head, she smiled at his vast understatement. At least her inner turmoil rested now that Jack was beside her. For whatever reason, his presence calmed her more intimate neediness, and he made her feel safe. He'd had that effect on her from the very beginning. It was only when he wasn't around that she let herself dream, and that's when the pain started. The hopeless yearning, wanting what she didn't have. Would probably never have.

"We definitely earned our keep," she said. "Everything was fine until a couple of the younger boys started teasing two older girls, who shifted in the deputies' cafeteria and turned into wildcats. Shocked the boys, who, obviously were expecting wolves, and the deputies were no help. They were laughing hysterically at the girls chasing the boys, who were too freaked out to shift. Janine and I were there as chaperones, and I think we were laughing harder than the deputies."

"Thank the goddess they weren't my kids. I bet their teacher was traumatized."

She raised one eyebrow and just stared at him for a long moment. "The boys were yours last year. This was Jace's group."

Jack covered his eyes and moaned when she added, "The ten-to-twelve-year-olds. Your seven-to-nine-year-olds are all taking notes."

"Thanks for that!" Laughing, he shook his head and then banged his forehead against his upraised knees. "I had no idea it was Jace's group. I haven't had a chance to talk to him all week." He wrapped his arm around her shoulders and hugged her close. Mary's whole body went stiff. She froze and Jack's smile slipped. He released her immediately and rested his hand on the rock behind her instead, as if nothing had happened.

Mary hung her head. She'd done it again. Totally overreacted to a touch made merely in friendship. No wonder he didn't see her as a potential girlfriend. According to her father she was ruined for any man, but even if he was wrong, she'd never be able to relax, never learn to enjoy simple touches, much less the sex everyone here so easily took for granted.

The sexual release all of them needed. She loved being a shapeshifter, but knowing that the need inside would grow each time she shifted was killing her.

Tears stung her eyes. Staring blindly at the dark spikes of the Rocky Mountains to the east, she tried to accept what she could no longer deny. She was all used up. Twenty-two years old and her only sexual experience had come from whoring, when she was forced to service terrible men who treated her like the garbage she was. Her own parents had disowned her. They didn't care that she'd been kidnapped by sex slavers, sold like so much merchandise. They only cared that she was no longer pure. Mary knew that wasn't important, but she feared that Jack would never understand, not a man as beautiful as he was, not one who every single woman around thought was the sexiest thing alive. She knew he was more than that—Jackson Temple-Fuentes was kind and gentle and he honestly cared about the kids he taught, the friends he kept, the men and women he loved.

He'd had sex with just about every single woman she'd met here at the pack's headquarters in Montana. With a lot of the men, too. It was no secret, something the Chanku talked openly about, something they did without a second thought. When your entire existence was ruled by an unstoppable libido, a person's sexuality was a given. Yeah, he'd slept with just about everyone she knew. Everyone except her. No wonder. What could he possibly find interesting about a woman who flinched whenever he touched her?

She treasured his friendship. She just wished she knew how to encourage his interest beyond what they had—and how she could somehow accept that interest. It made her angry—at herself, not at Jack— that her stupid reactions had her permanently placed in the friend category. She didn't want to lose that. He was her best bud, a guy she could talk to, ask questions of, laugh with, but she wanted so much more.

She wanted to get naked with him. She wanted to find out if he might be the one who could make the aching loneliness, the overwhelming need, finally go away. The one who could teach her that sex wasn't something forced on a woman, it was something to enjoy, to share with a partner. Or partners . . . She glanced at him, caught him smiling at her. That beautiful open smile of his. So perfect, except he smiled at her the way he smiled at his students.

The seven-to-nine-year-olds.

Somehow, she had to get over her hang-ups, stop flinching whenever he touched her, and just do it.

"Look, Mary!" He raised his arm and pointed to a spot in the sky just to the north of the crescent moon.

A shooting star streaked across the dark sky, bright fire against the shimmer of stars, trailing sparkling embers in its wake. Without thinking, she made a promise instead of a wish. Tonight she was going to speak up, tell him that she was attracted to him. How was he to know, the way she always pulled away when he touched her? Tonight Jack would see she was a woman who wanted him. She bit back a laugh. She probably should add that she was also a woman with major issues.

• • •

It was almost midnight. Jack thought he could sit out here with Mary all night long, but he had his last day of classes with the little monsters tomorrow, and if a guy wasn't on his toes, chaos was sure to ensue.

"C'mon, m'dear. I'm going to walk you back to your cabin and then collapse into my own lonely bed. I've got one more day before I'm free for the summer." He held out his hand. Mary looked at it for a moment—she always did that, and at first it had hurt him, that she seemed not to trust him, but then he realized it was so ingrained in her that she probably didn't even realize what she was doing.

Now, even though she still had that first uneasy reaction, she always clasped his hand and let him tug her to her feet. She'd even reached the point where she'd let him hold her hand when they walked. Spending time with Mary was like gentling a wild creature—a silly analogy, maybe, given that she could become a wolf in less than a heartbeat—but he knew her past, knew she'd been hurt and hurt badly. He knew she'd been a virgin when she was taken, that a man had paid a lot of money to be the one to take her virginity in a brutal rape that left her traumatized and bleeding.

She'd had no chance to get past that trauma, either. No time to heal from the bastard's cruel treatment. No, she was sold again and again, until the various men blurred into a single creature that became all men. Jack was still included in that group, but he was working on it. Working on building his friendship with Mary. Working on earning her trust. She was worth it, and he was positive there was a strong, vibrant woman hiding beneath all her layers of fear.

If anyone discovered the real Mary, he hoped like hell it was him.

They walked along the trail toward her cabin, not talking, but it wasn't an awkward silence. It never was with Mary, even though her shields were always high and tight. He didn't breach her trust by prying. It was common knowledge among the pack that she'd been victimized for over a year. He didn't want to rush her. They were Chanku. Almost immortal, which meant they had all the time in the world.

Lost in thought, he stopped in his tracks when she caught him by surprise with a sharp tug on his hand. He turned and she held her finger to her lips.

Listen.

Voices. And not all that far away. *I hear them. Janine and Leo?*

They're arguing again.

She glanced at Jack with troubled eyes. Janine was one of Mary's closest friends, one of the young women who'd been held by the same sex slavers as Mary. Leo Cheval had attached himself to Janine the very first week the girls arrived at pack headquarters. He was mostly a good guy, sometimes a controlling jerk, but Janine had appeared to handle him pretty easily. She was tiny but wonderfully strong-willed. He heard Leo's crude curse and tugged Mary forward. *I think it's time we say hello, don't you?*

If you think it's okay?

The question, along with the trust in her mental voice, shook Jack. He'd been hoping she would come to trust him. *Don't worry. Leo can be pushy at times, but he's mostly okay.*

Mostly?

She smiled at him as they walked toward the sound of their packmates arguing. She still held tightly to his hand. They rounded a curve in the trail. The two were focused on each other and appeared unaware of Jack and Mary. Their argument seemed to have morphed into angry silence between the two of them.

Mary was the first to speak. "Hey, Janine. Leo."

The two spun around. Jack noticed the relief on Janine's face first, but he felt Leo's anger just before the jerk slammed his shields down tight.

"Hey, guys." Jack used his calmest voice. Anything to offset Leo's swirling emotions, and Janine's obvious fury. There were red spots high on Leo's dark cheeks and his green eyes flashed. If Janine had been a cat, her back would be arched and her hair sticking on end. The image fit her so perfectly, Jack couldn't help sharing it with Mary, though he wasn't sure she was listening for him. She looked more concerned about Janine, but her choked giggle and the tight squeeze of his hand was enough to keep him from glancing her way.

"What are you guys doing out so late?" Janine stepped away from Leo, closer to Mary. If they hadn't just been yelling at each other moments ago, it wouldn't have caught Jack's attention, but he wondered if she was afraid of the guy.

"We've been sitting out by the pond, discussing the joys of herding Jace's kids on the field trip last week." Mary glanced at Jack and he rolled his eyes. "Jack, of course, knew nothing about it."

Janine laughed. "Head in sand, maybe?" Grinning at Mary, she said, "A little ostrich in his shapeshifting bag of tricks?" She turned and wagged a finger under his nose. "Jack. The two boys who started it all were yours last year."

"Thanks for the reminder. Mary already filled me in. I'm gonna catch hell from Jace next time I see him."

They talked for a few minutes, just the three of them since Leo stayed off to one side with his arms folded across his chest. Then Janine flashed a bright smile at Jack and Mary. "I'm headed back to the cabin. It was good to see you two." She turned and slipped off the trail toward the main route back to the cabins before Leo reacted.

He watched the way she'd gone, muttered a curse and left in the opposite direction.

"Should we follow?" Mary stared in the direction Janine had gone.

Jack shook his head. "No. She made it clear she was through with him for tonight."

"I wish she'd *stay* through with him." Sighing, Mary glanced at their clasped hands. "I'm exhausted. I think I'll catch up with Janine. You don't need to walk me home." She rose up on her toes and kissed him, just a quick peck on the lips that was absolutely void of any sense of passion. But it *was* a kiss, which was better than he'd ever gotten before. Still, she looked sad and sort of lost when she turned and went after Janine. She turned as she reached the fork in the trail and her pensive smile touched him. "G'night, Jack. I hope I'll see you tomorrow."

He watched her go, wondering how their night might have ended if they hadn't run across Leo and Janine. There'd been something about Mary tonight, almost as if she had something planned.

Unfortunately, he doubted it had anything to do with getting naked. He turned and headed in the opposite direction, toward his own cabin. Alone.

2

Yellowstone National Park
Thursday, 10:40 p.m.

This was a truly wondrous place, this fierce land called Yellowstone. It was even more magical after the sun went down. Reko crouched beside Ari, his brother. He'd been told they were almost identical, the way they were marked, their massive size. Two enormous wolves much larger than their wild brethren. He and Ari had paused here to watch the boiling mud bubble up from beneath the ground. The ambient starlight illuminated wisps of steam as it danced overhead before disappearing into the darkness. Fi would have loved it, would have wanted to know everything there was to know about the boiling muck that flowed up from the ground and smelled so foul, but their littermate—their sister—was gone.

She'd been killed by a rabid wolf somewhere north of here in a place the humans called Idaho.

Thank the goddess she'd bled out after fighting the beast rather than die a slow, agonizing death from the sickness.

I hear your thoughts, Reko. We've no reason to thank the goddess. That bitch forgot us long ago.

Reko turned his head slowly and stared at Ari. Like their father before them, Ari blamed the goddess for just about everything. Reko, however, preferred to believe as their mother had. *We don't know that for sure, Ari. Our kind stopped honoring her long ago. Maybe, after we forgot her, she just couldn't find us.*

Ari's snort was all the answer Reko was going to get. Carefully he stood, sniffed the air, and immediately went flat to the ground. *Ari! To the right. Men. It's hard to smell them over the sulfur, but if that's their scent I caught, they stink of fear.*

Ari raised his head. His nose twitched and he sucked in a great breath. *Fear and adrenaline. They're excited about something, but afraid, too. We need to get away before they find us.*

No. Reko glanced at his brother. *They're afraid of getting caught, which means they're doing something wrong. I'm going to see what I can find out.*

Idiot. This isn't our concern.

We live in this world, for better or worse . . .

It's usually worse. Ari shot him a dirty look.

For better or worse, and we need to protect it when things are wrong. Whatever they're doing feels wrong.

Be careful, Reko. Ari's eyes filled with sadness, as if he, like Reko, already knew their future. What little they might have. *You're all I have left. With Thor dead, with Fi gone . . .*

I know. I promise. Reko gave his brother one final glance before quietly blending with the shadows. Moving with great stealth through the darkness, he crept around the rocks, drawing closer to the group of men.

Reko heard the muffled shot at the same moment fire streaked across his skull.

His legs crumpled beneath him.

• • •

Chanku pack headquarters
Thursday, 11:00 p.m.

"Hey, Jack! It's been too long. Wondered if you were going to show up."

Jack waved at Gabe Cheval, grabbed a cold can of beer out of the ice chest and then wandered over to sit with Gabe and Jace Wolf. It had been way too long since he'd hung out with the guys, but he knew they'd be taking off within the next couple of days. "Don't harass me," he said, taking a long swallow. "I bet you haven't seen much of Jacc, cither." He tipped his beer to his fellow teacher.

"Yeah, but I'm making up for lost time. This is my third." Jace tipped his head back and emptied his can. "Going on my fourth, and I may need a fifth." He pointed at Jack. "You owe me one, bud, after what your little monsters pulled on the field trip last week."

Laughing, Jack sat down on top of the picnic table across from his buds. "Mary reminded me that the girls proved once again that women are the smarter sex."

"No doubt in my mind. But not my worry for the next three months."

Jace held his beer up to acknowledge Gabe. "We're headed out on our annual wild wolf survey tomorrow."

"Romy and Emeline are going with us," Gabe said. "I was afraid they wouldn't want to, but they're both really excited about the trip. Of course, Romy's seen a lot of that country before, since we picked her up halfway through the route last year."

Jack sipped his beer. Things had definitely changed, now that both Jace and Gabe were mated, but in a good way. Both his friends were still just as much fun as ever, but they were more mature, too. More settled? It wasn't easy for him to describe, but he admired them in a way he hadn't before.

Which led Jack, in a somewhat convoluted journey, to thoughts of Mary. For whatever reason, that woman was stuck in his mind. Gabe and his mate, Em, had been the ones who'd freed Mary and the other young women from the sex traffickers. Mary and three others had turned out to be Chanku and were now part of the pack.

And Mary? Mary, for whatever reason, haunted him. In a very good way.

Gabe raised his head and grinned at Jack. "What's with you and Mary? I saw you two sitting out by the pond last night. She's so quiet that I can't see her hanging with a hound like you."

How the hell did Gabe do that? Sometimes Jack wondered if Gabe read minds the way his dad did. "Mary's okay." He shrugged, unwilling to say anything personal. "We're friends. I like her."

Jace snorted. "Friends? C'mon, Jack. You don't do friends. You do fuck buddies. Mary, though? I think she's a little too good for you."

Jack punched Jace's shoulder. He wanted to hit him a hell of a lot harder. "You're probably right. I'll try really hard to remember that." He laughed, but it wasn't funny because he halfway agreed with Jace. Mary *was* too good for him, but for some reason they'd actually become friends. He'd been drawn to her that very first day when they arrived from San Francisco. She'd been timid and shy, still traumatized by her experience and the fact she had just discovered her Chanku heritage. All he'd really wanted was to be her friend, to show her not all men were bastards, but it was an unusual experience. He was so used to women coming on to him, but Mary wasn't like that. Considering what she'd been through, he'd avoided letting her know just how much he'd come to want her; instead, he'd sort of been waiting around for her to make the first move.

She hadn't. Not even close, though last night was proof she was more comfortable spending time with him than she'd been. There was definitely some real chemistry. But Mary, obviously, wasn't ready to act on it. Jack wanted more, but it was hard to know how to approach the subject. You didn't just ask a woman if she wanted to have sex when she'd been kidnapped, held prisoner, and whored out by bastards who were absolute slime.

The sound of laughter had the three men lifting their heads and staring across the meadow. Jack glanced at Jace and they both cracked up when Jace sent the thought *Woman radar* his way. Em, Romy, and Mary walked toward the picnic tables where the guys had parked their butts. Jack took another swallow of his beer, watching Jace's and Gabe's reactions as their women drew closer. He might as well have disappeared off the planet, as focused as the two had suddenly become. Like predators stalking prey, except Romy and Em weren't trying to get away. No, they were coming closer, as focused on their guys as Jace and Gabe were on them.

His revelation was just that simple: Jack wanted what his buddies had. Wanted that kind of look from a woman. Not any woman, though. Only one. *Mary.* He dumped the rest of his beer out on the ground, tossed the can in the recycle barrel and stood. Romy walked into Jace's embrace, and Em wrapped her arms around Gabe. Jack took Mary's hand.

"C'mon," he said, playfully tugging her closer and spinning her around. Laughing, she went with it. She didn't flinch at all. "There are some things a nice girl like you should never see." Standing behind Mary, he covered her eyes with both hands and she laughed again.

When it appeared that neither Jace nor Gabe would be coming up for air anytime soon, Jack took Mary's hand again and led her down the trail toward the woods. It was a beautiful night, a perfect night for getting naked with a gorgeous woman. Mary was definitely that, with her most amazing blue eyes and her long dark brown hair waving over her shoulders. Unfortunately, he didn't see getting naked together in their immediate future.

He would never push her. Most of the females, at least of his generation, born and raised within the pack, saw sex as one of the necessities of life—sort of like eating, sleeping, and breathing. Mary's experience hadn't been anything like that. Which was why it would be entirely up to Mary to make the first move. That is, only if she was at all interested in *moving* . . .

There was an old fallen tree near the path and Jack lifted Mary up to sit on the massive trunk. He'd always liked this spot, right at the edge of the forest where you could look out at the houses scattered across the huge meadow and the little fairy lights that marked the pathways through the landscaped gardens. It was like living in a park, and when he sat beside Mary and took her hand, he realized it felt different tonight, sitting here and looking at the place that had always been his home.

Was it him? Was he finally getting older, feeling a bit jaded and yet at the same time lost? Where the hell had that come from? He almost laughed. Introspection really wasn't his thing. He glanced at Mary. "You're quiet tonight. Everything okay?"

Turning, she studied him for the longest time. After a minute, she took a deep breath, sucked her lips between her teeth. Then she exhaled, and absolutely floored him. "Jack? Do you find me at all attractive?"

He almost choked. "You're kidding, right?"

She pulled her hand away from his. "I'm sorry. I never should have . . ."

"Whoa. Mary." He reached for her hand, held on, and all his best intentions disappeared. Shaking his head, he tried to figure her out, but she wasn't an easy read. "You're absolutely gorgeous. The first time I saw you I couldn't look away. I still can't. Truth, Mary? I've had a case of blue balls since that very first day. Ever since we've gotten to be friends, I've become way too intimately acquainted with my right hand, if you get my drift."

She covered her mouth and actually snorted, and then she blushed a fiery red. Jack grabbed both her hands and laughed with her. "Are you coming on to me, Mary Ryder?"

"I don't know." Cocking her head to one side, she stared at him out of those amazing blue eyes. He felt as if she saw right through him. "I've never come on to a guy before." She stared at the ground. "I wanted to, last night, but then I chickened out." Raising her head, she looked him directly in both eyes. "What do I need to do, you know, to get it right?"

He hadn't expected this at all, but he slipped off the log and stood, reached for Mary, and pulled her into his arms. "This, for starters," he said. And then he kissed her.

At first she froze, her lips as still as her body. He kept it easy but intimate, continued his slow but thorough exploration of her mouth, and within moments she was kissing him back. When she tentatively slipped her tongue between his parted lips, Jack wanted to jump up and cheer, though that really wasn't necessary. His dick was doing that all on its own.

When he took her hand and led her toward his cabin, Mary didn't hesitate. Not a bit.

• • •

Yellowstone National Park
Thursday, 11:15 p.m.

Ari watched in horror as the four men reached his brother. They stood over him, speaking quietly among themselves while Ari's heart broke.

They called Reko a trophy, congratulating the one who had killed him with gunfire. No wild creature stood a chance against men and their guns, even if that creature was sentient, every bit as intelligent—if not smarter—than the one who'd pulled the trigger. As Berserkers, Ari and Reko were much larger than wild wolves, and though only a few of their kind—including their brother Thor—had been taken by hunters over the years, their skins were much prized.

Ari flashed back on Thor's death, the obscenity of his murder, the sudden pain that had brought Ari to his knees.

Reko and Fiona had said the same, that they'd known when Thor died, even though they were nowhere close. The three of them had avenged their brother's death. They'd found his body, tracked the hunters. Fi had ripped out the throat of the shooter while he and Reko took care of the man's companions. They'd buried Thor and hidden the human bodies.

Not long after, they'd gone in search of more of their kind. They'd only been traveling a few weeks when he and Reko had buried Fiona, careful not to touch the tainted blood or saliva from the rabid wolf that killed her.

But he and Reko had felt her death. There'd been a link that told them she was gone.

Ari kept his gaze locked on Reko. He hadn't sensed Reko's death, and had to believe that Reko lived. He would not give up on his only remaining sibling.

One large man reached for his brother's body, checked him over and then nodded to one of the others. The two of them grabbed Reko's legs front and rear and lifted him between them—a dead weight. The stench of sulfur and blood left Ari light-headed, but he followed as close behind the small group as he dared. He refused to accept Reko's death. Not without proof. He had to find out if his brother still lived.

Somehow, if Reko was alive, Ari would save him, as much out of love for his brother as for the fear of life without him. As far as he knew, with both Thor and Fi gone, he and Reko were the last of their kind. He stayed as close as he could, listening, but the men spoke quietly, their voices much too soft for him to hear with the hiss of steam and the bubbling mud blocking the sound. He stopped behind a large boulder when, still carrying Reko, they slipped between two rocks in the face of the mountain and disappeared from sight.

They'd taken Reko into a cave. Ari weighed the possibilities. If he followed, he would most certainly be killed and there would be no one left to save his brother. *If Reko still lives.* If they killed Ari and Reko was already dead, there would be none of their kind left.

He didn't want to be the last, and he had the responsibility of their species, the promise they'd made to their parents. Their mother and father had been dead for many years, but what if their father with his powerful anger had been wrong? Reko had always been the man to think things through, to use reason tempered by emotion. Maybe his brother was right to hope.

Slinking away from the rocks, Ari hid behind a huge fir tree, one of the largest he'd ever seen. Crouching in the darkness, he opened his heart, grasped Reko's spark of hope and opened his very soul as he called out to their goddess. Ari trusted Reko, and Reko believed.

For that alone the bitch owed his brother salvation.

• • •

Jack's cabin at the Chanku pack headquarters
Friday, 1:45 a.m.

Jack Temple sprawled on his big bed, his body bathed in sweat, heart pounding, his dick totally limp for the first time in forever. He lay there a moment, blowing like a damned bellows until his lungs quit straining for air and his heart rate settled down to something closer to normal . . . for a guy running a frickin' marathon.

His ears were actually buzzing! Between that and the pins and needles prickling his fingers and toes from what had to have been the most mind-blowing sex ever, he honestly felt as if someone had knocked his personal foundation totally out from under him.

Damned female! It was all her fault. He wanted to laugh, but instead he rolled to his left and propped himself up on one elbow to stare at the amazing woman sleeping beside him. She was beautiful. A little repressed sexually, but that was to be expected. What hadn't been expected was the experience of burying himself deep inside Mary Ryder. And whatever hang-ups she had about sex certainly hadn't kept her from totally rocking his world, just as he'd known she would.

Goddess knew, she had a good reason for her issues. But as far as Jack was concerned, Mary was utterly fascinating. For one thing, she hadn't thrown herself at him. It could get tiresome, the way women treated him like a piece of prime beef, though he had to admit that most of the time he hadn't minded.

He could be such an idiot sometimes, but it was difficult for a single guy to have issues with constant offers of sex from men and women, human and Chanku. He'd not been emotionally invested in any of them— or them in him—so it was all good times and, if nothing else, good exercise.

Now though? Tonight, sex with Mary had gone so far beyond his usual experience that it felt wrong to refer to their coming together as something so mundane as ordinary sex. Was this the difference? The difference between having sex and making love?

He certainly hadn't expected this tonight, but she'd been the one to touch him first, the one to ask him if he had ever thought of her sexually.

Well. Yeah. Most of the time, but he'd been very careful not to act like a slavering hound. Sometimes it was hard to believe that they hadn't been intimate before now. He'd never been known for his patience, but looking back, he wondered if somehow he'd recognized her importance to him, if he'd instinctively known to go slow and easy, to let this build. He'd grown to treasure her friendship over the past six months. Now? Now that he'd tasted her, touched her, made love to her, she'd effectively ruined him for any other woman. Ever.

He wrapped one glossy brown curl around his fingers. Mary sighed in her sleep.

It was almost as if she was meant to be his, and in spite of their totally different upbringings, tonight was proof they had something important. He'd grown up Chanku with a set of parents unique even among the sexually open shapeshifters. His mom, Tala, had two mates, and Jack and his twin sister, Star, had different dads. Since Chanku females had total control over their breeding, Tala had popped out an egg and mated with AJ, then she'd done it again with Star's dad, Mik. Miguel Fuentes, aka Mik, was Hispanic and Native American; Jack's dad, AJ Temple, was a man who had always identified as gay, but who loved Tala as much as he loved his other mate, Miguel.

AJ fathered one more with Tala, Jack's full sibling Andrea, and as much as the three parents loved each other, their three children knew that they were loved most of all. Loved in so many ways. In spite of some of the politics and issues with humans going on outside the pack, Jack, Star, and their little sister, Andrea, had grown up in an idyllic setting. They'd been protected from the world outside—protected until they were ready to deal with it, surrounded by packmates, loved unconditionally by their parents and their pack.

But Mary? She'd been orphaned when her single mother died, and adopted as an infant by an ultra-conservative family, members of a cult-like fundamentalist religious group that hated Chanku. Her father had been furious to learn she was no longer a virgin after her kidnapping, and then he'd disowned her when he'd learned she was a shapeshifter.

Mary still hadn't come to terms with the loss of her adoptive parents, or the way they'd cut her out of their lives, seemingly without any remorse at all.

When Jack thought of his loving family, how his dads had both welcomed Mary into their home the night they met, how his mom had put her arms around Mary and promised to be there for her whenever she needed a mom, Jack had been so proud of his parents he'd almost cried. Mary had cried, as much for what she'd never had as for the love the pack and his family had offered. Unconditional love, no strings attached.

It was something Jack had known all his life, something Mary had never experienced.

Maybe he could be the one to show her what real love felt like. He already knew that his feelings for her went well beyond the usual fuck buddy, or even good friend. Way beyond. He wrapped more of her curls around his fingers, gazing at her face as she slept. Then her eyes opened and her lips curved in a warm smile.

"What are you doing?" She reached up and gently brushed his messy hair off his forehead.

"Watching you." He leaned over and kissed her, inhaling her scent, tasting her mouth, delving deeper to sweep his tongue along her teeth, licking across the sensitive roof of her mouth. She moaned, arching her hips, pressing herself against him in welcome, her tongue dancing with his in a seductive parry and thrust that quickly had both of them panting. There was no sign of the shyness he'd noticed earlier when they'd first made love, none of the hesitation. Then, though she'd been the one to instigate it, she'd hardly met his eyes and he'd easily taken the lead.

Most of the Chanku females he'd been with were alphas, and that could create a battle of wills atop the sheets.

Not with Mary. She'd followed him so naturally, so easily, that before long their lovemaking had taken on a natural rhythm, smooth and effortless, as if they'd partnered like this forever, yet he didn't think he'd ever been as aroused as he'd been with her.

When she'd reached her first climax with him, the look of surprise in her eyes had been his undoing. He'd wanted to slaughter the ones who had taken her, every single man who'd hurt her. Instead, he'd given her everything he had until she'd fallen asleep in his arms, sated, exhausted, and smiling.

Now she was sleek and warm, her body still slightly damp from the perspiration of their earlier efforts. This time he wanted more. The first time . . . that first time, dear goddess, they'd come together in a shocking blaze of need, their bodies primed and ready after months of friendship, after consciously avoiding any expectation of actually getting naked together.

He'd not wanted to frighten her, hadn't wanted her to think he was anything like those men who had hurt her. But Mary? Foolish woman.

She'd thought he was too good for her. Somehow he had to make it perfectly clear that she was the one who was so far superior in this relationship that he was still trying to figure out why she'd chosen him out of all the other single guys.

And she had chosen him. He'd not pursued her at all, had merely offered friendship, and she'd taken his offer and expanded on it. He was the one she'd come to for companionship, yes, but also for advice, for safety. She'd told him some of the horror she'd survived, she'd honored him, showing she felt safe enough with him to curl up against his chest and cry harsh, ragged tears when her parents abandoned her. He still couldn't believe she'd come to him, of all people.

He knew she'd been with some of the women, knew that women weren't her first choice, but she was still healing. What had shocked him most wasn't her treatment as a captive, it had been the life she'd lived before. It had to have been horrendous for a young woman raised within a repressive religious cult, where women were treated as second-class citizens. She'd admitted that being captured meant she'd merely traded one form of slavery for another, that her parents had been trying to marry her off to one of the older men in the church. The only reason she'd gotten to attend college was that she'd earned an academic full-ride scholarship to UC Berkley. Her parents hadn't wanted her to go, but she'd been over eighteen and had defied them for the first time in her life.

Then, just a couple of years later, close to graduation, she'd been captured, and for a time she'd believed it was God's punishment for defying her parents that landed her in such a hellish existence. The other girls had quickly convinced her that God had nothing to do with it—that the blame was all on the men who'd kidnapped her and the johns who paid for her.

She would never be without choice again. Not if Jack had anything to say about it. He nuzzled her beautiful breasts, reveling in the freedom to touch her, knowing she wanted this with him—but did she want it again so soon? Arching her back, she thrust her taut nipple against his mouth, answering his unasked question. He sucked on one, pinched the other until she was squirming and thrashing beneath him.

"More, Jack. Please, harder."

He bit down gently on her nipple and she cried out. When he pulled away and moved down her sleek torso, she whimpered. Nuzzling her smooth belly, he ran his tongue around the rim of her navel and then moved even lower. She'd stopped him here the first time, closing her legs when he'd nuzzled the soft curls between her thighs. This time, he palmed her firm buttocks and lifted her hips, sitting back on his heels and holding her up for his pleasure—and hers.

The only sign of her distress was her tight grasp on the tumbled blankets. He chose to ignore that, for now. Instead, he dipped his head and licked once across the damp folds between her thighs, then the crease between her thigh and groin. When she showed no sign of wanting him to stop, he parted the lips of her sex with his thumbs, tasted her nectar, and licked her deeper still.

• • •

Arching into that unbelievable feeling of Jack's tongue between her legs, Mary had a sudden urge to giggle. She'd been totally fascinated with him since the first moment she saw him, but Jackson Temple was almost too beautiful, too kind to be true. She'd never known anyone like him and she'd never imagined being with him like this.

For that matter, she'd never imagined ever choosing to be with anyone like this ever. She'd only ever known ugly men who got off on some truly disgusting acts, things she'd never imagined. She had no idea they'd want to use her mouth for sex—or her bottom. That was something she'd never even heard of, and when it happened all she could think of was that it was painful and dirty and nasty. Of course, she'd not been taught very much about sex, not beyond the fact that it was for procreation, never for pleasure. Losing her virginity before marriage meant, according to her father and their church teachings, that she was damned to burn in hell forever.

When she'd told her father what had happened to her, that she'd been captured and forced, he'd told her she might not be able to come back home because she'd sinned. The fact she'd been taken against her will and held prisoner hadn't mattered—if she'd really believed that it was evil, she would have found a way to escape. When she'd explained that their captors always kept one of the girls as collateral so that the others wouldn't try to get away, he'd said they didn't matter. They weren't true believers.

That's when she'd first begun to doubt him. A few days later, he'd told her he managed to get some sort of dispensation from their church for her. It would require a lot of prayer and most likely severe punishment, and she'd never be truly forgiven. She could still live with them, but probably not until after her little sister, Rebecca, found a husband. Having a whore for a sister would hurt Becca's chances for a good marriage.

Thank goodness the other girls had convinced Mary she really didn't need to go back because she was better than those hypocrites, who hadn't even tried to find her when she'd disappeared. Instead, she'd been invited to join the pack and accepted the invitation to come to Montana—and then she'd met Jack. He'd introduced her to his parents, his mom and her two mates, one of whom was AJ, Jack's father. The other girls had already met AJ and couldn't stop talking about the guy because they thought he was movie-star gorgeous. He was definitely handsome, but she thought his son was a lot hotter. The thing she'd remembered about AJ was how nice he was, how he'd hovered over Jack's mom, how he'd hugged and even kissed their mate Mik like he really loved the man. These people weren't all sexual deviants like the church taught. No, they were good people, loving, kind, and thoughtful of each other. Of Mary, too, though they didn't even know her.

But Jack? He was just amazing, and he'd noticed her from the beginning. Unlike the human men and boys she'd known over the years, even before she was taken, he'd not pressured her for sex. Just the opposite. He'd been really sweet to her, had teased and laughed with her and helped her out during the past six months as she'd adjusted to this new life, but not once had he pushed her for anything physical.

The closest they'd been was the night she fell apart, crying over so many different things she doubted either of them had any idea what had hurt her the worst—being sold for sex or discovering how little she meant to her family. He'd held her, his arms strong, his chest broad and warm, the steady beat of his heart a reminder that he was there for her, that she wasn't alone. But that was it—he'd offered friendship, but no hint of anything further.

She still couldn't believe she'd been brave enough to make a pass at him.

Couldn't believe that had been just a few hours ago, and in that short period of time her life had changed yet again.

Only this change felt even bigger than finding out she was a Chanku shapeshifter. Her breath caught as his tongue swept over her sex once again. She'd never experienced anything remotely like what he was doing. He'd tried this earlier and she'd sort of freaked about it, but then she'd remembered what Emy Cheval had told her, that the Chanku were very sensual creatures and believed that any sexual act between consenting adults, as long as no one was uncomfortable or afraid, was okay.

She'd vowed not to let the horrible things her father had said affect this new life of hers, and that meant banishing him from her mind. He'd said she was breaking the rules that God had set down for his people, and she was a sinner for putting another deity in his place, but Mary'd actually seen the Chanku goddess. Eve was a living part of their world, a truly good and loving goddess.

She was the one Mary believed in because Eve believed in Mary.

Jack hummed against her clit and she felt the vibrations deep inside. Her nipples peaked and the muscles over her belly rippled. He licked her again; she was shocked to realize that the groan she heard was hers. She wanted him inside her, wanted him filling that empty space where she'd much prefer his rather large penis to his talented but much smaller tongue.

He raised his head, his beautiful black hair tousled and curling around his face and his amber eyes sparkling, and he grinned at her, a very wolfish expression that almost made her laugh. The thought was definitely apropos, but then he lowered his head again and his tongue swept inside her, laving swollen tissues already buttery soft from her arousal. Rising, he sat back on his heels between her legs, spread his fingers across her butt to hold her hips with one large hand and traced the crease between her cheeks with the fingers now freed. When he teased the tight opening on her bottom with a single fingertip, her first reaction was to move away, to tell him not to touch her there, except it felt good. Really good.

She was still lost in the sensation when he moved his hand again. His fingers swept between her cleft and he thrust inside her with two of them, filling her channel, curling his fingertips up against her inner walls. Then he pulled his fingers out of her, grasped both her hips and planted his butt on the bed.

Lifting her over him, he held her above his erection so that she knelt with her knees on either side of his flanks. Reaching for him, she wrapped her fingers around the upper part of his cock and held him steady while he settled her over the dark plum-shaped head, her feminine muscles grasping his thick shaft as he slowly lowered her down his full length.

He was big and she was tight, but her sheath opened for him. She felt every inch of his erection as he filled her, sensed Jack's desire to make this good for her. She rested there a moment, absorbing the sensations: her body balanced on her knees and shins, on Jack's muscular thighs, the dark tangle of their pubic hair closely meshed. He was larger than any man she'd ever been with—and over the past year she'd been with far too many—so at first she'd been afraid she wouldn't be able to take him, but her body adjusted perfectly to clasp him deep inside and hold him tight. She felt the subtle pulsing of her inner muscles, the thick head of his cock resting against the mouth of her womb, and yet, as large as he was, as fully as he stretched her, there was no pain.

Only pleasure. Such extreme pleasure that she consciously fought against her climax. No, not yet. She wanted to experience every sensation leading up to that amazing sense of fulfillment she'd discovered in making love with Jack.

That was something else Em had told her, that now that she was

19

Chanku, her body was designed for sex, even more so than before she'd had the nutrients. She'd said that different things like the difference in the size of the men, even oral sex and anal sex were much easier for Chanku than for humans, that their bodies could make the necessary adjustments that would allow her to swallow a man's cock without gagging or pain. If she wanted to try anal sex, it wouldn't hurt.

Tonight, now that he'd shown her what a gentle, thoughtful lover he could be, she knew that whatever Jack wanted to do with her, she'd at least be willing to try. He thrust his hips up and held her there, lifting her up to her knees. "Open to me, sweet Mary. Let me into your thoughts. You're blocking me, but if I know what you're thinking, what you're feeling, I can make it better for you."

She laughed, opening her mind. *I didn't know I was blocking. I'm sorry. And I don't see how you can possibly make this any better.*

There you are. When Chanku are intimate, we share our thoughts. Then you can feel what I feel, I know what you are feeling, and with that knowledge we can make it even better.

If you make this any better, I might melt.

He laughed. She felt the thrust of his laughter inside.

That's the point, sweet Mary. I want to make you melt.

She tightened all those feminine muscles. Jack groaned, grabbed her hips and rolled with her, flipped her over onto her back, driving into her harder, faster, taking her higher. And then his thoughts filled her mind, and she knew.

She knew!

This wasn't just sex for Jack. This went beyond the mere physical, beyond the melding of two bodies. There was no melting now, no easy slip and glide. This was hard sex, rough sex, and it grabbed her deep inside, made her feel herself as if she were Jack. His sensations, his feelings filled her thoughts, the way her muscles clasped his thick erection and how she appeared to him, like some amazing goddess, so beautiful he wanted to kneel before her, but he couldn't.

Not if it meant pulling himself away from her body, away from the most amazing sexual experience he'd ever had in his life. She was giving this to him. Mary Elizabeth Ryder, a woman whose own father had branded her a whore. She was giving something special to Jack, and he in turn shared that with her.

This man saw her as a goddess, and his feelings were so true, so powerful, she knew she'd never hold back the tears. Her climax was upon her, so fast, so powerful she screamed. Jack's fingers tightened on her hips and he drove into her harder, deeper, finding his own climax as Mary's was finally ebbing.

The thick, hot wash of his seed spurting so deep inside threw her up and over another peak, so closely entwined, mentally and physically, that the orgasm was shared, a loop that repeated itself in slowly receding waves of pleasure between the two of them. Finally, Jack lowered himself carefully and fell to one side with his forearm resting across her breasts. When her orgasm ended, when the tremors subsided, she couldn't stop weeping, overwhelmed by what Jack had given her. Overwhelmed by what she had discovered about Jack, about herself.

Finally, she turned her head, saw his face so close to hers as he lay beside her, watching her. His beautiful dark amber eyes were awash in tears, his lips curved upward in an almost shy smile.

"Is it true?" she asked. "You? Me?"

He nodded. "I think it must be. I've been watching you since the first day. Making up stories about what it would be like if you were mine."

"But . . . you . . . you're . . ." She shook her head. Laughed, except it sounded more like she was sobbing. "You're you. You're Jack Temple. Every single woman I've talked to who knows you wants you." She laughed again, embarrassed by how watery her laughter sounded. "I'm just . . ."

He laughed, lying there beside her, staring at the ceiling. After a moment he rolled to his side and kissed her gently. "I know who you are," he said, punctuating his words with another kiss. "You're just Mary Elizabeth Ryder, a woman who has fascinated me from the first moment she arrived. Making love with you has merely reinforced my original opinion. You are strong, and so brave, and yet so very good inside. There's nothing about you that I don't admire. There's no one who could possibly be any better, any more perfect for me."

He rolled back over her, holding his chest and shoulders off her body. His penis had slipped free but rested now between her legs. He was still partially erect, his legs tangled with hers, their bellies pressed tightly together slick with sweat. Propped on his elbows, he rubbed circles over her nipples so that it was hard to concentrate on what he said. He was growing hard again, his shaft filling the space between her legs, trapped so close against her, but not nearly close enough.

She realized she was concentrating more on the sensation of that thick, hot organ pressing against her sex than what he was saying. Until he tapped her nipples with his fingertips.

"Pay attention, sweet Mary." He grinned and kissed the tip of her nose.

She blushed and raised her hips just enough to press them tighter together. He settled closer. All her feminine muscles clenched.

"Mary, I want to see where this goes, whatever this thing between us is. I've been with a lot of women—men, too, for that matter—but no one has ever affected me the way you do. Are you willing to give us a try?"

She couldn't speak. She hadn't expected anything like this. She nodded, biting her lips to keep from sobbing. She'd never dreamed . . . Well, actually she had dreamed, but that's all she'd thought it would ever be. She reached for Jack, pulled him down to her and kissed him. Hard.

His lips parted and he deepened the kiss, lowering his torso onto hers, pressing her into the mattress as he tangled his hands in her hair, holding her for his mouth.

Her phone rang. A distinct tone she had to answer. Jack broke the kiss when she stiffened.

"It's my mother." Mary stared at the stupid phone. Why was she calling now, in the middle of the night?

Jack rolled to one side and grabbed her phone off the dresser. He handed it to her, left the bed, and stepped out of the room.

3

Blinking into the velvety darkness, Igmutaka wondered just what the hell had awakened him. He'd been sleeping so peacefully with his beloved Mikaela Star draped across his chest, tiny Sunny Daye curled tightly against his back, and Fenris, his beautiful Fen, pressed close to Sunny with his long fingers splayed over Ig's thigh.

It really didn't get any better, and he shouldn't be so anxious, not with all three of his mates surrounding him, but the visceral sense of need, as if he had to be somewhere *right now,* would not free him.

He had no idea where that somewhere might be or why, but the sensation was real. His skin was cold, clammy, as if he were bathed in the sweat of fear.

No. That wasn't it. It couldn't be.

Igmutaka had lived many lives, from wild puma to spirit guide and then to man, existing over countless centuries through every kind of trauma imaginable. He could be many things, but afraid wasn't one of them, especially when there was no one sneaking up on them, their home was safe, and his lovers—his mates—slept beside him.

At least the women did. Fen's fingers gently stroked his thigh—the big man was as wide awake as he, and obviously just as perplexed. Containing the immediate rush of arousal raised by the sensual sweep of Fen's hand, Ig reached for his mind. *Any idea why we're both awake in the middle of the night, my brother? Other than the fact you're obviously hoping for more playtime?*

Fen's mental laughter tickled his senses. *Not a clue, but something or someone is telling me we need to be awake.* A moment later, the mattress

23

dipped and rose again as Fen quietly got out of bed and left the room.

Reluctantly, Ig disentangled himself from the sleeping women and slipped away from their warmth. He carefully covered Star and Sunny with the soft down blanket they'd left twisted at the foot of their bed. Their earlier lovemaking had been sinfully heated, but the night had grown cool and the women would miss the warmth two large men generated. Ig paused, gently stroking Mikaela Star's glossy curls while thinking of all that they'd done to generate that heat. It was not easy to leave either the warmth or the women he loved.

After a moment he followed Fen, trusting the man's instincts to lead them in the right direction. Fen always seemed to know the answers. A surprise, actually, considering just how recently Fen had learned of his Chanku heritage, the fact that he, like Ig, could trace his origins to the ferocious Berserker wolves of old. Ig found him sitting in one of the Adirondack chairs on the front deck. The sweet scent of the freshly milled cedar they'd used to enlarge Sunny's cabin was a reminder why it had been so hard to leave that comfortable bed. He was tired and his muscles ached, as much from the hard work of remodeling Sunny's small home so they'd all fit as from the lovemaking they'd enjoyed last night. A perfect celebration for having finished the job.

Of course, they never needed an excuse for *that* kind of celebration.

Sleep—at least for now—was no longer an option. He and Fen were awake for a reason, and they'd find out soon enough. The Mother had told them—after they'd surprisingly ended up in a four-way mating—that they might be called upon to serve their kind by serving her. They'd all agreed, but had yet to be called. At least not for anything major.

Until tonight. This felt deadly serious. Ig greeted Fen with a gentle caress to his broad shoulders before dropping into the chair beside him. "Find any answers yet?"

Fen merely grunted.

Ig heard footsteps, sensed his Mikaela Star before she walked through the door, rubbing her eyes as she wandered, half asleep, out of the house. Sunny was right behind her. Ig held out his hand, and Star took hold. He tumbled her into his lap as Fen reached for Sunny.

Star nuzzled Ig's chest and yawned. "What's going on?"

"Did we wake you?" Ig brushed his woman's tousled hair out of her eyes.

"No." She glanced at Sunny. "We both woke up at the same time." She shrugged and snuggled against his chest, rubbing her arms. "Nightmare, maybe? I woke up feeling anxious and afraid, but I have no idea why."

"So did I." Sunny sat up in Fen's lap, then stood and stared past the railing surrounding the deck. "But I have a feeling I know why. Hi, Eve. What's going on?"

Igmutaka's gaze snapped to the glowing cylinder of light appearing just beyond the deck.

"Nothing yet. Praise the Mother." Their goddess was little more than a shimmering column in front of the cabin, but there was no mistaking her presence—or her voice. She grew brighter, gradually corporeal, until her aura shimmered like silver fire with streaks leaping within the silver, more flames covering the full color spectrum. Finally she stood before them, solid, unbelievably beautiful, and obviously feeling the same anxiety as her four Chanku.

"The Mother wants you to come to the portal. She's contacting Sebastian and Lily now. Bring Anton. We'll need his alpha strength as well. Something terrible is coming."

As she took form, Ig realized that their usually composed goddess wrung her hands nervously; the colors of her otherworldly eyes spun in wild flashes—green and amber, brilliant blue to subtle gray. Her long blonde hair usually hung straight to her ankles; now it floated wildly about her, as if caught in a burst of static electricity, and her voice faltered. "We don't know if you can stop them."

"Stop who, Eve?" Eyes blazing, Fen leapt to his feet, his wolf very close to the surface, though his voice remained soft, filled with respect.

Like Igmutaka, Fenris would protect his goddess to the death if need be.

Eve shuddered and then took visible control of her emotions. "We have sensed an apocalypse, an event of total destruction planned by men, but somehow involving an entity of pure evil. Bits and pieces are coming to us slowly, but the terror will happen quickly. You'll need to pass through the portal. We'll use the astral to travel more quickly. Time is of the essence."

Ig was already in motion, but he heard Fen's soft question. "Where are we going?"

Eve's answer didn't give him much confidence. "I don't know, Fen. I hope to find out when we reach the astral."

• • •

The home of Sebastian Xenakis and Lily Cheval-Xenakis
Friday, 2:10 a.m.

Sebastian had been dreaming, but then he wasn't. No, he was answering the Mother's call. Coming awake so quickly was disorienting, to say the least, but he gently stroked Lily's shoulder, calling to her mind, bringing her as gently as possible from sleep.

Staring blindly into the darkness, she took a moment to focus on him. "What's happened?" She sat up in bed, blinking furiously, already wide awake, mind and body in sync and ready for whatever was needed.

Seb was still trying to master that one. "We need to go to the oak. I feel the Mother calling me, but not with words. It's a physical pressure, as if she's pulling me there. I'm not sure what's going on, but we need to hurry." He reached for his jeans.

Lily's hand on his arm stopped him. "It's warm enough. I know you connect in your human form, but we can get there faster as wolves."

She was right. Lily was always right, and it was one of the many things he loved about her, but he hadn't been a shifter for all that long. There were some things a guy had to get used to. They shifted out on the deck, leapt over the railing and raced up the mountain. There was no moon tonight, but the sky was so perfectly clear that starlight lit their way. The oak stood on the promontory as it had for over a thousand years, its thick branches reaching forever into the sky. Sebastian shifted, pressed his palms against the rough bark and bowed his head to the tree.

He still found it absolutely surreal that a powerful goddess would choose to speak to him, here, through a tree large enough, old enough, filled with a strong enough life force that it could harbor her overwhelming spirit for brief periods of time.

But this time was different. Usually she spoke clearly to him, her voice so filled with power that it often left him physically shaken. Tonight there were no words, merely images, as if he orbited in space high above the earth and watched horrifying scenes of massive destruction, continents breaking apart, fire reaching into the sky. He saw it all in less than a heartbeat, then shook himself free of her connection the moment all sense of the Mother was gone from the oak.

He turned to Lily, realized he was practically hyperventilating. Taking a moment he felt he didn't have to give, he shook off the aftereffects of communing with a being whose strength was beyond imagination. "Lily, I have no idea what she just showed me, but it's definitely not good." He opened his thoughts to her, showed her the images.

Her eyes opened wider. She clasped his hands. "From the Mother?"

"Yes. C'mon. We need to go to your parents' house." Her eyes flashed in panic and he shook his head. "They're fine. It's so we can get to the astral."

"Thank you." Obviously relieved, she kissed him quickly and they shifted. The two wolves raced down the mountain toward the home where Anton Cheval, Lily's father and the pack's alpha, lived. His house wasn't merely his home—it was strategically placed atop an underground cavern that presented the closest portal onto the astral plane.

There was only one tiny problem that Sebastian couldn't quite shake. He hoped someone knew where they were going, and just what the fuck they were supposed to do once they arrived, because whatever the Mother had shown him in that vision? Well, it was a hell of a lot bigger than anything any of them had ever dealt with before, and he could say that without even knowing what it was.

• • •

Jack's cabin
Friday, 2:15 a.m.

Mary stood beside the bed and answered the call. Her mother's face appeared on the small screen. She looked pale and exhausted, and it was obvious she'd been crying. Mary hardened herself—the last conversation Mary had had with this woman had been filled with recriminations and threats. Her first reaction was anger. It was stronger even than the curiosity over why her mother was calling, why her face was streaked with tears. Why did the woman who'd so clearly denied her have to call now, when she and Jack were just starting to talk?

"Mother? Why are you calling? The last time we talked you called me a whore and told me you never wanted to see or speak to me again. What's going on?"

Her mother stared at the screen, tears flowing, and Mary thought she looked as if she'd aged a good twenty years. "I was wrong," she said. "Dead wrong. I should never have listened to your father. Mary, I think he's crazy, he's doing crazy things. The church we've always followed? It isn't a church at all. You need to listen to me, try to find a way to stop them." She took a deep breath. "Your father and Brother Thomas have found a way to hasten the Apocalypse. They believe that Armageddon is here, in this country, that the signs are right and the Apocalypse is coming. He says there is a gateway to Armageddon, and they have a spirit guiding them, an angel." She drew in a harsh breath, coughed and doubled over, covering her mouth with a tissue. After a moment, she faced the screen again, but her lips were tinged in crimson, her voice ragged and halting. "They're wrong, Mary. It's not an angel helping them, it's a demon. A being who is evil, someone powerful enough to help them blow up the world."

"What? That's impossible . . . they can't do that! That's crazy." This was so not like her mother; something was terribly wrong. "Why are you saying this? What happened? Are you bleeding? Mom? What is it?" Mary glanced wildly about. Where was Jack?

"Mary. Listen to me. There's no time. I heard them talking. It's going to happen in Yellowstone, and if you're in that Chanku stronghold in Montana, he's not all that far from you. About four hundred miles, if that. Your father thinks he's a soldier for the Lord, but Brother Thomas has lied to him. He's lied to all of us and they have some sort of bomb that's huge, like an atomic bomb. You have to stop them!"

Mary hadn't even heard him come back into the room, but Jack grasped her shoulders, his big hands steadying her. "Mom, you're not making any sense. How could Dad get a nuclear bomb? That's crazy. Why would you believe something like that?"

Her mother looked directly into the screen, staring at Mary as if she could reach out and touch her, and her voice was strong again. Strong and angry, not the subservient wife at all. "Because your father is evil. He killed your sister, Mary. At least a day ago . . . I don't know how long. I'm so sorry; I've been unconscious. He strangled Becca in front of me. Then he shot me. He said he did it so we wouldn't have to die in the chaos that was coming. He thought he killed me, but I fooled him. I played dead and he left, but Mary?" She took a deep breath and said, "I won't see you again. Not in this world. I'm hurt, bad, Mary. Worse than I realized. I should have called you weeks ago, but I was ashamed. Now this. I prayed and I prayed, but Becca didn't come back. She's really gone." She shook her head slowly. "It's too late for shame. Too late for forgiveness for me, but not for you. I never should have doubted you, Mary. You're my daughter and I love you, but I'm dying."

Then she panned her phone slowly away from her face, focused on the body of a little girl with dark hair, lying on the floor. Becca was obviously dead, eyes open wide, the purple, almost black bruises on her pale throat an abomination.

Mary gasped and shoved her knuckles against her mouth. Jack tightened his grip on her shoulders. His harsh curse echoed inside her skull. Her heart pounded, her ragged breath rasped unnaturally loud and she couldn't stop staring at the horrific image of her baby sister. Rebecca was nine, her father and mother's natural daughter. A blessing, they'd said, after so many years of trying.

The image on the screen was unsteady as her mother turned the phone back to herself, but she held it away from her face and there was no missing the huge bloodstain across her midsection. "I love you, sweetheart. I never wanted to say those awful things to you, but your father made me. Now I wish I'd left him years ago, when you first went to college. I so wanted to be with you, to be that young girl tasting freedom for the first time. It's too late for me. Do whatever you can to stop Brother Thomas and your father. They follow one of the devil's minions, a demon they call Master Aldo. Your father thinks he's a saint. He's not. He's the one who told your father to kill us because he needed our life force. Saving us from the Apocalypse had nothing to do with it. That's not how God works, is it? God loves his children."

She started coughing again. Blood spattered the screen, obscuring much of her face. Mary wanted to wipe the screen though she knew it was the lens on her mother's phone now covered in fresh blood. "You have to stop them, Mary. Maybe that man who rules the Chanku? Mr. Cheval? He can do anything, can't he? Go to him, if he'll see you. Beg him if you have to. Your father and the others must be stopped. From what your father said, you only have two more days at the very most. Master Aldo will be ready then. I'm trying to stay alive. I don't want him to get my life force. I am so sorry, Mary. So very, very sorry. I love you."

The call dropped. Mary stared at her phone and felt the numbness settling in, the same emotional disconnect that had helped her survive her year of slavery. She turned to Jack, studied his beautiful face, the expression of . . . what? Anger? Sadness? She couldn't tell, but when she blotted out her emotions it was difficult to read those of another.

He shook himself and grabbed his phone off the dresser. "What is your mom's address, Mary? I need to call for help for her. She might still make it."

Struggling to shake herself free of the creeping sense of oblivion, Mary shook her head, a short, sharp jerk that just might shake her senses loose. The pain that arrived was a visceral thing, a pain she immediately buried.

"The address, Mary. I need it now."

She rattled off the familiar numbers, the street, city, state, but it didn't make any sense. She'd been so angry at her mother, but now . . . "Jack?" Tilting her head, she frowned, wondering who this person was who spoke, curious at her lack of emotional distress. This was something awful, wasn't it? It must be. Jack was talking to someone, reporting a murder. Giving Mary's address.

"He killed my sister, maybe my mother, too? I don't understand. What was that about?"

He didn't answer. Instead, he gave his personal information and ended the call. "Sweetheart, I don't know." He pulled her into a close hug. Then he clasped her shoulders, made her look at him. "We need to get to Anton. He can help us figure this out. Get dressed. It's too late to call, but if we're close I can reach him with my mind. Let's go to his house."

Still numb, Mary went into the bathroom and grabbed a damp cloth off the towel rack. Carefully, methodically, she washed away the evidence of their lovemaking.

None of this made sense. Her mother didn't make sense. Her father wouldn't have murdered his daughter. Tried to kill his wife. He loved them. At least he said he did, but he'd loved her, too, and look how well that had worked. Jack was right. Anton would know. He knew everything.

Mary tied her hair back in a ponytail and grabbed a piece of fabric hanging near the closet. She'd grown used to wearing the sarong-style dresses—easy to change in and out of when she needed to shift. Another example of the changes in her life. Jack had put on a pair of running shorts and a T-shirt. They both slipped on lightweight sandals.

He had a tight grasp on Mary's hand as they practically ran down the trail toward Anton and Keisha's house. Small solar lights illuminated the broad path, but little beyond. She glanced at Jack, at the taut line of his jaw, the determined look in his eyes. "What's going on, Jack? How can Anton help us? I don't get it, not anything my mother said. What could he be doing that she's warning us about here? Why would my father shoot my mother, strangle my sister?"

She should be inconsolable right now. All she felt was numb. Except where their hands linked. She felt alive where Jack held her.

"I don't know, Mary. But your mother mentioned that their minister was talking to a devil spirit, they called him Aldo. It's impossible, but maybe not. Aldo's an unusual name. You've met Sebastian and Lily, right? Sebastian's father was named Aldo Xenakis. He was a totally sick son of a bitch who hated Chanku. He was also a powerful wizard, but his magic was dark. Sebastian called it 'blood magic.' His spells needed the life force of young women that he raped and murdered. Sebastian killed him, but I'm wondering if part of Aldo survived."

"That's impossible."

"Is it?"

She really didn't want to think of that, but they'd reached Anton's house. It was ablaze in light. Mary glanced at Jack as they raced up the steps to the front porch. "They must be awake. What time is it?"

"Almost three," he said. "Something's definitely going on." He pounded on the front door.

Anton flung it open before Jack had time to lower his arm. "Did the goddess call you two as well?"

Mary shook her head. "No. My mother called. She was talking crazy, about an apocalypse, and I thought she was nuts when she said my father had killed my little sister and shot her—my mother. That a demon spirit had ordered it. Then she showed me Rebecca."

She turned to Jack, her muscles clenched tightly, all that held her from exploding into a million pieces. "You saw her, right? She's dead, isn't she?"

Wrapping his arm around her shoulders, holding her close, Jack nodded. "Anton, she warned Mary, said her father was in Yellowstone, that he has 'some sort of an atomic bomb.' Her description. She said we need to get out of here, that something terrible is going to happen within the next two days."

"Crap. That fits with other things we're hearing." He opened the door wider, stepped aside.

Jack shook his head. "There's more, Anton. The devil spirit, the demon Mary mentioned? They call him Master Aldo, said he ordered the killings because he needed their life force. Isn't that what Aldo Xenakis did? Killed those young women for their living energy? I called 911 and gave them Mary's home address and they said they'd send someone to the house to check, hopefully in time to save her mother, but the thing is, I'm wondering if Aldo Xenakis isn't quite as dead as we'd hoped."

"Come in. Both of you. We'll fill you in with what we know, but it sounds as if a lot of what we're learning fits much too closely to your news." Shaking his head, not looking nearly as in control as Mary expected from a man who never, ever appeared at all flustered or ill at ease, Anton gestured for them to come into the house. "So far," he said, straightening his spine, somehow finding that laser focus she'd grown to expect, "none of it looks good, but I'm glad you're here. You can either answer some questions or add to the confusion." He shook his head, obviously frustrated. "Either way, welcome to the madhouse."

• • •

Anton Cheval's home
Friday, 2:56 a.m.

Sebastian and Lily shifted as soon as they reached the house. Lily's mom, Keisha, met them at the back door that opened directly into a mudroom and then into the kitchen. Sebastian grabbed robes off the hook by the door and handed one to Lily. Covered in warm terry cloth, they followed Keisha through the door into the kitchen. Stefan and Xandi Aragat, sipping at steaming cups of coffee, greeted them just as they would any other morning at the pack alpha's house—if it weren't almost three in the morning, and if that unfamiliar look of fear wasn't so clearly etched on each person's face.

Even Keisha looked worried, and Sebastian knew how difficult it was to ruffle her amazing composure. "Is Anton . . . ?"

"He's in the cavern with the others—Ig, Sunny, Star, and Fen. Jack and Mary. They're waiting for you. Hurry."

Lily quickly hugged her mom. Sebastian followed his mate as she took the door to the stairs leading down into a large basement. A heavy door disguised as part of the pantry was open, and in less than a minute they'd reached the cavern where Anton and the others were gathered in front of the portal.

Sebastian wondered if he'd ever get used to looking directly into the astral, a world of brilliant hues, of trees and grass and sky so perfect it made him think he was looking at an artistically rendered high-definition photo of the world's most perfect park. He slipped his arm around Lily's waist, and the two of them joined the others. Anton turned toward them, nodded at Sebastian and then drew his daughter into a tight hug.

"Eve is conversing with the Mother," he said. "It appears that Eve heard a cry for help, a voice she didn't recognize. They've pinned it down to Yellowstone, but so far it's not specific enough. She's trying to reestablish contact."

Frowning, Sebastian glanced at Lily before turning to Anton. "This seems like a rather large response for a single call for help." He thought of the brief connection he'd had with the Mother, the terrifying images he'd glimpsed.

Shaking his head, Anton glanced once again toward the portal. "The Mother linked with Eve just before the original contact and sensed something absolutely apocalyptic. End-of-the-world stuff, somehow associated with the creature who called out for help moments later. She explained, through Eve, that this sort of prescience happens very rarely, but she's learned to take heed."

Now those frightening images made more sense. "That explains the visuals she showed me. I woke up knowing I had to connect with the Mother." He described that brief but frightening period filled with apocalyptic visuals. "That was it. No explanation other than the knowledge that we had to come here."

Anton nodded just as Eve appeared in the glowing portal. She looked badly shaken, but after a moment she raised her head and was once again composed as ever. Still holding on to Lily, Sebastian moved closer to the portal to hear Eve.

"We have connected once again with the one who warned us. His name is Ari." Eve focused on Igmutaka and Fenris. "He is a Berserker who has never shifted from his wolf form. He and his brother are in Yellowstone, traveling in search of the Chanku they've heard of, hoping to find what they need to be able to shift. They don't know of your compound here, only of Chanku in San Francisco. That was their destination." She shook her head and took a deep breath. "They've never had the grasses. They are from many generations of wolves with the thoughts of men, knowledge of what they should be able to do, but they don't know . . ."

Clasping her hands in front of her, she shot one very frustrated glance at Anton. Sebastian knew the alpha had done everything he could to get the word out about the grasses, but still there were more shifters out there. It was even more difficult reaching those Berserkers who had never been able to shift.

"Originally there were four of them. Their brother was shot by hunters about a year ago and their sister was killed along the way here. Tonight . . ." She took a deep breath. "Tonight, Ari's twin brother was shot and taken by a group of men who are planning something terrible. Ari's not sure exactly what, but he's followed them as far as he could. They've gone into a cavern that leads to a series of tunnels. He said they spoke of a nuclear device, something they hope to detonate deep inside the great volcano caldera that lies beneath Yellowstone. Their goal is to trigger an eruption."

"Holy shit." Totally out of character, obviously shaken, Ig turned and looked to Anton. "That volcano is huge, and it's still active. If that thing blows, it could wipe out most of the population in the U.S."

"Even worse." Sebastian tightened his grasp on Lily, as if holding her close would protect her. If what he'd seen was true . . . "The Mother showed images to me. Massive worldwide destruction. If they know exactly where to set that device, and if it's powerful enough to set off the Yellowstone super volcano, the explosion could be enough to cause slippage along the Ring of Fire. That's the series of earthquake faults and volcanoes that runs from the tip of South America and circles the Pacific all the way down past New Zealand."

"You're not just talking about a massive nuclear explosion that would only disrupt life in this country, are you?" Anton looked as if he'd aged fifty years.

"No, Anton."

The small group glanced from one to another, as if trying to recognize the source of the powerful voice that seemed to come from everywhere. From nowhere. Only Sebastian knew her as intimately as if they'd been lovers. He fell to his knees and bowed his head, with Lily dropping to her knees beside him.

Eve immediately knelt as well, and the others followed suit. A brilliant glow filled the portal, spilled out into the dark cavern, bringing with it a sense of immeasurable power. It pulsed with the beat of his heart, breathed with Sebastian's breath.

And then she spoke, her voice inside their heads even as it echoed off the walls of the cavern.

The Mother, the supreme being, an entity filled with unimaginable power, and yet one unable to stop or even begin to understand those pitiful humans with their free will and foolish, uneducated minds. Sebastian felt her touch, the intimate caress of one growing tired of the foibles of mankind.

"Eons ago your ancestors faced a similar threat, but they had mastered space travel and knew where there were planets that could harbor life when the destruction of their world was imminent. Earth was one of them. You don't have that option. From what I can tell, the fools planning this terrible act are too stupid to realize what they're doing. They think the volcano will explode and kill only unbelieving Americans and Canadians from Yellowstone east. They don't understand the science behind the tectonic plates or the danger of a nuclear winter, when so much ash fills the sky that all life on this world will die, if any at all survive the destruction of so many continents.

"Fools. They are all fools, but there's more. Sebastian, I don't want you to learn it at an inopportune time, but these idiots follow the teachings of your father. This heinous act is being carried out in the name of Master Aldo Xenakis. His evil does not reflect on the man you are, nor does it have any bearing on the man you will become. But if his dark magic is involved, if a fragment of his spirit still exists, you and your mate might be the only ones who can stop him."

Blindly Sebastian reached for Lily's hand as she took hold of his. He bowed his head, fully aware of the weight of his father's sins. "Thank you. You're right. I much prefer knowing the evil we'll face, the one we must defeat." He raised his head and gazed at her, the entity he had grown to honor and love almost as much as he loved his beloved mate. "How can we stop them? What do you want us to do?"

Rising, standing before her, he gazed directly at the supreme goddess, unafraid of her power. She had only ever used it to help him. Her light should have blinded him, but instead he looked into the swirling glow and felt peace. The Mother was on his side, in spite of his father, despite the evil Aldo Xenakis had created and nurtured. She was always on his side.

Why the Mother favored him, Sebastian had no idea, but one thing he was certain of—he trusted her.

"I can show you where they are planning this heinous act," she said, speaking to Sebastian but allowing the others to hear her. "How you can access them through the astral. Eve will share whatever we are able to learn, but she and I cannot stop them ourselves. Eve will be permitted to aid you where she can, but this fight will rest in your hands."

He felt her sigh of frustration. "There are rules. Always rules that even the gods are unable to break. Think of yourselves as chess pieces on a very large board in a game only marginally controlled by fate. Move with care, Sebastian. What you, Lily, Mikaela Star, Sunny, Igmutaka, Fenris, and yes, Jack, you, and Mary with your knowledge of the humans involved, do in the next few days could determine whether this world and all upon it live or die."

"How do the Berserkers fit into this?"

The Mother's light pulsed. "We don't know. Only that they somehow hold the key. You must save them first." Her glow began to fade.

Sebastian tightened his grasp on Lily's hand and asked one last question. "When do we leave?"

"In one hour. Sooner if possible. You will know what you need to gather, and then you will return to this place."

Her light winked out, the portal closed. Sebastian turned to Anton. The weight of the world rested on his shoulders, and he thought of the warning his mother had given him when he'd told her he wanted to know about his father. She'd been right. The man had been evil personified, and Sebastian could never pretend Aldo Xenakis's blood didn't run in his veins.

But if he'd followed his mother's advice, he never would have met Lily. Never would have found a father figure who loved him as if Sebastian were the man's own son, and that knowledge gave him the confidence to face Anton Cheval, an über alpha if ever there was one.

"Gather the pack, Anton. I have a feeling we're going to need all the strength—and more—that they can give us."

4

Sound carried from the cavern, so the men couldn't be too far inside. Once again Ari reached for Reko's mind, but there was nothing. No sense of his brother, but he would not accept that Reko was gone. Not until he'd touched his brother's lifeless body, felt for a heartbeat that didn't exist. The goddess had answered him, proof that miracles did exist. Now, crouched beside the entrance, hidden behind a tumble of boulders, he waited for their goddess to speak to him again.

She had spoken to him. He still couldn't believe the sensation of a woman's melodic voice in his head, her words more comfort than he could have imagined. She was gathering help, other Chanku and a couple of Berserkers like Reko and him. They weren't the last, and if Reko was alive and if they could get out of this in one piece, they'd get the nutrients they needed to shift.

He couldn't wait to tell Reko. It would be worth admitting he'd been wrong, just to have the chance to tell his twin he'd been right. But if Reko died without knowing? That was something so terrible he didn't even want to consider it. Ari stared into the darkness, but he didn't call to their goddess again. Not yet. She might be busy bringing men to him, those who would help save his brother. At least he could listen to the men in the cavern. Hopefully learn something more.

They appeared to be arguing. Whatever they were planning was big enough to interest a goddess, but they didn't sound either smart or organized.

"I think that's all we can do here tonight. Brother Thomas? Are you sure Aldo can get the device deep enough to actually set off the volcano?"

"That is Master Aldo to you, Ryder. I've seen his power and have no doubt. Are you certain you wish to question him? You didn't lie to me, did you? Your daughter is dead. Your wife, too? Master Aldo needs their life force if we are to succeed."

"Yes." His sigh was audible, even to Ari outside the cave. "They are both dead by my hand."

Ari shivered at the man's words. The human sounded more resigned than sad over killing his wife and child. An abomination like that was unheard of among the pack. Ari had never heard of Master Aldo, but he must be a terrible, evil man. Powerful enough to convince the human to kill both his child and his mate. Evil enough to ask for such a sacrifice.

"Did Master Aldo tell you why we need to wait until Saturday night? This place will be crawling with tourists then."

"He is most powerful beneath the dark of the moon. Have you got everything? We have the coordinates marked as he requested. We have to leave. It'll be light soon."

"Brother Thomas?" Ari recognized yet another voice. Four men had gone into the cave. He'd now heard three of them. "What about the wolf? He's huge. He'd make one hell of a trophy."

"Leave him for now. We'll get him out of here before Saturday. It's cold enough in here that the carcass won't spoil. If anyone finds him, they'll just think he crawled in here to die. Everything out of sight? Good."

"What about the fire? It's almost out, but . . ."

"Forget it. Let's go. We'll check back tomorrow night, make sure everything is set. We can grab the wolf then. Right now we need to get the equipment out of here."

Ari watched them leave, each of them carrying large cases or bags, though he had no idea what the stuff was. He waited until they were long gone, but it would be light soon. He had to get Reko out of the cave before daylight, but how? And where could he take him that he wouldn't be found? He stared at the opening to the cave, checked to make sure no one was around.

Then he stood and looked to see the way they'd gone. They'd hiked south along the paved road. There was a campground nearby, one where they must be staying, or where they might have left a vehicle. He glanced once more toward the cave. At least he could find out if his brother lived. With another quick glance to make sure he was alone, Ari slipped through the narrow opening, into the darkness beyond.

• • •

37

Montana cavern portal to the astral
Friday, 3:30 a.m.

It was barely three thirty in the morning when they gathered again in the cavern beneath Anton and Keisha's kitchen, nine of them, counting Anton, standing in front of the portal to the astral well ahead of the time the Mother had given them. They'd all changed into more serviceable clothing, following Eve's silent instructions. Jack wasn't sure what he and Mary could add to this venture, but he was glad they'd been included, even though Mary's father's involvement left him feeling ill. He actually hurt for her, but she'd not said another word about the man, nor had she mentioned her mother and sister.

She had to be in shock. Mary had been uncharacteristically silent since speaking with her mother, but she'd not wanted to talk about it, about her feelings, at all. He'd not pressed her, but he worried. Her shields were high and tight, but he didn't know if that was on purpose or merely her natural shielding. So often she didn't realize she was closed to him, but they were still new. She might not feel that comfortable yet. Sharing thoughts was more intimate even than sex—intimate enough that it took sex to a totally different level.

But this wasn't about sex. It was about seeing her baby sister dead, her mother bleeding, hearing that her father was involved in a plot with a demon that could destroy their world. She had every right to keep her own counsel, but he worried about her. Worried that she might be blaming herself when she was entirely blameless.

Anton had promised to check on her family once they'd gone through the portal. He said it was good that he had a job to do or he'd probably drive Keisha nuts because he wasn't in the middle of the hunt, but he knew he was needed here with the pack. He'd be the one to pull them all together if their power was needed. He'd already sent out a call that they be ready at a moment's notice, at least for the next day or so. Knowing their sexual energy might be crucial to success actually helped increase that energy when the time came for action.

Jack had a feeling they were going to need whatever help they could get.

He glanced at the others, at Sebastian and Lily, hands clasped, eyes forward as the solid stone of the cave walls slowly faded to reveal the perfect world that was all he'd ever seen of the astral plane. He'd never once crossed over from this world to that one, but that was about to change.

So much change, so quickly. After so many years just drifting, from the time he'd graduated from college and realized he still didn't have a clue what he wanted to do with his life. He'd met Mary and felt the first stirrings of the new course he'd follow; last night they'd finally come together and it had hit him like a lightning bolt.

She was the one he wanted. He'd been floating with the knowledge that there was a purpose in everything they did. When her mother called and that purpose had taken on a frightening significance, he knew how he and Mary reacted to the news would affect their lives from this day forward.

Their lives, and the lives of everyone they knew and loved. No more going with the flow, figuring that he'd know when it was time how to do what needed to be done, whether it was finding work that he could pursue with passion or learning to be the kind of man Mary could love. No, it appeared that life was going to just slap him upside the head, as his mom would say.

Funny how that worked—he and Star were twins, and both he and his twin had let life push them forward. They'd never really pushed back. She'd put her energy into avoiding her fate, but when she'd finally quit fighting the inevitable, she'd found her passion with the one man she'd hidden from all her adult life. Two men and a woman, actually: Igmutaka, Fen, and Sunny.

Leave it to Star to break all the rules. He loved his twin dearly, but sometimes she drove him nuts.

"Jack?"

As if his thoughts had conjured her, she was there, but before he could say anything, Star reached for him and hugged him close.

"What's that for?" He returned her tight embrace.

"I want you to know I love you, and I don't want to go into this without saying it to you. I'm scared of what could happen."

He kissed the tip of her nose. "You've got Berserkers on your team, sis. I think you'll be fine. I'd be more worried for the bad guys. I love you, too."

She squeezed him one more time and then let go with a quick smile for Mary. He caught her private comment. *You and Mary?*

It feels like it. I hope so.

Good. Igmutaka grabbed her hand and lightly tugged her forward. Star, Fen, and Sunny followed him from this world onto the astral. Jack watched them go, seeming to walk far from the cavern in very few steps. Sebastian and Lily were next. Jack held tightly to Mary's hand. She turned and looked at him and he had no idea what she thought, what she felt. Her mind stayed blocked. He brushed her cheek with his fingertips, and then the two of them followed Lily and Sebastian.

He wasn't certain what made him pause, turn, and glance over his shoulder at Anton just moments before the wall reformed behind them. There were tears on the alpha's face, his hand raised as if to bless them— or was he saying good-bye, knowing they might not make it back?

Jack mentally shook himself. He didn't need to be thinking along those lines, not if they wanted to come out of this alive. Facing forward, he saw Eve waiting for them, smiling.

How could she smile at a time like this?

"You're early," she said. "I'm glad. We have some good news. The Mother has reopened a long-neglected portal that's actually within the cave where Ari waits with his brother. Reko is injured, but he lives, so our plans have changed a bit. The Mother wants you to bring the two of them through the portal first so we can heal him. Sunny, I'll need you to help me, but Igmutaka and Fenris, you'll go in first and bring Reko and Ari back with you. We'll wait on this side of the portal, but should you need us, we'll be close. Come."

She turned and quickly moved through the forest, gliding really, with her feet barely skimming the surface. They all followed, moving at a quick jog to keep up until Eve paused at a spot that seemed no different from any other part of this strangely beautiful world. With a wave of her hand, the trees shimmered and slowly faded to darkness, lit only by the glowing embers of a dying fire. There were two wolves in the shadows, one lying on his side, his head smeared with blood, the other crouching over the injured one, watching them, teeth bared and snarling. Ari and Reko. Jack glanced at Igmutaka, who had easily taken the lead at this point.

"Give me a moment," Ig said, stepping through the portal. *Ari?* The wolf stopped snarling and went low, belly to the ground, responding instinctively to Igmutaka's dominance. Ig nodded his head in greeting, but mindspoke to all of them. *I am Igmutaka, a Berserker like you. We are all of the same pack. You, me, your brother, those behind me, we are all Chanku. This doorway leads into the world our goddess inhabits. She wants us to bring you and your brother into her world so that she can heal Reko. Will you let us help you?*

The wolf rose to stand between Ig and the injured wolf. *He's badly hurt, an injury to his skull. I don't know if the bullet penetrated or not. There's too much blood.*

Ig nodded and turned to glance over his shoulder at his mate. *Fen? He's huge. You're stronger than I am. Do you think you can carry him, or do you need help?*

No. I can do this. Fen moved past Ig and knelt beside the injured wolf, but he turned first to Ari. *I need to lift your brother. I'll do my best not to hurt him. Follow close behind me so that we can take you onto the astral plane with us. You'll both be safe there.* Gently he ran his hands over the unconscious wolf before carefully lifting him in both arms and holding the huge animal against his chest. Ari stayed close beside Fen, his gaze locked on his brother. It was only a matter of seconds before Fen and Ig with Ari and Reko were back on the astral plane, where Eve and the others waited.

Sunny immediately sat beside the big wolf when Fen gently placed him on the soft grass. Eve sat directly across from her on Reko's other side, but she turned to Sebastian and Lily. "I don't know how long this will take. It's going to be light soon. Take Ig and Fen back into the cavern, see if you can find anything that will give us an idea what they have planned. Ari, I want you to stay with us, in case your brother awakens. We're strangers and I don't want him to be afraid. Star, if you, Jack, and Mary could stand sentinel while we work on Reko, I would appreciate it."

"Will do, but do you really think you need guards here, on the astral?"

Eve merely shook her head. "Honestly, Jack, I don't know anymore." He thought she looked terribly sad, as if tears were a definite possibility. He had no response, but he watched as Eve studied the wolf for a moment, placed one hand on his shoulder and the other at the back of his neck, and closed her eyes.

Ari curled up on the ground in front of his brother while Sunny mimicked Eve's moves, placing one hand on Reko's hip, the other on the curve of his chest, then she closed her eyes as well. The trance appeared so peaceful, but their minds and whatever energy they used allowed them to go inside the injured wolf with the ability to manipulate cells, repair damage, and ultimately heal what had been injured. Jack had watched this before—he wanted to learn. He was almost certain he'd be able to do it. He sensed the process while the women worked on the big wolf as nothing more than energy, and yet . . .

Jack held tightly to Mary's hand, the two of them standing off to one side, his wolven senses alert to any disturbance here on the astral, though his thoughts had slipped to another question. They'd just jogged no more than a couple of hundred feet from the portal in Anton's cavern to one that put them inside a cavern in Yellowstone, a distance of over four hundred miles in the real world.

How the hell was that possible? There were so many mysteries. Would they ever have all the answers? Would they have time to find the answers, or would the crazies finally win? He glanced at their connected hands, his and Mary's. Her hand belonged in his, just as she belonged beside him. Whatever it took, whatever price he had to pay, he would protect her. Always.

41

. . .

Anton stared at the portal long after his packmates had gone through. He hated staying behind, but there was really nothing he could add. His magic was still strong, but Lily's was stronger, and when she melded her power with Sebastian, Anton knew of nothing that could stop them. He wondered if the two of them might actually have the ability to contain a nuclear explosion if one did occur.

But if they couldn't . . . he turned and went back to the house. It was nearly four in the morning, close to dawn on the East Coast, but he knew one person who was always up by now. He went straight to his office and unlocked the drawer with the special mobile phone that was renewed by each new administration in the White House. Presidents and congressmen alike had learned to trust the Chanku, but Anton rarely made a direct call.

He picked up the phone and stared at it a moment. He really had very little to go on at this point. Not nearly enough to disturb the powers that be.

"Anton, love? Any news?"

He turned as his mate stepped into his office, aware of his stress melting away in Keisha's presence. He moved close to her and rested his hands on her hips. "No, my love. I was thinking of calling the White House, but realized there's not enough yet to raise an alarm."

"It drives you crazy though, doesn't it?" She kissed him, smiling with such love in her eyes that he tucked the phone in his pocket and pulled her close.

"It does. I used to be in charge of all this stuff. Now even the pack defers to Lily and Sebastian."

"Which is good, I think." Looping her hands around his shoulders, she forced him to meet her direct gaze. "It means we can go back to bed. I think Stefan and Xandi are in our room, and I hate to waste another minute."

He laughed. "Don't pull that one. They only live down the hallway. You can find their bed in your sleep." Then, sighing, he held her close. "We going to have to call on the pack before this is over. They're going to need our power, all our power, if there's any chance of surviving this."

"Anton?" She raised her head, reached up and cupped his face in both her hands. "I almost lost you the last time you did that."

Nuzzling against the warmth of her palm, he thought of that last time, of the blast of power from so few of them, yet strong enough that it almost destroyed his mind. Lily had saved him, yet she'd only been a small child. He thought of her now, of her amazing strength. Of Sebastian, almost as powerful as their daughter, linked so tightly to each other they acted as one, combining their power, pushing their strength beyond measurable limits. "That's true. But we saved our president's life. Prevented a horrible act of treason."

Slowly shaking her head in denial, her voice thick with tears, Keisha pressed her fingertips to his lips, hushing him as if he were a child. "The pack is so much larger, so much stronger now. Combined, their power will kill you."

"Ah, Keisha, my beloved mate." He kissed her, tasted the salt on her lips. Pressed his forehead to hers and sighed. "One death to save a world? I would give my life gladly if the only life I saved were yours, but I don't think that's going to happen."

Sobbing, she clung to him. Then she pulled away and glared at him. "How?" she demanded. "How can you possibly believe you can do this and not end up an empty shell or worse? Is your arrogance still so great, Anton Cheval? Hubris has long been your downfall."

He almost laughed, she was so beautiful when she was outraged. Outraged because of her love for him. Her anger was such an amazing gift. He reached for her, took her hands, hated that she trembled. "Think of me as the director of a large orchestra, controlling the power of the music, bringing it to a mighty crescendo with every instrument perfectly synchronized to reach that perfect note. But the sound isn't for me, my love. It's for Lily and Sebastian, the two of them linked with the Mother in the ultimate fight against evil. The two of them with more power in a single cell of their bodies than I have ever known in my life. My job will be to collect the power, channel it, and pass it on without ever touching it myself. It's not a weapon for me. It's theirs to wield. Theirs to defeat whatever evil now controls the spirit of Aldo Xenakis."

Keisha bowed her head. He wondered what she thought but didn't attempt to look into her mind. She needed time to absorb the enormity of what they faced, of what their beautiful daughter had evolved into—a being strong enough to work with the Mother. Lily was a woman grown. A woman with more power than her father, even more than her powerful mate. Together they were invincible.

He brushed the wisps of hair back from Keisha's face and kissed her gently. She would always be his lodestone, the one who kept him focused on what really mattered in their lives, but he had to remember that there were times when he could be hers as well. "We have created a most amazing young woman, my love. Lily is the best of us, a creature far beyond any other of our kind. We have to trust her and the man she loves, and we will do whatever it takes to help them."

He waited while she considered his words, until she slowly nodded. "It's hard," she whispered. "So very hard."

"I know." He wrapped his arm around her waist and turned out the light as they left the office, his mind whirling. "I think you're right, that we need to spend what's left of the night with Steph and Xandi. There will be no more talk of this until tomorrow."

"Good." She smiled at him, dark amber eyes sparkling with tears. He tightened his hold on her, this most precious woman. He couldn't let her know that he was actually terrified of what tomorrow—or the next day—might bring. Afraid that those days might never come at all. But tonight was theirs, and he had to agree with his mate. There was no point in wasting another minute.

• • •

"Mary?" Jack and Mary both turned toward Fen, who, with Igmutaka, was preparing to return to the cavern. "Before we go . . . Ari's heard a couple of names. I'm wondering if they're at all familiar to you. Check with him, would you?"

"Of course." Mary shot a quick glance at Jack, and then went to sit beside the large wolf. Jack followed her, sat beside her, but his was a silent, supportive presence and no more. She wasn't sure what made her do it, but she reached out and stroked the wolf's shoulder. He looked at her with his dark amber eyes, and she saw so much pain in him, worry over his brother, sadness at the loss of his siblings. She focused on his eyes when she connected. *My name is Mary. I am so sorry for the death of your older brother, for Reko's injury, for your sister's death. Please accept my sympathy.*

The wolf closed his eyes and dipped his head, acknowledging her words. She knew all too well what Ari must be feeling. She'd gained a pack, but she had lost her family—a family that had, essentially, already been lost to her. She couldn't allow those feelings to overwhelm her now. There would be time to grieve; at least, she hoped there would be time. She pushed those thoughts aside, focused on the wolf. *Ari, what are the names you heard the men use? I might know who they are.*

Leaning into her touch, he sighed. *The one who did the most talking was called Brother Thomas. There were three others. I only heard one name. It was Ryder.*

She nodded, but she couldn't stop the tears. *Ryder is my father. I hope he wasn't the one who shot your brother. I am so sorry.*

It's not on you. The wolf rested his chin on her leg. *Never take on the guilt of another's sins. You are not that man.*

Thank you. She would do well to remember Ari's words. *Did you see the men? Can you describe them?*

There was very little ambient light. Only the stars with but a sliver of moon, and the air so filled with foul-smelling steam around the hot pools, I couldn't make out any details. One of the men was short and round and had short dark hair. Another was a tall man with hair both dark and light, worn long and tied back. The other two looked alike. I thought they might be brothers. Average height for human men, no hair on their heads.

Nodding, Mary glanced at Jack and spoke aloud. "The heavy man is probably Brother Thomas, since you heard his name and voice. He's the leader in their church. Ryder, who has to be my father, is the tall man with his hair tied back. It's dark with some gray—does that sound right?"

When the wolf nodded, she continued. "You're correct that the other two bald guys are brothers, Derek and Eagan Schmidt. All three men are deacons in the same church—that means they're leaders—and the church is one that has come to base their teachings on the words of a saint they call Master Aldo."

Looking at Jack, she added, "A man that is more likely one of the devil's own minions, from what you've told me."

"Hopefully this will help Anton, though I have no idea what they're planning. If anything."

"We need to get the information to him."

"I know. I'll ask Star. She may be comfortable moving on the astral, but if not, we'll let him know as soon as we're back." *Stay with Ari,* he silently added. *He shouldn't be alone.*

She nodded as Jack went to speak with his sister, who had taken a position on the other side of the injured wolf. Sitting beside Ari helped calm the anxiety that had been driving her since her mother's call. There had to be something more they could be doing right now, but healing Reko was going to take some time, and they had very few details. She wondered if it would be better to get Anton involved. She hadn't realized he could get in touch with the president at any time with a direct line to the White House, but Jack had told her their alpha had been careful never to abuse that connection.

She hated waiting. She wondered what Igmutaka and the others were doing, if her mother still lived, if her father had any idea what he was setting in play.

Ari lifted his big paw and pressed it into her hands. *Sometimes,* he said, *we have to let things play out as the fates decree. I am so glad I don't have to wait alone. I thank you for being here.*

I needed to hear that, Ari. Thank you. So simple. When there isn't anything you can do, wait until there is. She needed to learn that, needed to think more like the wolf.

• • •

Reko sensed he was not alone, that whoever was close to him was helping, not harming him. He thought he scented his brother, though he hadn't tried to reach him. His mind felt foggy, as if something tamped down his thought processes, slowed his ability to think, but it wasn't frightening. He knew that he was recovering.

It was still damnably inconvenient. He'd been shot, assumed he'd been captured, but he remembered nothing beyond the sharp crack of the gun, the sharper pain of the bullet. Would his brother hear him? *Ari? Are you near?*

Reko! Yes. Don't move. The goddess and another are working to heal your injury.

Goddess? What goddess? You said she doesn't exist. You don't believe in her, remember?

Smart-ass! You haven't changed, but I believe now, Reko. I believe in a lot of things I doubted. Never again. We are among our own kind, both Berserkers and Chanku, but even the Berserkers call themselves Chanku. They're treated as the old stories tell us, as valued protectors of the pack. They have the ability to shift. When you open your eyes, you will see humans surrounding us, but they are shifters. Shifters the way we should be, men and women who can move between human and animal. And one of them, the most beautiful of all, is our goddess. She lives, Reko! Her name is Eve. She answered my call for help.

That's good, Ari. He still felt so fuzzy. Was Ari telling him the truth?

I'm opening our conversation to the others, Reko. They have shown us nothing but kindness. What's good is that you are alive, my brother. I thought I had lost you, and when the men carried your body into the cavern, I called on the goddess.

And she really answered?

She did. And she is now at your back, with a woman who is Chanku sitting by your belly, both of them working inside your hard head, putting it back together.

Thank you, Ari.

For what?

For calling on the goddess. For making her hear. He sensed more than heard Ari's soft sigh.

I didn't believe, Reko. I thought she didn't exist.

Truth? Neither did I, but I wanted so much for her to be real.

I am most definitely real, Reko. My name is Eve and we are finished now, putting your hard head back together. Sunny has been working on you, too. The injury wasn't too severe and you should feel good as new by tomorrow. A headache, maybe, but when you're ready, you can open your eyes. Don't move too quickly—we had to replace some bone fragments and things need to settle before we can consider you truly healed. Your skull was like a badly fractured piece of stone, and according to your brother, every bit as hard.

Reko opened his eyes and carefully rolled from his side to his belly, blinking to focus on a forest so perfect it didn't look real, at two women who sat beside him, both with long, light-colored hair. Both were beautiful, but one was so perfect he wanted to kneel before her and ask for her blessing. Instead, he asked her the first thing that popped into his mind. *Why are you healing me when there are men planning to destroy the world?*

"Because the Mother says that you and your brother are keys to stopping them. And if you're going to do that, you need to be healthy." Eve leaned close and kissed him on the tip of his nose.

Reko reared back. *Ari? What is going on here?*

I have no idea, but you were dying and now you're not. And that was our goddess who just kissed your nose. I suggest we pay attention.

5

Caverns in Yellowstone National Park
Friday, 3:30 a.m.

Sebastian opened the portal and walked through first with Lily close
behind him. They split up and moved to either side of the gateway,
protecting it from interlopers as much as providing magical protection to
Ig and Fen. The two Berserkers stepped into the cavern next, each
carrying a small but powerful flashlight. The scent of Reko's blood was
still strong. Fen pulled out a small whisk broom, knelt where the wolf had
lain, and quickly brushed the loose sand on the cavern floor to disguise
the amount of blood Reko had lost.

Lily stopped beside him, whispered a quiet spell, and the scent
immediately disappeared.

"Thank you. Unless they look closely, they'll think he was only
knocked out, not hurt as badly as he was." Fen stood and tucked the
broom into the small pack he wore tied to his waist. "I doubt they spent
much time checking him or they would have known he was still alive."

Lily moved close to her mate. Fen frowned at the two of them. "What
do you sense?"

"Power," Lily said. "A lot of power, and the signature is way too
familiar. Damn it, Sebastian. What do you think?"

"I have no idea if he's dead or alive, but this definitely has my
father's signature." He stared off into the darkness before giving vent with
a sharp bark of humorless laughter. "I can't believe the bastard is still
giving us grief."

Lily took his hand. "We'll stop him. Permanently, this time." She
glanced toward a dark cleft in the rock. "That way, I think. Will you fit?"

"I will, but Ig and Fen won't make it through."

"Go ahead." Fen glanced toward Igmutaka. "There are things I want to check here. Let us know if you find anything."

Sebastian nodded and shared a private look with Lily. "Thirty minutes. It's almost four. Sunrise isn't for an hour and a half, but it'll be growing light shortly. The sense of his magic is through that opening, but it's faint. I doubt we'll find him, but I want to check it out."

"Go. I want a closer look here. Just a feeling of something evil, if that makes sense."

Sebastian shook his head. "My father is involved, Fen. Of course it's evil." He sighed and gazed sadly at Lily. "C'mon, Lil."

She pulled him close for a kiss. As Fen watched, they ended the kiss and stood a moment, Sebastian leaning close to press his forehead against Lily's. That moment filled Fen with warmth and, unexpectedly, a sense of joy, that love as powerful as Lily's and Sebastian's never wavered, no matter the threat. A moment later Sebastian raised his hand and a glowing ball of light appeared just above his fingers. Then the two of them disappeared through the dark slash in the rock, their way illuminated by Sebastian's mage light.

Fen stared after Lily as she followed Seb out of this section. She was a beautiful, brilliant young woman, and everyone in the pack knew just how much her father adored her, how much trust he had put in the man who was her mate. "It must just kill Anton to know his daughter is doing dangerous shit like this." He turned to Ig and shook his head. "How's he do it?"

"He trusts her," Ig said. "And he trusts Sebastian to do all he can to keep her safe. I think that's the ultimate display of love, when you can trust your child to find the kind of mate that will always be there for them."

Good enough, he thought, but Fen's concern was much more personal. "What the hell are we going to do when we have kids, Ig? Unless we totally screw this up, our first big assignment from the Mother, you know it's going to happen someday. Our women will want babies, but our lives are fraught with danger. There's always a risk we won't come home, that we won't be there for our children, that our children could become targets. I don't know how the others do it."

"Women are a lot stronger than we are, Fen. At least our women are. They will give birth and protect our children, and they'll know that we'll be right there beside them. If Mikaela Star ever gifts me with a child, she'll do it with the certainty that I would give my life to protect both her and our young. And you? You would do the same, for my child, for your own child. We're luckier than most of the mated pairs in our pack. There are four of us equally invested in one another."

Fen studied the man he loved—a love every bit as strong as what he felt for Sunny, for Star, and he realized something he'd never really considered in this context. "You've just reminded me of something even more important. This whole pack is equally invested in the safety of all. I have never doubted that. Just as I will never doubt you or the women who chose us. We have to believe that we'll succeed in stopping whatever these men have planned, and then we'll just have to learn to relax and let our goddess and the Mother watch out for us and our families."

He shook his head and stared toward another dark fissure in the rock. "Now we have work to do. I feel a tug in that direction." He pointed at the opening in the cavern wall, a relatively narrow crevice, considering his size. "I want you to check this area carefully, where most of their energy is concentrated. Ari said they talked about clearing everything out before they left. Generally something is overlooked. See if you can find it. I'm going in there."

Then he headed toward the narrow crevice at the back, opposite the entrance to the cave where the four men had gained access. Ig watched him for a moment and then went back to examining the rest of this small cavern. If the men had left anything, he certainly didn't see it. He took a step and something clattered against the rock wall. Leaning over, he picked up a partially burned stick. He almost tossed it back to the floor, but then decided to hold on to it.

A few moments later, Fen called out, "Ig. Come look at this."

He spun around and headed toward his mate's voice. "What've you got?" The opening was tight, but he managed to follow Fen's voice into an oddly shaped cavern.

"Recognize this?" Fen pointed to a symbol marked on the rock wall. He rubbed his finger over the lines, smudging them. "Charcoal," he said. "No way to tell how long it's been here, but I have a feeling it's fresh."

Ig held up his stick. "I present the first piece of evidence. Ancient tool for writing."

Grinning broadly, Fen took the stick and made a mark near the symbol. "Could have been the one they used."

Ig focused on the drawing. It looked eerily familiar. "That's a satanic sigil, isn't it?"

Frowning, Fen looked closer. "I thought it was a pentagram."

"Sort of," Ig said. "Except it's upside down." He traced the two points at the top with his fingertip. "Represents the horns of the goat, among other things, but it's definitely satanic. Certainly not a neo-faith group, which is how this sect thinks of itself, according to Mary Ryder. Are there others?"

"Don't know." Fen ran the narrow beam of this flashlight over the walls. "There. Isn't that another one?"

They continued searching and eventually found five, roughly positioned to match the five points of the symbol placed equidistant along the uneven walls of this part of the cavern system. Ig slowly walked the circumference of the cave, checking on each of the five satanic symbols. He turned the narrow beam of the flashlight to the floor in the very center of the room.

It was there, right where it should be, a large but faintly drawn black circle sketched on the rock floor with the upside-down pentagram inside. Except this one had a clear drawing of a horned goat inside the symbol. Ig stepped inside the circle. A shiver ran along his spine, a sense of otherworldly power. It was disturbingly familiar.

"Fen?" Ig held out his hand. "Stand here with me. Close your eyes, open your senses. What do you feel?"

Frowning, Fen clasped Ig's outstretched hand and stepped within the symbol. He stared at the darkly sketched circle, but his thoughts were shuttered. "Both hands." He raised his head, his face still caught in a frown. "We need to make a complete connection."

Nodding, Ig took Fen's outstretched hand, completing the link. They faced each other, fully inside the symbol. Linked with Fen, Ig led their thoughts, searching the energy of the men who'd drawn what could only be a focus point, a link to an entity of some kind. He felt their presence, though the echoes of their actions lacked a sense of power.

I wonder if Master Aldo is listening? Fen's soft mental voice sent another chill along Ig's spine.

I'm not sure if we should even mindspeak his name. Don't say it aloud. If he's truly demonic, acknowledging him could give the demon strength or even call him to us.

Good idea. I feel it though, and so do you. Fen squeezed Igmutaka's hands. *The men who drew this were powerless, but I believe they were working under the direction of someone or something with power. We are standing in a place of power. There are ley lines that converge in or around Yellowstone. I don't know the exact coordinates, but Eve can help us. I think we're going to need Lily and Sebastian close before we do anything to bring our attention to . . .* He shot a sexy grin at Ig. *He who shall not be named.*

Chuckling, Ig tugged Fen out of the circle. "I remember reading those books to Star when she was little. C'mon. I don't want anyone to catch us here, and the portal is close to the earthly entrance to this place. I know it's off limits to tourists, but that didn't keep those jerks out. Sebastian and Lily are due back any minute, and I want them to see this before we go. I think we've got enough to get Eve or the Mother working on whatever it is these idiots might be planning."

• • •

Sebastian placed his hands on the first symbol and bowed his head, obviously deep in concentration, while Lily did the same with one across the room. They both raised their heads and looked at one another before turning to Ig and Fen.

With only the pale light from Fen's flashlight to illuminate the dark cavern, their eyes glowed—Lily's molten gold, Sebastian's electric blue. Chills ran along Igmutaka's spine. Since their mating and the deep bond that went with it, both Sebastian and Lily had said their power was increasing. So much power that they were still learning how to control it, especially when the two of them worked in tandem. If Ig felt the magic, they must be wielding one hell of a lot.

Without speaking, Lily and Sebastian moved to the larger circle on the floor, but both of them stayed outside the line. Fen shot a concerned look at Ig, who immediately turned to the two wizards. "Fen and I both stood inside the circle. Wanted to see if we sensed anything. Was that a mistake?"

Sebastian shook his head. "No. I don't believe he would have sensed you unless you were casting a spell, or vocalizing a need to speak with him. Lily and I have a lot more magic and we often shed power. That's even worse inside a spell-casting circle, which this one is."

"Do we have enough?" Lily glanced at Sebastian and then stepped farther from the circle, rubbing her arms. "That thing gives me chills. It's oily and foul, and I can feel sunrise coming close. We need to get through the portal before anyone senses its existence. We're going to need it later."

"Works for me." Fen leaned over to brush away their footsteps, but Sebastian stopped him. "We can do it magically. Let's get going. Lily, go ahead and open the portal, okay?"

She nodded and went into the next room. Fen followed her with Ig right behind him. Ig paused in the doorway and turned in time to see Sebastian sweep his hand through the air. The sand and gravel within the cavern shifted, now undisturbed as if no human had set foot inside for years.

When Sebastian finished his spell, Ig asked, "Did you and Lily find anything in the other cavern?"

"More of my father's stench. He's been here in his demon form, though I'm not sure what that form is. Hopefully we can capture the men and get them to tell us. I can't believe that bastard is still alive."

"Is he, really? Alive?" Ig waited for Sebastian to precede him through the portal. "I mean, his body was burned by the lightning, the sheriff's deputies hauled what was left off the mountain, and then they cremated him. You can't get much deader than that."

Ig followed Sebastian, Fen and Lily through the portal she'd opened, and it was obvious Sebastian was trying not to laugh.

"You forget this is Aldo Xenakis we're talking about, Ig. I doubt his ego will ever die." Seb waited and then closed the portal once they'd all stepped out onto the astral plane. The air felt cleaner, the miasma of sulfur and the sense of evil merely a bad memory. Two wolves immediately stood, the larger of the two snarling. The snarling wolf relaxed his aggressive stance with a quick nip from his brother; this had to be Reko, the one who'd been injured.

Fen immediately went to him, but he was laughing, obviously glad to see the beast upright. "Be nice to me," he said. "I'm the one who carried your carcass out of that cave. I'm Fenris." He held his hand out, the wolf sniffed his outstretched fingers and palm, and his hackles went entirely flat.

He stared at Fen a moment and then softly said, *My apologies. I thank you for saving me.*

"You're one of us, Reko. We never leave one of our own behind."

"Fen's right, Reko." Lily introduced herself and Sebastian to the wolf, but Sebastian quickly excused himself.

"I need to let Eve know what we've discovered," he said, "that it's definitely my father involved in whatever those men have planned. Involved, and from all the signs, no longer human, definitely demonic. I can't figure out how he managed that, but hopefully Eve or the Mother will know."

Lily touched his arm. "We'll need to know how he's become whatever he is if we're going to fight him."

Sebastian kissed her, she touched his cheek, and the tenderness in that brief moment had Ig looking for his Mikaela Star. When he saw her with Sunny, when he caught the moment she realized he'd returned, he felt as if his entire world righted itself.

• • •

The astral plane
Friday, 4:45 a.m.

Lily watched Sebastian as he spoke with Eve, but the curiosity she sensed from the wolves couldn't be denied. She knelt in front of Reko, running her fingers through the thick fur on the back of his neck. Much of it was stiff with dried blood, but until he could shift they'd need to clean him the old-fashioned way. "Reko, my father is going to be thrilled to meet you guys. You're proof that there are more wolves out there, part of the wild population but still aware of their sentience as thinking men and women."

Your father is the pack's alpha?

That was Ari speaking. He stood slightly behind her, off to one side, and she recognized his voice. He and his brother looked almost identical as wolves, but their mental voices were unique to each. "He is," she said, turning to look at him as she spoke. "His name is Anton Cheval and he was the first of the modern Chanku to begin gathering those who were lost, building a pack, reconnecting with the goddess. All of us exist and our pack is strong because of him and the ones who were his first packmates."

We owe him much.

That was Reko speaking. Lily shook her head. "No, Reko. We owe you and your brother a great debt. By calling Eve, you helped our goddess and the Mother tie all the pieces of information together. What you overheard confirms our worst fears, but without you, we might never have been aware what these men were planning. We will stop them. We have to, but I hope we all survive this mess long enough for us to repay our debt to you. It appears we're dealing with some powerful dark magic. My mate and I are hoping that our magic is stronger." She glanced up as Sebastian joined them. "Ari, and Reko," she said, "This is my mate, Sebastian."

Sebastian nodded in greeting. "Magic for good generally is." He walked over to sit beside Ig, still speaking to the two wolves. "When I first discovered I was Chanku, I was already a magician with a lot of natural talent. My father practiced dark magic, working with energy he stole from the lives he took. The life force of his victims gave him unimaginable power, but it was finite. Anton Cheval is just the opposite. Lily mentioned her father—Anton is the über alpha for all of us who are of the Chanku species, and that includes Berserkers like the two of you." He glanced at Ig and then at Fen, who'd come to stand behind his mate. When he turned back to Ari and Reko, he shared a smile with Lily. "Those two reprobates as well."

Ig threw a tuft of bright green grass at him. Laughing with faked outrage, Sebastian ducked, but the mood of the gathering felt lighter. "We are basically all one pack with a few smaller groupings within the whole, and we work together." He shot a look at Ig and added, "Most of the time." Ig rolled his eyes and Sebastian winked before returning his attention to the wolves. "Anton is a wizard even more powerful than my father was when he was alive, but what gave Anton the edge is that he practices white or 'light' magic. Lily, you explain it best."

"Maybe," she said. "But I've never practiced dark magic, and you came awfully close." That one-time event still frightened her, to think how close Sebastian had come, how he'd been seduced by the need for more power. "Dark, or black magic, is inherently evil because of the source of the power. Sebastian's father used the life force of living creatures, killing young women in horrible ways in order to increase the strength of the energy he stole. The thing is, once that energy is gone, it's gone until the wizard kills again."

Sebastian took Lily's hand. "That's where the power that Anton draws from makes him so much stronger. He works with the power of love, with sexual energy that can burn stronger and hotter, and is ever renewable."

"Thank goodness for that."

Fen's heartfelt comment had all of them laughing. Lily realized the entire group, including Eve, had come together.

Sebastian squeezed her hand. "Lily's dad has learned to harness the sexual energy of the pack, and he's a strong enough wizard that he can use that power to increase his own abilities."

"Or share it." Lily looked into her mate's beautiful teal blue eyes and smiled. "That's how Sebastian was able to defeat his father in battle, when Dad gathered the pack together to share their love, the energy from that love, with my guy."

Sebastian tugged Lily's hand and pulled her close. He wrapped his arm around her shoulders and kissed her. "Which is why, once we figure out exactly what these idiots have planned, we should be able to stop them."

Lily wrapped her arms around his waist and leaned close. As always, Sebastian brought her both peace and strength. It was as if they fed off one another, renewing each as they drew from their mating link. "Aldo Xenakis might be a demon now—we don't know for sure—but he's still working what feels like the same kind of magic he used before. No matter what he does, it appears it's going to be based on death magic." She didn't mention Mary's sister, maybe even her mother as part of the power behind Xenakis. "We work with love, we have Eve and the Mother behind us, and while we know it's not a fated conclusion, we're hoping to change the outcome of what the Mother has seen."

"And this is where I interrupt." Eve wrapped an arm around Star's waist, the other around Sunny's. "It's almost six in the morning at home for all of you. The Mother has determined that Aldo Xenakis is definitely working with demonic power, but he intends to complete his task at the dark of the moon. His minions—because that's all those men are—are destined to provide the power he needs for his magic through their deaths." She sighed and glanced at Mary. "Mary, I'm sorry. Unless we can stop Aldo well ahead of time, I don't see any way we can save your father, though we are hoping to stop his plans before he can complete them."

Mary glanced at Jack and then focused on Eve. "I understand. If he took my mother's life . . ." She straightened her spine as if taking strength from those around her. "My mother might still be alive, but we already know he killed my little sister." Glaring in the direction of the portal, now hidden, she said, "He's an evil man who killed an innocent child. He doesn't deserve to live."

"Thank you." Eve reached for Mary's hand and held it. "I think that we, as Chanku, understand that. I often worry if those who have been recently changed, who are not so accustomed to our rather bloodthirsty methods of justice, will have issues with the way we tend not to protect or even forgive evil. Mary, you're right. What he did was evil, though your mother still lives. The Mother searched for her life force, and she is fighting her death, determined not to give Aldo her energy. She's a very brave woman. I'm sorry she didn't stand up against your father when he disowned you."

"Thank you."

Mary's obvious sigh had Lily grinning. "We'll get your mom out here for a visit when this is all settled, okay?"

"That would be wonderful."

Lily's heart went out to Mary. She'd never known a truly loving family, while Lily had grown up with not only the unconditional love of her parents, but the love of every member of her pack. It was times like this when she realized just how lucky she'd been, to be born the child of Chanku parents. Glancing away from Mary, she focused on Jack just as he raised his head and caught her eye.

Thank you, he said. *We're going to figure out how to stop those bastards and get rid of Sebastian's sperm donor permanently. And then, once things settle down, Mary Ryder is mine.*

Lily shot him a big grin, when what she really wanted to do was cheer.

• • •

The astral plane
Friday, 5:30 a.m.

Jack was aware of a subtle tingling along his spine, a sense of power he'd felt before but couldn't identify. Rather than shake it off, he reached for it, curious to see what could be affecting him here on the astral, surrounded by the pack. He sensed Eve, wondered if she wanted something from him, but then Mary leaned against his side, her arm loosely wrapped around his waist.

"So what do we do now?" Mary's soft question immediately redirected his focus.

"I don't know." He shook his head, thought of that sensation of the goddess somehow linking to him. "Eve? What now?" She was already watching him, and he knew he'd been right. She'd been checking him out for some reason.

"We rest. The moon will be darkest at midday tomorrow, just after noon, but evil works best under cover of darkness. The Mother says nothing will happen until after dark, most likely not until close to midnight. Go home and eat, sleep, gain strength. Anton has put out word to your packmates, wherever they are, to be ready to share every bit of sexual energy they can muster."

Then her focus on him sharpened until it was almost a physical touch, but only for a moment before she turned to the two wolves. "Ari and Reko, I want you to go with Jack and Mary. You'll meet Anton Cheval at the portal where you'll leave the astral. He's expecting you, but he also knows you need to rest. Once this is over, there will be time for you to meet the rest of the pack." She rested her hands on both Ari and Reko's shoulders. "I know they will welcome you."

"Is it okay for them to have the grasses right away?"

"Yes, Jack." She sat back, gazing thoughtfully at the two wolves. "I don't expect anything to happen for at least a few days, but you need to start eating the grasses or taking them in capsule form for your bodies to begin the process of shifting. Anyone in the pack will answer any and all questions you might have. Jack and Mary, I know you're probably wondering why I would send them with you, but I believe everyone who knows you two realizes you're the obvious guides for their new lives. You are both compassionate and loving, entirely without ego. Mary, you are new to our life, but you've adapted beautifully. I believe that with the two of you to help them, Ari and Reko will assimilate into the pack without any trouble at all."

As she spoke, Eve stood. She held her hand out to Mary and tugged her to her feet. The rest of them stood and followed Eve back to the spot where the portal led into the cave. She waved her hand and the portal opened. Anton and Keisha, along with Jack and Star's parents, AJ, Mik, and Tala, waited in the cavern, standing back from the portal to allow everyone to walk through.

Ari and Reko paused at the doorway. Eve stood between them, hands on their heads. "We're bringing two new members for your pack, Anton. Say hello and then please let them leave with Jack and Mary. They all need time to rest. Lily and Sebastian will fill you in on what's happening. AJ, Mik, Tala . . . thank you for being here. Mary and Jack will be helping Reko and Ari assimilate into the pack." She glanced at Anton and lifted one eyebrow, a perfect parody of his expression. "Since our alpha will be busy talking strategy with his daughter and son-in-law."

With a roll of his eyes, Anton wrapped Lily in a tight hug. "That's Eve's polite manner of suggesting I can be a bit intense, and she doesn't want me to frighten the new kids."

Laughing, Lily muttered, "Ya think?"

Eve nodded as Lily agreed. "That too," she said. Smiling, Eve moved aside as Reko and Ari stepped through the portal, but her expression shifted once they'd left the astral. "We have much to do. The Mother or I will contact you later this afternoon or tonight, once we know better what to expect, but all of you need to rest, to eat, to gain what strength you can. Anton, your pack is aware of our need?"

"We are." He stood with one arm around Lily, the other over Sebastian's shoulders. "Pack members are coming in from other areas. We've left just a skeleton crew in place in San Francisco—most of them are headed this way."

Directly into the face of danger. Jack's pride in his packmates was almost overwhelming, but never had they failed to heed Anton's call. Holding on to Mary, he passed Anton and went straight to his parents. AJ pulled him into a tight hug and held him close while Tala embraced Mary. Mik hugged Star tightly before his daughter and Ig left with Fen and Sunny. All of them were exhausted. Ari and Reko had stopped before Anton, heads down, tails tucked in deference to his leadership. Anton knelt in front of them, somehow knowing immediately which was which.

"Ari, Reko. Welcome. I'm Anton Cheval. In our pack, all are known as Chanku. Though you are Berserkers, according to our history you're still of the original Chanku bloodline. When this current crisis has ended, we'll have time to talk about our past connections, to find out more about your family. For now, do as Eve has said—get some rest, eat well, and Reko, you'll need to finish healing. Jack's parents have suggested you might be more comfortable at their home—it's bigger than their son's, and Jack and Mary can stay there as well, but it's up to you."

The two wolves looked at one another and then at Anton. *Thank you.* Ari spoke. He glanced at his brother. *When I asked the goddess for help, only half believing she existed, I had no idea what an amazing change it would make in our lives. We thank you for your hospitality.*

"Once things have settled and this crisis is resolved, you'll have a chance to meet more of the pack, to be formally inducted as members, but you are part of our pack already. We are your birthright. Your family. Welcome home."

•••

Tala, AJ, and Mik's cabin at the Chanku compound
Friday, 6 a.m.

Reko followed Ari into the large cabin that belonged to Jack and Star's parents. He couldn't get the alpha's words out of his head. *Family.* For so long he and Ari had felt they were the only ones of their kind left, but they'd been so wrong. They had family—a family that welcomed them, quite literally, with open arms. Welcomed them into their homes with what actually felt like love. It was amazing and, at the same time, rather frightening.

So many new things, new feelings, to assimilate. It was overwhelming, all of it. He wondered if Ari felt the same, but his brother had been quiet, most likely as fascinated as Reko by the many cabins they'd seen on their walk through the forest to this house of Jack's parents. That in itself was enough to confuse him—Jack had a mother and two fathers, though only one of the men had actually fathered him, but he obviously loved both men equally, and his mother most of all. Now that, Reko understood. He still missed his mother, missed her gentle nature and her fierce love.

He glanced up as they followed Jack and Mary inside the cabin. The rooms were large, befitting the large men who were Tala's mates, though she seemed small for an adult woman. Sunlight brightened the big room that appeared to be where the family spent their time. Comfortable furniture for human and wolf alike was grouped near a large fireplace, and what must be an area for preparing food took over one whole section of the room. Already there was much conversation—too much to follow with his head still aching and his legs less than steady.

How he and Ari could possibly be of much help in this coming battle was beyond him. All he wanted to do now was sleep. And eat. It had been much too long since either he or Ari had fed.

Tala, the small woman who was Jack and Star's mother, stopped in front of Reko and Ari. She was so tiny, she didn't even have to kneel to speak directly to the two of them.

"Reko, Ari, I know you must be exhausted and hungry. When Anton told us you'd be staying with us, I thawed venison for you. It's warmed and ready any time you are." She gently ran her fingers through the thick ruff of hair behind Reko's ears while stroking Ari's shoulder. He'd had no idea how much his body craved this contact until meeting up with these Chanku who lived on two legs. Who touched so easily.

"I'm so sorry you've been injured," she said, "but I believe that the nutrients will help boost your healing." She held out two large capsules. "These contain the Tibetan grasses that will eventually enable you to shift."

Such a simple statement, one that would have an immense impact on their lives. The grasses, the same grasses his father and mother had talked about yet never tasted. With a quick glance at his brother, Reko leaned close and sniffed the capsule. He almost groaned with the sensual pleasure of the scent. Chills skittered along his spine as he licked one of the pills off of Tala's palm and gulped it down. Ari took the other.

Reko stared at his brother, seeing himself in the other wolf's dark eyes. They were looking at a new beginning, one they'd long dreamed of. But if they didn't stop the ones intending to blow up a large part of this world, it could also be the end of everything they'd ever hoped for. His head hurt and the thoughts filling his mind weren't helping, but thankfully Tala was leading them toward a room that she said would be their place to sleep, that once they knew where it was, she'd give them their meal and they could rest. Reko was right behind her. He didn't even look to see if Ari followed.

6

Jack's parents' cabin
Friday, 2:30 p.m.

The heavy shades were still drawn and the bedroom dark when Mary awoke, but the soft murmur of voices from somewhere nearby reminded her that it wasn't early morning and she'd not slept in her own cabin. Not even close. She reached out, and when she felt Jack's solid warmth beside her, everything flooded back—the way he'd held her, the absolutely exquisite beauty of their lovemaking, then her mother's call and the horror when she'd learned her little sister was dead, that her father was involved in something beyond evil. Their journey on the astral plane, the two wolves they'd rescued—all of it now felt almost dreamlike.

Except she knew it had really happened. Every last bit of it, and there was more yet to come.

She lay there, going over everything they'd been through in such a short span of time, but something pricked at the edge of her thoughts, a sense of . . . what? Distress? Concentrating, she realized that yes, someone, somewhere close by, was afraid, but it wasn't Jack. No . . . Reko. His mental signature was different from his brother's, but she was somehow connected to his mind, and it was the mind of a sentient creature who was very much afraid.

Without waking Jack, Mary slipped out of the bed and wrapped herself in a warm robe hanging beside the door. Barefoot, she left their darkened bedroom and padded down the bright hallway to the room where Reko and Ari slept. The sun was high in the sky, but then it had been around eight in the morning before they'd finally gotten into their room, pulled the shades, and almost immediately fallen to sleep. She wasn't really rested, but still felt as if she'd slept for hours. When her stomach rumbled, she was sure of it, considering the huge breakfast Tala had prepared for them when they'd first arrived. She could definitely eat again.

Mary paused at the open door to Reko and Ari's room. There was a king-sized bed in the center, but the wolves each slept on large round pillows on the floor. Ari slept soundly, but Reko whimpered in his sleep. His feet twitched as he dreamed. She went to him and sat on the floor beside his bed. She thought of petting him, but he was in a strange place, still recovering from a gunshot wound. The last thing she wanted to do was startle a sleeping wolf, especially a Berserker. They were, after all, bred to kill.

She used her mindspeech rather than her voice. *Reko? It's Mary. Are you okay? I think you might be dreaming—I can sense your unease. Wake up, Reko. Let the dream go. Everything is okay; you're in a safe place.*

After a moment, his eyes opened and he blinked slowly, coming out of what must have been a very deep sleep in spite of the dream. She touched him then, stroking his shoulder. He rested his chin on her knee.

I was dreaming, but not about the men who shot me. It was someone else, someone . . . His mental voice tapered off. *Someone or something completely evil. I don't remember who, but he was definitely bad.*

Could you see him?

There was another pause. Longer this time. Then, *Shadow and fog, not a true visual. He said a lot of things to me, words I don't recall, but one thing I remember. He said I would be his conduit. What does that mean?*

I don't know, but I know how to find out. She continued stroking his shoulder and back, doing her best to offer comfort. Reko and Ari had suffered their entire lives. They'd never really known peace. She wanted badly to give him at least some peace. *Go back to sleep, Reko, and I should have answers later. You're safe with the pack. Evil can't touch you here.*

Sighing, he turned his head and licked her wrist, curled into a ball, and tucked his nose under his tail. Mary watched him until she was certain he slept. She wished she hadn't had to lie to him.

Obviously, if he was dreaming about Aldo and the demon was speaking to him, evil had already touched the wolf.

• • •

A few minutes later, Mary crawled back into bed beside Jack. He rolled close, wrapped his arm around her, but never actually awakened. She'd checked the clock and it was getting close to three. The sound of voices had tapered off, the house was completely quiet, and she was still tired. Unfortunately, her brain hadn't gotten the message. Her thoughts hadn't stopped spinning since she'd talked with Reko.

She had to let Sebastian and Lily know, and Eve as well, but not until everyone had rested. The Mother had said—through Eve—there was nothing more they could do, at least until they knew more, or Aldo acted. Lily and Sebastian needed to be at full strength. If Aldo had somehow established a connection with Reko, they'd have to sever it as soon as possible, and that would probably take enormous amounts of energy. Even Sebastian was afraid of the man—his own father—which meant that Aldo Xenakis must be a truly fearsome enemy. Reko and Ari had suffered enough; she hated the thought of evil invading Reko's dreams.

But why would Aldo warn the wolf? Could it be he wasn't aware that Reko was sentient? Could Aldo think he was merely dealing with a wild wolf? It made her head ache, considering all the dangers they were about to face. She'd grown complacent since coming here to Montana. When she'd been in San Francisco and still a captive of the men who'd taken her, Mary had always been alert to danger. She'd faced it nightly—no girl could ever relax when they were forced to have sex with a multitude of strangers each night. Their pimps could only stay just so close, and every one of the girls had been hurt—some badly—on more than one occasion.

Of course, a lot of those injuries had come from their pimps, the men who were supposed to protect them from the customers. Her concept of trust had flown by the wayside, until Jack.

Mary knew she'd survived because she'd learned to block her fears. She'd learned to deal with them only when she had a solution, or at least understood what she could do to keep herself safe. In the long run, nothing could have kept her safe. Nothing, no one. Until Gabe and Em had rescued all of them. Until Jack Temple had come into her life.

Could he protect her now? She knew he wanted to, but it was a demon they were after. A fucking demon! Growling under her breath, Mary scrunched up her pillow and tried to get comfortable, but she couldn't turn off the memories, or the worry.

"Hey? What's the matter?"

All sleepy-eyed with his dark hair mussed and that gorgeous smile clearly visible in the shadowed room, Jack threaded his fingers through her tangles and then nuzzled her throat and kissed her.

"Nothing, now." She arched her neck, bared her throat to him for more of his kisses. What was it about this man? The minute he touched her, that touch—that connection—became the most important thing in her world.

The only thing in her world.

How in the name of the goddess had they lasted so many months without touching?

He pushed the warm blankets back and uncovered her body. Whether it was from the cool kiss of air or the moist heat of his breath, her nipples puckered. He lingered over one aching, turgid peak for much too long, breathing softly. She clutched the sheets, arching closer. Shivers of sensation raced across her damp flesh. She whimpered when he finally drew the taut bud between his lips. Swirling his tongue around the tip, he gently nipped and dragged, drawing her whimper into a moan before he moved on to the other one. Groaning, she slipped her fingers through the cool silk of his hair and held him to her breast.

Back and forth, he worried one nipple and then the other. Her breathing was reduced to harsh gasps, and the stinging sensation of those sharp little nips sent current sparking from her breasts to her clit. Jack plumped one full breast with his hand before drawing his fingers over her abdomen. He circled her navel with a single finger and then traveled south, slipping his fingers between her folds. She was already wet and ready for him, her feminine muscles throbbing and clenching with need, her heart pounding so hard she was positive he had to feel the beat against his lips. Those perfect lips, wrapped tightly around her nipple, his tongue flicking the tip, his fingers thrusting slowly in and out of her oh so ready sheath. She undulated against him, silently begging Jack to get serious because his fingers weren't enough to do the job, but he continued his erotic teasing until she grabbed his hair in both fists and pulled him away from her breast.

"Enough! Your cock, my pussy. Now!"

His eyes went wide and he saluted. "Yes, ma'am!" Then, laughing like a damned fool, he sat back on his heels between her legs, lifted her hips and, without any further foreplay, thrust hard and deep. Her first climax slammed into her at the same time he bottomed out. She was still clenching around him when he withdrew and plunged deep again. Like an electric shock, her nerve endings seemed to light up from her toes to her scalp. Wrapping her legs around his absolutely amazing ass, she held Jack close, her muscles rippling over his thick erection until he arched against her, filling her with his seed, groaning as if his orgasm turned him inside out.

Long minutes later he rolled to his side and, still connected, plucked at her nipples again, this time with his fingertips. She tried to bat his hand away but didn't have the energy to do more than brush her fingers over his wrist. Turning his hand, he held hers, drew it to his lips and kissed each of her fingers.

"I was in your head."

"Hmmmm?" She turned and stared at him. He wasn't teasing her. No, his look was terribly serious. "What did you see?" She tried to remember what she was thinking at the moment of her climaxes. All she could recall was sensation. Sensation, and how very much she loved him.

He curled one long, dark tendril of her hair around his fingertip and tugged her close. Kissed her gently. "I saw the woman I'm going to mate. Whenever you're ready, Mary. You're mine. I planned to wait and ask you when this was over, but I don't want to wait. Tonight could be our last night, if this doesn't work out. If the worst thing happens and we don't make it, I want to go into the afterlife with my mate beside me. I love you, Mary Ryder. For now and always."

The sincerity of his words melted her, the love in his eyes claimed her. "I love you, Jack. More than I ever imagined loving anyone. I have for so many weeks now, but I never thought you'd feel the same." She ran her fingers along his jaw, touched the curve of his lips, no longer wondering how or why, accepting what was. "Just say the word. Whenever you're ready, so am I." There was nothing to think about, nothing more to consider than the fact she loved him. Had wanted him the first time she saw him, wanted him even more now, already the best of friends who had finally made love. Two people who had come together on every level, who had discovered, each in the other, exactly the one they needed. She kissed him gently and smiled. There was no way she could keep a straight face "But if you need orders before you can act . . . Now, Jack. I'm ready now."

. . .

They shifted and trotted out to the main room. There was no sign of Mik, but Jack spotted his mom and dad on the front deck, sitting under the arbor talking with Anton and Keisha. He and Mary went out through the open front door and paused beside AJ and Tala.

Mary and I are going for a run. We won't be long, but wanted to make sure someone would be here when Reko and Ari wake up.

Anton's smile let Jack know he was well aware of their reason for running. "Is there anything we need to watch for?"

Mary glanced at Jack and then spoke directly to Anton. *I haven't had a chance to say anything to Jack.* She must have felt Jack's question because she turned her head and gave him a look he'd already learned to interpret. *Well, you distracted me, Jack!* There was no ignoring his mom's snort when Mary turned back to Anton, continuing as if she hadn't been interrupted. *Reko woke me earlier. He was having a nightmare. For some reason, we seem to have developed a close mental connection, but I felt his fear. When I went to their room, Ari was sleeping but Reko was restless, so I woke him. I was worried because he was obviously afraid of something. He said he'd been having a bad dream, that someone had spoken to him though he didn't remember much of what he said, only that the voice was that of a man and he was terribly evil. Reko was very specific about the evil part. When I asked if he saw anything, he said no, only shadows and fog. He said he remembered one phrase from the dream, the man telling Reko that he was now the speaker's conduit. Could Aldo have contacted him? Maybe cast a spell on him?*

"I don't know, Mary." Anton shook his head. "We don't really know exactly what we're dealing with, but it could be. Reko was unconscious and weakened when he was in the cave, so his natural shields would have been badly compromised. I'll wait until he awakens and speak with him, but in the meantime, I'm going to see if Sebastian and Lily are awake. This is something they might be able to figure out with their ability to sense Sebastian's father. That man was definitely evil. If he's a demon now, he'll be many times worse. We just don't know enough about the dark side of our world, or the evil that inhabits it."

Anton turned to his mate. Keisha rested her palm on his knee, a subtle connection that seemed to steady the alpha. "As much as we've dealt with darkness over the years," she said, "you'd think we'd have a handle on it by now."

Anton leaned close and kissed her. "Ya think?" Smiling now, obviously calmed by Keisha's dry comment, he turned to Mary and Jack. "Go. Don't worry about this now. Get your run while you can. Then come back here so we can congratulate you."

Mary's head whipped around and she looked at Jack, who merely rolled his eyes. *No,* he said, looking at the woman who was soon to be his in all ways, yet speaking to the others as well. *I have absolutely no idea how he does that. Drives us all nuts. C'mon. Let's hope his good manners won't allow him to stick around for the details.*

They leapt over the railing at the edge of the deck and raced into the woods with the laughter of Jack's parents, Keisha, and the man who was their alpha following them into the forest.

• • •

Anton watched the two young lovers race toward the bank of evergreens bordering the huge meadow. He'd always thought there was so much more to Jack than met the eye. Even more beautiful than his amazing father, intelligent and inherently good, Jack would be the perfect mate for Mary. He loved seeing this younger generation find their true mates, partners who would make them even stronger, better than they already were.

Dear goddess, he hoped they would survive what was to come, but Mary's news changed everything. He rubbed his hand over the black phone still in his pocket. He'd not felt comfortable putting it back in the locked drawer in his desk with so much going on right now, with so many unknowns. There'd not been enough confirmed information to take to the president, but if what Mary said was true, they were fighting an even more powerful foe.

He really needed to talk to Lily and Sebastian, and if they could bring Eve in on the conversation, so much the better. He touched the back of Keisha's hand. She turned it palm up and held tightly to his. He was convinced his blood pressure dropped at least ten points whenever she touched him like this.

"Go," she said. When he cocked one eyebrow, she just shook her head. "Of course I've been eavesdropping on your rambling thoughts. How else do you expect me to keep you out of trouble?" Smiling, she kissed him. "Meet with Eve in the den. She could probably use some of your cognac about now. You know how much she hates that there's no Hennessy on the astral." She smiled when she said that—it had become a running joke that the only reason Eve showed up was for Anton's cognac. "I've contacted Lily. She and Sebastian were already awake and they're on their way. It's time for you to speak with Madam President. Time to take those men into custody so that Aldo won't have their living energy to power his plans. You really need to concentrate on stopping him if you're planning to save the world."

He didn't even question her. Keisha always knew what was going on in his mind, but it was never an intrusion. "If we arrest the four men who are already guilty of so much, I'm afraid that Aldo might take the lives of four innocents."

"But if we have those men in custody, there's a good chance it will weaken Aldo enough that he won't be able to take any other lives. The only death we know of is Mary's little sister. Her life force was most likely very strong, but it is still a finite source of energy for him. Aldo had to convince her father to kill her, which leads me to believe that he's not capable of killing by himself. Talk with Lily and Sebastian, and I'll bring Reko to you when he awakens. Now go. I want you busy with important things so that you're not snooping on Jack and Mary."

His mate was absolutely impossible, the way she knew him so well. "I was not planning to snoop."

"Right."

The look she threw him spoke volumes. Anton kissed her soundly and left, but he didn't even try to hide his smile, now that he knew exactly how perfectly Jack and Mary loved each other. He held on to the image of them running into the forest, held on to the sound of their laughter, the depth of their emotions. In spite of the danger they faced, in spite of the horrible things that might lie ahead of them, they loved enough to want a future together. Everyone should be as brave as those two. He carried their joy, the love from his wife, from his pack, carried that laughter and love close to his heart as he walked down the trail to his home.

• • •

The forest north of the Chanku compound
Friday, 3:45 p.m.

I wish I could just keep running far enough and fast enough that we could get away from all that mess with Aldo. Mary ducked beneath a gnarled tree, following a well-traveled trail that led toward a small meadow.

I know. But at least we have today. Now is what counts, and we have it together. Jack followed close behind her, so aware of her scent, of the emotions that left him breathless. He'd never really thought about what love felt like, but if this was it, it was so much more than he'd imagined.

No wonder the guys had been pushing him to find a mate. He'd have to thank them, though they'd left with their mates on the annual wolf survey early this morning while he and Mary were still on the astral. With luck, they'd never know what almost happened here . . . unless, goddess forbid, it happened. Still, there'd been no actual pushing from Gabe or Jace lately. Not since he'd met Mary. He hadn't even realized he'd been after her. Had no idea how empty his life had been before Mary. She'd just sort of seeped in under his skin, filled every empty place in his heart. He raced closer and nipped her shoulder. *Follow me. I know a place.*

It wasn't far, the small meadow near the base of the mountain, but it was always green unless it was covered in snow. Only a few frozen patches remained in the shadows this early in June. An icy spring seeped from beneath the granite and wildflowers were beginning to bloom. Jack remembered his mother bringing Star and him here to play, remembered making daisy chains later in summer with his sister and hoping the other guys wouldn't catch him. They'd tumbled as pups, gotten muddy and rolled in stinky things that drove Tala nuts, but she always brought them back. It was a place filled with good memories.

He wanted to add the most important memory of his life, and he wanted Mary to be part of it. He shared the history of the small meadow with her and she snorted.

It's perfect, she said. *As long as I don't have to roll in anything stinky.*

Spoilsport!

She butted his shoulder with her head. *I love you, Jack. Love you more than I can ever say.*

He couldn't speak—his heart was too full, his mind locked on the beautiful black and tan wolf standing here surrounded by tall stalks of white flowering beargrass. Butterflies fluttered from bloom to bloom, bees buzzed, and he heard the scream of an eagle overhead. Glancing up, he made sure it was a wild one and not a member of the pack.

The only witness to their mating he'd allow was Eve—her witness and her blessing as their goddess.

Mary watched him. She looked a little apprehensive about this next step, but he sensed no doubt at all over her decision. Jack's only concern was that he do this right, that he not hurt her. He was confident that he was a good lover as a man, but he had absolutely no experience with this as a wolf.

That was about to change. There were some things you did only with the one you loved, the one you intended to keep forever, and he loved Mary Ryder. He raked her shoulder with his paw and Mary turned, waving that beautiful flag of a tail in front of his nose. Her scent enveloped him and his body hardened. They'd been intimate for the first time mere hours ago after dancing around their growing sexual attraction for months, yet so much had changed. Their friendship, powerful from the beginning, had exploded into an all-consuming love.

That love was a pulsing, living organism, driving him to make this beautiful she-wolf his. He mounted her then, the two of them in the small meadow teeming with birdsong and the hum of insects, their feet digging into the soft earth as Mary braced herself to take his greater weight. He'd always wondered what this would be like, this feral mating they all knew was something saved for the mating dance, and only between mates forever after. Immediately, he knew why.

The sensations were so powerful, the tight clasp of her vaginal muscles, the scent of her wolf a potent aphrodisiac that pulled him against her, into her, until he was thrusting hard enough to drive Mary to her knees, her front legs folding gracefully beneath her. Part of him registered the fact he was physically overpowering a weaker individual, but he sensed her growing excitement, her need for the intensity of their joining. Her back legs were still raised as he grasped her about the middle, his hips driving him in and out in a staccato rhythm. Within seconds he felt the mating knot slip inside her tautly muscled channel.

Physically, this was already the most amazing thing he'd ever experienced, as if his feral side had finally found its purpose. Then, though he knew it would happen, he realized he'd not had the slightest idea what the mating link was really like until their minds connected. Later he would swear there was an almost audible click as their thoughts came together, as he locked into Mary's mind, into her memories.

As she locked into his.

He absorbed everything that made her the woman he'd grown to love, every single thing in her childhood that had molded her into the amazing woman she was today. She'd been hardly more than a toddler when her mother died, but her memories of the woman who bore her were good ones. She'd not been mistreated, and it appeared that the stories of her mother's abuse and drug use were just that—stories her adoptive parents told her. But why? Why sully the only memories she had of a woman who'd loved her, a woman who'd died as the innocent victim of random violence?

For the first time, Mary relived that moment, a moment she shared with Jack. She'd been a toddler when her mother was killed. There were loud noises she recognized now as gunfire. Her mother cried out and wrapped her arms around Mary to protect her. She must have been hit while holding her. Mary remembered falling, remembered sirens and flashing lights. One more senseless death among so many, and yet it had changed Mary's life in so many ways.

She'd forgotten all of it. Thankfully the child hadn't remembered the violence of her mother's death, but she'd also forgotten her mother's love, a love that was returned to her in her mating with Jack. There were so many more memories and visuals, both hers and Jack's. His active sex life before he'd met Mary was like a kaleidoscope image of beautiful women and men, but there'd not been any connection other than the joy in the moment, and he'd not shared any intimacy with a single person since he'd met Mary.

That was the thing that stuck with her, almost more intense than the memories of her birth mother's life and death. There'd been no one else but Mary from the time Jack had first set eyes on her. For over six months he'd spent every free moment with Mary, befriending her, helping her assimilate into her new life as a wolf, and in all that time he'd remained celibate.

As the memories faded away and the link dissolved, that was the impression that lingered. He'd not loved her from the first—he hadn't known her well enough to feel that strong an emotion—but he'd recognized something in her that called to him. She'd felt the same way, that sense of destiny that she'd read about in romance novels but never really believed.

I hear your thoughts, he said, and shifted at exactly the same moment as Mary. "Do you believe now that somehow we were destined, that finding each other was supposed to happen?"

Lying there on the damp grass, held closely by her mate, Mary almost giggled. "I do, though I had no idea it included lying in cold, wet grass with a perfectly wonderful hot guy holding on to me. Emphasis on hot. I think my back and butt are the only parts of me not freezing." She turned her head to look into his sparkling eyes. "I love you, Jackson Miguel Temple. I liked you best from the very beginning, and it's grown into something so amazing that yes, if this wasn't our fate, it certainly is now, and I would never change it."

Laughing, he held her close and rolled to his back. "How about changing so I'm on the bottom?"

"That works."

They made love there in the cold, wet grass with birdsong and bees all around, and then they shed the mud and grass when they shifted for the run back to the cabin. *I feel different.* Mary shook out her coat and rubbed her head against Jack's shoulder. *You're in here with me, in my mind.*

We're both different. You're in my heart, too. Jack had a curiously vulnerable look in his eyes. *I feel you so close to me, so much a part of me, that I can't imagine even functioning without you. I think I finally understand the mating bond, why it works the way it does. Why it endures.*

We have to go back, don't we? She wanted to stay here in this small, damp meadow. Wanted to talk about what they'd done, how they'd both changed, but there was a pressure growing in her mind, calling her back to the pack. Back to Reko? But she didn't love Reko and she'd just mated Jack. It made no sense. Curious, she turned and gazed toward the pack stronghold.

I feel it, too.

Jack's voice in her head reminded her that their thoughts were now shared. She hoped he wasn't jealous, but she'd not asked for this—whatever it was—with Reko, so how . . . ?

Whatever bond you had with Reko, it's mine now as well. I'm not jealous, Mary. He's part of our pack and he's frightened. We need to go back.

Turning as one, they headed back down the trail.

• • •

Anton's Pentagon
Friday, 4:00 p.m.

Sebastian and Lily sat at the long bar in the five-sided room they'd recently dubbed the Chanku Pentagon, while Anton quietly refilled each of their glasses with cognac. The room felt empty, as if the energy had been sucked out, but it often felt that way after a visit from Eve.

She might be their goddess now, but Anton wondered if he'd ever get past the memories that lingered after visiting with her. He'd known her first as Eve Reynolds, a member of his pack, mated to Adam Wolf, occasionally lovers of Anton and Keisha's. Now she was an immortal goddess, privy to the Mother's thoughts, a gentle, intelligent woman with the heart and soul of a wolf.

And she was every bit as frustrated as Anton, Sebastian, and Lily. Anton lifted his glass and tapped the rims of Sebastian's and Lily's. "Here's to making the right decision." He tipped the glass back and swallowed, welcoming the mellow burn of good liquor.

Lily glanced at Sebastian before focusing on her father. Obviously his daughter and her mate had already come to a decision, and while he'd been the one whose choices had essentially ruled this pack since its inception, he had no problem with deferring to these two.

"So," he said, leaning his elbows on the bar, "what do you think?"

Lily nodded slowly, and Anton wondered if she spoke to Sebastian or Eve. Only his daughter would call a goddess her closest girlfriend. "I agree with Eve. You need to pull out that fancy little mobile phone of yours and contact the president. She should be aware of the risk we're all facing. If it was just our pack affected there'd be no thought of including her, but this goes far beyond our pack. It affects the entire world, all peoples, no matter their race, their beliefs, whether they're friend or foe. We don't want to realize too late that we should have had help."

"Good," he said. "I agree." He pulled the phone out of his pocket and set it on the bar. "Now that we have the names of the four men, we can have agents check on their families. It's good to know that Mary's mother is still alive and appears to be healing, and even better that they're keeping her location secret. If we can bring the four into custody, that leaves Aldo without his source of strength. Biggest problem for now, I think, is that if Eve and the Mother are correct, the nuclear device is already in the park, quite possibly already in the cavern."

"That's where Ig and Fen come in." Seb stared at his glass before shooting a grin at Lily. "They can move as spirit, which means they should be able to locate the device if it's in what would otherwise be an inaccessible part of the cavern system. I'll be there with Lily to stop Aldo, which means you need to have the pack ready for us."

He glanced at Lily and winked. Lily slapped her hand over her mouth as she burst into laughter. "Sorry," she said, still giggling. "Totally inappropriate, but I can't help but think this is why the pack is always so anxious to be of service."

"I'll make the call now." Anton stared at the small black phone, picked it up and hit the call button. It would only call one number, and only one person had the other phone.

The president answered on the second ring.

7

Jack's parents' house
Friday, 4:30 p.m.

How could Ari sleep so soundly? Reko paced anxiously back and forth in the room that Jack's mother had said would be theirs as long as they wanted it. He'd been okay after Mary left, but then the dream had come back. When he'd called out to Mary, she'd not answered. He had to tell someone that the voice was definitely evil, and beginning to demand things.

Terrible things.

He heard voices nearby, but he didn't want to leave Ari. His brother had been awake all night and needed to sleep, though he rarely slept this soundly. Reko walked over to Ari's pallet and sniffed at his brother's shoulder. He breathed evenly, his heart was beating. There was nothing wrong beyond exhaustion. And relief, most likely. Knowing they were among friends, that they'd been welcomed into this huge pack like long-lost family.

He wondered where Mary and Jack were. Wondered if he could go out in front and search for them, but he didn't want to speak to anyone else yet. Not until he'd told Mary that the voice was back.

Reko wondered if the voice realized he was sentient, that his mind was as good as any human's. His formal education might be lacking, but he and his siblings had been taught to read those printed words his mother had treasured. She'd said it was important, that she wanted them to be ready to make their way among the human population when they finally shifted.

Unlike their father, their mother had never given up faith in the goddess.

Yet the goddess had answered Ari, had healed Reko, but she'd never answered his mother. He'd have to ask her why, should he ever see her again. Already, last night's visit felt like a poorly remembered dream.

He paused mid-pace as the scent of strange wolves caught his attention. He planted himself in front of Ari, prepared to protect his brother, and snarled when two wolves stopped in the open doorway.

Reko, I'm Jack and that's Mary. She said you were upset, that she could sense it.

Reko walked over to the two wolves and touched noses with each of them. *Your mental voice as wolf sounds the same as it does when you walk on two legs. Ari's still sleeping, but I'm hearing from the evil one. How do I make him go away?* He turned and looked at his brother. *He wants me to kill. I don't think he realizes I'm more than a wild wolf, that I can think and reason. That I determine my actions, not him.*

Mary glanced at Jack and then turned back to Reko. *Who does he want you to kill? Does he just say "go kill humans" and expect you to obey?*

Essentially, yes. He tells me that if I kill all the people in this house tomorrow night after dark, I will be rewarded with all the meat I want, but if I don't, I will be punished. He wasn't specific about the punishment, but he wants me to kill them when he's there with me.

Here? He's planning to come here? Jack focused on Mary. *I don't like the sound of that.*

Reko merely shrugged. He didn't like the sound of any of this. *I imagine it's so he can take their life force to do whatever it is he's planning. I have a feeling that he will get it from me as well through my death, though he's not mentioned that particular part of the deal.*

Blinking slowly as he came out of sleep, Ari raised his head and stared at Reko. *What are you talking about? Jack? Mary? I'm guessing that's you two. I heard your voices.*

You've guessed right. Mary turned to Reko. *Do you want to explain to Ari?*

Not really. I imagine you can make it sound a lot more exciting. Dress the story up a bit, make me look better. And then Reko snorted.

Mary turned to Jack. *I think I really like this guy. He's almost as bad as you are.*

Reko was still thinking about that when he realized Mary was explaining to Ari what was going on, at least what they thought had happened. He listened, wondering if she had any ideas.

Ari, it appears the demon contacted your brother through his dreams. I haven't had a chance to tell you, Reko, but our alpha thinks that while you were unconscious from the head wound, your natural shields were compromised. The demon may have placed a spell on you. I imagine now that you're awake, Anton will take care of the connection. He's more than just our alpha—Anton Cheval is a powerful wizard, and his daughter and her mate are even stronger, so you're in good hands here.

Anton's here, Jack said. *Let's go see if they've figured anything out, okay?* He shifted and reached for a pair of sweatpants hanging on a hook by the door. "Once you guys can shift, there are clothes in the closet and that dresser over there. If you need help with anything, don't hesitate to ask. I imagine you've not had to deal with zippers and buttons before."

Thank you. Ari glanced at his brother. *Leave it to you, Reko, to end up with a demon invading that worthless brain of yours.*

Mary shifted and opened the closet door. For a brief moment, Reko ignored the brotherly insult. He much preferred admiring Mary's naked form. Even without her wolven coat, she was beautiful. Disappointment surged through him when she grabbed clothing from the closet and covered herself, but it was almost evening and the air was growing cooler. He returned his attention to his brother. *At least I've got a brain, Ari. That's probably why he left you alone. Couldn't find anything to invade.*

• • •

Jack looped his arm lightly over Mary's shoulders as they walked through the house. She glanced at him as Reko and Ari followed closely behind, bickering and teasing one another, fighting laughter as the wolves' comments flew between them. They could have been any two siblings in the pack—Berserker or not, they still acted just like brothers the world over.

The four of them stepped out onto the front deck. Keisha, Tala, Mik, and AJ were here, but Anton was nowhere to be seen.

The moment Tala spotted them, she jumped out of her chair and pulled both Jack and Mary into a warm embrace. "I hoped this would happen." She kissed Jack soundly and then wrapped her arms around Mary. "Welcome to the family, sweetheart. I was so afraid you wouldn't want our worthless son." She shot a big grin at Jack. "Thank you. I was almost afraid to hope!"

AJ hugged his son and held him close for a long, meaningful embrace. Then he turned to Mary and wrapped his arms around her. "Mary, I am so proud to be able to call you my daughter. Once this mess is cleared up, we'll plan a real celebration for the two of you."

She couldn't say a word. She hadn't even considered that Jack's family would now truly consider her one of them. Her chest ached with the surge of emotion, her eyes burned. She glanced almost frantically at

Jack, but Mik had waited until both AJ and Tala had their time with their son before stepping in and hauling Jack close for a rough hug.

Then he turned to Mary and took both her hands in his as she struggled not to embarrass herself by falling apart, suddenly a teary, emotional wreck. "Welcome to the family, Mary. And, as AJ has said, once things settle down, we'll have a real celebration. For now, I just want you to know that you are a welcome member of our family. Jack, you know I've always been proud of you, son, and probably never more than I am now. You have chosen well."

Keisha had stayed back while Jack's parents congratulated him, but now she stepped forward. "I've let Anton know, though I imagine he's well aware you two have mated. Mary, I am so glad you and Jack have found each other."

"Thank you." Mary reached for Jack, feeling anchored the moment he took her hand. She clung to him, knew he sensed her emotions, knew her tears were close, that she was terrified of making a fool of herself.

It's okay, sweetheart. His soft mental laughter settled her when he said, *You're going to be fine. This is merely the culmination of an unbelievably emotion-packed couple of days.*

Reko and Ari had remained quiet while all the hugging was going on, but Mary and Jack turned as one and caught both wolves studying them.

Reko cocked his head and his voice filled their minds. *We did not realize you were newly mated. Congratulations. That's something we have long wanted for ourselves, but by the time we were old enough, we had only our small family left. Now only Ari and I remain.*

"That's going to be different now, Reko." Mary knelt in front of him with her hands around his thick neck, fingers buried in his dark silver fur. "You're part of a huge pack now. Once you shift, you'll have the chance to meet a lot of young females without mates. You, too, Ari, and it's not that far off. In just a few more days, we'll get to see what you guys look like. You're identical twins as wolves, so I'm really curious if we'll be able to tell you apart as men."

Keisha glanced up from her conversation with Tala and frowned. "Anton wants you to come to the house. Eve just left, but Sebastian and Lily are there with him. Reko, are you still hearing commands from the demon?"

They're almost constant now. He doesn't understand why I'm not obeying him. His threats are getting worse by the minute, but I think they're only words. I don't feel any physical effect from what he's ordering me to do, though the ugliness of his demands makes my fur stand on end.

Shocked, Mary stared at the wolf. "You mean it's been going on while we've all been standing around here? Why didn't you say something?"

Reko gave a very human shrug. *He's no more than an irritating insect in my head, spouting threats and giving orders. I figure when Anton has the time, he'll help me get rid of him.*

Keisha laughed softly. "Anton just spoke to me, Reko. He said he's got the time." She stood, shaking her head, but she wasn't laughing anymore. "Though it may take more than Anton's skill to remove a demon. Thankfully, Sebastian and Lily are there. You need to go now. I'll be up later."

• • •

Anton and Keisha's home
Friday, 5:15 p.m.

Jack, Mary, and the brothers ran into Ig and Fen at the front door of the alpha's home. Anton opened the door before they had a chance to knock and led them back to the five-sided den, where Lily and Sebastian were going over a large map of the Yellowstone volcanic caldera.

"Whatcha got?" Jack stood next to Sebastian, immediately recognizing the area encompassed in the large topographic map spread across the huge wall screen. It showed a cutaway view of the land above and the magma chambers below Yellowstone National Park. Imaging had improved to the point that individual chambers could be identified, as well as which had molten rock and which ones were hollow extensions of the caverns above. The field of magnetotellurics had expanded into three-dimensional imagery that displayed either on the screen or in holograms that could be studied from all angles.

Sebastian selected a small section of the image, swiped his fingers across the area on the screen and pulled it into the room, where it hovered, solid and real. "We're trying to figure out exactly where Aldo might have placed or be planning to place the device." Sebastian pointed to an area close to the cavern where Reko had been rescued. "I think it's here." He stuck his finger through what looked like solid rock, but was actually the holographic image, and tapped a spot a bit north of the main cavern. "When Lily and I were in the cave, we sensed Aldo. He wasn't there then, but it was obvious he had been. The sensation of his presence was here, north and down. Way down."

He followed a cleft in the rock until he reached a dark tunnel separated from the magma chamber by what appeared to be a mere two meters of solid rock. There was a larger area at the end of it, almost as if something had blown up a balloon and left it there. Open, empty. Sebastian glanced at Ig and Fen. "That's where you two will come in. You have the ability to move as spirit, and I'm hoping that means you can get through existing cracks in the rock, check things out, see if you can find an actual device. If you can't, maybe you'll be able to figure out where and when he's planning to place it."

Ig glanced at Fen and both men nodded. "We can do that," Fen said. "It's a little tricky, but we can actually move through solid stone. It takes longer, but it's possible. If we find it, then what?"

Sebastian deferred to Lily. "You take it from here."

She grimaced. "You notice he leaves me with the tricky stuff. We are assuming this device is something the men have managed to purchase on the black market. We're also assuming, because of what Mary's mother said, as well as from the precognitive visuals the Mother received, that it is a nuclear device, capable of worldwide destruction should it set off the volcano. Unfortunately, there's way too much nuclear material floating around out there to ignore the signs, but until now no one has been stupid enough to actually consider building a bomb or detonating one. We think that we might be able to bring the device to the surface as long as it hasn't been armed. If it's armed, that's a different scenario entirely."

"As in get the hell out of there." Ig shook his head.

"Well," Sebastian drew out the word. "There is a small chance that by combining our magic with the added power of the pack, Lily and I might be able to contain the blast, should it occur. That's a big 'might,' but it's a last-chance gambit."

Anton folded his arms across his chest and focused on Sebastian and Lily. "A terrible risk I prefer you not take."

"Agreed." Ig shook his head. "Not only is it a huge risk to the world should you fail, but we can't afford to lose either of you in this battle. I actually think we might be better off disarming the device belowground, depending on the mechanics involved."

"That only works if we've got room to return to our physical bodies, and if we can do it without tools," Fen said. "That's a couple of really big *ifs.*"

"I agree." Anton ran his fingers through his hair. "With any luck, I hope we can stop them from setting the device in the first place. I doubt the men Mary knows have the technical ability to arm a nuclear weapon, so I'm guessing that's something that Aldo is planning to do by magical means. If he is able to steal the life force of the four men, he might have the strength to do it, but there's another thing we need to keep in mind."

Jack glanced up from Sebastian's map. "What's that?"

Anton rested his chin on his steepled fingers. "We have four humans who are willingly working for a demon. They can't possibly believe he's an angel or a man of god, not at this point, unless they're complete idiots." He paused, glanced at Jack, but otherwise ignored his derisive snort. "We can only assume that Aldo has plans to kill them. Reko, I think that's probably where you come in. If he thinks he can control you, then he'll be counting on your killing the men for him, at which point he's going to go for their life force."

If I'm hearing you correctly, you're saying you want me to keep Aldo hanging around. That's something my father used to quote, that you should keep your friends close and your enemies closer. You don't fear this is taking that concept a bit far? What if he gets control of me and I snap? What if I turn on one of you at Aldo's command? I could not forgive myself.

Jack stared at the wolf, a creature he'd known for but a few short hours. He felt the same connection now that Mary had developed almost immediately with Reko, as if they had a bond almost as strong as that on the level of a mate. Almost as if Reko had imprinted on Mary when he'd first awakened, and that connection had been passed to Jack when he and Mary mated. What if . . . ? "Anton, Mary has had a very close connection to Reko from the beginning. When we mated, I . . ."

"You mated?" Sebastian's eyes lit up. "Congratulations to both of you. I had no idea."

"Neither did I." Lily actually pouted. "I pride myself on knowing what's going on around here, but you guys are sneaky." She grabbed Mary's hands in hers. "I'm really happy for you, Mary. You got one of the good ones."

Mary turned to Jack. Her eyes sparkled when she said, "I know. He's been reminding me of that very fact."

Even Reko laughed at her comment, his wolfish chuffing close enough. Ari had stayed quiet, though, sitting back from the group, observing but not commenting.

Anton interrupted. "What are you saying, Jack? About the connection with Reko?"

"I'm wondering if there's a way you can help us connect with him on a deeper level, sort of act as guardians to protect him from Aldo." He glanced at Mary. "Does that make sense?"

She nodded. "It makes excellent sense." She frowned and stared at Jack a moment before turning to Reko. "Would you allow that? Allow us to build a connection that would bring you into our mating bond? That should connect us on a deeper level, allow us to protect you from Aldo's constant yammering." She turned to Lily and shrugged. "I think it sounds like something we should be able to do. What do you think?"

"I think that if Reko is willing to go along, at least until this mess is over, it's an excellent idea. It wouldn't be a true mate bond, but he would have access to your thoughts as you would to his. I think it would also let you hear Aldo, though I don't believe Aldo would be privy to your thoughts. He doesn't appear to read Reko's. Dad, what do you think?"

"I think we need to give Reko a chance to comment." Anton walked around the bar and plopped his butt down on the floor in front of the big wolf. "We're standing around, planning your life for you, wolf. What do you choose? It's really not our place to make decisions for you."

. . .

Reko's first instinct was to lower his eyes, turn his head to bare his throat to the powerful alpha who had, most amazingly, lowered himself to Reko's level. But when he gave in to instinct, the alpha gently tipped his fingers beneath Reko's chin and forced him to meet his steady gaze.

"One thing I've learned as alpha of this growing pack is that we are all equal members, each of us as important to one another as we are to the pack as a whole, and that means we must remain true to ourselves. What Mary and Jack are offering to you is unprecedented—a newly mated pair willing to bring an almost complete stranger into their mating bond for the good of the pack, but the burden on you is unprecedented as well. You're the first of us to be possessed by a demon. It can't be a pleasant experience, but your strength in fighting a man who was a powerful dark wizard in life is impressive. If I thought this were a danger to either you or Mary or Jack, I'd probably figure out how to put a stop to it, but with Lily, Sebastian, and the others monitoring you, I think it will be okay. The question is, Reko, are you willing to share your thoughts, give up much of your personal privacy to Mary and Jack?"

This was one of those times that Reko was thankful for his father's and mother's teachings. They'd always said family had to come first, and wasn't that exactly what this pack was? A family. One that had welcomed his brother and him with open arms. It was also the most amazing adventure he'd ever been part of in his life. It was easy to answer Anton's questions.

I probably would have died in that cavern, and my brother would have been left alone. Your pack's rescuing us has also given us the opportunity to give back. He glanced at his brother, sitting quietly beside Fen and Ig, and felt Ari's approval. *I don't understand the connection with Mary and now Jack, but it gives me a sense of belonging I've never known before. I agree to do whatever needs to be done.* He wished he had the ability to laugh as humans did, or at least as Chanku with the ability to take on human forms did. *My life has been pretty dull and predictable up*

81

until now. From what I've seen of this pack so far, it's more exciting here. I think I'm getting the better part of the deal.

Anton laughed for him. "Seb, can you and Lily take Reko, Jack, and Mary somewhere quiet and help them figure out a tighter link?"

Reko followed them out of the room. He could already feel Mary's love for him, right there with Jack's. He glanced at Ari as he walked by. Should he feel guilt that his brother wasn't included?

No, Reko. I think this is your adventure. Mine's still out there, waiting for me. His dry humor showed in a final, fleeting thought. *I do, however, expect details . . .*

• • •

Anton stood and went back behind the bar. Ig always thought of it as the alpha's version of a throne, but it was where he appeared to conduct most of his business. "I wanted to let you know that I spoke with Madam President a little while ago. She's leaving us in control of whatever is done directly with the potential device while it's in place, and with Aldo. She was quite adamant that the U.S. government has very little experience dealing with demonkind."

"No special demon forces? Interesting." Fen glanced at Ig. "What about the four men? They're U.S. citizens involved in domestic terrorism."

"Which is why she's sending an FBI agent to act as a liaison between the Chanku Nation and the U.S. military and law enforcement—in this case, rangers with the National Park Service. He should be arriving in about an hour. He's been on special assignment in Seattle and will be coming in by jet helicopter. Tinker's got the landing pad lighted up for them and I'm sure we'll hear when they go over."

"Who are they sending?" Ig's demand probably said more than he wanted about his low opinion of government agencies, but they'd had years of being treated as if they were barely a step above dogs in intelligence.

"Agent Remington Caruthers. She said you should remember him."

"Thank the goddess." Fen slapped Ig on the back. "Someone we don't have to tie up and leave in a closet if we want to get things done."

"Rem's one of the good ones," Ig said. "He's smart, and he doesn't have a problem working with shifters."

Fen snickered. "Well, it didn't hurt that Star and Sunny shifted in front of him. Went straight from big, bad wolves to two absolutely gorgeous, very naked women."

Anton almost choked on his coffee. "Why didn't I hear this story?"

Ig merely laughed. "Because it wasn't imperative to the operation, though it did a lot toward building better FBI/Chanku relations. But Fen's right. After we shoved Rem's eyes back in his head he was okay, though he might've still been in shock when he dropped us off at the cabin."

Fen raised an eyebrow and turned toward Anton. "Actually, Anton, Ig's exaggerating. It was more exhaustion than shock. He went way out of his way to get us home that night, and he took care of the bodies. You can't downplay the importance of that."

Anton turned his alpha stare on Ig. "You never ignore the importance of someone willing to hide bodies. Especially when it's plural."

"Well, he didn't really hide them. Just managed to get them taken care of without involving any of us, so yeah. Rem's probably in the 'friend' category."

"Now that we have that settled." Anton reached for the coffeepot. "More coffee?"

"If you throw in a shot of Hennessy."

Anton topped off their mugs with fresh coffee and a shot of cognac. "Anyway, once Agent Caruthers gets here, I'm wondering if we can take him to the scene via the astral. I forgot to ask Eve if that's allowed, but it would sure make it easier to arrest those four and get them out of Yellowstone without anyone being the wiser."

"What are we going to do with the men once we have them?" Ig thought of all the things he'd like to do, but figured none of them would pass muster with Rem. He was a good guy, but still more "by the book" than Ig liked.

"That will depend on how much control Aldo has over them. He's got some, obviously, or I doubt that Mary's father would have murdered his little girl and then . . ." Anton paused and took a deep breath. "And then he shot his wife." He had to be thinking of Lily, his eldest, of his younger daughter Lucia, and his beloved Keisha. Wondering how any man could do harm to the women he loved.

Anton gripped the edge of the granite bar and his voice broke. The man who was usually so well-spoken stumbled over his words. "Mary's sister, the little girl was strangled. It . . . that is, it's a very personal attack, one that no loving father would ever consider." He sucked in a breath, obviously searching for control. "Of course, that's why it was so perfect for Aldo. He wants his victims afraid. Their fear gives him more power." He took another shaky breath but his voice was a steady monotone. "There's more dark energy in a fearful death. That little girl had to have been so terribly afraid."

He turned away and stared out the window for a few moments, a man beyond anger, and yet so terribly, terribly sad. Without thinking, Igmutaka walked around the long granite bar and wrapped his arms around Anton, the man who had been as a brother to him for so many years. Anton's chest heaved as he fought the tears, before finally giving in to the wracking sobs of a man pushed to the edge.

Ig thought of the time Lily had disappeared. Just six years old, she'd gone on a days-long journey on the astral, and Anton hadn't been able to find her. What had been almost two weeks to the family had felt like only hours to the little girl, but even knowing she was safe, the long separation had just about broken her father.

People, both human and shifter, knew Anton Cheval as a powerful man, the brilliant, charismatic leader of the Chanku Nation, both a financial wizard as well as a wizard in the true sense of the word. But only those closest to Anton understood what a deeply emotional man he was, that he loved deeply, empathized with the pain of others, that he took their pain into himself, but that was part of his strength. His ability to put the powerful alpha wolf aside and feel what his people were feeling, share their joy and their pain.

Sometimes, though, Ig worried that the pack forgot to share Anton's.

He stroked his friend's back without words. Finally he asked, *You okay? I can get Keisha.*

She's on her way. Thank you, Ig. Raising his head, Anton's smile was self-deprecating, a man well aware of his own failings. *You're one of the few who recognizes when I need a hug. My mate is the other. She sensed my emotions, seems to always know when my inner four-year-old is having a meltdown. She said she's bringing Sunny and Star. They just woke up.*

The loud roar of a jet helicopter rattled the windows. Suddenly all business, Anton stepped back into position behind the bar. "It appears Agent Caruthers has arrived."

· · ·

"Remington! It's good to see you." Fenris stepped up and took the agent's hand. "You remember Igmutaka, Sunny, and Star."

Rem chuckled as he focused on the women. "Impossible to forget such beauty," he said. "Not to mention the simple fact either one of you could easily whip my ass. It's good to see you, ladies." He turned to Ig and grinned at him. "You're just too pretty for words, man. You need to work on that." Ig laughed. He got that a lot, from both men and women. They shook hands as well.

Then Ig turned to Anton. "You've not met our alpha. Anton Cheval.

Agent Remington Caruthers is the man we worked with on that mess last year."

"I've heard good things about you, Agent Caruthers. Thank you for managing to get here so quickly. My mate, Keisha."

"It's my pleasure." Caruthers took Keisha's outstretched hand in greeting.

Keisha grasped his hand and, as was her habit, covered their right hands with her left. Ig bit back a grin at the startled look on the agent's face, and the sudden relaxation as Keisha's calming presence filtered through her grip. She swore she didn't do anything on purpose, but they loved to tease her about the tranquilizing properties of her touch. She smiled at poor Rem, who gazed at her with absolute adoration. "As my husband said, we are pleased that you were able to get here so quickly. Our daughter and her mate and two other packmates are also involved in the preliminary investigation, along with one of the Berserkers who first discovered this plot, if we can call it that. They'll be here shortly."

Anton interrupted. "Reko's brother is here, though, and I'd like for you to meet him." Remington slipped his hand free of Keisha's light grasp with an audible sigh and followed Anton across the room to Ari, who was lying quietly on one of the big pillows Keisha kept around the house.

• • •

"Ari, this is Agent Caruthers . . ."

Ari raised his head and looked at the alpha. Anton had knelt in front of him, putting the two of them at eye level. The agent went to his knees next to the alpha.

"Please." The agent interrupted Anton. "Remington or Rem . . . either is fine. When I hear Agent Caruthers, I think you're talking to my father. He was FBI for almost forty years."

"Good. We're rarely formal here. Call me Anton. And this is Ari." Ari tilted his head and focused on the agent rather than Anton. It was difficult, still, for him to meet the alpha with a direct gaze. Anton ran his hand over Ari's thick ruff at the back of his neck. It felt so good, better, even, because the strength of the alpha was in his touch. Ari had heard of what it was like to have a strong alpha, but with only their family to learn from, he'd never felt such a powerful touch. Nor realized the power of praise from an alpha. He actually shivered when he heard what Anton had to say.

"Because of Ari's bravery, Remington, we have a much better idea of what we're facing. Ari went into the cave in search of his injured brother at great risk to himself. Ari, are you able to communicate with the agent?"

I'm not sure. Ari projected his thoughts to the one who said to call him Remington. He'd never tried to speak to a human before. *Remington, are you able to hear my mental speech?*

After a moment, the human shook his head. "That's odd. I can feel a buzzing in my head, but no actual words. I'm sorry, Ari. If you shift, we'll be able to talk, right?" Remington glanced at Anton.

"Ari and his brother have been living in the wild up till now," Anton said. "They've just started taking the nutrients, so neither of them has shifted yet. Not much longer, we hope."

Ari dipped his head, acknowledging Anton's comment. *It can't be soon enough. I'm anxious to see what it's like, looking and acting human.*

Rem merely shook his head, as if he were as bemused by the night's events as Ari.

Anton glanced at Remington. "Ari said he's hoping it won't be much longer. He's anxious to see what it's like to look and act human." Then the alpha smiled at Ari. "That's when he'll probably realize he much prefers to be the wolf."

Standing, Anton glanced at the others in the room. "I want everyone over here," he said. "We need to catch Remington up on everything, and you've all got stuff to add to the conversation. You as well, Ari, so don't hesitate to interrupt me."

Ari waited while the others gathered. Sebastian, Lily, Jack, and Mary walked into the room. Reko stayed close to Mary and her hand was twisted in the thick fur at his neck. *You okay?* Ari had no real idea what they'd done to his brother.

I am, Reko said. *For now.*

8

Friday, 9:30 p.m.

Remington had listened carefully while Sebastian and Lily filled him in on Aldo's background. Jack noticed the man's eyes occasionally bugged out a bit, but he didn't interrupt and didn't ask any questions. Then Anton talked about their plan to capture the four men so that the demon Aldo couldn't steal their life force.

At that point, Jack was almost sure the agent started to twitch. He sat close beside Mary but he was afraid to look at her, especially when she softly mindspoke. *You realize,* she said, *the poor man thinks we're all crazy as loons.*

Fucking nuts is closer, I think. I'm surprised he's not asking questions.

Like, where's the exit?

That comes to mind.

Anton's voice slipped into their conversation and Mary clutched Jack's hand. She shot him a worried glance, but he merely nodded to Anton.

Stop it, you two. Once we tell him everything, Eve's promised to drop by. That should be all we need to convince him we're not, as Jack so eloquently puts it, fucking nuts.

"Okay," Anton said, leaning his elbows on the bar as if he'd not been reading the riot act to both Jack and Mary. "I know that's a lot to swallow, but it is exactly what we're dealing with. The president is aware that we work with magic on a level far beyond your standard Las Vegas magic show. I understand you've seen what Igmutaka and Fenris are capable of."

Remington nodded. "Touché." He glanced at Ig. "Last year when you disappeared right in front of me, and then reported from inside the terrorists' vehicle, I decided it's a good thing to be open-minded when dealing with shapeshifters."

Anton paused a moment. "Okay. Eve's asking the Mother if we can take you onto the astral to . . ."

The agent raised his hand. Jack thought he definitely looked a bit shell-shocked now. "Wait a minute. So far I've been following everything and doing my damnedest to make sense of all this, but the astral?" Laughing, he shook his head. "That's a bit too much for me to swallow, at least without—"

"Proof," Lily said. "Give me a minute." She closed her eyes and after a moment nodded. "Eve said to come down to the cavern. It takes more energy for her to materialize here and she's trying to save what she can. Remington? We have a portal in the cavern beneath the house. I know it's late and you're probably exhausted, but I think you'll sleep better knowing we're being totally honest with you and not spinning a wild tale. Well, it is a wild tale, but what makes it even wilder is that it's true. C'mon."

• • •

Friday, 9:47 p.m.

As he followed the shifters through the kitchen—one that looked like any other kitchen in a modern upscale American home—Rem reminded himself he had to remain open-minded. He'd learned to trust Ig and Fen, as well as Star and Sunny, but this whole thing was so far out of the realm of normal that verification was necessary before he could act.

But what would it take to convince him? He'd been an FBI agent for most of his adult life. He'd served in the Marines, fought hand-to-hand combat in some places that most people had never heard of, before joining the bureau. He'd been involved in clandestine operations so over-the-top that they still felt as if they'd been held on a Hollywood set. But never in his life had he followed a group of shapeshifters, three of whom claimed to be wizards of immense power, into a cavern beneath a perfectly lovely home to meet a goddess and check out the astral plane.

He should probably be running the other direction, but everyone was so perfectly normal on the outside—until they started telling him the story of why he'd been yanked off a top-secret investigation into an arms dealer in Seattle to check out a story of a demon in Yellowstone. It truly boggled the mind.

But if what these people were telling him was true, the arms dealer was small potatoes.

"Watch your step." Keisha, the alpha's lovely mate, touched his arm as they reached the staircase leading down from the kitchen.

"Thank you." There it was again, that sense of calm, of peace, even, that settled over him when Keisha touched him. Probably explained why nothing ever seemed to throw Cheval. The guy was the epitome of calm. He'd have to ask Igmutaka about that. About what the power was that Keisha seemed to wield so naturally. The big guy had never hesitated to answer any of Rem's questions before. So far, all of his answers—no matter how outlandish Rem's questions—had proved to be truthful.

He followed the group through a large pantry and storage area, past a heavy door standing open, and into a huge cavern where the humidity reminded him of the tropics. A large, shallow lake filled one side of it, and tiny lights set into the walls and ceiling softly glowed. Lily led them around the lake to an area on the far side, where they all stood together staring at a natural stone wall. There was nothing special about it, at least until he noticed what appeared to be hieroglyphics carved into the stone. And handprints. They were almost too perfect to have been carved, as if someone had pressed their hands into soft clay and left their prints, except this was obviously a natural interior wall of the cavern.

Lily walked over and pressed her hands against the prints. Then she just stood there, staring at the wall. Rem was ready to start fidgeting when the stone began to glow, starting at a pinpoint of light in the center that reminded him of the opening of the aperture of a camera lens. When the glow spread outward, he saw an amazing green forest on the other side, colors so brilliant, a sky so blue they couldn't possibly be real.

Something shimmered in the middle of the frame, shimmered and grew as a vertical glow before it coalesced into something corporeal. Corporeal and so absolutely mesmerizing he had to fight his first reaction, which was to fall to his knees in front of a woman of such beauty. She walked closer, and then she stepped through the light, out of the perfect forest and into the cave.

She gave Lily a quick hug and then walked directly toward him. He didn't know what to do, whether to bow as if to royalty or maybe just turn and run like hell. The sense of power about her sent hot and cold shivers running along his spine and the hair on his arms stood on end. If this was verification, damn it all, he believed!

Before he'd gathered his wits about himself enough to react, she stopped in front of him and reached for his hands. He lifted them, moving as if he'd been drugged, and she clasped his in hers. She was warm with life, her hair falling in long blonde waves to her ankles, but when he raised his head and saw her eyes . . . when he saw her eyes, he suddenly understood. He was in the presence of a creature that was so far removed from humanity as to be completely *other.*

Her eyes were rimmed in dark lashes, but they were of no discernible color. No, they spun in shades of green and gold, brown, blue, and amber. The pupils stayed dark in the center, but her irises never settled on a single shade, and it was impossible to tell what their true color might be.

Blinking, he realized she was smiling at him. "Remington," she said. "I'm Eve, and yes, I know my eyes are totally weird, but that's what happens when you get this job." She laughed, and the sound was music. He blinked like a complete idiot, but she was just so perfect. So unbelievably perfect.

"Lily has told me you're here to help us. Thank you. I've gotten the Mother's permission to allow you to walk the astral with our people. You'll be safe with them, and it will save much time since we have a portal that goes directly into the cavern in Yellowstone."

She'd talked to him directly. He'd just spoken with a goddess . . . had been touched by a goddess. He knew the import of this was something he'd have to absorb slowly, if at all. It really was too much. She released his hands and stepped back through the portal, addressing all of them now.

"I've heard from the Mother," she said, and her words sounded like music, too. Just like her laughter, so pure, so beautiful, each sound sent shivers along his spine. But this was different than the intimate conversation she'd had with him just moments ago. Now she spoke with authority, like an officer addressing her troops, and yet . . .

"The men haven't come back to the cavern, but the Mother expects them to arrive sometime around midnight. I suggest you eat, get some rest, and return to this place when we call you. I'm guessing around midnight, though if we need you earlier, I'll enter your dreams and tell you to come quickly. Don't set alarms, just in case they don't return right away. Sleep, now. You're going to be wishing for the chance by tomorrow, I can assure you. From all portents, it looks like Aldo's plans are supposed to come to fruition just before midnight tomorrow night. Our goal is to try and stop him tonight, instead."

The eye of the portal slowly closed, until they were all standing there in the dim light of the cavern. A shiver flashed across Rem's shoulders, down his back, a sense of touch that left him feeling energized, as if he'd gotten a charge of electricity directly into his veins. Anton glanced at him and raised one very expressive eyebrow. "Well?" It was obvious he was fighting a grin.

"You win," Rem said. "She's too beautiful to be real, but too real not to believe." He shook his head, forcing his body to relax, his spirit to calm. He was totally exhausted. Maybe that was why she'd affected him so strangely. Of course, she was, after all, a goddess. "I need sleep. I've been up for over twenty-four hours, and it doesn't sound like we're getting much rest tonight. I think this will all make a lot more sense after some shut-eye. But thank you, Lily, for introducing her to me. You're right. There's no reason to doubt anything you've told me."

The soft laughter around him was at least good-natured, but what these people lived with, the knowledge they had of things he'd thought of as fairy tales, was hard to imagine. Then Keisha's hand was on his. "We have a room ready for you, Remington. Come with me. Your bag has already been taken to it and there's a hot shower with your name on it."

He knew he looked like a total sap, but he took Keisha's hand and kissed the back of her fingers as if he were a Renaissance courtier and she was the lady of the manor. Which, he figured, she was. "I knew you were a queen among women. And men, for that matter. A shower sounds like pure heaven and I will follow you anywhere."

She laughed, but so did Anton. "Ah, my love," he said. "It appears another swain has fallen beneath your womanly wiles."

"Hey," Rem said. "So I'm easy and your woman is gorgeous. What do you expect?"

"Exactly what just happened. Sleep well, Agent Caruthers. I imagine tomorrow will be even more of a shock. I have a feeling the Mother will be speaking to us." He turned toward the doorway leading out of the cavern. "That entity still shrinks my balls and dick with a single word. I'm curious to see your reaction."

"Thanks for that," Rem said, but he was smiling when he followed Keisha out of the cave.

• • •

Reko? Ari stopped his brother in the kitchen. Mary and Jack waited for the two of them just outside the room in case they wanted privacy, but Reko included them in the conversation. *Sebastian and Lily have asked me to stay with them. They're staying in this house tonight, so I'll be close. Will you be all right without me?*

I'll be with Jack and Mary. They'll keep me safe. Don't forget to eat the pill with the grasses.

I won't. Good night, my brother.

Rest well, Ari.

Jack watched Ari follow Sebastian and Lily along the hallway to Lily's room. Whatever Lily and Sebastian had done had definitely improved his and Mary's connection to Reko. Unfortunately, now Jack was fully aware of Aldo in the background. The demon's threats were truly ugly, but Reko had quickly learned to tune the demon out.

Jack, however, had to monitor the demon, make sure he wasn't gaining control over the wolf. He watched Reko as he followed his brother with his gaze. The wolf's thoughts were private, but he and Ari had gone through so much over the past hours that a separation, no matter how minor, had to be hard for them.

As Lily, Sebastian, and Ari walked down the broad hallway to the wing where the extra bedrooms were, Jack and Mary, with Reko sticking close by, went toward Anton's den. He was already behind the bar, pouring a glass of cognac for the FBI agent. He waved them in.

Jack took a seat at the bar next to Remington. Mary settled on the closest couch, patted the cushions, and Reko leapt up to lie beside her. Jack watched them a moment before turning to Rem. "And here I thought Keisha had seduced you with promises of a shower and a comfortable bed. Instead, it appears Dr. Cheval's magic elixir has won the night."

Rem merely raised his glass before taking a sip. With his usual enigmatic smile, Anton merely said, "Something like that. Whatever you call it, it'll help you sleep." He poured two glasses and set them in front of Jack, then grabbed a ceramic bowl and filled it with fresh water for Reko. Jack delivered the glass to Mary and set the bowl on a small table next to the couch for the wolf.

Then he went back to the bar. "That's what I'm hoping." He held the glass up in a silent toast to Anton. "Thank you."

"I'm glad you stopped by here before heading to your parents' cabin, Jack. I'm curious how well Seb and Lily were able to help you and Reko."

Jack shook his head. "Probably a little too well. Aldo is a constant presence in Reko's mind, and now in mine and Mary's as well. Reko's taught me how to tune him out, but we're connected closely enough that if Aldo picks up strength and becomes a threat, Mary and I should know. Right now I'm trying to monitor him without tuning him out too much, at least until I can figure out how to still hear him without letting him interfere with the rest of my thoughts." He shot a glance in Mary's direction. "He's a damned irritating bastard."

Mary gave him a thumbs-up. "We just have to hope that my mother doesn't die." Mary ran her hand over Reko's shoulders, touched her forehead to his for a moment, and then walked over to the bar to sit beside Jack. "Her life force would give him more strength, and that could be enough to bolster the commands he's giving to Reko." She glanced at

Remington and shrugged. "My mother gave up any claim to my affection when she disowned me and labeled me a whore, but I don't want her to die. I really don't want her death to power a demon."

Anton covered one of her hands with his. "I understand your feelings, Mary. Don't ever feel you have to explain yourself. I know your decisions aren't made lightly. However, she's recovering, according to her doctor." Anton took a sip of his cognac and closed his eyes for a moment as he swallowed. He looked exhausted, but Anton carried the burdens of every member of his pack. Usually, though, it wasn't this obvious.

"I was thinking of bringing her out here once she's healed so we can keep her close," he said. "We don't know yet if Aldo is in her mind or not. She's not said anything, but she might not be aware of his presence. If he tries badgering her into taking her own life, I'm not sure she's strong enough now to fight him."

Mary nodded. "I would like that. I know she feels guilty over the way they treated me, and the fact she didn't recognize that Dad was changing so terribly. Its sounds like he's totally under the power of Brother Thomas, who seems to be nothing more than Aldo's minion."

Anton brushed a loose curl of hair out of Mary's eyes. He had easily stepped into a father role for her, just as Jack's parents had pulled her into their family unit. Such was the strength of the pack.

"Your mother should feel guilty." Anton's attention was focused entirely on Mary. "Don't excuse her and never, ever tell her you understand, because we both know that would be a lie. She needs the guilt to make her strong. If she doesn't carry some of the blame for your sister's death, she'll not fight as hard to stay alive to protect you, and we can't let Aldo have her."

Mary nodded. Jack took her hand, but he was focused on Anton. A thought had come to him, something that might be totally off base, but if not, it might answer the question they'd all been asking themselves. "I thought of something weird, Anton. You might think it's crazy, but remember the night that Aldo died? He was trying to steal Sebastian's life force, but he also wanted his immortality, wanted what it was that makes Sebastian Chanku, but obviously that's not something you can take from another. You have to be born with it. That spell, though? It had to go somewhere. We know it gave Sebastian a lot of his father's power, but I can't imagine that Sebastian would have accepted, consciously or otherwise, any of Aldo's dark power. Do you agree?"

Anton nodded. "Yeah. That makes sense." He glanced at Remington, probably to make sure the agent was paying close attention. "What are you getting at?"

"There were twelve rogue wolves that night. Twelve of them, every single one a powerful Berserker, and when the Mother killed Aldo with that bolt of lightning, all twelve of them died at the same instant. What if their life force got sucked into Aldo? What if it was enough to allow him to live on as a demon, demanding more life force to stay alive, to function? Could it have, in essence, turned him into a vampire feeding off the energy of his victims? Not a regular demon, if there is such a thing, but one who needs to kill to survive, because he was both created and empowered by the deaths of those who served him?"

Anton stared at him for so long Jack was convinced the man thought he was an idiot. Except he reached for Jack and clasped his shoulder. He studied Jack for a moment with a rather bemused expression before giving his shoulder a squeeze.

"You're right." Then he actually laughed! "I'm positive you're right. That would explain so much. I wasn't there. I was down here, so caught up in juggling all the energy from the pack, I never even thought of the energy from the wolves' deaths. Sebastian wouldn't have absorbed the life force of any creature—his magic doesn't work that way, would naturally repel it. Aldo, on the other hand, would suck it up like a sponge, most likely in the instant of his death. That's how he has the power to control four otherwise healthy men. How he could force Mary's dad to murder her sister, attempt to kill her mother. I can't believe none of us even thought of that."

He turned toward Reko. The huge wolf took up half the couch. He was probably four feet at the shoulder, his jaws wide enough to decapitate an adult with a single bite. His life force was strong enough that Anton felt it, felt the power of it here in this room that was so attuned to magic. He needed to consider what Jack had just said. Needed the quiet and the time alone to figure it out.

He glanced at Remington as the man finished his cognac. "Go to bed, Agent Caruthers, before you fall off the bar stool. It would ruin your tough-guy image, and we need to depend on you."

"Good night, all." Rem stood and nodded to no one in particular. "If anyone finds me along the way, it means I couldn't make it down that long hallway. Just haul my ass into the bedroom." He tipped a salute and left the room.

Mary grabbed Jack's hand and stood. "Good night, Anton. Reko? Let's get some sleep."

As they walked out the door, Jack glanced back once more. Anton stood quietly behind the bar, staring at the lights reflected in the big picture window that faced the east. He thought the man looked a little better than he had when they'd first walked in here, possibly because he had a puzzle to work on before he slept. That was good, because Jack didn't want to be worried about his alpha. He just wanted to crawl into bed with Mary. She was puzzle enough this night.

• • •

Mary could hardly keep her eyes open. Reko found a spot out of the way on the floor, but Mary sensed his loneliness. She touched Jack's hand and spoke to him privately. *I want to shift and invite Reko to sleep with us on the bed. Is that okay with you?*

He leaned close and kissed her. *Good. I was trying to figure out how to bring it up without it sounding a bit kinky. It is our first night as a mated couple, after all, but I think he's really unsettled tonight.*

With Aldo yammering nonstop in his head, can you blame him? The demon is driving me nuts, but I'm glad we're linked in and aware of it. Anyway, my wolf sleeps better than my human form. She kissed him. *I think because my senses are more acute, so I'm more alert. I know that no one can sneak up on me.*

Jack kissed her again. *I won't have to sneak up on you. I'll be sleeping really, really close.*

Mary slipped out of her clothing and shifted. Then she walked over and touched noses with Reko. *Sleep with us tonight, okay? We only have a few hours, and I don't want you to be alone.*

You're newly mated. I shouldn't intrude.

We're pack, and that's more important. Besides, we only get a few hours tonight, if what Eve says happens. They'll be waking us before we know it.

She glanced at the bed. Jack had already shifted and was curled up near the headboard. Mary leapt up beside him, walked a small circle and flopped down with her nose tucked beneath her tail. When Reko jumped up and joined them, he found a spot beside Jack, but his nose rested on Mary's shoulder.

Mary had never slept as wolf with anyone other than a few of the women, but immediately she knew this was a great idea. She liked the sense of being surrounded by warmth and love, and she was already thinking of Reko as part of her family—not on the same level as Jack, obviously, but definitely more than others in the pack. She wasn't certain why the link had been there since the first time she'd touched him, and it was definitely stronger now, after Sebastian and Lily had opened their mental pathways.

Aldo was still ranting in the background, though she'd mentally dialed him back to a soft murmur. Jack had already fallen asleep. Reko's soft breathing was a steady counterpoint to her own. It had been a long, eventful day and the night would be short before they had to face the demon and his minions. That meant she'd have to face her father, knowing the man had killed her little sister and tried to kill her mother. His daughter. His wife. He was not the father she remembered. That one had always been controlling and somewhat sanctimonious, but she'd never doubted his love.

Obviously, something major had changed, but how? Why?

Consciously she pushed those questions aside, something much easier to do as a wolf. Thinking instead of the man she loved, the one who was now her mate, as well as the more feral wolf sleeping beside her, was much more conducive to sleep and sweet dreams. With Jack's scent filling her senses and Reko's soft breaths tickling her ear, she drifted off.

• • •

Friday, 11:23 p.m.

Reko hovered in that mystical place between sleep and awareness, paying only slight attention to the demon ranting in the background. What had his attention were the scents of the two wolves he lay so close to. Mary had fallen asleep—through the new link that Sebastian and Lily had helped them set up, he was viscerally aware of both Mary and Jack as if they were truly linked as mates, though he couldn't hear any private conversations between the two. Still, it was an honor to be so close to the two of them. He wondered what it would be like when he finally had a mate of his own.

Reko? Awaken, but do it quietly. Don't disturb Jack or Mary.

The goddess? Why would she be contacting him? *Eve? Is that you?*

Yes. Hurry, Reko. We're being attacked. I need your help now!

Reko sat up, quietly so as not to disturb Mary or Jack, but that made no sense. Why would Eve want him without the two Chanku?

He thought about it for a moment, about the tone of her voice and the feverish haste in her directive. She wouldn't.

Reko? What's taking you so long? What are you doing? I'm out on the front deck waiting for you. Hurry. There's no time.

He pawed at Jack's shoulder, licked Mary's nose, but neither of them moved. *Jack! Mary! Wake up!*

What? Jack raised his head. *What's wrong, Reko?*

A voice that identified as Eve woke me, said not to wake you, that we were under attack. I don't believe it's really Eve.

Probably not. What did the voice tell you to do?

She said she's waiting on the front deck. How do I tell if it's really the goddess?

Good question. Mary? Wake up. Jack scraped a paw across her shoulder and she startled, sitting up quickly and blinking away her confusion.

Reko told her what he'd heard.

Reko! I can't wait much longer. Hurry—you have to hurry!

Okay. I heard it that time. Jack shook his head. *That's not Eve.*

Can he hear us? Mary glanced at Reko when she asked.

I don't think so. I've been speaking to Jack and no mention was made of that.

Jack jumped down from the bed. *I think we all need to check and see just who's waiting out on the deck.*

Mary and Reko followed. *Should we let Eve know?*

Not yet. Jack moved carefully, slipping out of their bedroom and walking as quietly as possible for a large wolf on a wooden floor. *She's probably got her hands full right now. I don't want to make contact with the demon, but I do want to know if he's actually able to materialize.*

You two need to hide in the cabin. Let me go out and look for him, but stay hidden or he'll know I'm not following his orders.

Be careful, Reko.

Mary's soft plea moved him.

Yeah, Jack added. *We're sort of getting used to you. Don't do anything stupid. We don't want you hurt.*

Reko chuffed quietly. But Jack's silly sarcasm following Mary's concern felt even better, as if Reko were truly a member of the pack. It was much more effective than merely telling him he belonged. These two showed him how they felt. He stopped in front of the door. There was a latch he could operate with his foot. He pressed it.

Eve? He sat on the deck and searched the area as if he truly waited on Eve. *I've answered your call. Where are you?*

A shimmer of light flickered in the darkness, but it wasn't the silvery glow he'd seen with the goddess. Instead, it was dark, as if lightning flashed and sucked up the starlight. He wondered what color it was, but it was most assuredly not Eve. Mary had told him how things would look differently to his human eyes.

He wondered what Jack and Mary saw.

• • •

Mary shifted as soon as Reko walked out onto the deck. The pressure in her skull was growing, the sense of evil building. She wondered if Aldo had killed tonight, if he had grown stronger, but she waited out of sight, still able to see the dark shimmer in front of the cabin.

Jack? What do you see with your wolven eyes? It's dark purple to me, like those black lights that make things glow in the dark. It's taking on a physical appearance, blotting out the trees behind it.

Imagine black lightning, but it looks oily, and yes, it's got enough substance to it to look solid, but I don't see a solid shape of any kind. It's very fluid. I'm aware of Aldo, but I can't hear his voice as clearly as I should. Reko? Is he speaking to you?

Silence. Mary glanced nervously at Jack. Did Aldo have control of the wolf?

Give me a moment. I'm listening to his instructions.

Mary sighed in relief when she heard Reko. She curled her fingers into the thick fur at Jack's neck and held on. Long moments later, Reko spoke again.

He's speaking in a feminine voice, as if he's the goddess, telling me I'll need to kill Chanku tonight. He says all of you are under the demon's control, and you'll attack Eve tonight because you'll see her as a demon. He says it's up to me to stop them, to protect her, that I'm the only one who knows the demon that we see is really Eve. You're not hearing this?

Not as clearly as I'd like, Jack said. *Did he say what the demon looks like? The one he says is really Eve?*

He said she'll look like a man named Aldo Xenakis. Is that him? The Aldo in my mind?

Yes. He's Sebastian's father, Mary said. *When Sebastian killed him, he became a demon. He's the one causing all the trouble.*

His voice is growing weaker. This must take a lot of energy for him to manifest in any way that allows us to see him.

I think you're right. The light is fading.

Reko sat there a moment longer before turning and walking back into the cabin. None of them spoke until they'd reached the bedroom again. Mary shifted and the three of them leapt up on the bed. She leaned against her mate. *Jack, have you let Anton know what's happened?*

I have. And Sebastian and Lily as well. She said she'd tell Eve. Lily advised us to try and get more sleep. It's going to be a long night.

Mary snuggled between the two wolves. *I'm exhausted. I really don't think falling asleep is going to be much of a problem. Rest, Reko. And thank you for facing the demon tonight. Your bravery is amazing.*

I'm not so sure about that. He's pretty scary. I hope he didn't see me shaking.

Jack raised his head. *If you hadn't been shaking, I'd think there was something wrong with you. Go to sleep, my friend.*

Reko lay there beside Mary with Jack's words ringing in his mind. *My friend.* He hoped Ari was sleeping soundly. Hoped his brother was finding friends among these Chanku who welcomed them so openly. He only wished his entire family could have lived long enough to know that he and Ari had finally found their pack.

9

The call came simultaneously from Eve and the Mother just before midnight. Fifteen minutes later they were all in the cavern, standing before the opening portal as the astral slowly came into focus.

Eve had already materialized, but she waited to step forward as the world around her fully took shape and color. The first thing Jack noticed was her hair—she wore it plaited now, in a single braid pulled severely back from her face. Instead of the usual white, full-length diaphanous gown, her long legs were encased in dark green leggings with brown leather boots, and she wore a tunic top the same reddish brown as the bark of the trees surrounding her pristine meadow. Her clothing might be somber, but Eve's eyes sparkled as they spun in their myriad colors, and if Jack wasn't mistaken, she was no longer afraid. In fact, she looked ready to fight.

"Come," she said, beckoning them forward. "You must hurry. The Mother says you only have eleven more minutes to reach the cavern ahead of the men. You'll need to capture them without injury. We don't know if merely spilling their blood will empower Aldo. Every demon is different. Some have the power to mark their victims so that no matter the cause of death, their life force belongs to the demon."

She glanced at Rem. He followed her quietly with an expression of awe and disbelief on his face as he walked upon the astral plane for the first time. "Agent Caruthers, you're responsible for bringing the men out of the cave and turning them over to the park rangers. Anton has spoken with the chief ranger and explained what's happening, that this is under the president's direction. His rangers will remain in hiding until they're needed, but they are aware that you, representing the FBI, will be in charge. The prisoners are going to be arrested and held by humans until we can question them, but your agency has given the Chanku Nation command of this because of our abilities. Once the four are in custody, that will leave Sebastian and Lily free to capture the demon."

"Yes, ma'am." He shook his head. "Wow. This is going to be a story for the grandkids."

Star turned and smiled at him. "Do you have a family, Rem?"

He laughed softly. "Nope. Not even a girlfriend, but I have a feeling I'm going to have to work on that once this is over, if only to have someone I can tell the stories to."

Eve shook her head, but Jack heard her soft laughter.

She turned, moving quickly toward the Yellowstone portal as they walked the astral plane. The others followed, with Jack and Mary bringing up the rear with Ari and Reko. Aldo was filling their minds with last-minute instructions. Jack knew Eve was listening, well aware of the orders the demon had given to Reko, and both Lily and Sebastian were in the same loop.

Did Aldo expect Eve to be there tonight? After the convoluted plot the demon had spelled out for Reko, Jack wondered how much the demon actually knew about any of them. He'd only ever dealt with Lily and Sebastian—his son. The rest of them were strangers, but what sort of powers did the demon have? There were so many variables—how could they actually plan anything?

Eve was in full fighting form, and other than her eyes, there was no physical way to tell she wasn't human. It was difficult to know exactly what she had up her sleeve because so much depended on Aldo's actions. She glanced over her shoulder as they drew close to the portal. "Ig, are you and Fen prepared to do a search for the device?"

"We are. Hopefully while Sebastian and Lily have Aldo otherwise occupied. What about Reko and Ari?"

"Reko's going to lie down in the spot where the men left him, so they don't suspect anything's changed, and hopefully that will be enough to keep them from noticing the rest of you. Rem will be at his side, and he'll make the initial confrontation. All of you, please be careful."

Lily slipped her arm around Eve's shoulders. "Yes, dear. We promise."

Eve laughed. "Your father's right. You really are a pain in the ass."

"Yeah, but you love me anyway."

Eve stopped at the portal, turned to Lily with tears in those sparkling eyes. "I do. So very much, Lily. Don't you dare get hurt. I never, ever expected we would do battle with a demon. I didn't even know demons existed!"

Rem muttered, "Now she tells us!" Mary covered her mouth to stop the laughter that was so terribly inappropriate right now. Jack grabbed her hand and squeezed. Lily hugged Eve.

"I hear ya on that one. I'll do my best to be safe. Let's go."

Eve nodded and waved her hand across what looked like another section of forest. The trees and grasses shimmered and the portal slowly opened.

The cavern was empty, the sandy floor where they'd walked last night untouched since Sebastian had magically hidden their footprints. "Go," Eve said. "I'm following, but you won't see me. Don't worry, I'm still here." With her words, she blinked out.

That was a first. It was so easy to forget Eve was a goddess, that she was no longer a physical member of the pack. She was just so *normal* most of the time.

And then she went and did something like that.

Ig, Fen, Star, and Sunny slipped into the next room, where they'd found the pentagram. It made sense to start their search within the boundaries of a room already suffused with power. Mary, Jack, and Ari went into the other, smaller room that Sebastian and Lily had explored the night before, but Jack stayed by the cleft in the rock so he'd have quick access to the larger cavern. Reko lay on the floor of the cavern, as planned.

Remington Caruthers knelt beside Reko, as if examining the body, but it was very dark inside the cavern, and even with his small penlight, he wouldn't be noticeable unless someone was very close. Jack could hardly see him and he was only a few feet away. With luck, the men would be so startled by Rem's presence, it would throw them off, make them reckless thinking they had a single man to focus on.

The closer they could get the four men to come to them, the better.

Sebastian and Lily had only a few moments to set their plan in action. Already the soft whispers of the men carried into the cavern. One sounded angry. They paused close to the entrance, but Jack could hear them quite clearly.

"I don't know why we have to come back here tonight. Master Aldo's not gonna be here until tomorrow."

"We don't know that, Eagan. Besides, I wanna get that wolf. His hide's goin' to make me a pretty penny once I get him skinned."

"We're going to be setting off a fucking A-bomb tomorrow night, Derek. A wolf skin will be the least of our problems."

"He promised immortality. Right, Brother Thomas?"

"That he did. God's servants do not lie."

Harsh laughter. "He gives me the creeps. Talking to a cloud of smoke is fucked."

Mary grabbed Jack's hand. *That's my father, but he never used to curse. Something has changed him.*

"That's heresy, Ryder. Be careful he doesn't just strike you dead. C'mon. We need to be sure everything is in place. We've got too much invested in this to ruin it now."

They slipped into the cavern, their way lit by a tactical-style flashlight with a high-intensity beam. Rem turned and stood once they were all well inside the cavern. "Who the hell are you?" he demanded. Standing, he towered over the four men, except for Mary's father. They met almost eye to eye.

Jack moved closer to Remington, but he remained hidden in the dark shadows. Aldo's voice was a constant threatening murmur in the background.

"Take him. He will not stop us!"

Jack moved quickly to stand beside Remington as the men charged. Aldo shrieked in his mind. Lily and Sebastian stepped out of the shadows, Sebastian on one side, Lily on the other. They raised their hands, stretched them out to grab a net only the two of them could see. Yanked hard and drew it tight.

The four men were stopped mere inches from Jack and Rem. Weaving invisible strands, the two wizards had the men entirely bound within seconds. Eve appeared in a flash of light. Two of the men fell to their knees, while the one Jack recognized as Mary's father and the shorter, portly man he figured was Brother Thomas remained standing.

"Turn us loose, now. Who are you to stop me?" Thomas glared at the brilliant light that was Eve.

But Rem answered. "Remington Caruthers, FBI." He flipped the badge out under Brother Thomas's nose. Then he turned toward the wolf still lying on the ground. "Okay, Reko. Why don't you help me get these four out of here."

Reko stood and shook the dust off his coat.

"I thought you said he was dead." Brother Thomas glared at one of the shorter men.

"He was. I swear it."

"Idiot. He's obviously not even a wolf! He's one of those Chanku." Glaring at Reko, he shouted, "Spawn of Satan, creature of darkness. Be gone!"

Reko snarled and slunk around the small group until he was closest to Brother Thomas. Snarling, he lunged at the man. Ari slipped in beside Reko and added his voice. Growling, jaws dripping saliva, they forced the men closer together while Sebastian and Lily pulled the net tighter, until the four stood tightly bound together in the center of the cave.

A dark glow filled the room, eclipsing Eve's brighter light, almost as if it sucked the light out of her. In the background, Jack heard the sound of a vehicle outside, but his focus remained on the dark light—the same dark light that had come to Reko at the cabin. *Seb, Lily—hold your captives. Eve, that's Aldo.*

There was no answer from Eve. The four men started gibbering, and if not for Sebastian and Lily's net would have fallen to their knees.

Aldo's speaking to me in Eve's voice, Reko said. *Do you hear him?*

Yes. Listening closely, Jack held tightly to Mary's hand. He shot a quick glance at Sebastian and Lily. Knowing they concentrated on holding their spell, he doubted they'd be paying much attention to the demon. *Aldo's doing a pretty good imitation of Eve, telling Reko that the dark light we see is not the demon, it's Eve. He says, in Eve's voice, we've been bespelled, that the purple light is Eve and the brighter light is the demon. Aldo's telling Reko to attack us if we go after the dark manifestation.*

The darker light pulsed and shimmered in the cavern, but the bright light had disappeared.

Where's Eve? Mary clutched Jack's hand. *She was here a moment ago, but I don't see her. Eve?*

That dark glow is definitely Aldo, Sebastian said. *At least it smells like him. He's got his own stench. I think he's having trouble manifesting a corporeal body, but we can't cast a spell until we're absolutely certain he hasn't got Eve. Lily? Can you tell? Is Eve still here? Can you find her?*

Lily frowned. She shook her head and tears filled her eyes. *No,* she said. *Eve's not here. Unless he's trapped her in that . . . that thing.*

She stared at the dark, pulsing malevolence before them.

• • •

Saturday, 12:10 a.m.

Igmutaka, Fenris, Sunny and Star gathered close. Working together, they'd finally sensed the nuclear device, hidden in a crevasse far beneath the cavern. The demon Aldo must have planted it—there was no way any human could reach the location so far below the earth's surface, close to the molten rock that seethed beneath the huge Yellowstone caldera. The others were busy in the main cavern. Ig had no idea what was going on other than the fact they'd trapped the four men in a spell and it was keeping Aldo's demon occupied. "It's now or never, Fen." Ig reached for his mate's wolf amulet.

"You might try sounding a bit more optimistic." Grinning at him, Fen offered a middle-finger salute to Ig before wrapping his hand around Ig's jade panther.

The amulets linked each man to his spirit guide past, gave each of them powers directly from the Mother. With a last look at Star, Ig focused on Fen and winked out. No longer a man, Ig was now nothing more than spirit.

As was his large, usually solid mate, now invisible to anyone's eyes. *Be safe,* Ig said to their women.

We love you, Fen said. Sunny and Star clasped hands and nodded. Ig felt the strength their women shared in the four-way mating link.

Swirling through infinitesimal seams in the bedrock, he and Fen narrowed in on the device. It was a foreign thing, easy to lock onto in their spirit forms because of its alien nature. It felt wrong among the natural minerals in the stone that made up the solid cap over the magma field.

They were well aware of molten lava surging beneath solid rock.

The device was there, nestled in the remnants of an ancient gas bubble that had formed during the last great eruption well over half a million years ago. Unfortunately, this volcano was due for another, whether in one year or one million years.

A nuclear explosion could trigger an event today.

Any idea how we do this? Ig hovered in and around the bomb, testing its properties, building a visceral awareness of the thing. He and Fen were nothing more than a collection of molecules that shouldn't be able to exist in this form. But they could, they did, and together they had the power to move the device. But where?

Fen, with his modern education and knowledge of things Ig was still learning, explained their next steps. *We'll move it into an area of molten rock where it will melt rather than combust.*

You're certain it won't blow?

I am. Exploding a nuclear device requires precise timing in order to start nuclear fission, the splitting of atomic particles, or fusion, which is joining them together to release the energy that is a nuclear explosion, and . . .

I think that's more than I need to know, Fen. Do you know how to disarm it?

Yes. Though I don't believe it's necessary.

You sound awfully cocky, Fenris. Ig continued staring at the thing. It wasn't all that large, considering, though it was definitely more than he could lift, especially in his spirit form, but . . .

Tap into the Mother, Ig. She's here with us. I knew nothing about nuclear fission or fusion, but I do know that the Mother knows all of that, and she is graciously sharing that knowledge. I've been paying close attention while you've been worrying. Have faith, man! Here's how we'll move this into the molten pool beneath the cap.

Fen shared knowledge with Ig of skills he'd never used and didn't know he had, possibly because they took the strength of both men. Working with a partner was a new and truly beautiful experience, but merely with the power of their minds he saw how they could act telekinetically. With what felt like very little effort, they lifted the large device, breaking it down into an invisible molecular mist and moving it into the molten center far beneath the caldera itself, deep within the red-hot core of the Earth.

Together they directed it to reform when it reached the hottest part, where it immediately melted. Fen and Ig felt its small death as a lightening of their souls. The risk was averted. For now.

We need to go back. Quickly. Something's happening.

Ig didn't question Fen's orders. He followed his mate through the cap of stone, arriving in the same small cavern where they'd left the women.

Their women were gone, but the sound of a battle raging in the next section of the cave had them taking human form and racing for the narrow exit.

The four men were restrained in a magical net held entirely by Lily. Sebastian battled a dark entity that could only be his father, but Ig wondered why he refrained from a killing strike.

Two men, park rangers by their dark green uniforms, stood in the doorway with guns drawn, but Fenris ran to them, spoke quickly, and the men holstered their weapons. That was when Ig spotted Star, Sunny, and Mary. They stood in the shadows with Lily. He felt the pull on the mating bond, knew they shared more strength to hold the spell intact.

Jack knelt beside Remington, who leaned against the stone wall; a large gash across his forehead spilled blood over his face and down the front of his shirt. Ig went to them. "What happened?"

"The dark light is Aldo," Rem said. "Somehow he sucked Eve in and he's got her trapped with him. Sebastian can't kill Aldo without harming Eve. The Mother can't interfere. One of those stupid rules of the immortals, but Brother Thomas was carrying a gun and shot me. Just grazed my forehead, but you know how head wounds bleed." He cursed softly.

Ig chuckled. "Well, if I didn't know before, I do now."

"Jerk." Rem flipped him off, then nodded toward two men standing on the other side of the cavern. "The guys with Fen in the doorway are the ones here to pick up the four, but we're afraid to shut down the spell while the fight's going on. Sebastian told us to get out of his way."

"Thanks, Rem. Hang on. I've got an idea." Ig raced across the cavern to Fen. "I say we go inside the demon and pull Eve out. That'll give Sebastian a chance at him."

Fen nodded, turned to the two rangers. "Watch those four. The women can hold the spell, but we can't allow those men to get hurt or bleed. Or get loose. That's the reason for the spell—it protects them from Aldo and it holds them prisoner. If the demon gets to them, hurts them or causes them to harm one another or any others in this cave, he gains power, and that puts the whole fucking world at risk. Just watch them and don't hurt the bastards. You okay with that?"

The younger of the two shook his head. "Shit, man. I'm not down with any of this. But yeah. Whatever you say."

"Good. Don't let this spook you." Fen grabbed hold of Ig's panther amulet while Ig wrapped his fingers around Fen's wolf. In seconds, they blinked out.

Fen, can you see Eve? She's there, caught in the demon's light.

I see her. How do we get her out? Telekinesis? Or just go in after her?

We can grab her. Sebastian? We can see Eve. She's trapped inside the demon. Fen and I are going to bring her out. When the wizard nodded, Ig took Fen's hand. *Can you feel her? See her?*

I can. We take her on three and set her beside Lily and the girls. Sebastian? As soon as we've got Eve, he's all yours.

One . . . two . . . three. Ig counted and both he and Fen reached for Eve. In spirit form, their arms still slid through the foul light that was more than it appeared—Aldo's form was manifested in a disgusting substance that felt like a thick, slimy, gelatinous mass. It covered Eve, held her close, wrapped her in slime, but the stuff pulled away from her when they reached in and tugged her free.

Aldo's shriek echoed off the walls; Sebastian struck—they felt the power surge in the very air around them. Successful or not, both the dark light and the mass winked out. Eve appeared, gasping on the ground beside Lily, who momentarily faltered but then continued to hold the prisoners inside her spell.

Star knelt beside their goddess and Sunny grabbed her hand. Sebastian melded his power to Lily, and the net strengthened. They held their prisoners steady while Ig and Fen searched for evidence that Aldo remained. Ari and Reko snarled, their focus entirely on the prisoners.

"He's gone," Ig said. "He's not dead. I sense his life force, but . . . Sebastian? Did you have a chance at him?"

Sebastian shook his head. "I hit him with a blast of power, but I think he either evaded it or maybe even drew it in. Sorry. I just don't know if he's weakened or not."

"But he lost this battle." Fen glanced toward Eve. "I think we call this skirmish a win. For now. We've got Eve, and we've got his four men. Four men who have sworn fealty to a demon, yet still live. I doubt they realized that oath of loyalty means they've also offered themselves as blood sacrifices."

"You lie." Brother Thomas glared at Fen, but Ig noticed how the other three men watched their leader. Obviously, none of them had realized until now that if or when Aldo came back, they probably wouldn't get out of this alive.

• • •

"Ig?" Sebastian stood back while the two park rangers cuffed Aldo's four acolytes. "Do you and Fen mind riding into Mammoth with these men? I don't know where Aldo is, or how much strength he has, but we know he wants these four. Badly."

Ig nodded. "Fen and I were planning to. I agree, and I don't want to put two innocent men in danger because of the prisoners they've got. We need to make sure they're kept in separate cells, too. Otherwise, Aldo might direct them to kill one another."

"I hadn't even thought of that. At least it's only for a few more hours." Sebastian sighed and then gazed toward Lily. She sat with Eve, holding the goddess's hand, speaking quietly, but she pulled Sebastian into their link. As he'd guessed, Eve had been badly shaken by Aldo's strength. She hadn't expected the power the demon could wield, hadn't thought he'd be able to overtake her in a battle.

He had. Without even putting forth much effort he'd captured Eve, held her within that evil mass of whatever substance he'd manifested. Anton had filled them all in on Jack's theory. They'd agreed it made perfect sense, but Aldo had obviously been carefully guarding the power he'd stolen from the twelve dead Berserkers, and the death of Mary's sister must have given him more strength than any of them had realized. Sebastian's father had always been a mean and sneaky bastard. There was no reason for Sebastian to think he might have improved with death.

He glanced up as Ig and Fen stopped in front of him. "We've got the prisoners loaded in the van out front. Fen and I are going along with the rangers. Remington, too. He's pretty woozy, poor man. We're calling him our token FBI guy, but we'll get him bandaged up, make our report, and then stay to keep an eye on him. And the prisoners."

"What about the prisoners? When will they be turned over to us?" That had been the deal, after all. The president had told Anton that he and the Chanku Nation would be responsible for both the men and the demon, since dealing with demonkind was entirely out of the expertise of any branches of U.S. service. Not that the Chanku had all that much experience with demons either.

Precisely none, in fact.

"Tomorrow." Fen glanced at Ig, who nodded. "We've been in contact with Anton, let him know Rem's been injured. The women don't have anything left to heal him. Holding the prisoners safe took a lot out of all of them. Star and Sunny will stay with us tonight. Tinker's going to fly down in the chopper in the morning and we'll grab Rem and take the men back then. Eve doesn't want them on the astral. She said there's some of Aldo in them, part of his spirit or something, but it's a link that connects them to him. It presents too great a risk to let them have access, even as prisoners."

Nodding, Seb had to agree. There was definitely something off about the four, but what the hell were they going to do with them now? He stood, moving slowly. The fight with Aldo had taken a lot out of him, too, and the knowledge that he could have injured Eve during the fight with a single wrong move was something he never wanted to experience again.

But his father had lost this fight—that much he knew. Possibly weakened, but not ended, and he had to wonder—how did one kill a demon, a creature that was already dead?

10

Saturday, 1:45 a.m.

Mary and Jack crossed over onto the astral with Reko following. Relieved to be out of that dark cavern and headed home, Mary relaxed even more when she saw that Ari stuck close beside Lily and Sebastian. She'd worried about Reko's brother. He was quieter, not as outgoing as Reko, and she wondered if he might be feeling overwhelmed by all the changes in his life. The fact he'd paired up with Seb and Lily was a good thing. They could watch over him, keep him safe . . . in spite of the drama.

This hadn't been a particularly normal day in the life of the Chanku. In fact, though she was still new, Mary figured it was probably unlike anything any of them had ever experienced. She was ready to go back to the way things had been, but that wasn't going to happen—not while Aldo existed. Too much had occurred in a very short time, and all the bad stuff could be laid at the feet of that one very evil practitioner of dark magic.

It was difficult to believe that such a beast could have fathered a man as kind and honorable as Sebastian, but Aldo Xenakis truly was a beast, and he'd left so much pain in his path.

Her little sister was dead, her mother gravely injured, her father a murderer in the service of the demon. Such terrible, unbelievable events, traumatizing things that might have immobilized her but for Jack. He had so quickly become her strength, this most amazing man she'd ever known who was now her mate. A man she loved beyond any sense or reason, other than the irrefutable fact she knew her life would never be complete without Jackson Temple in it.

She wondered if he was in her thoughts just now, and he gently squeezed her hand. She squeezed his back, savoring the connection that was both physical and mental, holding them close on so many levels. She still wasn't comfortable tuning into his thoughts. Maybe, once things settled down, she'd feel more comfortable keeping that continual link, but for now she was happy just keeping him close.

But what of Reko? He walked quietly beside her as they traversed the short distance across the astral, his mind closed to her now, though he'd been wide open to her and to Jack for the past hours since they'd strengthened the link with Lily and Seb's help. Even shut away, she felt him, a quiet, almost peaceful presence in her thoughts. She was connected to him in so many ways that felt right to her. Yet where did that fit in her connection to her bonded mate?

Jack interrupted her convoluted thoughts with a question for Reko. "Do you still hear the demon?"

No!

"So, Reko, tell me how you really feel." Mary bit back a giggle.

The wolf snorted. *That obvious, hmm? The demon's voice went quiet in the cavern, once he became visible. I think all his energy went to holding on to the visible mass, but when Ig and Fen pulled the goddess free, when Sebastian hit him with that surge of power, I felt a snap, as if the link he'd held with my mind had broken. I think he's gone, though I won't be surprised if he reappears once he's rested.*

"You're probably right," Jack said. "I've been searching for his voice since we left the cave. There's nothing there." He laughed. "Just your hard head, Reko. So hard you already feel like one of us."

The wolf turned and stared at him a moment, and then shook his head. *I take pride in my hard head, Jack Temple. It kept the bullet away from my brain.*

"Excellent point." Jack yawned and gave Mary a lopsided grin. "I am so frickin' tired right now, all I can think of is sleep."

You're newly mated, Jack. Shouldn't you be thinking of this lovely woman?

Reko's dry comment hung in their thoughts a moment. Laughing, Mary said, "I would think that would be uppermost in his thoughts, Reko. Thank you for reminding him." She glanced at Jack. He leaned over and kissed her.

"You're always in my thoughts, sweet Mary. So much so that I don't think of the fact I'm always thinking of you as long as you're close to my heart."

Reko rolled his eyes, but Mary had been linked to Jack when he was speaking. She knew those words came straight from his heart—knowledge she held close to her own heart.

They stopped at the portal to the Chanku compound. Eve paused before opening the gate. "Rest," she said. "Aldo's not dead. I expect him back, sooner rather than later. As soon as we know anything, the Mother or I will call you." She shook her head and softly sighed. "I fear he is stronger than either of us realized. I couldn't fight him. I had nothing. Nothing!" She glanced away, not facing any of them. "I failed to protect you."

Jack stepped up to Eve and hugged her as if she was just any of their packmates, someone he cared for. "You didn't fail at anything, Eve. You stood up to him but he was stronger. That does not make you less brave, or your fight inconsequential. Ig and Fen helped free you, but we know more about him because you were there. Think of what you learned tonight so you can share it with us, and remember that we are a pack. None of us is as strong alone as when we work together."

Eve hugged him tightly and then stepped back, but her eyes glistened. "Your mate is a lucky woman, Jack Temple, and I imagine your parents are very proud of you. They should be." She turned quickly and hugged Mary, then Sebastian and Lily, before turning to Reko and Ari.

"If you hear the demon's voice again, please tell me. I'm listening for your voices, so all you need do is call out to me in your mind." She brushed a hand gently over each of the wolves, and then stood. "I will hear you. Now go, all of you. Sleep. We have no idea how long it will take before the demon regains his power."

She waved her hand across the portal and the forest slowly parted before them. Lily was the first to step through. It was no surprise to Mary that Lily's parents waited impatiently on the other side.

• • •

Saturday, 2:00 a.m.

Mary thought of shifting so that Reko wouldn't sleep alone, but she wanted Jack to hold her. Wanted his strong arms around her, his lips against her hair, the heat of his body surrounding her so that she had nothing and no one to fear.

Besides—she bit back a giggle—this was still their first night together as a mated pair. Inviting another male into their bed probably wasn't the best idea, though it had certainly worked for Jack's mom.

What a bizarre couple of days this had been. And to think it all started when Romy and Emeline invited her to hang out with them and their guys in the meadow to have a few cold beers and celebrate the end of the school year. When they'd told her Jack would be there, she'd really had no choice.

Had there ever been any other option than to choose Jack? It still felt like a dream that he had chosen her as well.

Showering quickly, she toweled dry, went into the bedroom quietly, and slipped between the sheets naked. Jack had stayed back to speak with his parents and fill them in on what had happened tonight, but he was only a few minutes behind her. She heard him go into the bathroom, heard the sound of the shower. She shivered, knowing he'd be with her in moments.

Reko had chosen the large soft pillow that had been in the room he'd shared with Ari the night before. Tala must have moved it into their room when she realized Reko had shared their bed last night, but tonight, when he explained his choice of bed, he'd been adamant—she and Jack needed time together, but he really didn't want to be alone in his room.

Still, when he'd finally curled into a ball in the center of his bed, it was with his back to Mary.

And when Jack walked out of the bathroom followed by a billowing cloud of steam, Mary sent a silent *thank you* to Reko.

Jack crawled beneath the sheets behind her. He smelled of the citrus shampoo she liked, but underneath the crisp tang of lemon was his own scent, a subtle, musky aroma that was all Jack, a scent she was quickly growing addicted to. He scooted closer and wrapped his strong arms around her body, tugging her back against his chest.

It wasn't enough. Mary rolled within his embrace, pressed her face against his chest and sucked in a deep breath that filled her senses with everything that was her mate—his scent, the smooth expanse of pectoral muscles, his warmth and the steady beat of his heart. She sighed as her body relaxed into his, the dips and valleys of her form fitting perfectly into his.

He tightened his arms around her and rubbed his chin against the crown of her head, tangling her hair in the bristly shadow of beard he'd not shaved for the past couple of days.

So much had happened in such a short time. They'd been mated less than twelve hours. Mary let her mind drift back to their mating, and felt laughter bubbling up inside.

What are you laughing at, Mary Ryder?

We've been mated for almost twelve hours and I just realized that we've never made love as a mated pair except when we mated.

We've been a tad busy.

She buried her face against his chest to get her laughter under control, thought better of hiding, and slipped down the length of him, planting kisses on his ribs, the rippled lines of his abdomen, the dark trail of hair running from his navel to his pubes. When he groaned and thrust his hips forward, she nipped the tender flesh on the inside of his leg. His fingers tangled in her hair and he tugged.

Don't bother me, she said. *I'm busy.* He was already erect and growing. She ran her tongue around the broad head of his cock, slipping gently along the small slit at the tip. He tangled his fingers deeper into her damp hair as she circled his thick length with her lips and sucked him deep, but he was no longer trying to tug her away.

He groaned again, but there was laughter in the sound. His mental voice filled her head and her heart. He slipped his hands free of her hair and rested his palms on her shoulders. *I love you, Mary Elizabeth Ryder. Love you so much. When this is over, when the demon is no more, will you marry me, Mary mine? I want you to have my name and one day I want to have babies with you. I know that for some mating is enough, but I want it all. I want all of you. What do you say?*

Smiling around her mouthful, she slowly pulled her lips away from his erection, spending just enough time working her tongue around the crown that she had him shuddering, his hips thrusting. Then she slipped him completely out of her mouth and sat back on her heels. Gazing at him, his heartfelt request like a huge hug holding her safe, she finally got herself together enough to respond. *I would be more than honored to be your wife, though you know you already have me in every way possible. I love you, Jackson Miguel Temple. I will always love you, and I can't believe I was ever afraid of your touch. Now I can't wait to see what our future has in store. This mess with the demon now? It's just a bump in the road. We are stronger than Aldo Xenakis because we have the pack. You were right, what you told Eve. None of us is as strong alone as when we work together. You? Me? We will always be together. Now make love to me, Jack. Remind me why I think you're so special. I think I'm forgetting . . .*

She leaned over and kissed the very tip of his erection. Laughing, he flipped her to her back and knelt above her. *You need proof, eh?*

Of course I do. Then she opened her innermost private thoughts, opened to the sensations and needs, the desires coursing through her body. Desires and needs her mate had taught her not only to accept but to crave. She showed him in graphic detail what she wanted. This link, this amazing mental connection was all so new, so far beyond what they'd shared before, deeper, more detailed and immediate. The proof was there when he lifted her hips in his big hands, held her up to him and put his mouth on her, his lips, his tongue, the warm gusts of his breath teasing her tender folds. All her fantasies, her unspoken needs, things she'd only dreamed of in the dark of night were there now in every little move Jack made, every touch, every loving glance.

When he took her to the edge and held her there, she fell into his desires. Where before she'd only known her own deepest needs, now Jack's were right there with hers. She tasted herself on his tongue, reveled in the buttery soft tissues between her legs as he nipped and sucked, teasing with lips and teeth.

That was followed by another stronger, more visceral pain verging on ecstasy, an ache so deep and powerful, the gut-wrenching sensations he felt in his balls and cock, the sharp pressure to drive deep inside her to take her, to reclaim Mary once again and take what was now his forever more, this woman he'd been wanting since the first time they'd met. Those thoughts, unfiltered and so intense she shivered in his embrace to know the power she had over a man who was everything and more that she'd ever dreamed.

The power he had over her. *Now, Jack. Now!*

He lifted her close, filled her in a single hard thrust, bottoming out against her cervix. Her climax coursed throughout her body, building on itself, building on Jack's as he flew off the ledge with Mary. She felt the residual shocks they shared for long minutes after, even when their breathing had slowed and hearts had quit thundering. Finally, Jack pulled Mary back into an embrace against his chest. Again he nuzzled her hair, placed a rather chaste kiss on her forehead.

Replete now, as her body melted against his, she tried to empty her mind and seek sleep. Instead she thought of all the changes that had come so quickly into her life, which led her to thoughts of her father. He was no longer the man she remembered. She wondered if his disowning her had come before or after he'd gotten involved with Master Aldo.

No. She was trying to find a reason to excuse his behavior, but Anton was right. There was no excuse. If he'd been directed to do evil things by the demon, it was only because he'd let the demon into his mind. He had given a demon the freedom to control his thoughts, damn him.

"We're going to be okay," Jack whispered softly and kissed her again, finding her lips this time. "You . . . me? We have so much to live for, so many blessings in our lives. We'll get through this, Mary. We'll find out what's going on with your dad, figure out how he got hooked up with Aldo. Your mom is healing, growing stronger. We'll find out from her more of what happened. For now, though, you need sleep. We both do. I'll watch over you tonight, and so will Reko. You've got two big guys here to make sure you're safe."

He ran his hand gently along her spine. Up, down, soft strokes that relaxed her, reminded her how much they had together. She turned her thoughts from all the awful things going on, turned instead to Jack, to the loving family he had that was now hers, to the love of the pack. She let her thoughts linger on Reko for a moment, so aware of him sleeping on the big round pillow in the corner of the room, and then, just as her consciousness began to slip, she returned once again to Jack.

His arms tightened around her. She snuggled close, and realized they were breathing in sync, the two of them drawing each breath and exhaling in tandem. Smiling, she drifted away.

• • •

Saturday, 11:03 a.m.

Jack lay there in bed, so warm and comfortable he really didn't want to move, though even with the shades drawn it was obviously daylight outside. He rolled over carefully so as not to wake Mary, but she was already awake, smiling a warm, sleepy smile that had him instantly aroused.

So this is what it's like to wake up with the woman you love.

She ran a fingertip from the edge of his eyebrow along his temple and cheek to the corner of his mouth. He pursed his lips and turned to kiss the very tip of her finger. *If it's anything like waking with the man you love,* she said, *it's wonderful.*

At the same time, they both glanced at the clock. It was already after eleven. They'd slept almost nine hours. Jack turned and looked for Reko. He was sound asleep as well. It appeared all of them had needed the rest.

Mary frowned. *No one called us. Aldo must not have returned. This is, at this moment, the narrow point in time between the old moon and new. He hasn't come back yet. I wonder what that means?*

It means we go out and look like we're starving so Mik will make one of his really wonderful breakfasts for us. "Hey, Reko! Wake up, man. The day is half gone!"

Is he always this cheerful in the morning? Reko raised his head, but all the fur on one side of his face was flattened. He probably hadn't moved all night long. He yawned, a huge spread of jaws and display of sharp teeth that was a vivid reminder of the Berserker's strength and killing power.

"He is, Reko. But he says if we go to the kitchen and look really pathetic, like we're starving, Mik will make us something yummy to eat." Mary crawled out of bed as she spoke, and Jack wondered if she even realized she was entirely nude. Reko had certainly noticed, and he watched her with such abject longing in his eyes as she walked to the bathroom that Jack took pity on him. "It's okay if you look, Reko. She's pretty amazing, isn't she?"

Reko didn't respond, but then Mary walked back into the room. She had a robe on now.

Jack's right, Reko. We're really open about our sexuality. Even mated couples will take other lovers without any problem. She glanced at Jack and grinned. *Are you okay with that?*

Reko merely shook his head. *It's all new,* he said. *Not what I expected, but now I'm even more impatient to make my first shift!*

Mary wrapped her arms around his neck and hugged him. *We are all impatient for you and your brother to shift. Hopefully not much longer.*

Jack made a quick trip into the bathroom, washed his face, combed his hair, and slipped on an old pair of sweats. Then the three of them walked down the hall to the kitchen. Jack held the door for Reko to go outside and waited until he came back in. It was chilly out this morning—too cold to leave the door open.

Anton sat in the kitchen with Jack's parents, sipping a cup of coffee. The kitchen was warm and filled with wonderful aromas. Mik had an apron wrapped around his waist and his long hair tied into a single braid down his back. He stood in front of the big stove, frying bacon. "Good morning, Mary, Jack, and Reko." He glanced at the clock over the door and grinned. "Almost good afternoon. You're just under the wire. I've got bacon, eggs, fried potatoes, corn bread and, for you, Reko, scrambled eggs with cheese and bacon, and a couple of fresh rabbits."

Mary walked up to Mik and gave him a hug from behind. "I think I'm in love."

"Hopefully with the boy." Mik turned and kissed her cheek. "I'm taken."

"I know, and Tala would probably murder me in my sleep if I tried to poach, but there is nothing sexier than a man who cooks."

"Pay attention to him, Jack." Anton tipped his coffee in Jack's direction. "You can't imagine the points you can make when you put a meal in front of a hungry woman."

"I've never seen you cook, Anton." Tala walked into the kitchen and refilled her coffee cup.

He laughed. "Touché. You have, however, seen me do dishes."

"That I have. Big points there, too. Good morning, Mary, and no, you can't have Mik, but I'm sure you've made the man's day by asking." She walked over to Jack, kissed his cheek and told him good morning before plopping down on the floor next to Reko's pillow. "Brought your pill, Reko." She held her hand out to him. He used his long tongue to lift the capsule from her palm.

Jack loved watching his mom. She was such a tiny little thing and yet she had two huge men wrapped around her little finger. They still did their search and rescue, though it wasn't necessary to hide the fact anymore that her "search wolves" were actually her mates. He'd gone with them on a few of their jobs, and she was one of the bravest people he knew. Watching her now, curled up next to Reko, who probably outweighed her by well over a hundred pounds, was like watching a little kid with the family dog. She had no fear, loved everyone she met, and had been an absolutely amazing mother. He thanked the goddess on a regular basis for the wonderful parents he'd been lucky enough to have—and not just one terrific dad, but two.

Mary had never known love like he had, and yet she was so loving. He worried about her, about how she would handle it if her father died, or almost worse, if he ended up going to prison for the rest of his life. She was doing well, but he knew she buried things. She'd admitted to burying her time in captivity, the rapes and abuse she'd suffered, and what she hadn't told him, he'd seen when they mated. He knew that at some point she'd probably need to talk about a lot of those terrible things, but his mom was aware of Mary's past. If Mary needed to vent, Tala was tough enough to handle anything. She handled Mik and AJ, didn't she? And her own past had been every bit as violent as Mary's. The two women definitely needed some time together.

He sat there, watching and listening as his mom talked to Reko. The big wolf had his ears pricked forward and his steady gaze followed every expression on her face, each gesture of her hands. Jack wondered what the wolf thought of this tiny woman who was so obviously in charge of her household. It certainly appeared Reko had fallen under her spell.

"I don't know how it is when Berserkers make their first shift, Reko," she said, "but with humans, we start hearing better, and I remember my skin itching a lot. Probably just cellular changes that allow the fur to grow when we make the shift, but you can already hear like a wolf and you've got a beautiful fur coat, so I can't offer any advice."

Reko merely snuffled, but then he rubbed the side of his face against her shoulder and sighed. Yep, Tala had definitely added another male to her harem. Jack made eye contact with Reko. *She reminds me so much of my own mother,* Reko said. *I think I want to keep her.*

Too late, Reko. I think she's already adopted you.

And you don't mind?

She's tiny, but her heart is huge. She's got love enough for all of us. Jack glanced up as Anton walked across the kitchen to the coffeepot. *So does Anton, for that matter. It's all good.*

"I can tell you a little bit, Reko." Anton refilled his cup, and then turned to Reko and leaned against the countertop. "You've met two of the

Berserkers in the pack already. Ig was a spirit guide born as a puma and then turned to spirit. He went puma, spirit, puma and then to human, but the nutrients had long been part of his diet. He merely hadn't wanted to try his human form. Fen was born a wolf but shifted to human when he was a child and had forgotten that he knew how to shift, but his adult shift came after just a couple of days on the nutrients. According to Eve, Berserkers are closer to their feral side, but for some reason that appears to make it easier to access the human side. I imagine you'll shift at some point today or tonight. Fen only needed a few of the capsules."

Thank you. Reko slowly shook his head. *I just realized I'm going to have to learn to walk on two legs.*

Laughter followed Reko's comment, and then the conversation sort of flowed over the room. Jack took Mary's hand in his and sat back to listen. His mom was talking about her first shift, that she'd had no idea the big brown capsules Mik told her to take would help her shift.

"Nutrients, he said. Vitamins to help your body heal." She snorted, and Anton laughed.

"They worked, didn't they?" Mik glanced up from cooking.

Tala glared at him. "Well, yeah. I managed to shift in time to rip out the throat of the bastard who wanted to put me back in his stable of whores." Then she blew Mik a kiss. "And I got not one but two really hot guys in the bargain."

Jack was still laughing when Mik called out that breakfast was ready, so they all lined up at the buffet he'd put out, filled their plates, and found places at the big kitchen table. Tala filled a big bowl for Reko, adding the two rabbits Mik had warmed, and set it on the floor next to them. Jack, Mik, Tala, Mary, and Anton took their seats and Mik yelled at AJ to come in and eat. He'd gone outside to clean up some broken branches from one of the big pines, but he came in, washed up at the kitchen sink and grabbed a plate. After he filled it, AJ leaned over and gave Tala a kiss, and then took the seat beside her.

"You just missed Mom's story of her first shift," Jack said. "Tell Mary about yours."

AJ laughed and shook his head. "Does Mary know what reprobates your parents were?" He turned his charm on Mary and said, "Obviously, Mik and I have both cleaned up our acts."

"I certainly hope so," Tala said, pointing at Mik with her fork and then at AJ, but she was smiling. "You were no worse than I was, just a lot bigger, and there were two of you."

AJ just shook his head. "We weren't saints, that's for sure. Mik and I were inmates at Folsom Prison down near Sacramento, both of us in on crappy charges that a good lawyer might have gotten us off of, but we were still doing time when Ulrich Mason came by the prison and wanted to see me. He was the original head of Pack Dynamics, the search-and-rescue team that Mik, Tala, and I still work for, but I'd never seen him before. Anyway, he showed up at the prison after meeting with me, loaded Mik and me into his car and hauled our butts out of there. We had no idea where we were going or what they wanted us for, but we were so glad to get out of there we didn't even ask. Mik and I were already lovers, and we knew we could communicate telepathically. We thought that might be what had interested him, the telepathy."

AJ glanced at Mik, and both men held one another's stare for a long, telling moment. Jack had known from an early age that his two dads loved each other so powerfully that it sometimes almost overwhelmed them. This looked like one of those moments, but then AJ sort of shook himself and smiled at Mary. "Ric took Mik and me back to his home office in San Francisco. He didn't tell us anything about being shapeshifters or why we were there, just closed his office door and stripped down until he was standing there buck naked. Mik and I thought he was nuts. Then he shifted." Laughing, AJ shot a grin at Tala. "I just hate it when they do that. Scared the shit out of both of us."

Chuckling over a story he'd grown up on, Jack glanced at Mary, sensing her fascination with everyone else's tales. *My generation had it easy,* Jack said. *We knew what we were from the beginning, grew up loved and encouraged to shift. Our parents' lives were tough. My dad's a perfect example. I'm surprised you handled your shift so well, considering.*

Mary laughed outright at that, and took in everyone in the room when she spoke. "Jack just complimented me on my first shift." She turned her head and planted a kiss on his cheek. "Not true. I was in denial because my parents thought shapeshifters were the devil's own minions. I took the nutrients when Gabe and Emeline gave them to us, but I didn't tell anyone. Then I shifted, alone in my room, and ended up a catatonic whimpering ball of panic until Em and Annie showed up and talked me down. I was terrified. I knew my life was forever changed, that my parents would probably disown me, that I had nowhere to go, no home left. Then I found out what it was like to be a wolf, I came here and discovered what it meant to be part of a pack, to be loved because of the very thing that made my family hate me, and I realized it was the most wonderful thing that had ever happened to me."

She squeezed Jack's hand and turned to look at him. "Until I met Jack."

His mom sighed and conversation picked up, and they all turned away from them as if everyone wanted to give them this moment alone together. Jack's heart actually felt as if it wouldn't fit in his chest, so he tuned out all the talk in the kitchen and focused on Mary. Maybe, if they were really subtle, they could sneak away, go back to their meadow and make love there again. Their mating had been rushed and he wanted to explore more of her, the two of them together as wolves. Maybe . . .

Jack? Anton's mental voice landed right in the middle of Jack's fantasy. *Tinker just got in touch. He's here with the prisoners. Do you think Mary would be willing to speak with her father? She might be able to get more out of him than I could.*

If you had any idea what I was thinking just now . . . He sent Anton an image of himself gnashing his teeth.

His alpha merely gave him a cocky grin. *Actually, Jack, I was listening. And feeling jealous. I'd like to take Keisha to that same meadow, but it's not going to happen today. We have prisoners. And a demon to fight.*

So if you can't go, neither can we?

I wouldn't put it quite so bluntly, but yeah. I guess.

Jack sighed, and it wasn't all for show. *At least you're honest. I'll ask her.*

Actually, Jack . . . and Anton. I've been listening. And while the meadow is definitely my preference, I need to speak with my father, if only to tell him what a hypocritical bastard he is. She glanced at Jack. *Should we take Reko? I don't want to risk him having his first shift without us there to help him.*

He's definitely going with us. Jack kissed Mary. *I have a feeling Reko's going to be hanging around with us for a very long time.*

It certainly seems to work for your parents. She glanced toward Reko, who was watching the two of them closely. *C'mon, Reko. Anton wants us to go check out the prisoners. They just arrived. You can be the token bad guy.*

Okay, but one of these days I want to be the guy who gets the girl.

Mary glanced at Jack and they both burst into laughter. *Reko?* Jack stopped and pointed at the wolf. *I think that can probably be arranged once you've shifted.*

Reko stopped dead in his tracks. *Mary? What's he mean?*

Probably exactly what it sounds like. You're ours, Reko. Until you find a woman of your own, you're welcome to share our bed. Of course, that means you get Jack, too.

"You folks coming?" Anton paused at the door. "I'm going on ahead."

"Okay, right behind you. We were just giving Reko a brief lesson in Chanku social dynamics."

Obviously hiding a grin, Anton left. Jack and Mary hugged his folks and left a few moments later, with Jack fighting laughter at Reko's soft muttering as he followed close behind.

Social dynamics? So that's what they call it . . .

• • •

Anton and Keisha's home
Saturday, 1:15 p.m.

Keisha was waiting at the front door when Jack, Reko, and Mary arrived. Mary hoped her sigh of relief wasn't audible, but the fact Keisha was waiting relaxed her even before Anton's mate drew her into a warm embrace. Mary actually snuggled against her for a moment before blushing and standing back. "I know you're not a warm puppy, but hugging you has the same effect. I hope you don't mind."

Laughing, Keisha hugged her again and then held both her hands. "Mary, I can't think of a nicer compliment. Thank you. Okay . . . Anton wanted me to tell you, he's told your father that your mother died. We don't want him to think she's still a target. Jack, Reko, come in. Mary, your father is here with the other men. They're in the Pentagon. He's angry and extremely vocal. I don't want you hurt by his words. Remember he's not himself. Anton and I both believe the demon is controlling him."

"I hope that's it. But Keisha, he killed my sister, tried to kill my mother. The man I remember could be a sanctimonious jerk, but he wasn't cruel. He wasn't a murderer. Only a very sick man would confuse a demon's ravings with God, but that's because he believes in a god whose people preach fear and hate. He was primed to do evil things." She shrugged and glanced at her mate and Reko. "After meeting Eve and hearing the Mother's words, it's hard to believe in a god like that. Eve and the Mother are all about love. I know where my heart lies."

Keisha didn't say anything, but she was smiling when she led them down the hall toward Anton's Pentagon. Mary was surprised that Anton would choose to bring the men into his home, especially knowing they were controlled by a demon, but he was a powerful alpha. Maybe this was part of his strategy—show no fear. She wished she could be as fearless.

They reached Anton's room. There was no conversation to hear, no sound at all. Frowning, Mary followed Keisha through the door. Anton stood behind the bar with his customary glass of cognac. Sebastian, Lily, Ig, and Fenris had taken up positions on either end of the long couch that was up against one of the walls across from the bar. Four men, their legs shackled but hands free, sat on the couch. The air shimmered around them, and Mary sensed a spell. When she glanced at Lily and caught Lily's wink, she was positive.

That was good. It meant she'd have a moment to consider just what she wanted to say to her father. Holding tightly to Jack's hand, her other buried in the thick fur at Reko's neck, she walked into the room, paused near Anton, and waited to see if her father would acknowledge her presence.

11

Jack held tightly to Mary's hand. He felt her trembling, but it was so subtle that unless you knew what to look for, no one would ever pick up the slightest hint she was at all nervous. She paused a moment near the bar, and then the two of them walked across the room. They stopped about four feet in front of her father.

Ryder stared at her with a slight frown on his face, almost as if he didn't recognize her. Jack squeezed her fingers. *Any idea what he's thinking?*

No. I don't think he knows who I am, which is really weird. I haven't seen him in person in a few years, but we spoke on a video call a couple of months ago.

Anton? Can you pick up what Ryder is thinking? Mary says there's no sense of recognition.

She's right. Anton came out from behind the bar and stood behind Mary with his hands resting lightly on her shoulders. "Mr. Ryder. Don't you have anything to say to your daughter?"

Mary's father started, turned and stared at Anton with a perplexed expression that quickly shifted into anger. "That one's not my daughter." His snarl sounded more bestial than any wolf. "My daughter is a beautiful, pure little girl. That . . . that woman is a sinner and a whore. She consorts with beasts. She is no longer one of my family."

"Your little girl." Anton paused, nodding slowly, his demeanor deceptively calm. "You must be talking about Becca. The child you strangled. She's dead, you know. So is your wife. Both of them dead by your hand. Mary, here, is the only one left."

Ryder frowned and glanced at Brother Thomas, sitting to his right. "You told me I failed, that she still lived. I didn't fail after all." He smiled, a sick, demented expression in an otherwise average-looking face. "Good. Master Aldo will be pleased."

"They're lying." Thomas shook his head. "He would have felt the power upon her death. There was nothing. Only when the girl died. Master Aldo said there was a huge burst of energy when we gifted him with little Becca's sweet soul."

Ryder turned and glared at Mary. "You're lying, aren't you? Lying whore. Where is she?"

Mary shook her head, and her quick-thinking response had Jack squeezing her hand in support. "Before she died, we had a priest do an exorcism. He removed Aldo's commands. She died in peace without his taint on her soul. You failed. You have all failed. So what now, Father? What's your next plan for world domination? Or should we just call it world destruction? Such lofty goals." She let out a deep breath of frustration and anger. "To think I once loved you. You were always a sanctimonious fool, but you were my father. Not anymore." She turned her back on him.

Brother Thomas's eyes went wide. Jack waited, watching to see what he was going to do as his face twisted into the caricature of a man totally off the rails. He smiled. It made Jack's skin crawl. "There's another bomb, you know. Aldo will win, and we will be the power that launches Armageddon here, on these shores. None of you will survive. No one. But Ryder and me? We'll live forever."

"You really are a complete nutcase, aren't you? What about Derek and Eagan? Oh. That's right. Aldo didn't give them the platinum package." Jack glanced at the other two men, but they were totally caught up in whatever spell Lily and Sebastian must be using. This time, Jack turned away and Mary followed.

"Wait."

Mary paused and looked over her shoulder at her father. "What do you want?"

Ryder frowned at Jack. "Who is that with you?"

Mary turned to Jack and smiled. "This is Jackson Temple. My mate and soon to be my husband." Then she stroked Reko's broad head. "And this is Reko."

Jack added softly, "Soon to be our lover. C'mon, Mary. Reko." He led them across the room to Anton's bar. Reko jumped up on the couch beside Lily, and Mary and Jack took seats at the bar. Anton followed. "What now, Anton?"

Anton glanced at Fen and Ig. Fen nodded and walked across the room and took a seat at the bar next to Mary. "What happened last night was all much too easy," Fen said. "If that idiot's right and there's a second bomb, we're going to need to find out where it is, and quickly. Anton, as much as I dislike the idea of breaking into a human's mind, I have no qualms at all in this situation. Aldo will be back in demon form, and he'll be even more dangerous. We have to remain alert, ready for anything. And we cannot allow anything to happen to those four. They're essentially the fuel the demon will need for whatever plans he's got."

"I just contacted Eve." Anton glanced toward the wall where she often appeared. "I'd rather have the goddess do it." He exhaled loudly, frustration evident. "Do you think they'll try and plant the bomb in the same place? I mean, you and Ig were able to get it without too much trouble."

"That's why we need to take a quick look at the man's mind. He may or may not know. Somehow, we need to find out what he knows."

Jack had been watching the part of the room where Eve usually appeared. The air shimmered. "Anton? Eve's here."

He flashed a quick smile at Jack and walked over to the goddess as she morphed into a corporeal being. Ig had taken a seat near the two prisoners, but he stood as well once Eve was fully in the room.

"I heard your call, Anton. A second device is definitely not something we need right now. Just give me a moment with the one who made the claim."

She strode across the room and stopped directly in front of Thomas. He scooted back against the couch and glanced to his left, at Ryder. Eve slapped his face.

"Bitch."

Thomas glared at her, but Eve glanced at Anton and shrugged. "See, Anton? Women never get any respect. And you know what?" She turned toward Thomas and planted her hands on the couch on either side of his head. "I'm tired of fucking around with these bastards. Look, stupid. I'm going to give you one chance, and one only, to tell me where the device is hidden. If you choose not to cooperate, I promise this will not go well for you."

He stared at her without a word.

"Ig? Do you mind restraining him for me?"

Igmutaka's grin was almost as scary as Eve's new attitude. Jack and Mary stepped back, to give them more room. Ig grabbed one of Thomas's arms and yanked him off the couch, turned him quickly and locked his arms behind his back with one hand. He put his other arm around the man's throat, immobilizing him. "This okay?"

"Perfect." Eve stepped closer. When Thomas jerked toward her, Ig tightened his arm around his prisoner's throat. Glaring at him, Eve said, "Don't hesitate to cut off his air if he won't hold still." Jack had never seen their goddess this pissed off. She smiled when Ig tightened his hold.

"Just don't kill him. Yet. I don't want Aldo getting his life force, but I can get a clearer read if I touch him." She glanced over her shoulder at Anton and smirked. "Which is just the most disgusting thing ever. Probably why you want me to do this, right?" When Anton folded his arms across his chest, smiled slightly, and nodded, she mumbled, "Figures." Then she placed her hands on Brother Thomas's temples. His body jerked and twitched, in spite of Ig's powerful hold on him. He opened his mouth to scream, but Sebastian waved his hand and no sound came out. The cords on Thomas's neck stood out, his face turned red, and Eve continued standing there with her hands pressed to his temples.

Jack shot a quick look at the other three, all solely focused on Eve and what she was doing to their leader. In spite of Lily's spell holding them in place, they looked terrified. After a moment, she pulled her hands back from Thomas's head and wiped them on her pants.

She watched while Ig placed Thomas back on the couch. The other three watched but made no move to help him as he came out of the spell, grabbing at his throat, coughing and choking. Then she turned her back on the men and used her mindspeech to tell them what she'd learned.

There's definitely another device. I can see it quite plainly. Not quite as large as the first one, but it's nuclear and capable of too much damage. I don't know if the planet could survive an explosion if it's placed to break the cap separating that huge pool of live magma from the surface. He has no idea where Aldo hid the thing, and he doesn't know if it's even been placed yet. I'm sorry. Closing her eyes, she bowed her head, looking absolutely exhausted. *I'd hoped for more information.* Straightening her shoulders, she turned toward the wall, the spot where she usually entered the room. *I need to get back.*

She walked over to Anton and kissed him. Then she softly said, "Thank you for calling me. I really needed to let go on someone who deserved it. That felt pretty darned good." Then she quickly faded from sight, leaving behind the sense something wonderful was now missing from the room.

Jack shook off the feeling. It always felt odd when the goddess departed. As if she took a special life force with her. In spite of the bad news, he smiled. Eve was so damned nice, it made him feel better, knowing she could get just as pissed as the rest of them.

"Okay." Anton caught everyone in the room in his all-encompassing gaze. All eyes turned his way. "We've got a series of small rooms in the cavern where we're locking them up tonight. They'll be under guard. It's been a long day and we haven't heard a damned thing from Aldo. I want to see if there's any contact from him over the next twenty-four hours, because there's not anything we can do until he makes a move."

Fen asked, "How's Rem feeling?"

"Has a headache. He's in his room resting. I don't think he got much sleep last night, but I'll fill him in on what Eve's discovered."

Reko sat up and whined.

Mary was on her knees beside him in a heartbeat. *What's wrong? Is Aldo back?*

No. He's never left, but he's quiet right now. I think maybe he's still recovering from the fight yesterday. He turned and looked at Anton and then swung his head around to Jack. *I know how to shift, but I don't want to do it here, not in front of them.* He stared at the prisoners a moment before looking away.

C'mon. We're going outside, Mary said. *There's a beautiful little garden that Keisha just finished.* She turned to Anton. *Jack, Reko, and I will be back in a little while. Is that okay?*

It's perfect. Come back as soon as you can so we can welcome our newest packmate.

Jack took Mary's hand. "Let's go out the back, through the kitchen."

"Can we get to Keisha's garden quickly from there?"

"We can. We can also snag a pair of sweats for Reko off that rack by the mudroom door."

Good idea, Reko said. *I'm not sure I want to be waving my manly parts in front of the world, no matter how comfortable you appear to be with nudity.*

Laughing, Mary hung on to Jack's hand as they ran to the back door, snagged a pair of sweats off the hook on their way by, and quickly led Reko around the side of the house toward Keisha's newest garden.

She'd created a fairy-tale glen with small maples, larger oaks, black cottonwood and mountain ash. Patches of thick green grass grew in the sunny spots, other groundcovers added texture to shaded areas, with all of it banked by large blocks of granite. Jack and Mary went straight to a sunny patch and sat on a bed of closely cropped grass. Reko paced back and forth in front of them, obviously nervous.

Mary went up on her knees and held out her arms. Reko stepped into her embrace, lowered his head until he pressed the top of it against her chest, and sighed. *Why am I so afraid? This is something I've wanted forever.*

Mary ran her fingers through the thick fur at the back of his neck and laid her cheek against him. His entire body trembled, now that he was so close to actually shifting. "Reko, it's okay. You're afraid *because* you've wanted it for so long. So many things must be going through your mind.

What if it's not everything you've hoped for? What if something happens and you end up caught in the midst of your change? So many what-ifs . . . That's not going to happen, but I remember worrying about that one before my first shift. The thing is, Reko, this is a huge step. You won't be merely a huge wolf anymore. You'll be Chanku. Able to become any predator on the planet. Did you know we have that ability? One time I spent the day shifting, just to see what I could be.

"Over the course of an afternoon, I was a puma, an eagle, a big grizzly bear and a snake. Each one felt unique, but I was still me in every animal I chose. Just like you will still be Reko when you're standing in front of us as a tall, handsome man. Shift for us, Reko. I want to see who my new packmate will be."

He didn't move away. If anything, he pressed closer, and then she was hugging a very large man with long, wild dark hair, broad shoulders, and thick, sooty lashes. She held him close, his face pressed against her breasts, offering him a sense of sanctuary while he held on to her just as tightly. Jack went to his knees beside them and wrapped his arms around Reko from the back. The man in her arms had always been a wolf, had shared space with his littermates, with other members of their pack until none were left. Mary sensed the moment when Reko realized he was no longer a wolf, and when he also knew he wasn't alone.

• • •

Saturday, 2:15 p.m.

It happened so fast he didn't even know he'd shifted. Not at first. His packmates held him. Jack hugged his back and rested his head against Reko's shoulder. Mary embraced him, her arms holding him close—so close that his face was pressed against the warm swell of her breasts and he inhaled her familiar scent with every breath.

That was something different. Scents were muted in this body. Where before he'd been aware of the fresh smell of the grass and the musty scent that told him a harmless garden snake was curled up in the rocks to his left, now he smelled only Mary's addictive aroma and the earthy, somewhat spicy scent he associated with Jack. And sounds . . . it was quieter in this body. Birdsong in the distance and Mary's soft breaths, the steady beat of her heart and Jack's as well, but not the rush of blood in their veins unless he really strained to listen.

Carefully, he slipped out of Mary's embrace. He turned his head slowly, gazing around the garden where they sat, mesmerized by the colors. He'd never seen color like this before. Anton had asked him shortly after they met to pay attention to the colors he'd see when he shifted.

Now Reko knew why. The grass was so green, flowers in the sculptured gardens in shades he thought must be blue and pink, yellow and purple. Mary had tried to describe color to him on the astral, and he saw enough to have an idea what she was talking about, but this was absolutely mesmerizing. He glanced up and the sky was a brilliant blue, a color he'd heard described as the color of a robin's egg. He'd love to see one of those for himself, see if it was really true.

No one spoke, and for that he was thankful. He wasn't sure he'd be able to say a word, not because he didn't know how, but because there really were no words to describe what his senses were telling him right now. He reached out and touched the blades of grass, felt the coolness against his fingertips, which meant he had to hold his hands up in front of his face and check them out. His fingers were long with flat nails at the ends, his hands were fairly broad, and there was dark hair growing on his forearms. Nothing like the fur that covered his body as a wolf—this was coarse and lay close to his skin, but not at all dense. It didn't look like it would do much to keep him warm. No wonder everyone wore clothing. It wasn't merely to cover their nudity. It would be cold here in winter without his fur.

He glanced down and saw the same kind of hair on his thighs, though there was a darker tangle around his sex. He was glad his prick wasn't erect because that might have been embarrassing. It looked like it was going to be huge if it ever got hard, and it was right out there in the open. At least when a guy was a wolf, that part mostly stayed hidden inside the warm sheath under his belly. The sheath on this one was right out there, front and center.

This belly didn't have hair, other than a trail that led from his bellybutton to his crotch. He ran his hand up his belly and across his chest. There was more hair on his chest. He glanced at Jack. He thought so . . . Jack's chest was almost entirely smooth, but he'd seen some of the other guys without shirts on, and some of them had hair on their chests.

Jack sat back on his butt with his arms wrapped around his knees, quietly watching while Reko stretched out his long arms and longer legs, while he inspected his hands and feet and figured out the patterns of hair on his body. He looked at his feet again. He had really big feet! Bigger than Jack's. Definitely bigger than Mary's. She was so petite compared to this huge body. He shook his head and shoved the thick mass of hair back from his face, sat up straighter, and slowly turned to Mary.

She raised up on her knees again. He was a bigger man than he'd thought he would be, maybe as big as Fen, though it would be hard to tell until he could stand next to him. Mary had to stretch out her arm when she raised her fingers so that she could trace the line of his jaw. Her touch was so gentle that he leaned into it and realized he was looking into the bluest eyes he could possibly imagine. The color he saw with his wolven eyes was grayer, not this beautiful, brilliant blue. She lifted her other hand and cupped his cheek. Rubbed her fingers over what felt like a slight shadow of beard. He wondered if he'd have to learn to shave. Wondered what he looked like. Wondered if Mary found his appearance pleasing.

He didn't think she was listening to his convoluted thoughts, but she must have been. "Reko, I've always thought you were a beautiful wolf, but you are an absolutely breathtaking man."

She traced his lips with her fingertips. He smiled beneath her touch. Her compliment left him feeling relieved, and he realized he'd been worried that she wouldn't find him appealing, though why he should think like that about a mated woman made no sense.

Laughing out loud, Mary turned to Jack. "I think you've just lost your position as the prettiest man in the pack . . . well, besides Ig." Jack whimpered, but then he was laughing as he unfolded his long legs and stood beside Reko.

"She's right, Reko. You are absolutely beautiful and the women are going to go nuts when they see you." Jack held out his hand. "Do you want to try standing?"

Reko let out a shuddering breath. Opened his mouth, shut it. He laughed, a short bark of sound that startled him so much he clapped his hand over his mouth. *I'm not sure how to speak. I've always thought my words.*

"Don't overthink it," Jack said. "The first time I became a wolf, I could howl. When I turned into an eagle and wanted to shout, what came out was an eagle's scream. It will happen the way it's supposed to."

"Jack's right. Say my name. Mary is such a simple word. So is Jack. Try it."

"Mary." He blinked at the sound of his voice. It was deeper than Jack's, kind of ragged-sounding, but he guessed that might be because he'd never spoken in this form before. Then he turned to Jack. "Jack," he said. Then he held out his hand and Jack carefully tugged him to his feet. Reko held on to him, waiting to find his balance. He stared at his feet for a moment and then raised his head. The world spun.

He grabbed for Mary with his free hand. "You okay?" She held tightly to his hand and grabbed higher on his forearm for a stronger hold.

He laughed again, knowing what to expect this time. "The ground is a long way down."

This time Jack was the one laughing. "That's because you're a very tall man." He stood back and looked at Reko, slowly shaking his head. "I'd say about six-seven, don't you think, Mary?"

"At least. Fen is six-six, though I think he's bigger overall. The guy's built like a mountain. Makes Sunny look like a little kid next to him."

"I don't think Sunny is at all intimidated by her mate's size, do you?" Reko was beginning to feel steadier on his feet. "I just realized that shifting for you the first time can't have been this complicated. You went straight to running on four legs; I've got to figure out how to balance on two. At least this brain appears to know how my arms and legs work. So far."

"He makes an excellent point, about the leg thing." Jack glanced toward the house. "Anton just checked in. He wants to make sure your shift went okay."

"I would like very much to show him." He saw the pants Mary had grabbed lying on the grass behind her and reached for them. "I should probably cover myself first."

Mary stepped aside so he could grab the sweats. "I guess this means the party's over, huh?"

Reko pulled the pants on and was glad they fit. The legs were almost long enough, but he'd recognized Mary's joke. "For now, anyway. I was thinking we might continue at a later time, maybe the three of us in Jack's cabin?"

Mary grabbed one of his hands, Jack took the other. They looked at one another and he saw Mary wink. Jack sort of grumbled, but Reko knew he was teasing.

"Guy catches on fast, don't you think?" Jack said.

"I certainly hope so." Mary grinned and tugged him along as she headed back to the house.

• • •

Anton was alone in the room with three round glasses sitting on the bar when they walked in. Reko paused for a moment in the doorway. Everything looked different to this form. Even though he was a vary large wolf, Reko had had to look up to see Anton's bar, or whenever he spoke with other members of the pack unless they came down to his level. Now he was much taller than Anton, though the man's shorter stature didn't take away from the power of his alpha command. He poured the dark amber liquid into each of the glasses. Reko recognized the bottle from earlier.

"Welcome, Reko. A toast to the newest member of our pack."

Reko walked up to the bar and carefully sat on one of the stools. He picked up the glass, holding it gently in his palm with his long fingers wrapped around the bowl. "I've watched you pour this for the others and wondered what it tasted like. It smells better to this nose than the wolf's."

Anton held his glass up. "Small sips, Reko."

Reko glanced at Mary and Jack standing to either side of him. They each lifted their glass and very gently touched them to his. The clear glass rang like tiny bells. He cocked his head, listening to the sound. Everything sounded slightly different to this set of ears.

He took a small sip of the amber liquid. It was nothing like he expected and not at all like it smelled. The burning sensation wasn't entirely unpleasant, but the taste made him want to sneeze. Blinking rapidly, he turned a level look on Anton. "You drink this for pleasure?"

Anton laughed. "That we do, which I imagine has lowered your opinion of our human selves quite a bit."

Reko took another small sip and rolled his eyes. He was learning things this body could do, and somehow that felt apropos. "I would never be so rude."

This time Anton laughed even louder, as if the weight of the past few days might hopefully scatter with the sound. "You, Reko, are a treasure. I'm so glad you and Ari are now part of our pack. And no, Ari hasn't shifted yet, though we expect it at any time. He does want to see you, though."

"I imagine he does." Reko glanced toward the door. "We're twins, and our wolves are almost identical. If he sees me, he'll know better to expect what he'll look like."

"Have you seen yourself?" Anton moved to the end of the bar, walked around to Reko's side. When Reko shook his head, Anton paused beside him and said, "Come with me."

They all followed Anton down the hall to the first of the spare bedrooms and walked inside. Anton flipped on a light, took Reko's arm and led him to a full-sized mirror. Reko gazed at the man looking back at him. He couldn't look away. This was the man his parents had never gotten to see. That was his first thought. The second was that Ari would probably look just like him.

His dark brown hair was thick and waving about his shoulders, shot with silver and lighter brown and coming to a slight V over his forehead. His eyes were dark amber, about the same color as Jack's and so many of the other Chanku in the pack. A fine pelt of dark hair covered his upper chest. Another dark trail began at his navel and disappeared beneath the waistband.

He was a big man, taller than Jack and even Fen, though not as broadly built as Fen or even Igmutaka. He was easily the tallest man he'd seen so far. He wondered if that made him an oddity among the men of the pack. He didn't want to be different, to be singled out. He was too new to this group of shapeshifters. He wanted to be like them, not something different.

"You're not an oddity at all," Anton said. "You're a well-built, strong, handsome man. Men and women alike will want to get to know you better, and from what I know of you already, they're all going to like the man you are."

The alpha appeared to hear everything any of them thought, but it was comforting to Reko that the one in charge of this vital pack was so closely attuned to its members. And that he seemed to know exactly what Reko needed to hear.

"You will be—you already are—a valued member of the pack." Anton paused a moment and gazed toward a large window that looked out over a big meadow to the forest beyond. "We used to fear the Berserkers," he said, speaking softly. "We thought they were too feral to be civilized. Then we discovered that both Fen and Ig were of the Berserker line, both valued members of our pack and beloved by both our goddess and the Mother, and that forced us to reevaluate what little we knew of your kind. We've learned we are not so different after all." He stopped and then smiled broadly. "Ari's headed to the bar. He's anxious to see his brother."

Reko didn't wait. *Ari? I'm coming to show you!* Spinning about, he left the bedroom and the reflection of his new body and headed toward the Pentagon, with the others following close behind. He met Ari in the hallway just outside the bar. His brother stopped the moment Reko stepped into view, turned and stood in front of him.

Reko? It is you, isn't it?

"It's me, Ari. I just looked in a mirror and got to see what I look like. Since we're twins . . ."

I should look very much like you. You're a big man, Reko. What is it like? Is it hard to walk on two legs? Does the shift hurt?

"No. It happens so quickly." He knelt in front of Air and hugged the big wolf's neck. *When it's time, you'll see it in your mind. Your body will know exactly what to do, and when you make the decision to shift, you'll wonder why you couldn't figure it out before. There's no pain, merely the sensation of being different. Your sense of smell, of hearing, they're not as good. But touch? My fingers are very sensitive, much more than paws.* He ran them gently through Ari's thick fur, then used his new voice again. "As far as standing on two legs and walking? My first thought was that the ground was a long way down!" He laughed, remembering how tightly he'd held on to Mary after Jack had pulled him to his feet.

I think I'm close. I'm getting small images that seem to have to do with shifting, but not enough. Not yet.

"It will happen. Probably very soon. We're much alike and we started taking the nutrients at the same time. I cannot wait to embrace you, my brother, as a man grown." Hearing voices, Reko glanced up in time to see Keisha and Lily coming from the kitchen. He could hear Sebastian, Ig, and Fen all laughing about something, and another voice that sounded like Remington.

They were coming to see him. His pack. He hugged Ari once more and then stood. Turning, he gazed down into Mary's bright blue eyes. "Thank you," he said, glancing toward Jack standing beside her. "Thank you both for making this so wonderful for me." Then he raised his head and waited to meet his pack as an equal, standing upright on two legs for the first time in his life.

• • •

Mary walked between them, her hands tightly clasped by the men escorting her through the night. Reko and Jack laughed and joked with each other, talking to one another over the top of her head after an evening that had turned into something beyond special. So many from the pack had arrived to welcome Reko that Anton and Keisha's house had rung with laughter.

But for Mary, the most special part of the evening had been when Jack's mom had taken her aside and hugged her tightly after watching the way both Jack and Reko had hovered over her during the evening.

Tala's eyes had actually twinkled when she and Mary stepped outside and found a quiet spot on the deck. "I'm not saying you're headed for a three-way mating, Mary, but don't let any preconceived notions keep you from following your heart. AJ, Mik, and I are proof that a triad can work." Then she'd laughed and glanced toward her son, who hadn't left Reko's side all evening. "And Jack certainly doesn't seem to have a problem sharing his woman with a man he could easily love."

"How is it," Mary had asked, "that Jack and I found love so quickly?" She rolled her eyes. "Once I figured out he actually was interested, anyway. And how is it that he and Reko and I have connected on such a deep level in just a couple of days? In the real world, that doesn't happen."

Tala had merely laughed. "Think about it. This is our real world, but outside of the pack, people can't see into their partner's thoughts, can't read their desires, or know what they're thinking. Among Chanku, there's no chance for subterfuge. What you see is what you get, quite literally, because you see everything."

Mary thought of that first night, making love with Jack, seeing the way he felt about her in his open thoughts. Knowing he already saw her as his mate had given her the freedom to love him in spite of her horrible past. Then the bond Lily and Sebastian had helped them open with Reko had shown both Mary and Jack the truth of the man inside the wolf, an intelligent, fun-loving male with a heart so decent and strong that both of them felt honored to be so closely linked with him.

She'd hardly allowed herself to look forward to tonight. She and Jack were so new, but so was Reko. From what he'd told them, he was a virgin. Mary took that responsibility to heart. She'd been a virgin when she was taken. Her first sexual experience had been rape, so ugly and painful that it had taken the last six months and Jack's love to make her see sex as something beautiful.

Whatever happened tonight with Reko, she wanted it to give him nothing but good memories. Whether he stayed on with her and Jack or went off and found a mate of his own, tonight was going to be as perfect as she and Jack could make it.

• • •

Jack's cabin
Saturday, 10:20 p.m.

Reko followed Jack and Mary into the small cabin, but this felt so wrong to him. Mary and Jack were newly mated, and yet they had insisted that he return with them. He'd offered to stay on at Anton's house no matter how much he wanted a chance to learn about intimacy for the first time with these two, but they'd both looked disappointed, as if he were doing them a favor by coming home with them.

He sighed. He'd been much too easy to convince.

He didn't get it. If he had a woman, especially one as amazing as Mary, he didn't think he'd be willing to share. And another thing . . . he still wasn't sure about sex with Jack, even though Jack and the other men acted as if it were the most normal thing in the world.

Of course, that could be due to the whole libido thing. They hadn't been exaggerating about that. Before his first shift, sex had obviously been something he'd thought about, but it wasn't anything he'd ever experienced, so he hadn't missed it.

Then he'd shifted. And he'd done it more than once, shifting back and forth between his wolf and human forms a couple of times tonight, just to make sure he could still do it, though he'd felt badly when Ari watched him a couple of times. His brother hadn't said a word to him. Not since that very first interaction. In fact, he hadn't said anything at all during the evening, but Reko hadn't realized that until just now. He'd been way too caught up in all the changes in his body.

The repercussions had been immediate and undeniable—shifting had been simple, but dealing with the aftereffects was a bit more problematic. There was no hiding that huge erection between his legs. The damned thing had wanted to poke out of the waistband of his pants, but he'd shoved it down so the cut of the pants held it somewhat in place along his left leg.

It was terribly uncomfortable trying to walk, hoping no one noticed he was aroused, but they all acted like it was no big deal, merely a part of being a shapeshifter. Jack had said it was something they all had to learn to deal with. Then Sebastian had said, "No shit, Sherlock," which meant absolutely nothing at all to Reko, but had left Jack and a couple of the other guys laughing so hard they had tears in their eyes. He knew they were laughing about issues they'd had, not at him, because he'd caught a few silly images in Jack's thoughts.

He tried to remember his pack when there were still other members, and he remembered teasing, but it wasn't as good-natured as what went on here. Or maybe he merely understood it better, now that he was a man grown. A man grown, now wearing a man's body, with a man-sized prick throbbing between his legs.

Mary walked into the kitchen and grabbed a bottle of red wine off the counter. She poured glasses for each of them and carried them into the main room. Jack sat in one of the single chairs. Reko quietly followed Mary and took a seat on the longer one. He knew it was called a couch. It was certainly comfortable, and when Mary set the three wineglasses on the table in front of it and sat down beside him, Reko decided it might be his favorite place to sit.

"To you, Reko." She held her glass aloft, and he knew enough now to touch the lip of his to Mary's, and then to Jack's. "You've had a long journey to come this far, but now that you've shifted, there is so much more for you to see."

"And sexually, more to learn," Jack added. "More to experience." He took a sip of his wine. "The one thing Mary and I want to make sure you understand is that we will never, ever push you to do something that makes you uncomfortable. Sex is a huge part of our lives, but it might not be the same for you. The other Chanku and Berserkers we know well have very few rules or boundaries, but they do exist. Incest is taboo, so there's no sex among family members related by blood, adults and children never have sex with each other, and we will never try to coerce, force, or otherwise manipulate a partner into any sexual relationship of

---

Kate Douglas

any kind. It's all about free will. We might ask you to try pushing personal boundaries, but no is always going to mean no."

"I'm not sure how much you know about our shapeshifter physiology," Mary said, "but we're immune to most human diseases. Sexually transmitted diseases are a non-issue. Cancer doesn't seem to affect us, or any other problems, including genetic abnormalities. A couple of our packmates—you've met Sunny and you'll meet Manda Quinn before too long—had incomplete shifts when they were young because they hadn't had the nutrients and their bodies weren't ready to change. They spent their lives crippled, their bodies twisted. Once they were able to shift, their bones realigned themselves into the bodies they were always meant to have."

"And they're okay now?" That was something Reko had wondered about. What happened when his body changed? Why didn't it hurt?

"They are," Jack said. "Both exceptionally beautiful and perfectly healthy. And don't forget Stef. He was caught in a partial shift for a long time with absolutely no idea what he was. He thought Anton had cursed him, but Stefan and Xandi, and then Keisha, once she was found, were the beginning of this pack. They knew very little about what they were, or how our bodies worked."

"You can't impregnate a female Chanku without her full knowledge and consent, and unless she's your bonded mate, it just won't happen. We women have full control over our reproductive systems." Then Mary laughed. "Which is why Anton ended up with Lucia when he thought he and Keisha were all through having babies. She still wanted more."

"But he's the alpha. How did she get away with that?" The alpha's word was law, wasn't it?

"In this pack, at least, the final word will always be Keisha's. Chanku are matriarchal—if a female were to challenge you, you'd probably back down without even realizing you'd done it. Anton is, for all intents and purposes, our pack's alpha. We tease him and call him our über alpha, but that's how we want the peoples of the world to identify him, because it's much easier for men to relate to a man in charge, and women think he's really sexy, so they believe him, too." Laughing, most likely at the foibles of humankind, Jack added, "His is the face the world sees when we go public on anything, but every member of the pack recognizes Keisha as the final word, including Anton."

"But how do we shift? Why can't I see the changes taking place? One minute I'm on four legs and then I'm on two."

"Would you believe me when I say we really don't know? We've never figured it out, but Lily was the one who learned our species history, and she said that when we shift, we actually slip into another dimension

138

where we make the shift, and time adjusts so that it appears instantaneous. It's really the most magical thing about Chanku and Berserker shifters— the way it happens.

"Another thing." Jack laughed this time, and Reko was sure it was at his expression. He had to remember to close his mouth. So many things he didn't know about who and what he was! "Right now you look like you're in your late thirties," Jack said. "Now that you're shifting, you won't age, and at some point you'll realize you actually look younger."

"When we shift, our cells somehow rebuild to their optimum level." Mary shoulder-bumped Reko. "I will be forever twenty-two years old. Men seem to stick at around thirty or so, which is a good age for guys."

Reko thought about a few of the packmates he'd met, men who seemed so knowledgeable for their obvious youth and yet received the respect of men much older. The wolves in his pack that had died of old age had been close to twenty, but they'd looked ancient. His mother had been seventeen, his father barely eighteen. If they'd been able to shift, they would still be alive. "I've been alive for twelve years as a wolf." He stared at his hands. "If Ari and I never shifted or managed to live a full life without dying young, we would have lasted maybe another seven or eight years." He raised his head. Everything was blurry, his eyes filling with tears. A new human thing, this obvious showing of emotion. "Our parents would still be alive. How old are your leaders? Anton Cheval? How many years does he have?"

Jack frowned and focused on Mary. "He was born in 1955, right?" When Mary nodded, he said, "That means he turned eighty-five in February. So yeah, you're right. I'm so sorry we didn't find you before this. They would likely still be alive."

Reko thought about that for what felt like a very long time. It really wasn't, but his mind cleared in small increments as memories flew behind his eyes. His mother and father teaching him and Ari to hunt, talking about their memories as young wolves, the hopes they had that at some point they might find the nutrients that would finally give them the birthright so long denied.

He and Ari had those nutrients now, they had reclaimed their birthright. He would not squander something his parents had yearned for all their lives. He glanced at Mary and then took her hand. Reached across the table for Jack's and held his as well. "I will always mourn the loss of my parents, of my brother and sister, but Ari and I have achieved what all of them hoped for. I will do my best to embrace everything that is new in my life, to stay wide open to this journey." He gently squeezed their hands. "With your help, I think I am ready to begin the trip."

Releasing their hands, Reko picked up his wine and drained the glass.

"I will wait for you in the bedroom," he added, carrying his glass into the kitchen. Then he tossed a wink at Jack and left the room.

Their laughter followed him, along with Mary's dry comment. "It appears he's going to be a very willing pupil."

He hoped Mary was right. He fully intended to learn everything he could, at least as much as he had time to digest before the demon showed up again to screw with his plans.

12

Reko stopped at the restroom first. Taking care of bodily functions was easier as a wolf—finding the side of a tree or a clump of grass to piss against made a lot more sense than aiming at a hole in an appliance. Leave it to humans to make things more complicated.

He finished and was washing his hands when there was a knock on the door. Jack stood outside with a small brush in his hand. "For brushing teeth." He handed the blue brush to Reko. Pointing to a wire rack holding two brushes of the same design, he said, "The red one is mine and the yellow one is Mary's. This will be yours."

Then he proceeded to show Reko how to brush his teeth, explained what some of the things in the cabinet over the sink were for, and pointed out the controls for the shower and where to find extra towels. When Jack left the small room, Reko stared at the silly brush in his hand and wondered just what he'd gotten himself into.

Teeth scrubbed—he had to admit the scrubbing made his mouth feel really good—and his hair brushed and tied back out of his face with a stretchy thing Jack had given him, Reko finally walked the short distance to Jack's bedroom. Mary's back was to him. She sat on top of the bed talking to Jack, covered in the soft black shirt Jack had worn earlier. It was rich with Jack's scent. Reko wondered if Mary realized Jack was marking her with his scent, but she was so totally without artifice that he doubted she'd even noticed. She loved Jack and probably wanted to surround herself in his things. That made perfect sense to Reko. He wished he could surround himself with Mary.

Jack smiled when he spotted Reko. There were no hidden meanings behind his expression, and Reko relaxed a bit, though he also felt guilty, knowing he was here for intimacy with his friend's mate. He still wasn't sure what this was about, this invitation into their bed, but his prick was pulsing with blood again, which meant his body was telling him not to screw up this opportunity. He stopped beside the bed and waited for Mary to notice him. She glanced over her shoulder and smiled. Then she grabbed Jack's shirt where it hung to her hips and pulled it up and over her head.

Reko sucked in a breath. He'd seen her naked before, but never with the knowledge that he could get naked with her, or that he'd be free to touch what she so casually displayed. All that beautiful, smooth skin suddenly took on an entirely new meaning. As a wolf he saw her as a beautiful creature, but not necessarily as a sexual object.

This form recognized the potential. He cleared his throat, realized that, for some reason, his voice was even deeper than normal. Or at least what he assumed was normal. "When I saw you unclothed in your human form," he said, "I thought you were a lovely representative of the female of the species. Now, seeing you like this, knowing I have your permission to look and appreciate you in a more personal manner, my reaction is totally different. You are more beautiful than anyone or anything I have ever seen." He laughed softly, knew his skin was probably dark with the flush of blood he felt rushing across his face and chest. These bodies didn't hide embarrassment well at all. No better than they hid arousal. "I know what I'd like to do," he said, and it was practically a growl, "but please, tell me what is acceptable. Tell me what I should do."

"What is your body telling you?"

It appeared Jack was ignoring the obvious. Reko glanced at his swollen prick and then raised an eyebrow in Jack's direction.

"Use the other brain, the one between your ears," Jack said. He tapped his forehead with one finger. "The one between our legs is always telling us to rut without thought. We have to keep him under control."

"Until you don't," Mary said, giving Jack a quick grin. "I know what I want, and honestly? Rutting doesn't sound bad at all." She threw a big pillow on the floor in front of Reko. Kneeling, she raised her head and smiled at him. Even with the pillow, she looked small kneeling before him, but her eyes were almost level with his groin. Her mouth. She licked her lips. His heart pounded, his prick stood high and hard. He wasn't certain what she was planning until she reached between his thighs and cupped his balls.

His knees almost buckled and a harsh groan startled him, exploding unexpectedly from his mouth. He struggled to control that other brain Jack talked about and concentrated solely on Mary and her gentle fingers.

Vaguely Reko was aware of Jack moving to sit on the bed behind him, but his attention narrowed to Mary as she lightly stroked the sac behind his prick. He groaned again when she rolled the hard orbs inside between her fingers.

He'd never imagined sensations like this, never once thought of a woman touching him so intimately, focusing totally on him, giving him pleasure.

Closing his eyes, he waited, hoping she'd stroke his prick or at least touch it, but Jack was behind him now, and Reko let out a strangled shout when Jack's calloused fingers pinched his nipples. He'd never thought those were sexual parts on a man, but the shock of sensation that passed from his chest to his prick left him shivering. His erection stood higher and harder than ever.

Mary turned his balls free and stroked along his full length. He arched his back, thankful for Jack's strong support behind him. His legs were already trembling. He was so sensitive now with the protective skin that Jack called a foreskin rolled back behind the flared head, his legs almost collapsed when Mary's hot mouth found his rounded glans, when her tongue circled the rim and dipped into his slit. She slipped more of him into her mouth. At first he worried about hurting her, about choking her with his size, but she sucked him even deeper, her tongue stroking the sensitive underside where the foreskin attached.

He was so caught up in the actual dynamics of what Mary's mouth was doing to his prick that he'd almost entirely tuned out Jack's hands on his chest, the amazing sensation of Jack's fingers slowly twisting and rubbing his nipples. Mary clutched his buttocks, holding tightly to the globes of his ass, separating them and exposing him to Jack.

Maybe he should have been embarrassed—he didn't know human customs, but these Chanku had no false modesty about their bodies—and Mary's mouth on him, Jack's hands on him, all of it felt absolutely amazing. His body was building toward something huge, something so monumental and unfamiliar he didn't know what to expect. Mary pulled him close against her mouth and her throat rippled over his prick as she swallowed him down. He couldn't believe she took all of him, but her lips stretched tightly around his thick base and touched the silky, softly curling hair at his groin. Jack pressed close behind him, his thick erection sliding now in the crease Mary had spread wide with her hands on his ass.

Her thoughts filled his mind, the taste of him in her mouth, how she loved the taut muscles beneath her hands, loved the sense of his prick in her throat, but she called it a cock, not a prick, and he wondered about the semantics. Still, he opened his thoughts to her, shared what her mouth felt like, the wet heat that was so absolutely perfect, the firm grasp of her hands holding him. He included Jack, shared the hot slide of Jack's cock over his ass, the exquisite pain as he continued to pinch and twist Reko's nipples.

Reko knew what an orgasm was, thought he might have had them in his sleep a few times, though he wasn't sure. There was no doubt in his mind now that one was coming for him. That had to be it, this sense of expectation growing stronger with every stroke of Jack's cock between his ass cheeks, the strong suction he felt and even observed when Mary's cheeks hollowed with each draw against his prick.

And this was just one small act of sex. They hadn't even gone near actual penetration, and when he thought of that, he realized he wanted his first time to be inside Mary—or even Jack, if that's what the man wanted. He shared that with them and they both reacted immediately. Jack sat back on the bed, though he continued to gently rub Reko's nipples, and Mary slowly pulled away from his prick, leaving him with a kiss on the tip and the cool air moving over the wet surface.

"How do you want me, Reko? On my back with my legs spread, or maybe on my hands and knees?"

He shook his head, overwhelmed by her amazing generosity. "What do you want, Mary? What makes you happy?"

"Really?" She scooted across the bed and lay down on her back. "I want your mouth between my legs first. I'll show you." She leaned forward and parted the damp lips of her sex. Pointed to a small nubbin of flesh at the very tip. "You can lick this. It's my clitoris but I just call it a clit. You can even lick inside me until I'm really wet and ready. Then I want you to push your cock inside me and let your instincts take over." She laughed. "I give you permission to think with that head." She pointed at his prick, standing high with white fluid already bubbling at the tip.

His heart thundered in his chest, his balls ached and he felt as if his prick was going to take off on its own to do as Mary said, push inside and let his instincts take over. Right now, his instincts weren't at all into this pause in all the action.

And wasn't that exactly what Jack was talking about? Using the brain in his head, not the one between his legs? No matter what Mary said.

Besides, he was the one who'd asked for the change in positions. He took a deep breath, let it out slowly. Tried to organize thoughts that wanted to zero in on that dark thatch of hair between Mary's thighs. Wanted to dive inside and . . . "What about Jack?" He glanced to his right. Jack sat there smiling like he knew a secret.

"We'll worry about Jack after you make love to Mary." Jack's voice filled with laughter. "Do you have any idea how hot you are, Reko? How much I want you buried in me or me in you? I'm not particular, but first I really want to see you make my Mary happy." He leaned over and kissed Mary, then he turned to Reko, stood to cup his face in his hands, and kissed him.

Reko hadn't expected the kiss. He really didn't expect it to feel this wonderful, not with a man. He was taller than Jack, though not much wider, but he grabbed Jack's shoulders to hold him in place, deepened the kiss, thrusting his tongue into his mouth, exploring Jack's teeth and the hot tangle of his tongue, tasting him, each exploring the other in a small duel that lasted until they were both gasping. Jack was the one who broke the kiss.

He didn't so much wipe his mouth as run his fingers across his lips before he took a deep breath and winked at Mary. "He's a fast learner, Mary."

"Good."

Her voice sounded thick and even Reko recognized her need behind that one word. He focused on Mary, fell into the deep blue of her fierce gaze. She caught him there, held him. She wanted this, wanted him. Like Reko, she was tired of waiting, though he'd waited a lifetime, not even dreaming that anyone like Mary might be here at this time and place for him. He turned and put a knee on the bed, then moved over Mary and knelt reverently between her spread legs. He stared at her for a long moment, learning her shape, the angles and curves and contours of her beautiful body. Then he gently slipped his hands beneath the firm globes of her bottom and lifted her to his mouth.

She rested her legs on his shoulders and clutched the thick bedding with both hands. Leaning close, he inhaled her scent and almost spent himself at that moment. She was ripe with the pheromones he'd only heard of, the musky aroma that drove males wild when they came close.

With just the tip of his tongue, he circled the tiny bit of flesh she called her clit. Her hips bucked in his grasp. He held her still with his hands and used his mouth as she'd asked him, lapping at the swollen lips of her sex, suckling her clit. It had begun to swell so that it peeked out from its fleshy hood—her reaction to his touch. He had no idea a woman had such a thing, like a tiny prick only so very sensitive. Mary's thoughts flooded him, the way his tongue felt when he swept the length of her sex, how she wanted him to lick inside her. Her instructions fascinated him. Willingly, he followed her lead.

As he drove his tongue deep inside, stroking her inner walls and lapping at her juices, his fingertips brushed the damp, crinkled ring between her cheeks. Everything between her legs was wet with her sweet nectar, and her whimpers told him just how aroused she was. How very much she loved what he was doing. Without really considering the move, he slipped one finger deep inside the opening in her butt. The ring of muscle clamped tightly to his finger and she cried out, arching her back, forcing his finger deeper and pressing her sex tightly against his mouth.

She flooded him with her arousal, flooded his mind with the sounds of her pleasure, and the connection exploded between them into a white-hot barrage of sensation. He licked and nuzzled, knowing instinctively to bring her down from her climax slowly, knowing when to pull his finger free of her body with care. Before she was totally slack in his arms, he lowered her hips and legs, pressed his prick against her opening, and slid all the way inside in one smooth thrust. He held himself there, his sensitive glans pressed against what could only be the hard mouth of her cervix, locked in place by her feminine muscles rippling through her climax. He wanted to move faster, harder, but at the same time he wanted to hold perfectly still and feel Mary, experience her inner tempo, the muscles pulsing with her arousal, adjusting to his size, enclosing him in a hot, wet embrace.

"Now, Reko. Hard and fast." She clutched his upper arms with both hands and lifted her body to him. Gazing into those beautiful blue eyes, he did exactly as she ordered. He filled her over and over again, the steady rhythm of his hips pounding into her, the thunder that was his heartbeat racing the echo of Mary's.

He knew his climax was coming and opened the link to Mary, brought Jack into it with them and moved in and almost out of her as if he was a huge piston in a mighty engine. She was so tiny compared to him, and if not for the link between them he would have been afraid of harming her.

But she wanted this, wanted him, and she reveled in the strength of his taking, gloried in the love of her mate, who watched her pleasure and took it into himself. The three of them, so tightly connected that there was no Jack, no Mary, no Reko. They were one, the three of them finding completion as Mary screamed, as Reko cried out and lifted her against him so that he knelt here, in the middle of their bed with Mary's strong legs wrapped around his hips, with Jack cursing and laughing, holding both of them from behind.

Reko bowed his head over Mary, who'd gone limp in his arms. Jack's arms stretched around Reko to hold Mary, to hold Reko. After a few moments of the three of them gasping for air, Jack's laughter filled the room. "Stay there," he said. "Don't move. I'll be right back."

Reko had no idea why he'd given the order, but he held Mary close, brushed her tangled hair back from her forehead with his fingers, kissed her lips lightly for one more taste. Jack crawled up on the bed behind him.

"That was a first," he said. Reko felt a warm, wet cloth on his back.

"What are you doing?" Glancing over his shoulder, he realized Jack was washing his back.

146

"Washing my spunk off your back. All I was doing was hugging you guys and soaking up your shared sensations, but when you both climaxed, I joined you. I wasn't even touching myself. It was all you, Reko. You and Mary. There. You're all clean."

Stunned by his own powerful response, Reko carefully lay Mary back down on the bed. He kissed her lips, just a taste, and asked, "Are you okay?"

"Better than okay. Reko, that was magnificent."

He stared at her, confused as much by the tears filling his eyes as the amazing woman he held in his arms. "Why, Mary? Why would you and Jack ask me to come here? Why did you choose to share yourselves, your love, with me? I'm a virtual stranger."

"Not entirely." She ran her fingers along the side of his face. "Not since we've linked. Reko, has Jack told you where I come from?"

"No, all I really know is that you are a woman without equal, yet your father is one of the demon's minions."

She nodded. "I know. I am so ashamed of him, but thank you." She kissed him quickly. "I hate that so much, that my father is quite literally in league with the devil, but my story might explain why it's so important to me that you be here with us. Almost two years ago, I was kidnapped by a man who was a sex slaver. That means he stole women away and then sold them into prostitution. I was a virgin, just like you were tonight. I didn't know then that I was Chanku. I'd never had sex, didn't plan to have sex until I found the man I would marry, but the men who took me beat me and then sold me night after night to strangers for sex. I was raped and beaten until I was so terrified of sex, so disgusted by men, that I thought I'd never enjoy any of this. When I found out I was Chanku, my libido kicked in, much as yours has, but I was still afraid. That is, until I met Jack."

She glanced at her mate, and the love in her eyes made Reko hurt, not because it wasn't for him, but because he wondered if any woman would ever look at him that way. "The thing is, Reko, I wanted your first time to be wonderful. I wanted you to have nothing but good memories of your very first sexual experience. And your second, and . . ."

"Your third, fourth, fifth . . ." Laughing, Jack glanced at the erection that was already coming back to life for Reko. "And it looks like you're ready for round number two . . ."

• • •

Jack was so proud of his Mary that he could hardly stand it. She'd been cautious at first, but the fact she trusted him enough to invite Reko into their bed was a huge step for her. He wondered if she realized the power of the link they were forging tonight with their Berserker.

Their minds were already in sync, and he'd felt a power in Reko when they climaxed that was very close to the mating bond. He knew that Ig and Fen had mated in their human form. Unlike Chanku, who were born in their human form and completed the mating bond as wolves, Berserkers were born as wolves or pumas and mated as humans. He certainly didn't want to accidently mate with Reko unless the man wanted it, but tonight, linking so closely to him during sex, had been amazing.

Jack had never linked even casually with another male during intimacy, and tonight had been a unique and powerful experience. He wondered what Mary would think of such a thing, if she was even interested in spending her life with two men instead of one. It certainly seemed to work for his parents—all three of them. Jack had to admit a certain amount of prejudice. He wanted what his parents had, that all-consuming love that still allowed each of them their freedom within their triad. It was, to him anyway, the ideal. And he'd hoped to have it one day, though he'd never really expected the opportunity to arise—or that he'd ever know the kind of woman willing to experiment the way Mary was.

Not physically, but emotionally. Chanku women were always open for sex with other members of the pack, but they guarded their emotions during the more casual couplings. Mary guarded nothing of herself, not with Jack and, surprisingly, not with Reko either.

Reko lay on his back with Mary sprawled across his chest. This time Mary had been astride the big man, controlling his orgasm while Jack held Reko's feet to the bed so he couldn't buck Mary off—something he'd playfully tried to do when she first crawled on top of him and teased him longer than he wanted.

He'd let Reko rest a few minutes, but then Jack wanted to make love to him, just the two of them. He had no idea if Reko would go for it, if he'd want to top or take the bottom once it was explained to him, but Jack needed a stronger connection with the man. He felt it deep inside, that tonight was important, well beyond the mere chance to have some spectacular sex with the new guy in the pack.

No, this was something more than that, but he wasn't sure if it was important for the three of them and their relationship, or if it had something to do with the danger to the pack. That thought had been niggling around the back of his brain for the past hour or so, and he couldn't quite let it go. Whatever the reason, Jack knew he had to have Reko tonight.

• • •

Sunday, 12:30 a.m.

Reko opened one eye and caught Jack watching him. Mary slept soundly across his chest, her lips swollen from their kisses, her legs sticky with his ejaculate and his semi-hard cock still planted inside her sweet body. *I don't want to wake her. Will you help me move her to the other side of the bed?*

Jack nodded, got off the bed and walked around to Reko's side. He carefully lifted Mary away from her lover and, when Reko pulled the covers back, lay her between the clean sheets. She whimpered, pursed her lips, and then settled back into sleep. There was still a spot of dried semen at the corner of her mouth. Reko had no idea if it was his or Jack's, but one thing was obvious—they would all need showers in the morning. Of course, Reko had already learned that shifting would leave them as clean as any shower, but a shower together sounded much more decadent. No matter. Mary appeared to be out for the night. He glanced at Jack.

Grinning broadly, Jack asked him, *Are you tired?*

Reko had scooted back against the headboard. He shook his head. Tired? Not with so many new sensations firing in his brain. He pulled his feet up close to his body and wrapped his arms around his knees. Jack walked back around the bed to sit beside Reko's legs.

Reko almost laughed, but he didn't want to wake Mary. Jack had no idea what was spinning through his head right now. *Not yet,* Reko said. *I still want to find out what sex with you is like. I know I definitely like what I did with Mary.* He shrugged, even though he felt anything but calm. He sucked in a deep breath for courage. Let it out. *I liked it even more when you were with us.*

Jack's smile blossomed into a stupid grin. *I wasn't sure if you were really interested or not. I don't want you to do anything you're not comfortable with.*

He hadn't been comfortable thinking about sex with Mary, especially with Jack sharing the bed, but it had turned out absolutely amazing, so it was hard to use comfort alone as a criteria for making a choice. *I want to know if I'm comfortable having sex with you. I won't know if I don't try, though I'm not really sure of the logistics.*

Those damned logistics can be confusing. Jack tilted his head and gave Reko a long stare. *How is it you know the language so well? Your vocabulary, your understanding of nuance and the subtlety of language, is better than some of the guys in the pack.*

Sadness, a sense of loss, settled over him. Sadness and memories.

Never mind, Reko. Not if it makes you uncomfortable.

He stared down at his toes and slowly shook his head. *It merely reminds me of what I've lost. I'm a man grown, but your question reminds me how very much I miss my mother. She taught us to read. She used to scour garbage bins for newspapers and magazines, a big, beautiful wolf risking her life so her children could be educated. We had to learn our numbers and letters and our mental voices had to be clear so that if we ever shifted, we would be able to converse as intelligent men. She was very smart, our mama. My greatest regret is that she didn't survive to see this world Ari and I have discovered.*

Jack's steady gaze never wavered. *I'm sorry, too, Reko. We can ask Eve if your parents passed through the veil where Eve lives. She might have news of their spirits.*

Reko nodded. *That would make Ari and me very happy. I would like to pursue that, when this mess with the demon is finally ended. But tell me, Jack Temple. How do men have sex? How do they make love with a partner who matters to them?*

He laughed, something Reko had discovered that Jack did a lot. He was a man with much joy in living. *With our mouths,* Jack said. *With our hands, with our cocks. There are many ways. Sit here.* He patted the bed beside him.

Reko glanced first at Mary. She still slept, so he moved to sit on the edge of the bed next to Jack.

Take my cock in your hand while I take yours. Stroke it in a way that would feel good for you and I'll do the same.

I don't know what feels good. Remember, I've only had these hands and this appendage for a few hours. Not enough time to get to know it all that well.

Excellent point. Follow me, then. Jack wrapped his hand around Reko's semi-hard cock and squeezed gently. Reko felt blood rushing through his veins, knew his prick was expanding beneath Jack's fingers. He groaned when Jack's grip tightened around his shaft, and he grew even larger. He took hold of Jack and slowly stroked him until his prick was standing high and hard—just like Reko's.

Like this?

Jack groaned. *Exactly like this.*

I like this. He held back a moan that wanted to escape. He had his pride to consider, after all. *What else can we do?*

I can take your cock in my mouth at the same time you take mine, or we can use the other orifice we have, and either you can insert your cock into me, or I can do it to you.

I wondered if that was so. When your prick slid over my ass, I felt it in my gut, as if I wanted you to go inside me there. When I touched Mary with my fingers, it felt perfectly natural to penetrate that opening as well. I think that is what I want to do next.

Okay. Jack gave Reko's cock one last squeeze and let him go. *Do you want to fill me, or do you want me to fill you?*

You. In me. I want to know what Mary feels.

It's not the same, but close, I think. On your hands and knees, or on your back, facing me?

I want to see you. I want to see the face of the man who fucks me.

Jack grinned at him. *I see your vocabulary is increasing.*

Smart-ass. I'll be on my back, waiting for you. And, for what it's worth, I have an excellent vocabulary. I merely like to maintain a certain amount of decorum, and both smart-ass *and* fuck *would warrant a nip from my mama.*

I can tell. Like I said, she raised you right. My mama would do the same when I was young. She might be tiny, but we never doubted her strength. Jack reached into the drawer in the bedside table and grabbed a small jar while Reko got himself situated on the bed, lying on his back with his knees bent, his feet planted flat on the rumpled bedding.

Jack glanced at him and frowned, then grabbed a couple of pillows that had fallen to the floor. *Put these under your butt to lift your hips up. It helps.*

Reko did as he was told and then lay back while Jack tended to him. He took his time, rubbing along the crease between Reko's ass cheeks, pausing at the tight opening and pressing there with the lubricant he'd taken from his jar. Jack's touch was magic, the way it made his body react, the sharp sense of need that grew with every little thing Jack did to him. Reko hadn't expected the level of excitement he felt, the need for Jack to press inside an opening he'd never once associated with sexual intimacy.

This human body had so many different attributes, but maybe he'd just never thought about them when he was a wolf. It definitely had more sensory nerve endings.

I'm going to stretch you a bit, so it won't hurt when I enter you.

That works. Reko tried not to tense his muscles, but the pressure of Jack's fingers sent arousal lancing along his nerve endings. He didn't even try to hold back the involuntary arch of his spine, or even the way his toes curled. He hadn't been expecting that. One thick finger entered his hole, then another. Breathing shouldn't be this difficult, but he was so caught up in the tactile sense of entry that it felt as if all those automatic senses like breathing and thinking just quit.

A third finger filled him, and this time Jack twisted them inside and rolled across something that made his prick stand even straighter, made his back arch and his body quiver with need. Jack scooted close and lifted Reko's knees, pushed his feet back close to his butt. Made him feel more naked. Entirely vulnerable. He lay there analyzing the feelings coursing through him. They were okay. He could do this because of Jack. Because he trusted him.

"I don't want to hurt you, Reko. Try and relax all your muscles."

He did. He honestly did try to relax everything, but when Jack pushed against that tiny little hole with his huge prick, Reko tightened every muscle he had. Jack didn't force him, but he didn't quit pushing. Slowly, in, out, and in again, barely putting any pressure on Reko's ass until suddenly, without any warning at all, the taut ring of muscle released and Jack's big cock slipped through, sliding deep inside Reko's body. There was a sharp burn that faded into warmth. A sense of fullness he should have expected.

A sense of connection to Jack he hadn't really understood. Not when they merely talked about this.

Both of them sighed. Jack ran his fingers across Reko's brow, shoving the hair that had pulled loose from its restraining band away from his eyes. "You okay?" Jack whispered, his voice low and filled with concern.

In answer, Reko lifted his hips and forced Jack deeper. This was amazing, this sense of fullness, of connection to another male. *I am,* he said, reverting once again to mindspeak. *How can we do this again and include Mary? I want all three of us connected this way. All at the same time.*

There it was again. Jack's beautiful smile. Just looking at him made Reko happy. *One of us makes love to Mary,* Jack said, *and the other comes in behind the one with her. All three of us in sync, all of us loving one another. That's one way, but there are others.*

I like that. We need to get really good at this, and then we need Mary.

Right now, Reko, I need you. Jack pushed Reko's long legs back against his chest and planted his hands against Reko's knees. The position opened him even more to Jack's steady thrusts, to the thick length of his prick deep inside Reko's body. This connection, man to man, was something he'd never imagined, and yet it felt every bit as right as when he had filled Mary. He glanced at Mary, expecting to see her still sleeping beside them.

Except she was wide awake, watching the two of them, plucking at her nipples with one hand, the other moving slowly between her thighs. Reko stretched out his arm, inviting her close, and she quickly scooted over to lie beside him. Then she reached for his prick, leaned in even closer and wrapped her lips around the dark crown.

He closed his eyes, awash in more sensation than he could easily handle. Awash in the love between Jack and Mary, the love they felt for him. It was more than he'd ever known, this kind of acceptance. All his life he'd hoped to one day find his pack, and now, so very quickly, they'd found him and made him one of them. He reached for Mary, lifted her as if she weighed nothing at all, and turned her along his chest so that she knelt over him, her knees beside his head.

She hadn't let go of him, still had him in her mouth while Jack continued his steady strokes. Reko knew he wasn't going to last much longer, but the least he could do was take Mary with him. Holding her thighs apart, he licked and nibbled at her sex, tasting once more the sweet flavors that seemed to drive him higher than ever. Her mouth on his prick, Jack taking him closer to the edge with every thrust, and his taste and scent receptors filled with Mary, Reko let loose of all semblance of control.

Jack must have sensed his growing arousal. He picked up speed, driving fast and hard, taking him to a perfect point where he hung in the balance between pleasure and pain. Mary sucked him deep, taking him into her throat, where the act of swallowing sent ripples of pleasure from one end of his prick to the other.

He sucked her clit between his lips. She pulled his prick from her mouth and cried out, her body almost doubling up against his. Gripping him in both hands, she worked his full length in perfect rhythm to Jack's short, hard strokes. Reko bucked his hips and cursed, Mary laughed and covered his spurting cock with her mouth, catching his seed. Jack's fingers dug into his hips and he arched his back and thrust his hips forward, going deeper still as he flooded Reko with his ejaculate. It felt as if he emptied himself a dozen times over deep inside.

It took a long time before they were able to catch their breath and take stock of what they'd done. Reko took one look at the rumpled, sticky mess of them and barked out a single laugh. That was all it took.

Jack rolled away to one side, holding his sides and laughing. Mary lay across Reko giggling, and Reko just lay there smiling. This was pack. This was what he and Ari had always wanted. Others to love them, others who cared enough to share laughter, to share love. This was what he'd wanted, and more.

He crawled out of bed and stretched out a hand. "We need a shower and we need to change the bed. Neither of you mentioned how messy sex as humans could be." Mary took his hand and tugged Jack along with her. They all trooped into the bathroom. Reko turned on the shower and the three of them stepped into the relatively large enclosure. His body felt ultra-sensitive, as if the climax they'd just shared had multiplied tenfold in the aftermath, and when Mary took the washcloth and gently swished it over his chest and belly, it didn't take him long to lift her high and bring her down on the erection that appeared to have no intention of going away. In his defense, he had a lifetime of celibacy to rectify. Her legs went around his hips and she settled against him while Jack finished rinsing the soap off of all of them.

He brought Mary to climax and followed her into his, his heart thundering and lungs inflating, mouth gasping for air. Mary laughed and kissed him. The pleasure of her mouth on his lasted mere seconds.

Pain exploded along his spine. Blinding, burning pain. Reko dropped to his knees, clutching at Mary to keep her from falling. Jack quickly caught her and grabbed Reko's arm to slow his fall. They all ended up on the floor of the shower with the water cascading all around.

Mary reached for the controls and shut the water off. Reko sat there on the tile with his head still spinning. When Jack went to speak, he held up a finger, silencing him. *It's Aldo. He's back. Do you hear him?*

Jack focused on the link he shared with Reko, and it was there, the slimy voice of the demon, taunting Reko, reminding Reko that he belonged to the master now. Threatening him with more excruciating pain should he disobey. Mary crawled into Jack's lap and held Reko's hand as the three of them listened to the demon's newest plan.

He was gone within a minute, but the essence of his visit left Reko slightly nauseous. They dried off in silence and Jack grabbed a clean set of sheets out of a closet near the bathroom. Mary went on ahead and stripped the bed, and they had it remade within minutes.

Mary crawled into the big bed and Jack and Reko got in on either side of her. "Should we let Anton know?" He stared into the darkness. "I hate to bother his sleep, though. It's almost two in the morning."

"Aldo wants you to kill the four men, so obviously he knows where both you and they are. Anton needs to be aware of that. Didn't Eve say she'd be listening for you?"

"You're right." He thought of Eve, and finally just spoke aloud. "Eve, Reko here. The demon Aldo came back. This time he sent pain, a spike of fire down my spine that dropped me to the ground. He wants me to kill the four men Anton is holding prisoner, among others. I'm going to try ignoring him tonight—we all need more sleep—but I wanted you to know he's returned."

He hadn't really expected a response, but a glow appeared at the end of the bed, and within a few seconds Eve stepped out into the room. "I'm sorry, Reko. I was hoping it would take longer, but thank you. I'll let Anton know and make sure he has extra guards on the men. They're all locked in separate rooms in the caves below the house, and pack members are taking shifts watching them. No one is alone with them, so I think you can sleep without worry. We can't let anything happen to them. They are where Aldo intends to find his strength."

She paused and stared off into the distance. "I've asked the Mother how to help you if Aldo tries to hurt you again. She will come to you in a dream—her power is much too great to actually show herself. I'm not sure what she has planned, but I know she'll protect you as best she can."

Within seconds she was gone. Reko lay back against the pillow with Mary's butt against his belly and her head tucked under Jack's chin. He tried to get comfortable, but there was just too much going on in his head. The Mother? Coming to him? And he was expected to sleep after an announcement like that? After a moment, he shifted. He'd slept his entire life as a wolf. Tonight he needed the familiar body before he could hope to relax.

Mary and Jack shifted as well, and the three of them curled into one another. Tuning Aldo down to a distant murmur, Reko slept. And he wondered if he would dream of the Mother.

13

Jack's cabin
Sunday, 5:00 a.m.

Reko awoke in the gray light of early dawn, yawned and stretched, stared at long arms stretching overhead and realized he'd awakened as a man, not a wolf. Sometime during the night he must have shifted. He glanced at Mary stirring beside him, beautiful even half asleep with her thick brown hair in wild tangles around her shoulders and her lips still kiss-swollen from the night before. It appeared all of them had finished the night in their human bodies. Jack was still out, dark hair mussed and flattened on one side, his lips parted and what looked like a bit of drool at the corner of his mouth. Reko almost wished for a camera, just to show the pack proof that Jack Temple wasn't pretty all the time.

Except that, even now, drool and all, Jack was beautiful to Reko.

His mind felt so fuzzy this morning, as if something teased the edges of memory. Not something, someone, but . . .

"G'morning, Reko."

He turned his head and then leaned over and gave Mary a kiss. "Good morning to you, too." He gazed into her brilliant blue eyes, quite different from most of the Chanku and Berserkers with their amber-colored eyes so like the wild wolves, and he remembered. "She was here, wasn't she? I'm recalling bits and pieces of my dream, but you and Jack were with me. Do you remember?"

"I do." Mary scooted up to lean against the headboard beside him. "She was beautiful, like a Nubian queen from olden times. Skin like obsidian—so dark! I've never seen skin that black."

"Her eyes were blue like yours." Reko ran a finger along her cheek to the corner of her eye. "I didn't expect blue eyes."

Jack shoved himself up on his elbows and glared at the two of them. "It's still the middle of the night. Why are you two awake?"

"Good morning to you, too, sunshine." Mary leaned over and kissed him. "We were talking about our dream visitor last night."

"She looked just like Queen Nefertiti, except her skin was darker. Honestly?" Jack shook his head. "She looked like a goddess should look. Crazy powerful."

"You're right about Nefertiti, Jack." Mary sat up and folded her legs in front of her. "Exactly like her. I've seen pictures of drawings from the pyramids. Of course, the Mother said it was a construct, that she couldn't appear to us as she really is because she's too powerful."

"I can believe that." Reko pulled his knees up and rested his cheek on them. "She said Aldo wouldn't be able to hurt me anymore. I've heard him ranting and raving in the background, but he seems surprised that I'm not doing what he wants me to do."

"Which is to kill the four men." Jack got out of bed and headed toward the door. "I wonder where he got the power to hurt you in the first place, 'cause that's a big step, from getting blown out of the cave to inflicting pain on a mortal. Back in a minute. If we're gonna be awake, I need to piss and I need coffee. In that order."

"And here I thought my mate was a morning person." Mary stared at the open door Jack had just walked through. She was smiling.

That was good. Reko had expected some awkwardness this morning after the intimacies they'd shared last night. If anything, it was just the opposite, all three of them appearing more comfortable with one another today. It made him think of Jack's parents, the way they made their triad work. Could that be what Jack and Mary wanted? He lay back and thought about it a bit.

He truly thought it might work for him.

His head and body were telling him it could be a perfect relationship, even though it was much too soon to be thinking of anything like that, but once the thought entered his mind, he had a feeling it wouldn't be leaving. "C'mon," he said. He got up, stood beside the bed, and grabbed Mary's hand. "Let's make it easy on him."

Mary sighed. "If we must." She cocked her head to one side and grinned at him. "I guess that means no more playtime in the bedroom?"

Reko slanted an innocent look her way. "You mean we're only allowed to play in here?"

• • •

Mary and Reko were both laughing when they got to the kitchen. Jack

157

was just pulling clean cups out of the cupboard and the scent of coffee was waking him up, bit by bit. He filled and handed cups to each of them. A few minutes later, Mary suggested teaching Reko to cook breakfast, which was what they were doing when Anton knocked on the door. It was barely six a.m.

Jack filled another cup and handed it to the alpha when Reko brought him into the kitchen. "What's got you out so early, Anton?"

He glanced at Mary and said, "We found out where Aldo got that burst of power that allowed him to hurt Reko last night. Eve told me what happened. Are you okay this morning?"

"I am. Thank you." Reko glanced at Jack and then added, "We met with the Mother during the night. She did something to prevent the demon from hurting me again."

Anton's eyes went wide. "You met with her? In person?"

"Not exactly," Jack said. "She came to the three of us simultaneously in a dream. We all saw a powerful woman with skin that was shiny black like obsidian. Other than the unusual skin color, she looked very much like images we've seen of Queen Nefertiti, right down to the headdress."

"Except she had blue eyes, like mine," Mary added. "At least she did in this version of herself. She said she can't show us what she really looks like because she's much too powerful."

"I can believe that." Anton shuddered. "She sort of leaks power whenever she's appeared. I can feel it, and it's so far beyond anything I can comprehend that I'm glad we've never had to look at her directly. I much prefer it when she speaks to me through Eve. That I can handle." He turned to Mary. "And that is why I am here. Eve spoke to me just a bit ago, Mary. I'm sorry. There's no easy way to say this, but your mother died last night."

Mary let out a long breath as both Reko and Jack went to her. "From her injuries? I thought she was getting better."

"No." Frustration evident, his eyes narrowed as he focused on her. "It was murder. Some charlatan contacted her at the hospital, said he'd been sent to exorcise the demon. She allowed him to come in, and the bastard killed her. Aldo was waiting and took her life force. The Mother had been watching her, felt her passing. She said your mom's life force was not very strong—she'd been weakened by both your father's attack and the death of your little sister. I don't think she wanted to live anymore, but she probably thought that by removing the demon from her soul, her energy wouldn't go to Aldo. He must have sensed her, known she was still alive. We believe the man who killed her might have been one of Aldo's minions, possibly from before his death. Aldo had a huge following while he lived. For all we know, they could be making blood sacrifices to him.

He's strong—stronger than he should be this long after his death. The life force of the Berserkers that died should not have carried him this many months."

Mary wrapped her arms around herself in spite of Jack and Reko holding her on either side. Jack felt her confusion, understood her ambivalence over her mother's death. She stared at the floor then she finally sighed and slowly shook her head. "I was looking forward to her coming here, to see what she was like without my father's influence," she said. "For missing that opportunity, I'm sorry she's gone, but any love I felt ended long ago." Mary leaned into Jack's embrace, but Reko still had his arm looped around her waist. He glanced at Jack and nodded. Jack acknowledged him with a tilt of his head. Already the three of them were forging a new connection.

"Understandable." Anton stepped close and kissed Mary on the forehead. "You will always have a home here, you know. You are much beloved, not merely by these two."

"Thank you." She glanced at Reko, then at Jack. "I've never known family the way I have here. Never felt so welcome anywhere else. Especially in my home. Even when I was young, I was apart from my parents. Any grief I feel is for the mother who gave birth to me. She loved me enough to give her life to save mine. Jack and I learned that during our mating when we bonded. I was so young, I'd completely forgotten what happened. The woman who adopted me lied about my origins, and turned her back on me when I really needed her. I'm sorry she's gone, but I'll not truly mourn her loss."

Her eyes swam with tears. She brushed them away. "I'll miss Becca, though. I'll miss her terribly. In spite of my parents' strange parenting, she was a sweet and loving little sister."

Jack hugged her against him and kissed the top of her head. *I love you,* he said. Then he stepped away from her and grabbed the coffeepot. "Anton, can you stay a few minutes? Have a seat. I want to tell you about our visit with the Mother last night and get your take on things. We're trying to figure out what to expect next."

· · ·

Jack's cabin
Sunday, 8:20 a.m.

Anton glanced at the clock in the kitchen. "Keisha's going to have my head. I told her I'd be back by eight." Reko had opened his thoughts to Anton, allowing him full access. For some reason, and in spite of the alpha's mind-reading skills, he couldn't pick up the demon's voice without Reko's invitation, but he'd not said much about what he heard.

Now as he stood to leave, he clasped Reko's shoulder. "I know you've said you're blocking Aldo, but have you listened closely to anything he's saying? What he wants you to do for him?"

Reko exhaled, knew he sounded disgusted. "All I hear is death and killing, and that he wants me to start with the four in the cavern. He knows where they are, but he doesn't have the power to do anything about them. Then I think I'm supposed to go after the Chanku and work my way through the pack, killing one at a time so he won't waste any of the energy."

"I thought that's what he was telling you to do, yet you're ignoring his orders. Why do you think he figures you'll do it?"

Reko merely shrugged this time. "I think he still believes I'm a wolf. He's never seen me in this form, only as a wolf. He also thinks I'm still reacting to the pain he hit me with before. That was pretty effective—he dropped me to the ground with whatever he did—but the Mother has done something to block that, so it appears he can't hurt me anymore. Even if he could, Anton, please believe me when I promise that it wouldn't matter what he did to me, I will not hurt anyone in your pack, including the four prisoners. I won't do anything to help the demon."

Anton appeared lost in thought as he moved toward the front door. "I've never doubted you, Reko. Believe me, if I did you wouldn't be here with Jack and Mary. I see you as an asset, not a threat. But Aldo? Now that he's a demon, I don't believe he has the same mind he had as a living man. I think he's always been crazy, actually, psychotic or even sociopathic are the words I'm looking for. Now that he's a demon he doesn't seem to understand the mortal world anymore, except how it might benefit him, but he's not picking up on clues that should have told him you're not a malleable creature, that you're a strong, sentient man. Maybe something got scrambled in the transition when he went from human to demon. I don't even know that he's truly demonkind. He could be nothing more than a construct, built entirely from the spell he cast the night he died, and the deaths of the twelve Berserkers who served him. Sebastian might have a better feel for him, since they fought magically in the cavern. I haven't asked him anything about his father's mental state, or if he could even tell what the man is like now." Raising his head, he glanced at Jack and Mary, and then turned to Reko. "Thank you, Reko. I'm sorry you're getting such a rude introduction to life among our pack, but I'm glad you're here."

He turned away then and went out the door, obviously distracted, probably still running all that they'd discussed through his mind.

Reko watched him walk away, Anton's head down in thought but his stride steady. The alpha respected him, something Reko had never imagined. He'd never thought beyond finding the nutrients, learning to shift, and now he thought of the experiences he'd had in the last four days. He wondered about his brother, if Ari had made his first shift yet. Anton hadn't said anything, and he'd not even thought to ask him.

He pulled Mary into his arms and held her for a moment. She wasn't his. She would never be his, but he knew he would always love her. He rested his chin on top of her head and gazed at Jack across the room. Mary's mate watched him with a smile on his lips. Reko smiled back. Yeah, he definitely loved Mary. Just as he would always love Jack.

• • •

Ari's room at Anton and Keisha's house
Sunday, 8:30 a.m.

Ari paced the wood floor in his room, the one next to where Sebastian and Lily slept. They were in there now, awake, their voices soft, their concerns over his inability to shift making it even harder to concentrate on his body, on what was going on with it.

Reko had shifted yesterday, numerous times, and Ari still didn't have a hint of how it should work. He'd tried looking into Reko's mind during one of his shifts, but there'd been nothing there but a huge black wall. He should have tried to speak to him afterward, but he hadn't, and that was his own fault. He'd been jealous, pure and simple. He was still jealous, and he didn't like this new side of himself. Reko never blocked him, but it might be something to do with the nutrients. He'd expected something to happen to him last night, but he'd awakened as four-legged, furry, and frustrated as ever.

So far, he'd not been as impressed with the people he'd met here as Reko seemed to be. Lily and Sebastian appeared to care for him, but they were mostly focused on the whole issue with the demon, as they should be. They were currently researching spells that might help them fight the demon in combat, if it ever came to that, which meant they were into some terribly intense work.

Ari felt more like an afterthought, but that left him with much too much time to think. Not always good for a guy who could find trouble wherever he looked. Reko was always the one looking on the bright side, while Ari knew he focused on the negatives. He'd heard of mirror twins, where they were identical but opposite in appearance. Maybe he and Reko had opposite personalities. Maybe that's why the two Chanku who watched over Reko seemed to be more attached to him than one would expect a newly mated pair to be. It was so much easier to love someone who was optimistic rather than a guy like Ari, who always felt as if he walked under a dark cloud.

It had all seemed so perfect in the beginning, at least once Reko was healed and Ari knew he hadn't lost his brother, but now? Now Reko was hanging all over that mated woman and her mate didn't have the balls to stop him. That was bizarre. If he ever had a woman of his own, he'd protect her with everything he had.

Reko said the demon talked to him. That was just wrong. Sebastian and Lily had said they could block the demon from his brother's mind, but they'd all decided to let the demon continue to have access to Reko, just so they could keep track of the bastard.

Did Reko have any say in that? Or were they just using him like a tool, something to make it easier to find and kill the demon, as if such a thing was even possible. Damn. There was too much going on to keep track of all of it, and he wasn't able to communicate directly with Reko without everyone else around. Was the pack purposefully keeping them apart? How could he ever find out, if that was the problem?

A soft knock on his partially closed bedroom door interrupted his thoughts, a welcome distraction to pull him out of his dark and convoluted musings. *Who's there?*

"Hi, Ari." Lily pushed the door open. "Sebastian and I are going down to the kitchen for breakfast. Do you want to join us?"

He thought about it a moment and wondered if he'd enjoy his meal more if he went out and killed something for himself, but Lily was kind to him even though he wasn't entirely sure what she was thinking most of the time. *Thank you. I was hoping to meet you as a man this morning. Maybe one of Keisha's delicious meals will help move things along.*

"One can hope. I wish I knew what was taking you so long, but we know you're one of us, so it's going to happen." She sighed and held the door wide for him to leave the room. "Unfortunately," she added, "I'm not a very patient person."

Neither am I, he thought. But he kept that one to himself.

• • •

Jack's cabin
Sunday, 9:30 a.m.

Reko helped Jack clean up the kitchen while Mary showered. It was interesting, how easily some things came to him, as if there was some sort of genetic memory that allowed him to know exactly what was needed for certain acts.

Like the sex he had last night and this morning with Jack and Mary, or the simple chores he was helping Jack with in the kitchen. His body had instinctively recognized the sexual triggers that aroused him when they were in a sexual situation, and now he knew exactly what was involved in drying dishes and putting them away.

"Reko, what do you think of going for a run today? The demon is quiet . . ."

"I know." Reko set a stack of freshly washed and dried dishes on the overhead shelf in front of him. "It doesn't even feel as if he's present right now. Nothing like last night, thank goodness. At least he's not invading my thoughts. That gets old, fast."

He rolled his eyes at that one and Jack laughed. "He really is a pain in the ass, isn't he?"

"That he is, and yes. I would love nothing more than a chance to run and explore this area. Would Mary like to go, too?"

Jack snapped his butt with the dish towel. "It was her idea."

Reko laughed and grabbed the towel and held it up. "I'll go, on one condition. You show me how you did that."

"How you did what, Jack?" Mary walked into the kitchen with her eyes on Reko and the towel.

"I want him to show me how he snaps it to make it sting. I can't pay him back if I don't know how it's done."

Laughing, Mary grabbed the towel. "Don't you dare, Jack Temple, because I know exactly whose butt will end up the target."

Rubbing his palm over the curve of her rump, Jack looked at Reko when he said, "But it's such a perfect butt, sweetheart."

Growling, Mary dropped her robe and shifted. She was out the door and gone before the guys had even stripped off their pants.

• • •

Mary loved nothing better than running through the forest here at the compound. It was mostly safe, though no matter where Chanku went they needed to remain alert. Even here they'd had trouble with poachers coming onto the well-marked property, but regular patrols kept most of the troublemakers out.

The trails wound through beautiful stands of cedar, fir, and pine, across bare granite worn smooth during the last ice age, along rushing creeks and others that slowly meandered through sunny meadows this time of year. Those would fill with wildflowers come fall. Oaks had sprouted new pale green leaves at the lower elevations, and clear spaces created sunny breaks where sometimes a herd of deer or even a mother bear with her cubs might be feeding.

There was no sign of human habitation once she entered the forest.

Mary was aware of the sounds of her men following her—they made absolutely no effort to be stealthy as they chased her down—but she also picked up familiar voices ahead. Slowing her headlong dash for freedom, she turned off the main trail to follow another that wound through rocky outcroppings and thick stands of aspen. She loved this area where she and Jack had occasionally picnicked during the friendship she'd not realized was Jack's subtle form of courtship.

She heard someone running toward her full tilt and stepped aside. The huge wolf tearing around the bend in the trail was easy to identify—Leo Cheval's wolf carried the markings of his mother's snow leopard. His white coat was covered with black rosettes, his ears and tale tipped in black. He snarled as he raced by her. Obviously Leo was not having a good day. Curious now, she trotted in the direction he'd come from.

Janine sat on a fallen tree, looking small and cold, naked with her knees pulled up and her arms wrapped around herself against the chilly air. She stared off in the distance, totally unaware of Mary's presence. Mary paused and watched her friend, noticed when Janine brushed her hand over her eyes. She was crying.

Mary trotted along the trail toward Janine and paused a few feet away. *Janine? What's wrong, sweetie? Did you and Leo have another fight?* When Leo had latched on to Janine at the very beginning, she'd clung to him then—all of them had been equally traumatized, terrified, and excited about this huge change in their lives. Sex slaves one day, shapeshifters with untold freedoms the next.

It had not been an easy adjustment for any of them, though Mary had learned to fit in surprisingly fast. She wondered how much of that had been due to Jack's influence. Probably a lot.

Janine turned toward her and shrugged. "Hi, Mary. I don't know if you'd call it a fight. I told him I wanted to break it off. After what happened the other night, I realized I'd had it, that he was too controlling. This is the first time I've seen him since Wednesday, but I knew it was time. He didn't take it well."

I wondered about that. He seems to have an opinion on just about everything and everyone you interact with. I wish you'd said something when Jack and I ran into you guys. I had a feeling you were biting your tongue the whole time we were walking back to your cabin.

Janine burst into laughter. "Thank you for that. I was, and you're right. It's exactly what I told him. I think he took his job of teaching me how to be a shapeshifter a bit too seriously. I kept telling him I wanted to experience things for myself, and he'd get angry and say that was stupid, that I shouldn't have to take risks. He didn't get it, that I need to take those risks to prove I'm still strong, that I can still do the things I want to do without a keeper." She shook her head. "He's a lot like his father, I think. Emeline warned me about Leo, that he liked to be in control, and at first I didn't mind because I was so scared of everything. It was all so new and wonderful." She shook her head in disgust. "I kept thinking someone was going to come along and make me leave, or tell me I didn't really belong here."

I'd shift so I could hug you, except it's still too chilly to lose the fur, but yes to that. I was so lucky to have Jack. He's never doubted my strength and pushes me to do more. Did you know we're mated?"

"No! Oh, Mary. That's wonderful!" Janine jumped off the log and put her arms around Mary, nuzzling the fur around her neck. "I really love Jack. He's a terrific guy, his parents are fantastic." She laughed. "And damn but his two dads are gorgeous men. I'm envious of Tala."

Jack and I are in a sort of temporary triad right now. You've heard about the two Berserkers that Ig and Fen rescued?

"I have. Everyone's talking about them, and about the fact that Sebastian's father is back and he's a demon." She laughed. "But you're in 'sort of' a triad? Explain, please."

One of the Berserkers, Reko, the one who was injured, has been staying with Jack and me. Yesterday he made his first shift. We sort of, um, introduced him to sex.

"And?" Janine's sapphire blue eyes, so much like Mary's, actually sparkled.

Mary's wolf huffed, the closest she could come to laughing. *I will say that the man is not only gorgeous, he's a natural.* She leaned close to Janine. *I think Jack and I are both falling for him. He's a truly amazing, honestly good man. They'll be here any minute. They're chasing me.*

There you are!

She turned at the sound of Jack's voice. Reko followed close behind, his wolf almost twice the size of Jack's. They didn't appear to mind the chilly breeze; both of them shifted, and Janine's eyes went wide when she saw Reko for the first time. Mary gave in and shifted, but she had to bite back laughter. The girls had all gotten used to the casual nudity among the pack—it was hard to avoid when clothing didn't make the shift—but there was a lot more of Reko than most men. So far, Janine was handling it pretty well.

"Hey, Janine." Jack walked over and leaned over to give Janine a hug. She was tiny, more like Tala than most of the other women, not much over five feet tall, and maybe a hundred pounds. "I want you to meet one of our newest packmates. This is Reko. Reko, remember when Mary told you about her kidnapping, when she was held prisoner? Janine was held by the same bastards that took Mary. They all escaped together. Of the six girls who were rescued, four of them turned out to be Chanku, and Janine's one of them."

Reko stayed back, but he nodded toward Janine. "It's good to meet you, Janine." He glanced at Mary. *Is she afraid of me?*

I honestly don't think that's fear, Reko. We'll talk later, okay?

He nodded and seemed to relax, but Mary noticed a hint of a smile on that sexy mouth of his.

They talked Janine into joining them for their run. Reko said he was hoping to see Ari out on the trail. Jack had mentioned that Anton and Keisha and a bunch of their friends were going to be running today, barring any issues with Aldo, and there was a chance they might cross paths. With that in mind, the four of them took off. Janine and Mary took the lead with the guys following close behind, racing for miles through the wild land. They hunted. Reko brought down a small buck. There was very little left for the vultures and ravens when they finished. Later they stalked rabbits, but with full stomachs they didn't try to catch any. After a long day of nothing but freedom, forest, and clear blue skies, it was only natural that Janine come back with them to Jack's cabin.

Mary thought of it as Reko's second lesson in Chanku social dynamics. He seemed fascinated by the various sexual positions afforded four people. Janine was freer and happier than Mary had seen her since they'd arrived here six months ago.

Later, when both guys were sound asleep, tangled in a masculine pile of hairy arms and legs, Mary and Janine headed out to the front porch, bundled in warm robes this time, each with a glass of dark red port wine.

"And you say there are two like him?" Janine giggled and took a sip of her wine. "Reko's absolutely gorgeous and he's a truly nice guy. I'm going to watch for his brother because it looks like this one is all yours. Have you seen the way he looks at you? And at Jack?" She stared out into the dark forest for a few seconds. "I really want a man to look at me that way someday. Like I'm the only woman he sees, but not one he has to protect so much as . . ." She turned to Mary. "I don't know. I guess I want respect as much as I do love. Is that so much to ask?"

"No." Mary shook her head hard. "We deserve respect. We're survivors. What we lived through kills a lot of women. Leo's a great guy and someday he's going to find the perfect mate, but he was smothering you. I think it's harder for you because you're so tiny. The guys see you and don't realize that your wolf is every bit as deadly as any wolf in the pack. They see this cute little blonde with a pixie haircut and big blue eyes and they figure you need protection. That you're small and helpless. I know you're not, and the right man will come along and he'll know, too."

"I hope so. Tell me about Reko's brother. I'm curious, now that I've seen Reko!"

"Ari's been with Lily and Sebastian since he arrived. It's all such a mess, and Reko's still not free of the demon, though he's been quiet today. Jack and I are locked into Reko so we can help monitor his thoughts and keep track of what Aldo's threatening."

"He's lucky to have you."

Mary shook her head. "Not as lucky as we are to have Reko. He's very special, and even though Jack and I are newly mated, we both feel as if Reko fits perfectly within our bond. I'm hoping he'll choose to stay with us." She turned to Janine and shrugged. "I love Jack's mom and his two dads. They've accepted me as if I were their daughter. I see the three of them, and I want what they have."

She gazed into the forest, thought about life with two men. Other than twice the laundry, she honestly couldn't see a downside. And Jack knew how the washer worked, right? Sipping her wine, she reached across the small space between her chair and Janine's and took her friend's hand. "He's out there for you, Janine. I just hope you don't have to wait as long as Sunny!"

"Yeah, but she got Fen. Some things are worth the wait."

Mary tipped her glass to Janine's. "Truth," she said.

Janine's softly whispered *truth* echoed Mary's.

14

Ari awoke from a sound sleep. Something had awakened him, but he
wasn't sure what. He hadn't been dreaming . . . at least, he didn't think he
had. He lay there on his round pillow on the floor, listening to the silence
in the big house, searching for any sound that didn't fit. There were
sounds, but they were merely the house speaking its own language—the
hum of electronics, an old clock that ticked, the occasional creak of wood
as it contracted from the cooler night air and the subtle movements of the
ground as the earth breathed beneath them.

He trotted over to the sliding glass door beside his bed. It opened onto
a large deck that ran across the back of the house. The door was open for
him—Lily was thoughtful that way—and he stepped outside.

There was barely a sliver of moon tonight and the stars were a
magical river of twinkling lights flowing across the ebony sky. He
searched for Reko's thoughts, but there was only darkness where his
brother's mind had always been. Had shifting into a man changed him
that much, that he no longer needed that lifelong connection to his twin?
They'd never gone so long without speaking, at least not since this long
journey had begun, but then, a lot of things had changed.

For one thing, this sleeping inside on a comfortable bed was much too
easy to grow accustomed to. He wondered where Reko slept. Was he in
the same bed with the two who watched over him? Now that he could
become a man, had they welcomed him into their mating bond? Sex was
so open here, but Lily had explained that it was because of the shifting,
that it had a serious impact on a person's libido. His had been fairly quiet

168

all his life. Without a female to draw his interest, he'd learned to ignore the occasional urges of his body. He'd like to ask Reko about that. There were a lot of things he wanted to ask Reko.

He wished his brother had come to see him today, but there had been no sign of him. Of course, he'd not been here for much of it. He'd run today with Lily and Sebastian, with Anton and Keisha and their close friends Stefan and Xandi. Run with the largest pack of wolves he'd ever been with, and it had been magnificent! They'd hunted and brought down an older doe, one that was large enough to feed all of them. There'd been no fighting over the meal, no calling rank before feeding. Stefan and Xandi had made the kill and they'd taken the first bites, but they'd quickly invited everyone to join them.

People here were nice—so nice they made him nervous. It wasn't normal to accept strangers into your home, into your lives. Not without knowing more about them. He really wanted to talk to his brother. He needed to get his take on this pack, on the way they'd taken two strange wolves in so easily. How they seemed to trust them without any reservations at all. It wasn't normal. Not normal at all.

He walked quietly across the deck, not easy with his nails clicking against the wood, but he reached the steps and jumped from the top one to the soft dirt at the bottom. Everyone was exhausted after all the activity the past couple of days. He didn't think anyone had heard him, so he raised his nose to the sky and drew in a deep breath. The night called him. A little run would help him get back to sleep, and if he sniffed out Reko's scent, maybe they could talk. He wished he'd asked where Jack's cabin was. He only knew the one where Jack's parents lived. Silently, he trotted around the house to the main trail that ran through the little village of cabins and headed toward the mountain that towered over this beautiful valley.

• • •

Jack's cabin
Monday, 1:40 a.m.

"You sure you don't want to spend the night?" Mary finished off her port and grinned at Janine. "It's really toasty in that bed with Jack and Reko putting off heat."

Janine laughed at that one. "Hon, the sex was amazing. Two guys and you? I don't think it can get any better, and Jack's got a big bed, but he and Reko—especially Reko—are big boys. I'd be hanging on to the edge of the mattress all night hoping for a soft landing." She set her empty glass aside. "My place isn't that far, and honestly? I need some downtime. It was pretty intense with Leo today." If she were totally honest, it had been intense for the last few months. Why had she stayed with him so long?

"What set him off?"

Janine stared at Mary and then figured it couldn't hurt. She hated saying anything bad about the guy, but he'd finally just gone over the top. "I said something about wanting to explore the caverns with Sissy. Annie and Alex offered to take us through them when they've got some free time, and I said I'd love to go. When I told Leo, he said absolutely not, under no circumstances could I go into the caverns, that it was too dangerous and Alex wasn't all that trustworthy."

"Alex? I'd trust Alex or Annie with my life. I mean, they helped get us out of that hellhole, they risked their own safety for women they didn't even know. That's a stupid thing for him to say. What did you say to him?"

"Exactly what you just said, only not as nicely. It was sort of the proverbial straw, ya know?" She hated confrontation, but he'd had no right to give her orders like that. "Leo'd been nitpicking about stuff from the time we took off on our run, little things about me hanging out with Sissy all the time, and wanting to go back to school. The thing is, Mary, I really want to get my teaching credentials. I love kids, and I think I'd be terrific teaching middle-grade math." She laughed at Mary's shocked expression. "Hey, it's the one subject I was really good at. I love numbers. Anyway, Leo said that I was being foolish, that there were enough teachers here. Then when I mentioned touring the caves, and he put his foot down . . ." She rolled her eyes. "His hypothetical foot because we were both wolves and running while we were having our *conversation.*" She made air quotes around the word with her fingers. "I had enough of that attitude with our pimps. Do *not* need it with the man I'm choosing to sleep with."

"You made the right choice." Mary took her hand, which was unusual for her. She wasn't usually all that touchy-feely. "A lot of those things that you have issues with? They're red flags to tell when you're in an abusive relationship. I took advantage of the therapy the pack offered, and one of the things they talked about was how to recognize a potentially abusive relationship. Did you go?"

Janine shook her head. "I was going to, but Leo said I didn't need to, that I wasn't weak like the others." What an idiot she'd been. "Like any of you guys are weak. Did everyone else go?"

Mary nodded. "Yeah. We wondered why you didn't, but you were always with Leo. You might want to mention some of the things he's said, how he's acted with you, to Annie. She'd know if you should report it to Anton. He'd want to talk to Leo, maybe do a little one-on-one about how not to treat a Chanku alpha bitch." She laughed. "I take that label to heart. Keisha said the guys really can't manipulate us unless we let them, that they're hardwired to acknowledge our strength. Best thing ever about being a shifter. It's like we have our own set of really big brass balls that we can pull out when we need them."

Janine just about choked. Then she stood and slipped out of the robe. "On that note, my darling, I'm going home to my own bed." When Mary stood, Janine gave her a long, hard hug. "Thank you. I had no idea how much I needed girl talk. And sex. The sex was really good. Please tell the guys thank you for me. I think I need to hunt down Reko's brother."

"You should. Get him first before some other single female stakes a claim."

"That sounds so mercenary." She shifted, but then she paused and looked over her shoulder at Mary. *Probably why I really love the idea. Thanks!*

She took off down the trail toward the cabin she shared with Sissy. Of course, Sissy was rarely in their cabin. She and Mac had a sort of friends-with-benefits relationship, one that was a lot healthier than what she'd had with Leo. And that was a shame, really, because basically he was a good man, but Mary was right. He'd been smothering her. She was so ready not to be smothered. Not by anyone.

She noticed movement up ahead and wondered if it might be Leo. She really didn't want to see him right now, especially not with the scent of both men and a woman on her. Not that she didn't enjoy it herself, but Leo might not agree, and she really didn't want another confrontation. As she caught up, she realized it was definitely a wolf, and he was huge.

She got a little closer and he stopped. Obviously he figured out he was being followed. Janine stopped as well, about six feet behind him. This had to be Ari, Reko's brother. Even in the darkness she could tell they were almost identical. *Are you Ari? Reko's brother? I'm Janine, a friend of Mary and Jack's. I met Reko tonight.*

Met him and fucked him, it appears. He turned around and faced her. *His scent is all over you.*

That I did. He's a really nice man—and wolf. Did he get all the good manners in the family?

Ari growled. She probably should have been afraid, but she was still pumped up after her talk with Mary. The image of big brass balls came to mind.

Well, it's been . . . interesting. Nice meeting you, I think. Good night, Ari. She trotted past him and was almost to her cabin when he ran up beside her and stopped.

I'm sorry. That was uncalled for.

Apology accepted. She cocked her head and stared at him for a moment. *It can't be easy for you, coming into the pack in the middle of all the problems with the demon. And Reko said you hadn't shifted yet. I'm sorry. That's got to be frustrating.* She paused at the bottom step leading to her front door. The cabin was dark, and there was no sign or scent of Sissy. *This is where I live. Do you want to come up? I'm not really ready to go to sleep yet.*

He stared at her, long enough to make her uncomfortable. Then he shook his head as if he might be shaking off a bug or something. *I was rude to you, yet you're still inviting me into your den?*

You apologized and I accepted. C'mon up. She trotted up the steps to the small deck, shifted and opened the front door. "I'll shift back once we're inside, if it makes you more comfortable."

Please don't, he said. *I like hearing your voice. I like the way you look in this form, too.*

Janine smiled and winked at him, and then stepped inside. He followed her into the house and gazed around the small main room attached to an even smaller kitchen. The bedrooms, at least, were larger, but she wasn't planning to take him in there. At least not as a wolf. She left the front door partially open in case he wanted to leave, but he walked into the living room and leapt carefully up onto the couch. Sitting there on his haunches, he leaned against the curved back.

Janine sat at the other end of the couch and threw a soft afghan over her body. She was trying to remember if she had anything clean to put on, but she hadn't done the laundry today, and the blanket was going to have to do. Besides, she remembered something Reko had been talking about during their run. "I've heard a little bit of your story from Reko," she said. "Did you know he's been trying to contact you? He said it's like there's a block between your thoughts and his. Have you tried to reach him?"

No. I thought he was ignoring me on purpose. He's tried to reach me?

"He has. In fact, we went for a long run today looking for you, but you must have been in a different part of the forest."

I've tried to contact him since I last saw him. Nothing has worked.

"That's odd. Your mental voice is very clear to me, but then I'm sitting close to you. When was the last time you were able to communicate with Reko?"

When he first shifted at the pack alpha's home. He spoke as a man but switched to his wolf voice. I spoke as a wolf and we had no difficulty understanding one another. After that, I don't think we've actually had a chance to speak to one another. He sighed, and realized it sounded very much the same as when the humans did it. He hated to think he might look weak to this beautiful woman, but she was kind, and she was listening to him. She might even be able to help. *I miss my brother,* he said. *We've never been apart, yet here we're in a strange place with people who, even though they are kind, are still strangers to us. I don't like being apart from him.*

Janine scooted close to Ari and wrapped her arms around him. He was a massive wolf, and yet he leaned into her embrace and his huge body went limp as he relaxed beside her. She couldn't imagine what he must be feeling, separated from his only surviving family. She'd heard about his losses—parents, brother, and sister. There really were very few secrets within the pack.

"You can stay here with me, Ari. Tomorrow I'll take you over to Mary and Jack's place and we'll try and figure out why you and Reko can't speak to one another the way you've always done. That's just making everything even harder for you."

Janine, what does it feel like when you're getting ready for your first shift?

She hugged him even closer, opened her thoughts and her innermost feelings to him. Ari seemed lost, and she couldn't help but sympathize. She'd been lost for so much of her life. Lost until she'd been found. *I was one of the women who'd been kidnapped and sold as a sex slave. That's how I met Mary. She'd been taken, too. After we were rescued by members of this pack, I started taking the nutrients and we were almost positive I was Chanku, but until I actually shifted no one could be certain. I'd always dreamed of the forest, of running like the wind, but I never imagined what those dreams meant. The day I shifted, it was as if I found out who I was meant to be. I had value where I'd always felt as if I had no worth at all. And it was so odd. One moment I had no idea how to turn into a wolf, and then it was as if the instructions were right there, hardwired into my brain. I shifted, and when I looked in the mirror and saw my wolf, I wanted to cry. I was so beautiful. Strong and finally free.*

She rubbed her face against his thick fur. "I think that, when we're meant to be more than one creature, we're never truly free until we can reach inside ourselves and find that other self. When I'm a wolf, I'm a lot braver than when I'm a human."

Ari shivered within her embrace. She pulled back and looked into his amber eyes. "Do you know how? Are you ready?"

I think I might be. While you were talking, I felt myself falling into old dreams I had of walking on two legs. I'd forgotten about them, but in my dreams I saw Reko walking beside me. We were both very tall.

"Come over here by the fireplace. I'd hate for you to shift and fall off the couch!" Laughing, feeling Ari's excitement along with her own, she led him over to the soft rug in front of the hearth. He sat on his haunches, and then stretched out on his belly, panting. She felt his excitement as if it were her own, knew his nerves were strung tight, but before she had a chance to get nervous with him, the beautiful wolf before her was suddenly a very large, very naked man.

"Oh, Ari. You've done it." She wrapped her arms around him as he sat up and drew her into a tight hug. His big body shuddered and she knew he wept. She worried a man like Ari would see that as a weakness, so she didn't say a thing, but she didn't let go, either. She wanted to look at him, to see if he resembled Reko or if he had a look totally his own, but he held her as if he really couldn't turn her loose. They sat there, Ari sucking deep breaths, his body shaking, clutching Janine as if she were his lifeline, though he was easily twice her size.

Finally, she couldn't stand it. Janine leaned back from his broad chest and smiled at him. Tears streaked his face, but he ignored them, staring into her eyes and probably seeing her as a woman for the very first time. She remembered the differences when she was first a wolf, the increased sensitivity to scents and sounds, the dull colors that looked more like black and white and shades of gray, while for Ari it was just the opposite. Now he'd see colors brighter, hear sounds a bit muted, scents not nearly as sharp. He would if he looked, anyway, but he didn't look around the room or anywhere else but at her.

Probably the same way she looked at him. He was unbelievably beautiful. Every bit as large and handsome as Reko, Ari somehow had a wilder, more primitive look about him, though that might be because Reko had that day of learning to be human ahead of his brother. She realized she was stroking Ari's shoulders, running her hands over his chest and learning the contours of his body. Slowly, she backed out of his arms and he let them drop to his sides. Then she stood and held out her hand. "I've got a mirror in my room. Come. I want you to see how amazing you are."

He smiled at that and his eyes actually twinkled when his lips curved up at the corners. "That requires that I walk on two legs without falling."

His voice was even deeper than Reko's, smooth and so sexy it made everything between her legs clench and release and then tighten up again. Moisture trickled down her inner thigh and she squeezed her legs together. She'd been a prostitute before she was kidnapped, had twice as much sex as a sex slave, and regular sex with different guys in the pack, and she'd never once responded to a man this way. "We'll take it slowly," she said. "And I have to tell you, your voice is really sexy."

He laughed, and that sound went straight between her legs, too. She wriggled her fingers, still holding her hand in front of him.

He took her hand but didn't use her help at all to stand. If he had, she figured he'd probably have pulled her over, but he uncurled his long legs and rose until he was towering over her, at least a foot and a half taller than she was. Her much smaller hand completely disappeared inside his grasp. If she actually thought about the size difference, she might have been terrified, but she'd had his twin brother inside her just a few hours ago, and that had been absolutely perfect.

Leading Ari into her bedroom, Janine closed the closet door to expose the mirror mounted on the front. Ari stood there for the longest time, staring at his image. Then his focus switched to Janine standing beside him. She knew the moment it registered that she was just as naked as he was, and that his new body was attracted to her.

It wasn't easy to ignore an erection as big as his. Flaccid directly after his shift, he was bigger than a lot of men when aroused. Right now, he actually looked even larger than Reko. Turning slowly, he swept his hand over her short pixie cut. She watched the two of them in the mirror, looking beyond the size difference to see the man himself. He was so gentle, the way he touched her. His body had gone from slightly interested to fully aroused in less than a breath, and yet he touched her as if she were made of spun glass, his large hands barely brushing over her shoulders, along her arms. When he palmed her breasts, his large hands covered her. He rolled her turgid nipples between thumbs and forefingers. She moaned, lost in sensation as he stroked and explored her body.

Walking over to the bed, she tugged his hand so that he'd follow and made him sit on the mattress with his long legs over the side, extended out from the bed. Grabbing a pillow off the bed, she shoved it between his feet and knelt between his legs.

"What are you doing, Janine?"

His voice sounded strained. Good. That's exactly how she wanted him. "I'm going to show you one of the things this body of yours can do. I think you're going to like it." Smiling, she palmed his inner thighs and ran her thumbs up the creases where his legs met his groin. Then she leaned close, grabbed his cock at the thick base with one hand and pointed it toward her mouth. He watched her, his eyes glittering as she swept her tongue across the weeping slit and tasted him. He clutched the bedding on either side of his thighs and a deep moan echoed up out of his chest.

Palming his sac with her free hand, she gently rolled his testicles between her fingers. His breath hitched in his chest and his body jerked. Wrapping her lips around his glans, using her tongue to tease the sensitive spot where his foreskin connected beneath the broad head, she gently showed him exactly what a small woman with a talented mouth could do.

She'd never climaxed before from giving a man oral sex, but knowing that this was the first time for Ari, that he had absolutely no practical knowledge at all of this body, of what it could feel, what it could do, was probably the most intense turn-on she'd ever felt. Her arousal built, lick by slow lick, until he grasped her shoulders with his hands.

"Inside," he said. "I want to do this inside you. Reko and I have talked of this, and we both knew that if we were ever in this body, if we were ever fortunate enough to find a woman who pleased us, that we would want to find our very first release within her."

That's perfect. She slipped his erection out of her mouth and crawled up on the bed. "How do you want me? You on your back with me on top? Me on my back with you on top? Me on my hands and knees with you behind me?"

• • •

He laughed. Not in his wildest dreams had Ari ever imagined a scenario like this, a beautiful woman he'd never met before tonight helping him through his first shift, somehow understanding his fears and yet not making note of them, merely being there while he worked through the feelings and the odd senses of this new body.

And now she was willing to take him into her body, to give him pleasure he'd not even known how to imagine. But she was waiting for an answer, and there were too many options. "All of them," he said. When she laughed, he couldn't stop laughing either, because all the stress of the past days and weeks, months and years felt like nothing compared to the astounding sense of coming home, the welcome and the passion he felt with and for Janine, such a tiny, sparkling woman. There was such life in her! "I want to do everything with you," he said. "You'll have to show me how. Show me what I need to do to make this feel perfect for you."

She was so generous, lying on her back, pointing out her various body parts and how they corresponded to her wolf, showing him what his were called, and what he could do with everything. Not so very different from his wolven body, but that one had never had sex, either.

She showed him where to touch her, how to give her pleasure. Then she smiled at him and he thought his heart might explode with all the unfamiliar emotions that shot him through and through. He touched her, and he was so careful because her skin was softer than anything he'd ever touched. He remembered his mother teasing him when he was a pup, telling him how much she loved his soft tummy, and he wondered if Janine's skin was like that, soft like a young pup's belly. He stroked her breasts, rolled one nipple between his thumb and forefinger, and yes, her skin was just that soft, though her nipple was taut, the flesh wrinkled and darker than her skin. She arched her back and thrust her breast against his hand. Taking the hint, he tugged, not as gently, on the little bud, and she moaned.

That was a good sound, so he did it again and then she arched her hips and wrapped her hands around his prick and actually glared at him. "Now," she said. Her breath came in soft little pants, her eyes had a glazed, almost starry look in them, and he knew he would never, ever be able to deny her anything. He took himself in hand and placed the broad head of his prick between her thighs, and all he could think was that he didn't want to hurt her because she was so tiny, hardly bigger than a child, though he knew she was a woman grown. Slowly, gently, he pushed against her, and she was so slick, her tissues buttery soft and wet, that he ached with wanting her, but feared hurting her even more.

But she raised her hips and grabbed his and she was stronger than she looked, rising up and forcing him deep. He slid inside, and the walls around his prick were alive, grabbing hold like a warm fist, clasping him as if she used her hand to stroke him. He never would have believed he'd fit, but he slid through her hot, wet depths so easily, and when he hit the end of her channel, she didn't scream in pain.

No. She sighed. And then she began to move, raising her hips beneath his, showing him how to move inside her. He followed her lead, using muscles in his lower back and thighs that must have been developed specifically for this act. She licked her lips and he wanted her tongue tangled with his, so he kissed her, long and deep, and she whimpered into his mouth. Still her body moved beneath his and her hips rolled with each thrust he made.

When her climax came, he watched in wonder as her lips parted, her eyes squeezed shut and a deep flush spread across her fair skin. Arching into him, she drove him deep and deeper still. Knowing she had reached her peak, he let himself go and it was like leaping from a high cliff into darkness and then light. Brilliant flashes of light. He had no idea where he might land, or even if he would survive the fall, but he knew he would not be the same man after this.

His life had changed. He was changed, and Janine had made it all perfect.

She snuggled close to him and within seconds was asleep, her lips against his throat so that he felt the tiny puffs of air with each breath she took. His body had never felt this sated, this totally relaxed. For the first time since coming to this pack he felt as if the future might actually hold something good for him. Reko certainly believed it, but it had taken Janine to bring Reko's hardheaded brother over to his way of thinking.

Ari lay there grinning. Reko was going to have way too much fun once he found out that his brother had not only made his first shift, he'd found a woman who seemed to actually like him. He knew he liked her. A lot, but he needed to get some things worked out before he could think about any kind of future with a woman he'd barely met. Morning would be here soon enough. He'd ask Janine to take him to Reko. She knew where his brother was staying. He and Reko needed to get together, figure out why they couldn't speak to one another the way they always had.

Something was interfering, but he had no idea what it might be. He let his mind drift to thoughts of the woman in his arms. He'd never been so close to a female, never imagined what a male and female could do together. He let his thoughts fly free, until they ran into that same black wall, like a dark curtain that stopped them. Stopped everything.

• • •

Jack's cabin
Monday, 5:38 a.m.

Jack? Mary? Is Reko with you?
Jack sat up at Anton's frantic call. Reko was lying on Mary's other side, rubbing his eyes as Mary jerked awake as well.
Yeah. He's here. You woke us up.
Has he been with you all night?
Frowning, Jack glanced at Reko. *Yeah. I got up to take a piss around three and he and Mary were getting it on. What's up? Why do you want to know where he's been?*
Two of the prisoners were killed about an hour ago. Aldo got their life force. Adam and Doc Logan were on watch when a huge wolf that looked like Reko raced past them and tore out the throats of two of the men, the brothers named Derek and Eagan. He was gone before either Adam or Doc could get to him. They tried to catch him but lost him in the woods. No idea where he is.
Ari, maybe? He looks just like Reko, but why would he . . . ?
Wait for me. I'm coming there. We need to find him, but I don't want to hurt him. Whatever happened, I doubt it was Ari's idea. It appears Aldo has taken over a new wolf.

• • •

Janine's cabin
Monday, 5:45 a.m.

Janine rolled over and snuggled next to Ari. He was so big and warm beside her, his body like a furnace on this chilly morning. She crawled over his chest and kissed him. His arms came up around her and he held her close.

"Good morning, beautiful." He kissed her, a deep kiss that took advantage of her sleepy surprise when he used his teeth and lips, his tongue and his hands to bring her wide awake. She moaned into his mouth and he rolled her over beneath him.

His hands were everywhere, stroking her legs, her back, her throat. He kissed her over and over again, using his knee to force her legs apart. She opened her thoughts to him, wondering what had brought on this rough but totally sexy approach, but his thoughts were blocked to her.

Instead, there was a dark wall where the bright light of his mind should be. The same darkness he said he'd seen in Reko? Ari grabbed her shoulders and held her flat to the bed. He gripped his cock in his hand and pressed against her slit, pushed against her and slid inside. He groaned, but when she looked into his eyes, the man staring back at her could have been a stranger. "Ari? What's going on?"

He frowned. Shook his head as if he was shaking off a fly. His grasp on her shoulders released, and he looked down at their joined bodies, frowning. "Janine?" He shook his head again. "I'm sorry. I don't remember this. I don't . . ." Slowly he pulled out of her and rolled away. He stared at the doorway and suddenly stood and walked into the front room. Janine jumped out of bed and followed him.

She found him standing on the front porch staring at a scattering of dark flakes in front of the door. She flipped on the porch light—dawn was approaching, but she couldn't tell what he was looking at. Going to her knees, Janine sniffed and immediately recoiled. "Ari, this is blood. Did you go somewhere last night? Because this looks like you were covered in blood when you shifted. That's what happens when we've got stuff on our fur. When we shift, it all falls away. What happened?"

He stood there, his face twisted in confusion, in fear. Janine walked closer and put her arms around his waist and held him, but after a few moments he shoved her away. "No, don't touch me. I'm remembering things. Horrible things." He turned to her and his face was twisted with whatever thoughts he—

"I think I killed someone last night. Those men in the caves? I think I killed at least one of them, maybe two. I didn't even know where they were, but I remember killing men, ripping their throats, but why? What would make me do something so horrible? I need to find Reko. He'll know what to do, he'll . . ."

"Ari. Come inside. We need to talk. Please?" She took his hand and tugged. He followed her as if he had absolutely no will of his own, and when she walked with him to the couch and pointed at the leather cushions, he sat. "I'm contacting Anton. He'll know what to do."

"He'll kill me." He shuddered and stared at the floor. "I won't fight him. I deserve to die."

"No, he will not kill you. He's our alpha for a reason. He's smart and we trust his judgment."

Ari shook his head. "Those two men's deaths will empower the demon."

"Ari!"

He recoiled when she shouted, but at least he turned and looked at her. Really looked, and she knew she had his attention.

"Stop it. Anton's on his way. He's bringing Reko with him, and probably Mary and Jack, too. Come on. We both need some clothes and I want to put some coffee on."

She grabbed a pair of sweatpants Mac had left on the hook by the back door. They'd probably be too short, but that couldn't be helped. Mac Cheval was tall, but not anywhere near as tall as Ari. She went into her room and pulled some yoga pants and a sweatshirt out of the laundry basket and headed into the kitchen.

Ari sat at the kitchen table with his head in his hands. He looked broken. How could such a perfect night as last night end up like this? She walked over behind him and wrapped her arms around his shoulders. Leaning close, she kissed the side of his neck and nuzzled the soft skin under his ear. "You're mine, Ari, and I will not let anyone hurt you. Just answer Anton's questions and I'm going to tell him about the black wall in your mind. Because it's there, Ari. I felt it when I tried to speak with you earlier. If you did anything last night, it wasn't you. I'm convinced it was the demon. We'll get through this, but you've got to have faith. And promise me you will always tell the truth. No matter how awful it is. Anton will listen."

He shook his head. "I don't even know the truth. I barely remember what happened."

She kissed him. "It'll be all right. Please, don't worry, Ari."

They both heard them at the same time, Anton, Jack, and Mary coming up the front steps. Janine looked at Ari. Both of them closed their eyes and he held both her hands against his chest when it was obvious their three visitors were standing out front, staring at the pile of dried flakes of blood in front of the open door.

15

Reko raised his head and it was like looking into his own eyes. "Ari? That's you? But when?" He pushed past Anton and went straight to his brother. "Good goddess, Ari. When did you shift, and why did you . . ."

When his brother rose and just stood there, speechless, with tears rolling down his cheeks, Reko wrapped his arms around him and held him close. What a nightmare, but it had to be the demon. Aldo had been suspiciously quiet for the last day or so, but how could he have gotten hold of Ari? "Don't worry, Ari. We'll figure this out. Anton's here and he's called Sebastian and Lily. They were up at Sebastian's house, but they're on their way."

Anton stepped into the cabin and Ari raised his head and moved out of Reko's embrace. He went straight to Anton and dropped to his knees in front of the alpha, bowing his head. Reko felt his brother's shame practically rolling off of him in waves. His gaze flashed from Ari to Anton, and the sadness on the alpha's face almost brought him to his knees as well.

Anton gently stroked Ari's head for a moment, and closed his eyes. Then he knelt before Ari, just went right down on the floor in front of his brother, and pulled him into a tight hug. After a moment, he drew back and rested his hands on Ari's shoulders.

"I am so sorry this has happened to you. Somehow, some way, you are now hosting the demon. Reko? Do you have any idea when he might have left you?" Anton stood then, reached down and took Ari's arm and gently tugged until Ari stood. All of them moved into the kitchen and took seats around the table, but Ari still didn't meet the alpha's eyes.

Reko sighed and took the chair next to his brother, but he focused on Anton. "Aldo was such a nasty constant that I sort of blocked him out and let him rattle on in the background. He was there Saturday night when he zapped me with that sharp pain, and Sunday morning when you stopped by Jack and Mary's. You heard him then, right? When I let you in?" Anton nodded, and Reko continued. "Okay, but I didn't notice him at all when we ran."

Janine walked over to the counter and grabbed the coffeepot, then returned to the table and pulled out the chair beside Ari. He wondered how his brother had ended up with Janine. It had to have happened shortly after she left the bed she'd shared with the three of them.

She didn't appear to be paying attention to him as she filled cups she'd lined up for each of them, but after she'd filled them for everyone, including Ari, she stopped and, with one hand on her hip, looked right at him and said, "Reko? Would you do something for me? Would you try and mindspeak with Ari? He said he's been unable to reach you since shortly after you shifted."

"Really?" Reko sent a typical brotherly insult to his brother. He didn't react. "Ari? Are you blocking me? Try speaking to me."

Ari stared at him for almost a full minute. Finally, he shrugged. "I've not been able to see or hear your thoughts since you shifted. It was okay in the beginning, but I tried to link with you when you were shifting. I wanted to see how you did it, but all I saw was a thick black wall. I figured it must have something to do with the shifting." He shrugged and looked away. "I was jealous. I didn't try speaking to you again. I'm sorry."

"I don't blame you, though I do wish you'd said something. But that's all I see when I try and talk to you now. Darkness instead of the usual sense of light when we speak without words."

"Ari? You say you tried to link with Reko during a shift?"

"I was curious. I thought if I could see what he saw, I might be able to shift, but there was nothing there. Just black where I usually see light."

"That blackness might have been the demon following a mental bridge between you and your brother, or maybe just forging one to use at a later time. There's no denying you're closely linked—twins of both human and Chanku pairings often share a connection that the rest of us can only find in the mating bond. I'm not certain, but Sebastian and Lily might be able to figure it out. Aldo was stronger after the death of Mary's mother, and it wouldn't take a lot of energy to slip between minds that were completely open to one another. Ari? Did you notice any difference in your feelings about people or what was happening? Did your viewpoint change at all?"

He thought about that for a moment and then hung his head. Reko moved close and put his arm around his brother's shoulders. "It's okay, Ari. I knew I had the demon, so I was aware of wanting to be angry at everyone, and then I had Mary and Jack to help carry that burden." He rubbed his forehead against Ari's, the way they'd always done as wolves. "It's not easy to cart a demon around in your mind, brother."

"But I killed two men, yet I don't remember going to the place where they were held. If you asked me to go there, I might not be able to find it. How did I get into the cavern? The only way I know is through your house, Anton. You would have heard me. Someone would have."

"You're right." He paused, his brow furrowed, considering. "Just a moment."

Reko watched Anton while he silently communicated with someone. After a moment, he nodded. "I just spoke with Doc Logan. He said the wolf came in from the tunnels. There are any number of entrances on our property, so you must have come in from somewhere higher on the mountain, which means Aldo was actively directing you. He owned the property next to this for many years, so I imagine he's familiar with many of the cave entrances."

"Why don't I hear him now? How do we know if he's still in me?"

"We don't. That's why we're waiting for Sebastian and Lily."

"Why don't we go to them, or at least to your house," Janine said. "That was the last of my coffee, and there's nothing in the refrigerator for me to make breakfast." She smiled at Ari and Reko. "These are very big boys. I need to stock up!"

"Excellent idea." Anton stood and turned to Janine. "I'm going back now to help Keisha throw some things together and give you and Ari time to find some clothes other than just the pants. It's cool out this morning. I doubt there's much around here that's long enough for his legs." He laughed softly. "It appears I need to add a shopping trip to the schedule."

"I'd love to see that list," Jack said, pretending to whisper to Reko. "Make breakfast, get the demon out of Ari, shop for extra-long pants and shirts, kill the demon, take Keisha out to dinner . . ."

Anton merely shook his head. "I should probably put taking Keisha out to dinner at the top of the list. She loves taking care of everyone, but I need to spend more time taking care of her. Jack, Mary? I'll walk you back to your cabin in case you need to get anything. Let Reko and Ari have a chance to talk, and then we'll go eat way too much before we get busy on what needs doing. I have a feeling we're going to need that big breakfast before this morning is over."

Ari watched the three of them leave before turning to Reko. "He doesn't blame me. I don't understand. Why?"

"You've done nothing wrong, Ari. You had no idea the demon had taken over, you were under his control entirely. When Mary's mother died, he got more energy and that's probably what gave him the strength to control you."

"But I killed two men. They didn't have a chance against a Berserker bent on death!"

"Their lives were already forfeit. They were complicit in trying to blow up this part of the country. I have no sympathy for them. I'm just sorry you didn't kill all of them, but then Aldo would be even stronger. The demon had already claimed them, just as he's claimed the two who are still alive. They swore their fealty to their Master Aldo. One of those still alive is Mary's father." Reko shook his head. Mary was so torn by this. She hated being part of it, hated the man who was her father, if only by adoption. "I doubt he'll survive the coming battle, and believe me, there will be a battle. We need to be prepared." He hugged Ari, and Janine joined them, wrapping her arms to encompass both men.

"Being prepared means being strong. Ari, are you okay with the sweats you're wearing? I've got a big hooded sweatshirt that might fit you. I think it belonged to Tinker. He's not as tall, but he's really big. Talk to Reko. I'm going to shift to clean up. I don't want to take the time for a shower. I'll get dressed and be out in a couple minutes."

• • •

Anton and Keisha's home
Monday, 7:45 a.m.

Jack and Mary showed up at Anton's about the same time as Ari, Reko, and Janine. Sebastian and Lily had arrived a few minutes earlier and immediately latched on to Ari, most likely to search for the demon. Stefan and Xandi were putting the last dishes out on the buffet, Keisha was running the show, and Anton was at the bar in the Pentagon, hiding out. At least that's what Jack accused him of when they stopped in to see why he was there.

"She ran me out," he said, laughing softly. "I'm much better at cleaning up than cooking. Jack, you can help me bus tables after everyone eats, okay?"

"Whatever you need, Anton." Then he took a seat at the bar with Mary beside him. "Is there a plan to get the demon out of Ari? I know Reko's worried sick about his brother. He said that the whole time the demon was in him, he had Mary and me to lean on. Ari's doing this alone."

"I know. I've thought of asking if Janine would be willing to share the burden, but I'd rather just boot the bastard out now and get this over with. We erred by allowing him to remain in Reko."

His voice broke and he looked away, so unlike Anton, who always said he preferred to meet problems head-on. But now? Jack hardly recognized him like this.

"We underestimated his strength, never a smart move in any confrontation." He focused on Jack once again. "I have to take responsibility for that because it was my call. In my defense, what little there is," he said and cursed softly, "none of us realized he might move to Ari without our knowledge. We felt it was more important to know where he was, what he was planning. The situation now is much worse with Aldo empowered by the two deaths, so it's time to take him out permanently. If we can."

He stared out the big window facing the mountains for a moment, then sort of shook himself and focused once more on Jack and Mary. Jack wondered what Anton was thinking. It was obvious before he admitted it that he blamed himself. Not really fair, considering that none of them were versed in dealing with demonkind, including their alpha.

"We can't fight the demon until we get him on his own." Anton stood taller, resolute now that they were finally planning to act. "But we'll be ready the minute he's out. I've had the pack on standby. We're going to put out the word that I'll need energy available as soon as Sebastian and Lily do the exorcism, which is exactly what this will be. Lily just contacted me, said she and Sebastian have confirmed that Ari is definitely playing unwilling host to the demon. He's in there, though she can't tell how long since he took Ari over. Getting Aldo out of him is going to be tricky, and I won't lie to you. It could be dangerous for Ari. We'll be sure he understands that before we begin."

"What if he doesn't want you to do it? What if he's afraid?" Mary's blue eyes were wide, her fear for both Reko and his brother radiating off her tense body. She looked at Jack, though her words were for Anton. "I keep thinking how afraid he must be. This is all such a huge change for both of them. Ari's horribly upset about killing those men." Jack wrapped an arm around her shoulders and held her close. There wasn't much else he could do, not when he was every bit as worried as she was.

Anton shook his head. "We will never do anything to one of our pack against his or her will, but I have no alternative to offer. I'm afraid that if we don't remove the demon, Ari might attempt to take his own life, rather than harm anyone here. The demon was strong enough after taking the life force from Mary's adoptive mother to make the move from Reko to his brother. With two more deaths, I don't know how anyone could fight his compulsion. Ari's honor runs deep, as deep as Reko's. I want both of them whole and healthy. The pack needs them." He smiled and focused on Mary. "I think you and Jack need them. At least, you need Reko, and Reko needs his brother. Somehow Reko completes you. It happens rarely, but when it does, it's wonderful to witness."

Jack thought of his parents, that they weren't the only healthy triad in the pack. There were a couple of others who made it work as well. So many different pairings—couples, triads, even Ig and Fen and their mates in a quad, and yet all of them were, for the most part, harmonious. There were occasional disagreements even among the traditionally mated, but basically everyone got along. It was hard not to when you knew what your partner was thinking. There was no hiding problems, and that was a good thing.

"Dad?" Lily stepped into the room with Sebastian beside her. "I think we've figured out how we're going to do this. Before you argue, hear me out first. Okay?" Anton folded his arms across his chest, making it clear he'd listen, not that he would necessarily agree. Lily copied his stance and glared at him. Jack had to bite back a grin. Did all parents have trouble seeing their children as competent adults?

"Just listen, Dad. Face it, my magic's stronger than yours, but you're better at channeling power. You've had more experience with that. Right?"

Anton chuckled. "Yeah, like the time I burned out half my brain?"

Lily's aggressive stance melted and she hugged him. "That was a learning experience though. Do you agree?"

"I agree. And you're the one who saved my butt, so I'll listen." He smiled, unfolded his arms and planted his hands on the granite bar. "What's the plan?"

"You call on the pack for power since you're linked to everyone, only you channel it to me, not you. I catch it and hold it. I can hold a lot of power. Sebastian does the exorcism and you link with me, grab what he requires and feed the power from me to him as he calls for it. We have no idea how much he's going to need, so you'll have to stay in tight contact with him. You're the conduit between us. We do this in the cavern with Eve standing by in case we need her help. He's got a solid exorcism spell that should work without harming Ari. We're going to have Reko anchor him—the fight-or-flee instinct could kick in and we don't want him hurting himself or anyone else. He specifically requested his brother's help."

She paused and took a breath before glancing at her mate. Sebastian stood there looking so damned proud of her. Jack loved the dynamic between the two of them. Lily smiled, and continued. "We don't have any idea what will happen once Sebastian pulls Aldo out of Ari. Sunny and Doc Logan will be in the cavern so we have a medical team on hand for Ari, in case Eve is tied up and can't help him should he need it. I want both Liana and Adam on the surface in case they're needed for medical intervention up there. The thing is, the exorcism itself should be fairly simple, but once Aldo's out, we're going to have a very pissed-off demon who's juiced up on fresh energy. There could be power surges, and if Aldo breaks free of Sebastian's hold, goddess only knows what chaos he could cause.

"We'll have a trap and a bucket of salt to bury him in once we catch him. Of course, we're assuming that he has some of the properties of demons, and salt should control him, at least until we can destroy him. Igmutaka, Fenris, Star, and Sunny will be in the cavern with us. Ig and Fen can go spirit if they need to fight Aldo in that form, and we can channel power to them, but Sebastian will be wielding the power we get from the pack and working the spell to contain him once he's out, so hopefully it won't come to that. The Mother will be on hand to observe. She can't take part. One of those stupid god and goddess rules."

"Are you sure you can handle that much power? The pack is larger and this isn't a very scientific method for powering a machine."

Lily practically growled. "Which is good, because we're talking about sexual energy powering magic to fight a demon. I'm not sure that science is even remotely involved." Then she actually had the nerve to wink at her father. "I'll handle it, Dad. I have to. Mom's going to stay with me. She's got her own magic and we work well together. She tends to even mine out when I need a leveling influence."

"Will your mother be in any danger?" He shot a quick glance toward the hallway, where the sounds of meal preparation and conversations carried from the kitchen and dining area. "I really don't want to risk your mother in any . . . ."

"Dad." Lily forced him to look at her. "Stop thinking like a husband and father. You have to put that aside. We are all in danger. The entire fucking world is in danger, and it stops here. There's not just a risk for all of us who want to fight this bastard, there's a risk for every inhabitant of this planet, beast or human and those of us in between, if we don't stop Aldo. I've never heard of a demon who gains strength from the life force of those he kills, but if he succeeds in destroying most of the life on this planet, there will be nothing that can stop him. It's beyond imagination what he could be capable of—he could evolve into something totally and permanently unstoppable. None of us knows what could happen if he starts feeding from the massive number of deaths from an apocalypse. Not you, or me, or the Mother, or any of those gods who tend to look at us as game pieces on a very large chessboard."

Jack had been glued to Lily's face, caught up in her impassioned plea to their alpha. This was, at this moment, her alpha, not her father, she implored. Then Keisha walked into the room and all eyes turned toward her. She was a beautiful woman—tall and regal as any queen, with unimaginable power perfectly hidden behind her kind and caring nature. He was so used to Keisha's warm hugs and home-baked cookies that he often forgot she was the alpha's bitch, the one person in the pack that even Anton deferred to.

Her magic wasn't like Anton's, Lily's, and Sebastian's; wizards all, they worked the kind that needed spells. They drew their energy from the world around them, from love and sex, and the living energy of all creatures and even inert substances like rocks and soil and running water. Keisha's was magic sourced from a caring heart and a need to do the right thing for those she loved. Anton had once said that his mate was the strongest sorceress he'd ever known, and there were few who would dispute that.

Now, she simply paused in the doorway and smiled at all of them before focusing on Anton. "My love. You will listen to your daughter, and I will help wherever I am able. Now, enough of this. The meal is on the sideboard and you all should come in and fill your plates and your bellies."

With that, she turned and walked back to the kitchen. Anton merely looked at Lily, and the two of them grinned at each other. With a shrug and a shake of his head, Anton looped his arm over Lily's shoulders and walked with his daughter and her mate out of the room.

Jack held tightly to Mary and thought of the power those three represented, the hope he had that they would succeed. And then he thought how much more he now had to lose than he had just five short days ago.

• • •

The cavern beneath Anton's home
Monday, 10:45 a.m.

"Listen up." Anton stepped to a spot close to the open portal to the astral so that Eve could take part in the proceedings. Once again Jack noted that she was dressed for battle, her long hair braided and wrapped around her head, her clothing stretchy, fitting close to her body and totally serviceable. She carried a short sword in her right hand with a small crossbow looped over her left shoulder.

"We're going to start this in ten minutes." Anton gazed about the large cavern. "Stef and Xandi will stay in the house to coordinate pack energy. We'll be in constant communication."

"Those two might as well be mated," Lily muttered. She wasn't kidding. The bond between Stef and Anton was closer than mates, closer than brothers.

"Just about everyone is here. Waiting on Rem," Anton said, glancing about the cavern. Doc Logan, Sunny and Star and their guys, Ig and Fen, stood off to one side. Tinker McClintock was here with his two sons, Mike and Ricky. The two men were still "the boys" in the minds of the older pack members, but both of them were huge, even bigger than their father.

They were powerful men, all three of them, and over the years had become an important part of Anton's army, if there could be such a thing within the pack. Every single adult member had the ability to fight to protect this, their home, but Anton rarely asked. He hated putting anyone in danger.

Tinker and his sons didn't wait to be asked. They merely showed up. Always.

Exactly like Keisha. Jack watched her, standing quietly in the shadows. Even from his spot across the cavern, he could see that her entire focus was on her mate. Anton occasionally glanced her way, and Jack swore he could feel their connection, as hot and bright as any magic.

Jack glanced toward the back of the cavern, where the last two prisoners were being held—the one called Brother Thomas, and Mary's adoptive father, Ryder. He wondered how Mary was dealing with this. No matter what her feelings toward the man, he was the only father she'd ever known, but her thoughts were blocked, not because she was keeping him out, but because there was so much going on in her mind right now it was impossible to find a single cohesive thread.

He was going to be so fucking glad when this was over.

Still, as if she'd picked up Jack's concern, Mary glanced toward the area of the cavern where her father was locked up. "Is someone guarding the prisoners? I'd hate to see their deaths give more power to the demon."

"Tinker and his boys are going to keep an eye on them," Anton said. "We're leaving them down here as much for bait as anything. Their presence should keep Aldo close enough for Sebastian to be able to overpower him once he's out of Ari." He turned to Tinker and his sons.

"Tink, I want you and the boys back with the prisoners before we start this. Sebastian has no idea how long it's going to take him."

"Got it. The boys are going to stand guard as wolves. They'll be able to sense the demon's presence faster than if they're human." Tink nodded toward his sons, who had already shifted, and the three of them walked to the back of the cavern, disappearing down a narrow tunnel.

Ari and Reko stood off to one side, as if unsure where they should be. Janine waited beside Ari, holding his hand. Anton walked over to them and they spoke quietly for a moment. Then Anton hugged each man— Reko first, and then Ari. With Ari, he stood a moment with his hands on the taller man's shoulders, while Ari nodded as if agreeing to whatever Anton was saying. Reko stood by, a solemn expression on his face. Jack shivered, struck by the sense of how wrong this was, that after wanting the ability to shift all their lives, Ari and Reko had finally gained that ability, only to be faced with such horrible danger.

He silently prayed to the Mother as the brothers followed Anton to a spot near the water's edge and sat on a smooth section of polished stone. Reko settled behind Ari, prepared to hold his brother. Anchoring him? Jack wasn't certain, but from the serious expressions on both men's faces, Anton must have explained the risk. Janine sat off to one side, not touching Ari. There was probably too much danger for her to get too close.

A few moments later, Remington Caruthers stepped into the cavern. His head was still bandaged, but he looked a lot better than he had last night. He remained their official link between the Chanku Nation and the FBI, essentially sanctioning whatever happened here today.

"Anton?" He paused in front of the alpha. "Before this gets started, do you want me here where you're doing the exorcism, or should I help Tink keep an eye on the prisoners?"

"They're probably your primary responsibility at this point. I've already lost two of them on my watch."

"Don't blame yourself for that, or Ari either. The only one to blame is Aldo." Rem patted his shoulder holster, checked the handgun's position. "How about I take a spot in the doorway between here and their cells?"

"Good. But be careful, Rem. I like you. I'd hate to have Aldo decide to take up residence in our only human."

Remington chuckled. "I'll remember that. I'd hate to have Aldo move in even more than you would." He moved into position by the doorway.

Anton closed his eyes and tilted his head back. After at least a full minute, maybe longer, he opened his eyes and smiled. "One of the best orders I can give, for the pack to get down to the business of creating sexual energy. Lily, I'm going to let it build before I channel it to you. I want to be sure I have enough to create a solid pathway. You okay with that?"

"Definitely. Just don't let it build too much. I'd hate for you to knock me on my butt when you redirect." She took hold of Sebastian's hand and lowered herself until she sat cross-legged on the smooth stone at the water's edge. Glanced at her father and grinned. "It would totally screw with the diva image I'm working on."

Anton shot her a quick grin, but it was obvious he was somewhat distracted. The sense of magic was already growing, so strong now that even the totally non-magicals in the room felt it. The ancient indoor lake was shallow but constantly refilled from sources farther up the mountain. Its smooth surface slowly broke into ripples, as if the air above the water stirred. Lily, her father, and Sebastian had always agreed there was magic here, that the water had magic; the cavern with its portal to the astral was a magic unto itself.

But now? That magic was growing, coming in from all directions, flowing into Lily at Anton's request, where she would hold on to it until Sebastian had need. They still weren't sure how much power it would take. Sebastian had explained his thoughts to them the night before—he'd been studying demons, trying to figure out what kind Aldo might be. He'd come to the conclusion that Aldo was unique, not at all typical of demonkind. Since his existence was built entirely on the life force he'd stolen from the dying Berserkers the night he and Sebastian fought, everything he did now was to give himself more time, one desperate chance after another to survive as a living entity.

It could be very difficult to end him. On the other hand, once they destroyed what functioned as his soul, there should be nothing left. He would finally, truly die.

At least that was the theory—and the plan. Sebastian set an industrial-sized bucket of salt on the ground near the brothers, and beside it a small metal box. He'd explained how it was made of lead and he had a spelled lock that might just make it harder for the demon to escape. That was assuming they could get him inside the box in the first place.

Then he moved to a spot about three feet from Reko and Ari. He took a huge amethyst crystal out of a cloth sack and held it carefully in both hands. It was at least a foot long, with a diameter of about six inches. He lifted it up in front of his face as if he were a rock star and the crystal his microphone. His lips touched the crystal as he murmured too softly for the words to carry. The crystal glowed in his grasp, and after a full minute of some sort of incantation, he slowly pivoted the huge crystal and pointed it at Ari. A silver stream of light flowed from the pointed end of the crystal and spread out over Ari's body like crackling lightning looking for a way inside. Ari's eyes went wide. Reko tightened his hold on his brother and dug his heels into the smooth rock. Janine sat quietly, one hand covering her mouth.

A flash out of the corner of his eye caught Jack's attention. He glanced at Lily, sitting just behind and to the right of her mate. She'd taken the lotus position, legs folded, hands resting on her knees with her palms up. Her head was tipped back, her slim neck arched and her entire body glowed a deep golden shade. Her palms appeared to be filled with more of the golden glow, and power radiated off her slim muscles in shimmering ripples of energy.

Keisha had taken a spot directly behind her daughter, very much the way Reko now supported Ari. She had her hands on Lily's shoulders, her eyes closed, head tipped back. The power radiating from Lily seemed to spread over Keisha, but with her the golden shade took on many hues, until Jack realized it wasn't merely power he was seeing, it was the auras of both women, strong and beautiful, flashing with life and purpose, and more strength than he could possibly imagine.

Anton moved to sit beside his daughter. Resting his hand on her shoulder created a physical link that allowed power to move visibly from Lily to her father, a sparkling web of what looked like electrical charges crawling over their arms, from her body to his. Anton raised his right hand and held it toward Sebastian, with his fingers clenched in a tight fist.

Slowly, Sebastian set the crystal aside, the tip still pointed at Ari with lightning flashing within the purple facets. He studied the crystal a moment. "Ari?" Sebastian spoke clearly, his voice carrying above the audible crackle of power. "You okay? Whatever you do, don't shift."

"I won't. I'm okay. Do it."

Sebastian straightened, stretched his left hand out to hold on to Ari's, and reached back for Anton and shouted, "Now, Anton. Now!"

Anton opened his hand and grasped Sebastian. Power flashed between them, a golden arc from Lily to Anton, from Anton to Sebastian, and all of it poured into Ari. His body stiffened and he cried out, the long, agonizing howl of a wolf in distress. It raised goose bumps across Jack's flesh, had Mary curling against him, crying out in pain for their lover and his brother. Janine screamed and curled into a tight ball beside the men.

Reko's hair stood on end as the energy spilled over from his brother, but whatever the spell, something was definitely happening. Darkness spilled out of Ari, a thick cloud of black, oily smoke from his mouth, his eyes and ears, and still he howled, his wolf afraid, howling his fear.

The last bit of darkness stretched as if it tried to hold on to its host. With an audible whoosh of sound, it snapped free of Ari. Sebastian pulled back, but he held tightly to Anton and the two men stood as one, reaching for the curling, swirling blackness that was once Aldo Xenakis. Eve was with them and Lily stood to join them. Instantly they built their net, this one designed to hold a demon instead of human prisoners. Sparkling fibers of energy flashed into existence around the swirling mass. Igmutaka and Fen blocked his way to the prisoners in the back, and Remington held his position.

The moment Sebastian cut contact with Ari, the Berserker collapsed in his brother's arms. Janine crawled close to hold them both.

Mary and Jack moved as one, racing around the edge of the pool to Ari and Reko. Both men were unconscious, but at least they were breathing, though Ari's was labored. Jack looked for Sunny and Logan, but they were with Keisha. She'd gone down as well. Lily was channeling power to the others as she helped hold Aldo in their net, all of them drawing it tighter, shrinking Aldo's mass down to a fraction of its original size. Eve worked with them. She must not have seen Ari fall.

Jack had never helped anyone in medical distress, but he'd felt the ability growing in him, knew that if he didn't try to help Ari he'd never forgive himself. "Watch Reko," he said to Janine. "Mary, I'm going to see what I can do for Ari. I think I can do what Sunny and Logan do. I want you to watch over me while I'm inside."

"Hurry. I felt it, when we mated. I'm positive you have the gift. Go. I'll be here."

He sat close to Ari and placed his palms on the man's chest. Felt the erratic heartbeat, the irregular patterns in his heart, closed his eyes and willed himself inside. There was no sensation at all, but when he opened his eyes, Jack was there, deep within the chambers of Ari's heart.

And he had absolutely no idea what to do next.

16

Eve, I'm in Ari. His heart is fibrillating, you know, racing and then stopping and racing again? There was no one else to help him. How do I get it to work right?

There were no words, but suddenly he *knew* exactly what to do. But the knowledge came with the Mother's signature, not Eve's. Of course, Eve was trying to control the demon right now, helping Sebastian and Anton and Lily. It was only sensible the Mother would answer him, though totally unexpected.

But he was here, and he was Ari's chance, and it really was a fairly simple thing to do. Carefully massaging a particular muscle seemed to relax the frantic beat, and a touch to the right bundle of nerves, the *push* of energy to force them into compliance, and Ari's irregular heartbeat went from crazy to sluggish to absolutely perfect.

He stayed there a moment longer, making sure everything else was okay, and then he merely thought himself back into his body and he was sitting there, with his hands on Ari's chest, and the big man was lying there, smiling at him. Janine was at his other side crying and laughing, Mary hung on to Jack's arm with tears in her eyes, and Reko was awake, shaking his head in disbelief.

Mary glanced at the battle going on so close to them, where the wizards and their goddess were slowly but certainly bringing Aldo under control. "We need to get Ari out of here," she said. "He's still weakened from whatever the demon has done to him. Jack, can you and Reko carry him into the house, where Aldo can't see him?"

"I will carry my brother." Reko ran his fingers through Ari's hair. "He's carried me often enough."

"That's because I'm older than you."

"By two minutes, which makes me that much younger and stronger.

And better-looking." With a quick glance at the battle taking place, Reko knelt and slipped his arms beneath Ari. When he stood, his muscles bulged and he steadied himself before taking a step. "Lead the way," he said, and followed Janine and Mary out of the caverns and up the steps into the house.

Janine led them down the hallway, looking for an empty guestroom. Mary and Jack stopped in the kitchen to raid the refrigerator. Jack hadn't worked inside Ari for long, but he was shaky from hunger. Mary reminded him that Jace had said it took a lot of energy to do even a simple healing, and she filled a huge platter with sliced beef and cheese. They took it with them and found the room where Ari was lying on a bed.

They sat there, all five of them, feeding the machine, as Jack thought of it. This was far from over, there was still a nuclear device out there somewhere, and as far as they knew, Aldo hadn't been truly dealt with yet. But Ari was alive, and Jack knew he'd helped heal him. He hadn't been wrong. He'd always thought he could do it, but he'd never had the opportunity—or the nerve—to try. He wished he'd had the nerve to help Remington when the bullet grazed him. He knew better now. He'd saved Ari.

Thanks to the Mother, he hadn't failed.

• • •

The cavern beneath Anton's home
Monday, 11:40 a.m.

Sebastian was vaguely aware that Reko was carrying Ari out of the cavern, which was good thinking on their part, because he wasn't sure the four of them were going to be able to hold on to the demon. With the energy from the two men that died early this morning, Aldo was stronger than he'd ever been, and he desperately wanted the two prisoners that still lived.

Energy still flowed to them from the pack, a steady power that appeared to be endless. Anton's and Lily's—and now Sebastian's—was powered by love, by the physical expression of that love. Eve's just *was,* though she gratefully used whatever energy they shared with her. The sexual energy that the pack was currently providing would never run out. They loved, and when they loved, when they expressed that love physically, they could energize the world. With their Chanku sex drive, the odds of running out of sexual energy were pretty low.

It all depended on how Sebastian used that power. Right now he was helping Eve, Lily, and Anton shrink the net holding his father's demon spirit, forcing Aldo, within the net, down to a manageable size they could shove into that lead-lined box and then bury the whole thing in salt. It should hold him for a while, at least until they figured out what to do with him. Oddly enough, it was a silent battle. The crackling of magical energy, the sound of sparks snapping were all he heard.

He saw Keisha rise with help from Sunny, and the two moved back out of the way. Doc Logan slipped around beside Eve and flipped open the lid on the box. The net crackled and flashed with power, and the demon fought desperately as Sebastian, Lily, and Eve took over and slowly twisted the strands tighter.

As the net grew too small for four of them to easily work together, Anton handed his strands off to Lily and went straight to his mate. He held Keisha close, but the two of them were ready to help if they were needed. Lily continued to pull power from the pack, but now it was a simple thing to share it among the three of them. As long as Eve could pull from it, she could remain on this plane and not lose her strength, and there was no sign of their source of energy running out.

Anton had set their packmates up around the country so that they timed their lovemaking to keep a continuous line of sexual energy coming to the three wizards. Stefan and Xandi remained in the house, helping to coordinate those who, due to distance and the vast number of contacts, had to be organized by direct calls rather than Anton's mental orders.

Sebastian nodded to Eve, who turned her strands over to Lily. They'd finally gotten the net compressed to an area smaller than the box. Working carefully, Sebastian and Lily folded the strands over and over again until Aldo was little more than a golf-ball–sized lump of seething dark energy. Still wrapped in the glowing net snapping and crackling with power, Aldo's anger was a palpable entity in the cavern. Carefully, they placed the mass into the box that was half filled with salt, and Eve slammed the lid closed. Sebastian set the spell-protected lock and tucked the key in his pocket.

The silence was extraordinary. No one said a word. Physically and mentally exhausted, they all just sat there and stared at the box. Remington sauntered over and stared at it along with them. "You know," he said, "that was pretty damned impressive. But we still have a nuclear device out there somewhere."

"That has occurred to me," Sebastian said. "Any ideas where to look?"

"Can we question a demon?"

"Not really. He's totally incapable of telling the truth and he knows we intend to destroy him, so there's no incentive for him to tell us where it is."

Ig and Fen wandered over. "When we got rid of the last nuclear device, we transported it telekinetically into molten rock beneath the volcano, where it melted. What would happen if we were to do the same thing with Aldo?"

Sebastian raised his head, searched for Eve. She sat in the opening to the astral with her feet hanging over the edge into the cave. Close enough to hear them, but enough in her own world where she could recharge. "Eve? Would that work, what Ig's suggesting?"

"I've already asked the Mother. I'm waiting for her answer because I honestly don't know."

Keisha brushed off her hands against her long skirt. "I really don't want that thing in the house, so I'm going upstairs to get some lunch together and I'll bring it back down here. Give me a few minutes. Sunny? Want to help?"

Sebastian watched the two of them heading out of the cavern and turned to Anton. "How the hell does she do that?"

"Do what?" But he was smirking.

"Fight demons, get knocked out by a sexual power surge, come to and immediately want to feed everyone."

"Are you hungry?" That was Lily, of course.

"Well, yeah. I'm starving. Aren't you?"

"I am, and I bet Eve is, too." She glanced at Eve.

Eve raised her hand. "Starving goddess here."

Remington pushed away from the wall he'd been leaning against. "I didn't do anything, but I can always eat."

Tinker and his sons wandered back into the cavern. "Prisoners are hungry, too."

Sebastian shook his head and laughed. He turned to Remington. "That's Tinker's way of saying he and the boys are hungry and they just might eat the prisoners if no one feeds them."

"I guess when you can turn into a wolf that's a pretty good possibility." Rem stared at the box holding Aldo for a long time. "What's with the salt?"

"Demons don't like it," Sebastian said. "At least that's what our research tells us, though it's hard to do serious research on something most people think's a myth. I figured we'd use the salt to cover any bases we might be missing. I've got more if we need it."

"He had me pick up a ton of it when Mom and I did a big shopping trip a few days ago." Lily might be teasing, but her expression was thoughtful. "The guy at the store must have thought we were both nuts, Mom and I lugging huge industrial-sized bags of salt to the check stand."

"You could always make jerky." It was obvious Remington was trying not to laugh. Finally he raised his head and made eye contact with Anton. "Please tell me this is not a normal Monday for you folks."

Anton just shook his head. "Demons are a new twist, but there's always something going on. Tink, why don't you and the boys help me grab a couple of those collapsible picnic tables. Keisha and Sunny will be down here with a five-star meal before you know it."

The three of them headed toward the storage room between the cavern and the stairs into the house. By the time Keisha and Sunny, along with Stefan and Xandi, Janine, Reko, Ari, Jack and Mary, were back, all loaded down with food, tables had been set up and the rest of the guys working up top had come down to join them for lunch. Remington and Tinker carried sandwiches back to the two prisoners. Eve had gone to wait on the astral, but she stepped back into the cavern and took a seat at the table by Lily.

Sebastian had found a larger box that he filled halfway with salt, set the one holding the demon inside it, and poured the rest of the salt over the top. It made it a lot easier to sit and enjoy a meal among friends and family. For now, at least, they had the demon under control.

Unfortunately, they still had no idea where the nuclear device had been hidden.

• • •

The cavern beneath Anton's home
Monday, 1:15 p.m.

A bunch of the guys cleaned up the mess after lunch, and then Anton called a meeting. Doc Logan raised his hand, and when Anton acknowledged him, asked how they could have a meeting down here without the bottle of cognac. "It's not easy," Anton said, "but be strong, Doc. You can handle it."

"Yeah, but what about you?" Doc grinned at Keisha, who merely rolled her eyes.

"I'm tough. Besides, I think I've got one hidden down here somewhere if it appears anyone needs it." He looked around the group of them seated at the two tables set end to end and focused on Ari and Reko for a brief moment. Then he winked. Reko wasn't sure what that was all about, but he liked it.

Moving on, Anton planted his hands on the table in front of him and leaned forward. "Okay, now that we have that item cleared up, I need some suggestions. How are we going to find Aldo's bomb, and what are we going to do with Aldo?"

Fen and Ig shared a look, and then Fen spoke up. Reko had noticed that he often took the lead when speaking for the two of them, even though Ig was extremely well-spoken.

"When Ig and I had to find the first device, we had a general idea where it had been planted, and it was surprisingly easy to find. Once we were in our spirit form, working together, we were able to sense it as something intrinsically wrong in the natural world. I'm suggesting we go spirit and first check to see if it's in the general area around here. If not here, we can do another sweep beneath the Yellowstone caldera. We've been working on the prisoners' information that it hasn't been planted yet, but Aldo planted the first bomb, and there's no reason for him not to have planted the second. Not once he got the energy after Mary's adoptive mother died."

"How long would it take you to check the caverns first? I know they cover a big footprint, but so does the caldera."

"If we leave now," Ig said, "we should be able to scan the entire area before three." He leaned close and kissed Star, and Fen did the same with Sunny. Then the two men grasped each other's pendants—a jade puma hanging from a leather cord around Ig's neck, a similar jade wolf around Fen's—and disappeared.

It was more than obvious not everyone here had witnessed their shift from man to spirit, but Logan was the first to see the similarities. "That's essentially what Adam, Sunny, and I do when we're healing injuries."

"And now Jack." Reko focused on Jack, sitting directly across the table from them with Mary at his side. "He saved Ari after Sebastian pulled the demon out of him. You were busy working on Keisha. I don't think anyone except Jack, Mary, or I recognized Ari's distress."

"How did you know what to do?" Logan was smiling as if someone had just given him a gift. Reko had wondered if he'd be jealous, but there was no sense of that. None at all.

Jack merely shrugged, but he looked at Ari, and Reko felt the emotion, the pleasure he experienced, knowing he'd saved a life. "I've thought for quite some time that I might be able to heal. Just a feeling when I've been around one of you guys working your mojo, but there'd never been an opportunity when I felt comfortable enough to ask if I could try while you were helping someone. So often it's an emergency, and the last thing I'd want to do is interfere." He hung his head a moment. "I regret not trying to help when Rem was hurt at the cave in Yellowstone." He glanced at the agent, sitting quietly with his head still bandaged. "I would have felt a lot more comfortable practicing on his hard head than Ari's heart."

Remington snorted and flipped him off, but he didn't say anything.

Jack looked at Ari. "There was no other option when Ari went down. I sensed his heart was pounding like a runaway train and he was obviously in distress. I asked Mary to watch over me, sat down next to him and placed my hands on his chest. Then I just thought myself inside, and suddenly I was there, inside one of the chambers of his heart, and it was beating way too fast and out of sync . . . it felt wrong, but I didn't have a clue what to do. Nothing."

"And?" This time, Anton was asking.

"I called on Eve for help. I wasn't even thinking how busy she was, working with you guys trying to hold on to Aldo, but my mind filled with the information I needed. It felt as if it came directly from the Mother— the message had a lot of power behind it. I knew exactly how to massage a part of his heart and then to send energy to a bundle of nerves that were misfiring. As soon as his heartbeat was normal, and after I'd waited long enough to know it was going to stay that way, I just thought myself back into my body. Ari was fine and Reko carried him up to the house to get him away from Aldo." He shot a grin at Ari. "That was Mary's idea. She was afraid you might be more temptation than the demon could handle."

"And I'm very thankful for that. I don't want him back inside me ever again." Ari turned to Sebastian and Lily. "Not that I don't appreciate what you did to get him out of me, but that's an experience I don't care to repeat."

"Trust me, Ari." Sebastian took Lily's hand. "None of us do. I'm just glad the spell worked, and definitely pleased Jack was able to help. I missed that entirely."

"The way this group gets into trouble," Jack said, "I'm sure you'll get a chance to watch me at some point." He grinned at Sebastian and then turned to Logan. "The thing is, when we're spirit and inside someone's body, our bodies are still intact, stuck in position without any awareness. It makes a healer vulnerable unless there's someone there to protect them. Unlike Ig and Fen, who go entirely spirit. Their clothing, even their jade talismans go with them. Healing's not like that."

"You're not kidding." Sunny glanced at Star. "A couple of years ago Fen, Ig, Star and I were down near Mt. Lassen at one of the pack's cabins when Fen and Ig were both shot by men hunting Chanku. I was trying to heal a really bad belly wound before Fen could bleed out, but I was pulled away from Fen when I was in the midst of healing him. I finally got myself, quite literally, back together and healed him, once they locked us all up and left us alone."

"And then she healed Ig, and passed out." Star stared at Sunny for a few moments, while Reko watched them in pure amazement. The things these people could do! He'd never known of this ability to heal. "I wanted to be able to help him so badly," Star said, "but I lack the ability. Of course, that means we all work really hard at keeping Sunny safe."

"Works for me." Sunny leaned against Star and gazed up at her like a needy pup.

"Well, we can't do anything about Aldo until we hear from the Mother. Eve, let us know as soon as you find out, okay?"

"I will, Anton. And Keisha, thank you for lunch." She glanced at the box holding Aldo. "And the excitement. That certainly got the heart pumping. Do you think he'll be okay here?"

"He should be fine. There's a locked titanium safe in one of the side rooms. The box with the salt and the demon should fit inside."

Ari and Reko helped put the tables away and Tinker and his sons carried the box into the cavern with the safe. They'd returned to the main cavern and were just getting ready to go back up on top when Fen and Ig got back.

There'd been no sign of the nuclear device anywhere within the cavern system. They opened the portal to the astral and met Eve in the doorway to let her know they hadn't found anything. Sunny and Star went with them—the guys would go to Yellowstone via the astral in order to search for the device in and around the caldera, and the women would go as backup.

Reko had learned of their four-way mating, the fact they were favored by the Mother as a special team that worked to stop things like this demon with his bombs. He watched while they softly conversed with Eve and then said good-bye to Anton and Keisha and crossed onto the astral plane. The comfort with which these people interacted with their goddess amazed him. Everything about them amazed him, almost as if he and Ari had moved beyond the mere magic of shapeshifting and now consorted with the denizens of other realms.

It might have taken them a long time to finally connect with this pack, but so far it had been one amazing experience after another, and in spite of the danger, he wouldn't change any of it. He'd never felt so alive, never felt so close to his brother, had never at any time felt the kind of love that was finally part of his life.

• • •

Ari followed Reko up the stairs, suddenly overwhelmingly exhausted. Janine held his hand, and he was glad she'd not abandoned him when she discovered there was a demon inside him. Once they left Anton's house, they all walked the same trail that took them first by Jack and Mary's place, and from there to Janine's.

But Reko stopped him before he and Janine continued. "I talked to the goddess today, to Eve. I asked her if there was a way to find out how our parents and our siblings are, even though they've already passed through the veil and are no longer living. She said that sometimes it's possible to connect, to find people on the other side, especially if they've left something important unfinished. I asked her if she had a chance and could find them, if she'd let them know we made it. That we're shifters now, the way we are meant to be. I want them to know that their dreams were real, that we will carry them forward with us."

Ari's chest ached. So much emotion in this body. Weaker than his wolf in so many ways, but so much stronger in this, the capacity to feel. He welcomed it, even when the pain almost took him to his knees. "Thank you, Reko. I had no idea that was even possible."

"She might not be able to find them, but if she can . . ."

"You are an amazing man, Reko. An amazing brother. I know I can be a prick sometimes, but I do love you." He wrapped his arms around his brother, his twin, and hugged him close, but before he cried all over him, Ari pulled away.

"Thank you, Ari. We don't say it enough. I love you, too." Reko smiled, but his eyes filled with tears just like Ari's. Ari grabbed Reko's shoulder and squeezed it, but there was nothing more to say. He took Janine's hand and let her lead him along the trail. For whatever reason, he felt as if she was leading him home.

• • •

Lily and Sebastian's room at Anton's house
Monday, 10:20 p.m.

Sebastian! Into the caverns quickly. The demon has escaped! He's killed one of the prisoners and is consuming his life force now. The other prisoner is next. Go! Now!

Sebastian sat up, his mind spinning. Had that been a nightmare or . . .

"I heard it, too. Hurry!" Lily was out of bed in a heartbeat. She ran down the hall to her parents' room and pounded on the door. By the time Sebastian had grabbed a pair of pants, Anton was at the door and Lily was telling him what was going on.

Stef and Xandi had been in the same room. Stef was already dressed and followed them down the hall. He turned off at the Pentagon room. "I'll get the word out for energy—they'll channel it directly to you, Anton, so be ready."

"Got it."

Sebastian held the door for him and the three of them raced into the cavern. An eerie green light flickered outward from the stone cells where the prisoners were held. The two men who'd been guarding them were down, but Remington raised his head. Long bloody claw marks stood out across his left shoulder and down his arm. "Call a healer. Bay's got a head injury. Needs help now."

Anton shouted "Go!" to Sebastian and Lily, and stopped to check Bay. He sent out a call to Logan, Adam, and Jack, knowing at least one of them should be able to respond. Jack answered and said he was on his way. Anton passed the news on to Remington just as Lily screamed, but it was a scream of rage, not pain. Spinning away from the men, he raced down the tunnel toward the flickering light. It pulsed now, with a foul energy that sucked air from the tunnel, the dust from the floor, bits of rock and anything not nailed down.

Sebastian and Lily had the demon cornered up against a wall, but it was all they could do to hold him. They'd told Anton they hoped to use a containment spell, something that should work when he had a corporeal form. He appeared solid, and he actually resembled the living Aldo Xenakis, discounting the green skin, lack of clothing, and distorted features. The long talons at the ends of his fingers explained Rem's injuries.

Mary's father and Brother Thomas had served Aldo's purpose. Their bodies—eyes open and staring—lay in a twisted heap on the ground between Sebastian, Lily, and the demon.

Anton raised his arms and threw his strength into the mix just as a powerful wave of energy hit him.

Stefan had reached out to the pack. And the pack reached back. *Stefan? Can you split the energy, channel it evenly into Lily, Sebastian, and me?*

Yes, but warn them. There's a lot coming in, more than we had earlier. It's going to charge things quickly.

Lily! Sebastian! Stefan's sending energy directly to each of us. He said it's coming in stronger than this afternoon.

Eve popped into the room, armed with a longer sword and her crossbow. Leaving her sword in its scabbard, she cocked her small crossbow, loaded a bolt and fired. Aldo screamed in rage. She hit him with a second bolt, then a third.

Power crackled in the small room and sparks flashed against the dark stone. Sebastian glanced at Lily. Sweat poured down her face but power flew from her fingertips, bolts of pure white lightning encircling Aldo, wrapping him in blazing energy. Eve fired another bolt from her crossbow. Aldo pulled it out and flung it to the ground and charged.

Lily and Anton stopped him with a burst of energy and he shrieked. Reaching for Eve, he caught her as she leapt out of reach, raking her arm with his claws. She screamed furiously and shot him once again with a bolt from her crossbow. Sebastian hit him with a burst of white lightning, but he was looking for a miracle. It was going to take more than one to stop the demon.

* * *

Beneath the Yellowstone caldera
Monday, 10:25 p.m.

They'd split up to cover more area, but Ig disliked being so far from Fen. Their minds kept them connected, but he was used to his mate working close beside him. Here in this hellish place between the molten rock and the heavy capstone that was all that kept the volcano from exploding, Ig knew his otherwise immortal life could be snuffed out in a heartbeat.

Except, in this form he had no heart. Nothing but the essence of the man he was. It was hard to remember that he'd lived such as this for eons before finely taking a corporeal body. He'd been nothing more than spirit, a creature whose only purpose was to guide his charges from birth to adulthood. He'd done his job well, and damn it all, he was going to do this one, too.

He passed through an area where the earth's crust was thin, where the cap separating the molten rock from the surface was riddled with fissures. If he were a demon and wanted to do the most damage, this would be the ideal target. He paused here, absorbing the sense of this place that was the closest he could imagine to hell on earth.

He felt it, then. Felt the *wrongness* of the device. It was close—close enough for him to sense something else. A timer? Was this one already primed? *Fen! I've got something. Can you come to me?*

No. Dammit! I've got one here, too! There're two of them! It's placed against a weakness in the cap. If it goes, we're going to lose this damned volcano.

Shit. Does it have a timer? This one appears to have already been set, there's some kind of device . . .

Fuck! That's what I sense. Not a timer, something else . . . somehow . . . crap! It's linked to Aldo.

Can you move it by yourself? Get it into the molten rock and reform it where it can melt?

It worked really well the first time. Ig sensed words, realized it was more of Fenris cursing. *I don't know if I'm strong enough to move it without jolting the device, but I'm on the far side of the caldera from you. We can't meet at one or the other in time. I'm concerned this sensor on it might be tied to Aldo's life force. If he dies, they blow.*

And Sebastian and Lily are doing their damnedest to kill the bastard. Fenris, you can do it. I'll take care of this one, you've got that one. Let's hope like hell there aren't any more. Call on the Mother. She won't let us founder. But Fenris, if anything goes wrong . . .

If anything goes wrong, I will love you in the afterlife, Igmutaka. I will love you forever.

And I you. But remember . . . His heart clenched in his chest, though it was all merely sensation without substance, but . . . *remember Sunny and Mikaela Star's promise to us, that should we die, they will join us in the afterlife. They wouldn't take it back, and we cannot let that happen. Do not fuck this up, Fenris! I love you, but I love those women just as much, and I don't want their lives to end. Ours either, for that matter. Please, be careful.*

I will. I love you. Now let's hope like hell the bastard only had two of them. You be careful too, dammit. I can't lose you.

Ig took strength from his mate's love. He thought of their women on the surface, waiting for them at the doorway to the astral. He and Fen had forced the promise from Sunny and Mikaela Star, that they would go onto the astral should the bombs explode. With any luck, that plane should survive, and all who were on it, but if he and Fen died, it wouldn't matter. Sunny and Star would follow them. That couldn't be allowed to happen.

With a quick prayer to the Mother, he went deeper still, deep enough to sense the extreme heat even in his spirit form. He'd never lifted an object this large. Never performed any act with so much risk to everyone he loved, everything he knew. He crouched, in spirit form, beside the huge device. He'd only done this once before, working in tandem with Fen. This time he was alone, just as Fen was alone with his own fucking bomb.

Definitely a story for the grandchildren, should they be so fortunate to survive. Ig stared at the device and remembered how he and Fen together had broken the last one down into nothing but a molecular mist, had sent that mist into the depths of the molten rock pooling beneath this part of the caldera.

He focused on the device. Drew what strength he could from the Mother, drew even more from his love for his mates. He could not, would not fail them. Pushing with his mind, he began the process of turning solid matter into mist.

17

The demon showed no sign of weakening. The scrape of toenails sliding on stone was the only warning that Ari and Reko had entered the cave. Snarling, jaws wide, they launched themselves at Aldo. Ari went for his throat, Reko stretched his huge jaws around the demon's torso and clamped down.

Aldo screamed as the weight of the Berserkers took him down. Blood sprayed from his ripped throat and entrails spilled across the stone floor.

"Lily! Now!" Sebastian charged the demon, power rippling from his fingertips. Lily stood beside him, both of them practically standing on top of the demon, bombarding Aldo with their spell. Anton took Sebastian's other side, and Eve tossed her crossbow aside and joined them, until the room flashed and flickered with unspent power.

Grunting like a beast, Aldo shoved Reko away and grabbed Ari's jaws to pry them away from his throat. Twisting and turning, he morphed into a huge boar with long tusks, but even as his entrails disappeared back inside, the image shimmered. Ari clamped down harder as the boar shook his head from side to side, throwing the huge Berserker's powerful body back and forth as if he were nothing but a toy.

Sebastian grabbed Lily's arm and pulled her out of harm's way. Eve backed off but they kept up the barrage, careful not to hit the wolves. The Berserkers needed room to fight.

Reko scrambled to his feet and leapt, landing solidly on the beast's back. He clamped his huge jaws around the boar's spinal column and bit down hard, biting through thick hide and thicker muscle.

Sebastian shouted to Lily and Eve, "Harder! Hit him harder. More power. He's weakening." His hatred for his father had only grown with time. He felt no remorse, no sense of anything other than the potent desire to end this man who, in every form, was evil incarnate.

Aldo morphed again, and a massive cobra weighted down with the two Berserkers struck at Eve. She bounded lightly out of his way. He dropped his head and slithered backward across the cavern with Reko still holding on to his spine and Ari gnawing at his throat, both digging their claws into the stone floor, searching for purchase to hold the demon in place. He tried to strike, but Ari held the snake just beneath his jaw, too close for Aldo to sink his fangs into him.

Sebastian doubled down on the bolts of power he threw, careful not to hit either Ari or Reko. A flash of movement caught his eye. Remington raced into the cavern with an ax held over his head. "Ari! Turn him loose."

The Berserker opened his jaws and rolled out of the way as Remington swung the ax. The sharp blade caught the cobra just behind its head.

As strong as the snake was, Remington was stronger.

The head rolled away from the writhing body, only it wasn't the cobra's head. It was Aldo as he'd looked the night he died, his face crusted with burns from Sebastian and the Mother's lightning strike. His eyes opened. His lips moved, but his voice rang in their heads, not their ears.

You will die now. All of you. Two perfectly placed nuclear bombs, both set to my life force. When I cease to exist, they explode. Such a simple thing. Foolproof, really . . . and then I will see you in hell.

His eyes closed. The black mist, much smaller this time, escaped from his mouth. Lily swept in with a small energy net and scooped up the mist. She twisted the top, enclosing the black cloud within the shimmering strands. The moment she closed it, the cobra body disappeared and a man's body lay in its place.

The demon mist within the net turned to dust and fell through the glowing strands. Lily hung her head, and the net faded within her grasp. Sebastian turned to Anton. "Can you sense Ig or Fenris? Can you warn them?"

Anton shook his head. "Not when they're inside the earth." His tears fell as he pulled Lily into his arms. "You and Sebastian were magnificent. You held him." He turned to Reko and Ari, who sat beside one another, sides heaving, muzzles bloodied. "Your bravery knows no bounds. I am so proud to call you packmates." Then he raised his head and stared at Remington. "And you? I truly wish you were one of us, Remington

Caruthers. You are a man without equal and I am proud to call you my friend."

Remington let out a disgusted snort. "Friend? When it appears I may have just fucked over the world with my manly display?" His harsh laugh faded, and he shook his head. "I'm sorry. I had no idea he would have anything like that. How long, do you think?" He glanced at the head lying on the cavern floor. The blood pooled around it was drying, turning dark.

"I don't know. We should have heard from Ig or Fen by now, if they were successful. There's always the chance they might have destroyed both devices before Aldo died."

"Again." Sebastian cursed. "I thought we killed the bastard the first time." He turned to Remington. "That was a pretty amazing thing for you to do. How's Baylor?"

"Jack's almost done healing him." He glanced at Aldo's head, sucked in a deep breath, let it out. "The fucker never read the demon rulebook. A titanium safe? The salt? The lead container? Once he'd rested, they couldn't hold him. He turned to mist and escaped, reformed right in front of Bay and me and attacked, but we fought him off. He went for the two men because they were unprotected at that point. He must have spelled them. They were held in separate cells, but they're both in here. Easier victims than Bay and me." He took a longer look at Aldo's remains. "I really don't want to leave that thing here. We need to destroy it."

"If he was right, and the volcano goes off, we might not have to worry about it." Lily glanced at the walls of the cavern. "It seems pretty solid. Shouldn't we have felt something if two nuclear devices exploded?"

"Yeah, if Fen and I had screwed up, you'd probably have felt a whole lot of something." Ig stepped into the small room, Fen beside him, with Sunny and Star hanging on to their men.

"How?" Anton looked from one to the other. "He said there were two, that they were tied to his life force." He barked out a harsh laugh. "That was, of course, *after* Remington beheaded him." He shook his head, stepped closer to Ig and Fen. "We thought everything was over."

"So did we." Fen shrugged. "Ig found a device on the south end of the caldera at the same time I found another on the north end, the two as far apart as they could be, and no way we could work together. We realized they were somehow tied to Aldo, figured you'd be fighting him at some point and we had no doubt you'd win. We weren't sure we could do it." He glanced at Ig. "We'd never done telekinesis by ourselves."

"I didn't think I could do it without Fen, but the Mother was there for both of us." Ig stared at Star for a moment. She tightened her grip on his arm. "Mine exploded while I had it in mist form, in the process of moving it into the molten pool below the cap. That's probably the point when he died, but it scared the crap out of me. It was more like watching bubbles in a soft drink instead of a nuclear explosion. It caused a minor tremor, but not enough to set off the volcano." He laughed softly. "I think the tremor was me, freaking out." He focused on Remington. "Rem? How'd you kill the bastard? Even the Mother and Sebastian couldn't do it."

Remington glanced at Sebastian. "Hell, I'm human. No magic. I had to resort to a lower form of reasoning." He held up the ax. "I beheaded him, but Lily took care of what was left."

Lily merely shrugged. "There wasn't much left after you and the boys dealt with the bastard." She saluted Ari and Reko.

Remington rested the ax on his shoulder. "I guess even demonkind can't fight a pissed-off pair of wolves and a mere human with a honkin' big ax."

There was laughter all around, until a brilliant light flashed in the cavern. The wolves went to their bellies. Remington raised the ax and held his ground. The rest of them shaded their eyes against the glare. The light covered Aldo's remains, pulsed a couple of times, and then faded away. The body and the head were gone.

Sebastian turned to Lily, his teal eyes swimming with tears. "That was the Mother. She wanted to clean up the mess. He's gone. Permanently, this time."

• • •

The main cavern
Monday, 11:20 p.m.

Jack sat beside Baylor Quinn, resting his forearms on his bent knees, taking slow, steady breaths. Bay was conscious, his head in Manda's lap. Bay's mate stroked her fingers through his dark hair. Their partners, Jake and Shannon, sat with them, quietly celebrating as only longtime mates could do. Jack felt the love among the four of them. They each had only one mate, but they'd all been together for so many years that they might as well have been bonded, each to the other.

He glanced up, caught Mary watching him. There was so much love in her eyes, but sadness, too. He reached for her, held her hand. Her fingers were cold so he tugged her closer, then closer again until he could pull her into his lap. He knew her father was dead in the cell where he'd been held. Eve had told them just a few moments ago. The bodies of both Nathaniel Ryder and Brother Thomas would be collected by the FBI once Remington Caruthers reported in.

They'd beaten Aldo Xenakis, hopefully once and for all. And Jack had saved Baylor Quinn's life. Rather than celebrating, he felt a sense of quiet satisfaction that he'd been able to help someone he'd always admired. Doc Logan and Adam had both arrived a little while ago, but they'd not interfered. Instead, they'd checked over Rem's injuries before sending him in to help the others, and then watched to make sure Jack handled the intricate work of repairing an injured brain. He'd sensed the Mother beside him, inside him. She hadn't spoken, but somehow she must have shared the knowledge he needed. How else would he have known exactly what to do? He'd fixed the damage to Bay's brain so perfectly that the man had awakened with only a minor headache, the indentation in his skull carefully repaired.

As Adam had explained one time, all a healer had to do was go inside and fix what was broken. It wasn't nearly as difficult as Jack had thought it might be.

• • •

The cavern beneath Anton's house
Tuesday, 12:45 a.m.

Reko grabbed Ari and tugged him toward the doorway into the main cavern. "I'm ready to get some sleep, and I think I heard Janine out here."

Ari immediately quit fighting him. "Really? Do you think she'll let me come home with her tonight?"

Reko merely grinned and headed down the tunnel to the cavern. He saw Jack and Mary, and the man Jack had been healing when Reko raced past him appeared to be awake and talking. And Janine was there, talking quietly with Anton and Keisha. She turned when they entered the cavern, focused immediately on Ari and ran to him.

"I was so worried about you! You left in such a hurry."

He wrapped his arms around her and held her close for a long moment. Her head barely came to the middle of his chest, but his size didn't seem to bother her a bit. "I heard Reko call me." He held her even closer. "I knew my brother needed me, that my pack needed me." The moment he said that, Anton raised his head and gave Ari a thumbs-up. "We made a difference, Janine, but I'm tired now and ready for bed."

"Good. So am I."

She raised up on her toes and Ari bent to kiss her, so comfortable together that Reko had to laugh. "I guess I'll know where to find you. Good night, Ari, and good night to you as well, Janine. I'm so glad you're watching over my brother."

"Me, too." She flashed a smile at him, linked her hand with Ari's and gently tugged him toward the doorway that led to the exit.

Reko watched them go before turning toward Jack and Mary. He was absolutely exhausted. At least he was clean from shifting. The blood and other bits and pieces of demon that had matted his hair were now scattered about the floor of the cell. "I need to sleep," he said. "I never realized how much work it was to fight demonkind."

"Tell me about it." Mary huffed out a disgusted breath and took the hand that Reko offered. "You coming, Jack?"

"That I am." She reached out a hand to him and he took it, but Baylor stopped him.

"Thank you, Jack. I can never repay you for what you've done."

Jack squeezed his hand. "You already have, Bay. You didn't die on me. That's one hell of a gift."

"It certainly would have ruined my night." Bay reached up and touched Manda's cheek.

"Mine, too," she said. "Mine, too."

• • •

Jack's cabin
Tuesday, 1:30 a.m.

Reko and Mary slept soundly. Jack had crawled into bed with them, but his thoughts wouldn't allow him to rest. He'd finally gotten up, eaten a sandwich Keisha sent with him, and then checked in with his parents. He'd let them know what had happened tonight, and told them how he'd healed Baylor Quinn. His mom had nailed it when she'd said it was absolutely perfect that he was a healer—as a teacher, working with the youngest ones meant he was always dealing with banged knees and toes, and the occasional bite when a kindergartener made their first shift and accidently chomped on one of their classmates.

Now he sat alone in the front room with only a candle to light the darkness, staring at his reflection in the big window that looked out over the meadow. He was exhausted but so wound up over all that had happened, he couldn't unwind. When Reko told him about the fight with the demon, he'd almost panicked.

He could have lost the man so easily, and that terrified him. Already he loved Reko every bit as much as he loved Mary. It was a different love, this feeling he had for the man, but powerful and wonderful, and a little bit frightening. He'd known Reko less than a week, but they'd shared more experiences in that short time than he had with some of his lifelong friends.

He sensed Reko the moment he entered the room, leaned his head back over the couch and looked at him upside down. "I thought you were sleeping. What are you doing up?"

"You weren't there with us." Reko stepped over the back of the couch and sat beside Jack. "Couldn't you sleep?"

Sighing, Jack shook his head. "Too many things bouncing around inside my head. It was a rather busy day, don't you agree?"

"I do. Come with me. You need to sleep." He took a long look at Jack, leaned over and kissed him. "Besides, I missed you. You belong in there with your woman."

Jack stood, grabbed Reko's hand and tugged the big guy to his feet. "I belong just as much with my man. C'mon, Reko."

They crawled into the big bed beside Mary, with Jack in the middle. He was still wound up, but . . .

Reko was gently pulling Jack's boxers down his legs and cupping his balls in one big hand. *This will help you relax,* he said. His mouth found Jack's cock with unerring accuracy, his lips and tongue worked magic that only Reko could do. When Jack found his release, Reko swallowed his seed, licked him clean, and carefully pulled his boxers up over his butt.

I love you, Jack. Now sleep. We'll solve any outstanding issues tomorrow.

I have a feeling that's not a suggestion, it's an order.

Go to sleep, Jack.

Good night, Reko.

Good night, Jack.

Would you two please stop chattering and go to sleep? Grumbling, Mary crawled over the top of Jack and snuggled between him and Reko. In mere seconds, she was sound asleep. A minute later, Jack knew from Reko's even breathing that he'd joined Mary.

Listening to the two of them, knowing they were his, that the danger—for now—was past, was a truly satisfying feeling. That his life would be forever changed because of the two he loved, who loved him? That topped just about everything. Jack finally let it all go. And slept.

Works by Kate Douglas

The Spirit Wild Series

Dark Wolf
Dark Spirit
Dark Moon
Dark Refuge
Dark Terror

Paranormal Romances

DemonFire
HellFire
"Crystal Dreams" in *Nocturnal*
StarFire
CrystalFire

Erotic Romances

Wolf Tales
"Chanku Rising" in *Sexy Beast*
and as the ebook
Wolf Tales 1.5—Chanku Rising
Wolf Tales II
"Camille's Dawn" in *Wild Nights*
and as the ebook
Wolf Tales 2.5—Chanku Dawn
Wolf Tales III
"Chanku Fallen" in *Sexy Beast II*
and as the ebook
Wolf Tales 3.5—Chanku Fallen
Wolf Tales IV
"Chanku Journey" in *Sexy Beast III*
and as the ebook
Wolf Tales 4.5—Chanku Journey
Wolf Tales V

About the Author

Kate Douglas is the author of the popular erotic paranormal romance series Wolf Tales, the erotic SF series Dream Catchers and StarQuest, as well as the DemonSlayers series. She is currently writing the next book in the Spirit Wild series.

Kate and her husband of over forty-five years have two adult children and six grandchildren. They live in the beautiful wine country of Sonoma County, California, in the little town of Healdsburg.

Write to Kate at kate@katedouglas.com. She answers all her email.

Connect with her on Facebook at
www.facebook.com/katedouglas.authorpage or on Twitter @wolftales.

Made in the USA
Monee, IL
30 August 2019